BY NANCY KRESS

NOVELS

Prince of Morning Bells
The White Pipes
The Golden Grove
An Alien Light
Brainrose
Beggars in Spain
Beggars and Choosers
Oaths and Miracles
Beggars Ride
Maximum Light
Stinger
Yanked!
Probability Moon
Probability Sun
Probability Space
Crossfire
Nothing Human
Crucible

STORY COLLECTIONS

Trinity and Other Stories
The Aliens of Earth
Beaker's Dozen

CRUCIBLE

NANCY KRESS

A TOM DOHERTY ASSOCIATES BOOK

NEW YORK

This is a work of fiction. All the characters and events portrayed in this book are either products of the author's imagination or are used fictitiously.

CRUCIBLE

Copyright © 2004 by Nancy Kress

Edited by James Minz

A Tor Book
Published by Tom Doherty Associates, LLC
175 Fifth Avenue
New York, NY 10010

www.tor.com

Tor® is a registered trademark of Tom Doherty Associates, LLC.

ISBN 0-765-34603-6
EAN 978-0765-24603-2

First edition: August 2004
First mass market edition: June 2005

Printed in the United States of America

0 9 8 7 6 5 4 3 2 1

In memoriam

Charles Sheffield

ACKNOWLEDGMENTS

This book owes a large debt to my late husband, Charles Sheffield, who allowed me to use the McAndrew Drive he created for his own character, Arthur Morton McAndrew.

I would also like to thank my editor, Jim Minz, for his many valuable contributions.

PROLOGUE: DEEP SPACE

They had been traveling for two months, and they had been traveling for nineteen years. Every inch of the ship, which was not theirs nor even their own species', was as familiar to both of them as each other's skins: every mole, every alcove, every hair, every alien fixture they did not understand. At "night," an arbitrary concept since they had never figured out how to control the ship's lighting, they lay in each other's arms and whispered as if there were anyone within light-years to overhear.

"Lucy? Are you all right?" Karim Mahjoub said.

"Of course I am," she whispered back, trying to keep her voice free of annoyance. They both considered her the more fragile one. Sometimes she resented that.

"I wish we knew for sure how much longer."

"I thought you did the math."

"Yes, but I can't be sure. You know that," he said, with just a touch of reproach. He had been taught, very hastily, how to fly the ship, and how to aim it in the right direction. He had figured out on his own how to use the formidable weapons aboard. But the computer was too complex, too alien. They were accelerating at over a hundred gees, but he didn't know how much over, or how far away was the destination.

Lucy didn't apologize. "I'm going to check the prisoners again."

"They're fine," he said, not because he'd checked but because they were always the same. Once they had been warlike, dangerous, technologically advanced aliens. This had been their ship. Now they sat passively in their confined quarters, eating when food was brought, caring for themselves minimally, dreaming who knew what dreams in their virus-infected brains.

Lucy said, "I'm going to look."

She rolled away from him and got to her feet, a slight figure in heavy clothing; temperature control was another thing Karim had not decoded. The alien Furs apparently came from a cold planet. Lucy walked toward the prison room, her boots clomping loudly on the metal floor.

She opened the door without caution. At first she and Karim had been so careful, setting up the force-shield walls every time they moved among the Furs. But the Furs hardly seemed to notice. Now she stood in the open doorway without protection.

Most of the Furs seemed to be asleep, although it was difficult to distinguish sleep from their awake state. "Meditating," Karim called it. "Praying," Dr. William Shipley had said, back on Greentrees. Jake Holman, Greentrees' leader, had been franker: "They've been turned into the closest animal thing possible to moving plants." Two Furs in the corner, however, were active, mating again. All of them did that often, since they'd been infected. They were highly contagious to their own kind, and highly attractive. That was the point.

Lucy checked that the water trough was filled and clean. One Fur slowly raised its head and actually seemed to see her, and Lucy's heart stopped. They were so strong, so muscled with their powerful legs and even more powerful balancing tail, their teeth so sharp and pointed . . . But the Fur merely gazed at her, unblinking, and lowered its head again to endless silent contemplation.

Lucy shut the door. Karim came down the short corridor toward her. Even before she saw his excitement, she knew, because the floor began to change configuration beneath her feet.

The captured alien ship used a McAndrew Drive. That was what the humans called it, after the scientific genius who had described it in theory, Arthur Morton McAndrew. Humans had never built a McAndrew Drive ship; they had neither the materials nor the expertise. Furs had built them designed along the same principle, which was perfect balance between acceleration and gravity.

The ship consisted of a superdense disc, a long pole extending out from the disc, and living quarters that slid along the pole. As the ship increased acceleration, the living quarters slid closer to the disc, increasing the counterbalancing gravitational pull on the beings inside. Inside the ship, Lucy and Karim experienced a steady 1.6 gees, presumably the gravity on the Fur homeworld. But to equalize these forces at various spots inside the ship, the floor must bow when acceleration or deceleration changed and the living quarters moved up or down the pole. That was happening now. Gravity on Lucy's body remained constant; she had no sensation of being anything other than upright. But her line-of-sight knew.

"We're decelerating," she breathed at Karim.

"Yes. Rapidly."

"Can you see the planet?" A stupid question; she knew that as soon as she asked it. The ship drew energy from the quantum activity in the vacuum. It moved in a furious cloud of plasma that blocked all outside signals until they stopped.

"Nothing visual yet. But it can't be long now." Karim drew a deep breath, raised an arm, let it pointlessly fall.

Not long now. Not long until their arrival at an alien planet, and not one belonging to the Furs but to the third species loose in this part of the galaxy. A species far more alien to humans than the Furs. A species whose legacy represented humanity's only real chance at protecting Greentrees.

A sudden image invaded Karim's mind, unbidden and unwelcome. His grandfather in their beautiful, long-ago garden in the Terran city of Isfahan, intoning the Koran to a small Karim, who had been frightened of him. The old man's dark eyes had burned with passion and faith: " *'Every soul shall taste of death, and we will prove you with evil and with good for a trial of you, and unto us shall ye return.'"*

"Come on, Lucy," Karim said. "Let's go back to the bridge. We need to be ready for arrival."

1

MIRA CITY

The party was reaching its city-wide crescendo, the speeches would begin soon, and no one could find Alex.

Typical, Siddalee Brown thought grumpily as she pushed her way through the crowd in the park. Never where she was supposed to be. Off doing something else—probably a worthy something else, but not *here.* Not where Alexandra Cutler was supposed to be and Siddalee Brown was supposed to make sure she was. Typical!

"Have you seen Alex?" she asked Salah Hadijeh. Salah, dressed in some fantastic white flowing robe—you could never tell about the Arabs, likely to turn up in anything at a party except conventional clothes—only laughed. "Alex? I saw her ten minutes ago, in the Mausoleum. Drunk as a vat bug." He laughed again, swaying, and raised his glass to Siddalee.

Huh! Alex didn't drink. But Salah certainly had been, and weren't those Arabs supposed to stay away from alcohol? Against their religion, Siddalee had been told. Not that she cared, but it was just one more sign of everything wrong with the young people today. And Salah's information was useless; Alex certainly wasn't in the Mausoleum, which Siddalee had just finished searching, every single square foot, without finding anyone who'd even seen her boss. And Siddalee certainly wasn't going to search it again.

So where to look? She chewed her generous bottom lip, surveying the park, and as she looked the bottom lip pursed more and more until Siddalee was chewing the inside of a mouth clamped tightly shut.

The party was, in Siddalee's opinion, out of control. Practically every table in Mira City had been dragged out into the park for the fiftieth anniversary of the First Landing on Greentrees. Earlier, Siddalee had noticed pitchers of that new alcohol, Blue Lion, that those kids who owned the Chu Corporation were fermenting. That had been bad enough—a fiftieth anniversary should be a solemn celebration, to Siddalee's way of thinking—but by now you couldn't even *see* the tables. People stood on them and sat around them and probably lay under them, a seething mass of people, at least half of whom looked drunk. The pretty genemod flower beds were all getting trampled. The Chinese kids were setting off those awful things they called firecrackers, and a mixed bunch of Arabs and Cutlers were loudly singing that demeaning song that Siddalee heard everywhere now:

"On Greentrees we are
For good, but is it good,
How would I know, all I know
For sure is yooouuuuuu . . ."

Siddalee had never heard such stupidity celebrated—as if they hadn't all learned to "know" so much from being on Greentrees! And the song had a pretty tune, too . . . such a waste. To make it worse, she spied among the Arabs and Cutlers three kids that she knew for sure were New Quakers. Quakers! Acting like that! Their parents certainly didn't know.

At least the Quakers wore modest gray coveralls, which was more than you could say for some of the other young ones. Dress on Greentrees offered two usual choices: coveralls, modeled after the ones the First Landing wore (some of them *were* the ones the First Landing wore; Threadmores lasted nearly forever). Or the more popular "wraps," which had evolved on Greentrees. These were no more than pieces of bright holcum-fiber cloth cut into different shapes and worn tied around the body in whatever configurations happened to strike the wearer as interesting, from voluminous to skimpy. During the cool nights, wraps were worn over the thermal skinsuits that covered everything but hands and head. Days were warm enough that most people just tied their wraps over bare bodies. As fashion, it was both cheap and highly competitive, with much praise going to innovative wrappers, although not from Siddalee.

At the far end of the park, against the huge government building that everyone called the Mausoleum, a temporary platform had been built high above the crowd for the speeches. Siddalee saw Jake Holman's wheelchair being pushed up the ramp by a muscular Arab in another of those silly flowing robes. If anyone knew where Alex was, it might be Mr. Holman.

"Oh!" a girl cried as Siddalee pushed past her. Siddalee had spilled the girl's pitcher of Blue Lion, sending the bright blue liquid foaming down the front of the girl's coverall. "Watch what you're doing, you Furry shit!"

It was the worst insult on Greentrees. Siddalee stopped dead, stared at the girl, and realized she knew her. Star Chu, they'd worked on the reservoir project together. Star had cut her glossy straight black hair short and she wore one of those stupid fake-Cheyenne fake tattoos on her left cheek, a cluster of tiny stars, plus that new red lipstick that Chu Corporation had just put on the market along with its alcoholic drinks. But Star wasn't a bad person. She recognized Siddalee and blushed.

"Oh, sorry, Siddalee, you just startled me."

"Have you seen Alex Cutler?"

Something strange passed through Star's eyes, but she just shook her head. "No. Sorry."

"Thanks." Siddalee left, again chewing on her bottom lip. Star hadn't seemed drunk, or at least there hadn't been any slurring in her accented English. Star was smart and resourceful, Siddalee knew from the reservoir project, as smart as Siddalee herself, which was very smart. So why did she want to get herself up like that and

act like she was some sort of painted party girl instead of the re-
sponsible citizen of Mira City that she really was?

"You're a Puritan, Siddalee," Alex had said to her, more than
once. *"They're only ten years younger than you are, you know, and
fundamentally no different."* But Siddalee didn't feel the same age as
Star and Salah and their crowds, and she didn't know what a "Puritan" was, and she wasn't about to look it up in the deebees. Old
stuff, probably. Useless stuff. Alex wouldn't even know the word if it
weren't for Mr. Holman.

Where was Alex?

Siddalee fought her way through to the quieter area close to the
Mausoleum walls. Here the New Quakers sat decorously around
their tables, talking softly, trying to ignore the raucous hilarity behind them. Off to one side sat a group of veiled Arab women. Under
the veils, Siddalee knew, would be mostly wrinkled, gentle faces; the
new generation of Arab girls didn't go veiled and some even had the
genetic treatments that meant they would never have the wrinkles
of their mothers and grandmothers. Siddalee approved. She had
never understood the strict Arab division of sexes, and she was glad
it was weakening so much on Greentrees. That was one good thing
about her generation, anyway.

She reached the steep ramp leading to the speakers' platform
and hauled herself up it. No one tried to stop her. On top, Mayor
Ashraf Shanti argued timidly with a tech fiddling with the broadcast cubes. Behind them stood the weirdest group of people that
Siddalee had ever seen.

She expected the New Quaker representative, of course, sober in
his gray coverall, waiting his turn to make a brief speech commemorating the First Landing. She also expected the Chinese leader of
the dissident city, Hope of Heaven, although only yesterday had
Mayor Shanti become certain that the troublemaker (and that's
what they all were in Hope of Heaven, don't try to tell Siddalee anything else!) would show for the ceremony. Siddalee even expected
the Cheyenne chief. He stood to one side, a fantastic figure in some

sort of animal skins trimmed with feathers and beads, a tattoo on his deeply sunburned cheek. Didn't he know how bad that much sun was for him? Did the Cheyenne even take skin-repair genetic supplements?

But the weirdest figure by far was the woman who crouched at the very back of the platform, beside Jake Holman's wheelchair. Siddalee looked, and looked again, and thought, *It can't be*.

Alex had told her about Nan Frayne, tales that Alex had heard from Mr. Holman and from Alex's dead aunt, Gail Cutler, who'd been among the First Landers. Siddalee had only half believed the stories. Sometimes Siddalee had even doubted that Nan Frayne existed. Could this person possibly be—

"Siddalee," Mr. Holman called in his quavery old voice. "Come here. I want you to meet someone. This is Nan Frayne."

Siddalee approached warily. Nan Frayne didn't rise or extend her hand. She looked at Siddalee with such a straight, grim stare that Siddalee felt outraged—what had she done to earn that much dislike? Nothing. Nan Frayne was old, maybe sixty, but looked even older because her skin was so lined, burned, and discolored. Against that skin her pale gray eyes looked startlingly light. She had gray hair, cut very short, and on her wiry body wore a clean new coverall too big for her.

"Hello," Siddalee said politely—Alex insisted on politeness to everyone—but Nan Frayne didn't so much as answer her. "Mr. Holman, do you know where I can find Alex?"

An odd look passed across Mr. Holman's face, the same kind of look that had flitted though Star Chu's eyes. Something was going on here that Siddalee didn't know about. But all Mr. Holman said was, "Isn't Alex supposed to make a speech?"

Of course Alex was supposed to make a speech—Alex was the *tray-o*. Mr. Holman knew that. But Siddalee restrained her irritation. In addition to Alex's insistence on courtesy, Mr. Holman deserved great respect. He was the man who had organized the colony ship to Greentrees fifty years ago, he'd been the CEO of Mira City back when the city had been a corporation, and he had led the group that fought off the alien Fur attack all those decades ago. Plus, he was old, over eighty in both Terran years and Greenie years, and Siddalee Brown was not going to snap at him.

"Yes, sir, she's supposed to speak right after you and . . . damn, the mayor's starting!"

The tech had fixed the broadcast cubes, which, like so much other nonessential machinery on Greentrees, was falling apart. Then the tech must have left the platform, because Mayor Shanti was starting his speech and the only people left on the stage were the ones who belonged there and Siddalee Brown.

"Don't worry about Alex," Mr. Holman said quickly. "She'll show up or she won't. Just go sit down and enjoy yourself, Siddalee."

As if she could do that with her boss messing up again! Blushing darkly, Siddalee scurried across the platform, down the ramp, and into the anonymity of the crowd.

"—for half a century," Mayor Shanti was saying in his unaccented English. The crowd had quieted, mostly, and Siddalee could hear the translators' mechanical voices in the Arabic, Chinese, and Spanish that some of the older people needed. Everyone born on Greentrees, of course, had learned English at school, even the Arab women in the medina. It was the law. "—trials and triumphs no one could have foreseen, but—"

Where was Alex? She was supposed to speak third, after the mayor and Mr. Holman. Well, Siddalee had done her best. She dropped heavily to the grass, scowling. A sudden breeze brought the smell of moonflowers, a thick heady fragrance. Probably from plants crushed under some table, Siddalee thought crossly. It would take weeks to restore Mira City's beautiful park. Somewhere to her left another of those annoying "firecrackers" went off, followed by drunken laughter.

No one on the platform reacted. And, Siddalee noted suddenly, Nan Frayne was no longer up there. Siddalee hadn't heard or seen the woman follow her down the ramp, but nonetheless she was gone, as stealthy as the sweet-scented wind.

On the other side of Mira City, Alexandra Cutler ran through the deserted streets toward the genetics labs.

God, she was out of shape! Fear kept her moving until, winded, she was forced to stop and bend over for a moment, hands on her knees, a middle-aged woman who stayed lean but not fit. Or not fit enough for this anyway, although "this" should not be something anyone on Greentrees had to prepare for. "This" should not be happening.

Please let it not be true.

Her panting echoed in her ears, unnaturally loud. As soon as she could, she straightened and resumed running.

Finally the lab buildings loomed ahead, windowless foamcast structures, many large enough to contain negative-pressure safe labs and plastic-roofed growing beds. A virgin grove of Greentrees' tall narrow trees, their leaves purple from an analog of Terra's photosynthetic rhodomicrobia, grew beside the labs. Although they stood at the edge of Mira City, just before the river swept abruptly west, to Alex the labs were the heart of the city. Here the native flora and fauna of Greentrees were genetically adapted to fit two not always compatible ends: preservation of the native ecology and use by humans who had come from a different planet. Without the labs, humans might have survived on Greentrees, but they would not have flourished. As the tray-o, the Technology Resource Allocation officer, Alex meted out the largest share, by far, of resources to the gene labs. Too large a share, some said. Let them. The labs were key.

And someone had the arrogance, the stupidity, the sheer bad taste—to Alex, the three were nearly synonymous—to threaten the labs.

The solemn, pretty Chinese girl, Star Chu, had warned Alex just minutes ago. "Alex . . . I'm afraid there might be trouble at the gene labs. Soon. Now. I can't say more, but I think you should survey it. Take security with you." And Star had turned away, disappearing fluidly into the crowd, before Alex could question her, could in fact do more than numbly register that Star herself looked like the embodiment of what she had delicately referred to as "trouble": a hardworking, successful part owner of a Greentrees corporation who nonetheless wore fake Cheyenne tattoos on her cheek, used Blue Lion and fizzies, and wore discontent as blatantly as her red lipstick. Yet she'd warned Alex.

Alex's father had once told her that he thought the Arabs would cause eventual problems. *"Over time the Arabs might find Greentrees a real culture shock. The contrast between the traditions they bring with them and the ways pioneer societies evolve could lead to real factionalism among them, even violence. Watch out especially for their youth, Alex."* But the Arabs had settled in seamlessly, developing a sort of semisecular semiassimilated Islam that satisfied everybody, and the Chinese youth had splintered, rebelled, and exploded. Go figure.

The lab buildings looked quiet, an unlovely utilitarian series of connected foamcast cubes. Alex, who hadn't taken the time to wait for security, approached cautiously. The front door of Building D stood crazily agape on half its hinges. Someone had lasered it.

Alex could remember when no one on Greentrees locked buildings.

She took her comlink from a pocket formed by her red-and-green wrap, which she had tied in an elaborate, modest crisscross that didn't impede movement. Guy Davenport, Mira's security chief, answered immediately. "Alex here," she panted. "I'm at the gene labs, the door's been forced open, and there may be trouble."

"Don't go in," Guy said. "A detail will be there right away. Do you hear me, Alex, don't go—" She clicked off and entered the building.

The corridor was cool and shadowed, a sharp contrast to the sunlight outside. There was no lobby; this was a completely utilitarian structure. Alex walked past closed doors, some with Restricted signs. At the end of the corridor, the door to the animal labs stood open. Something crashed inside, and suddenly the air was thick with shrieking.

She sprinted forward. "Stop it! What are you doing here! My God, you can't—" And stopped dead.

Two groups of Chinese kids faced off across the room. Cages surrounded them, and half the noise came from a pair of lions, the only predator on Greentrees dangerous to humans. Tree dwelling, the lions had the long sleek bodies of cats but with tentacled forelegs and a powerful prehensile tail to wrap around branches. Like so much else on Greentrees, their skin was purplish blue. Alex knew that the geneticists were trying to modify the lions' genome to make them less aggressive without disrupting Greentrees' food chain. So far this had failed.

The female of the experimental breeding pair screamed in her cage. The male stood in the middle of the floor, baring its teeth at the unarmed group of kids huddled against a side wall.

"Get out of here, Alexandra Cutler," one of the others said. That group stood beside the door Alex had just burst through, their leader armed with a laser gun he should not have been able to obtain.

She forced herself to calm. "You're Yat-Shing Wong, aren't you?"

"Wong Yat-Shing," the boy sneered. "In Hope of Heaven, we've reclaimed true Chinese usage in our naming."

Hope of Heaven. Alex's heart sank. Hope of Heaven was the dissident settlement established ten miles downriver from Mira City, and this was some sort of youth war between the Chinese of Hope of Heaven and the Chinese in Mira. Alex couldn't imagine anything more stupid, or more dangerous. The lion growled softly.

"Mr. Wong, you don't want that animal to hurt anyone."

Wong only smiled.

"Ms. Cutler, it's coming closer!" a captive girl in a brief red wrap said, although the lion wasn't. Alex considered her chances of seizing Wong's gun and shooting the beast; not good.

"Stay calm," Alex called to the girl. "Yat-Shing, you don't want to be charged with murder. I know you don't."

There had never been a murder on Greentrees, not in fifty years.

Wong snarled, "You don't know anything about what we want in Hope of Heaven!"

The lion gathered itself to leap.

The girl in the red wrap screamed. The three others in her group tried to run toward the door, one of them tripping and sprawling facedown in front of the lion. Alex grabbed for Wong's gun and was easily shoved away. As she fell, pictures of the scene registered on her numbed mind, each preternaturally hard edged and clear:

The girl in the red wrap with her hands over her face, long slim hands with rings on each pinkie.

The sprawled boy, raising his head from the floor as the lion soared over him toward the girl, his look befuddled as he glimpsed the underbelly of the attacker.

The spear arcing through the air and catching the lion in mid-flight, so that it shivered on the air and then dropped short of the girl, pierced through the soft tissue of its right scent organ and into the brain.

A spear?

Alex rose slowly and turned her head. If she had expected anything at all, if she'd been able to think of anything, it would have been a Cheyenne brave. There were Cheyenne in Mira for the celebration. The Cheyenne, those southern romantics reviving a primitive lifestyle from an earlier planet, used spears. A Cheyenne might have—oh yes, *this* made sense—just wandered by and happened to hurl a spear at a deliberately loosed lion deep inside the genetics lab building—

Framed in the doorway stood an alien Fur, seven feet high, balanced on its jumping tail, a second spear in its tentacled hand.

The room went absolutely silent, even the sobbing rescued girl. Probably half the kids in this room didn't even believe the Furs existed. No more native to Greentrees than were humans, their population was small and their history completely improbable. Almost no one in Mira had ever seen one. The primitive Furs lived far to the south, in the same subcontinent as their enemies the Cheyenne, countless light-years from their space-faring cousins who had sworn to destroy humanity.

Alex scrambled to her feet and lunged a second time for Wong's gun, before he could shoot the Fur. She was too late. Nan Frayne stood beside the Fur, the boy's gun in her hand, his arms laced painfully behind his back to a thonged stick she held casually in her other hand.

"Nan—"

"I was with a security detail when they were comlinked," the old woman said. "Old"—not the right word, no. Nan Frayne looked old as boulders looked old, weathered and strong and something not to get crushed by. "You need better security people, Alex."

And now Guy's forces came puffing through the door, two men as middle-aged as Alex but much fatter, guns drawn, looking helpless.

"Security's fine," Alex said crossly, which was stupid because clearly it wasn't. Nan Frayne, the two times she'd met her before, made Alex feel like an idiot.

"Could have fooled me," Nan said. "Gang stomper?"

Alex didn't know what the words meant; Nan was First Landing and they all used Earth words that had slipped out of the language because there was no need for them. Alex didn't answer. Nan said something in a low, growly language to the Fur, who answered her. The kids gaped at the alien. The security men began to yammer at Alex. Yat-Shing Wong, or Wong Yat-Shing, began, "If you think you—" and Nan gave a casual twitch of the stick holding him that made him yelp in pain. Through this babble Nan turned to Alex and spoke as if the rest of the din didn't exist.

"I was coming to see you anyway. Your mayor wants you. He just got word. There's a ship approaching Greentrees."

Alex opened her mouth but no words came. No ship had approached Greentrees for thirty-nine years. There were only two possibilities whose ship it was. Finally she managed, "Is it—"

"I don't know if it's Karim Mahjoub—or if it's the enemy. You go find out. I've got better things to do."

A moment later Alex found herself holding the stick that tethered the furious Wong, and both Nan and the Fur had melted out the door.

2

MIRA CITY

Jake had warned them. For thirty-nine years he'd warned them, and it had done very little good. Now he slumped in his wheelchair, his old bones aching and his mind struggling to stay awake, because they hadn't listened to his warnings and the time had finally come to pay for that.

Maybe.

The hastily called meeting included the triumvirate, Jake, and the physicist in charge of Mira's dwindling array of space sats, David Parker. Contain the information, Jake had said immediately, and for once Alex had actually listened to him.

"The ship is coming in at a tiny fraction of c, and it's just beyond Cap," said Butler, and everybody shut up because that put a new spin on everything. Cap was the farthest-out planet in the star system; in Mira City, major landmarks were given nonsense-syllable names to avoid favoring any one of its three dominant cultures. So the planets were Mel, Jun, Greentrees, Par, and Cap. Cap was 2.6 new AUs from the sun, David said, while Jake tried to remember what a new AU was and failed.

"So if it's coming in that slow," Alex said, "it isn't using a McAndrew Drive? And it's not Furs *or* Karim Mahjoub?"

"No way to tell," David answered. He was a thin, nervous, balding man with startling blue-green eyes, undoubtedly the legacy of a vanity genemod three or more generations ago on Earth. He was some sort of distant cousin to Alex, Jake remembered, but, then, three-quarters of the scientists on Greentrees belonged to the vast Cutler clan. As Parker spoke, he plucked at his left ear. "There's no reason I can think of why either Karim or attacking Furs wouldn't use the drive to come in, if they had it. If this ship keeps on the way it is, it won't be here for eleven days. Our orbital probes are giving us plenty of warning."

Mayor Shanti said, "Then I don't see how it could be Furs. An enemy wouldn't do that."

Lau-Wah Mah said, "I don't think Karim would, either."

The Cheyenne leader, whose name Jake had forgotten (he forgot too much these days), and who had been asked to the meeting only because he was in Mira City for the celebration, said nothing.

In the general silence that followed Mah's remark, Jake shifted his chair for a better view of the Chinese governor. Shifting the chair cost Jake effort and pain. Once the chair had been powered, but a few years ago the parts had worn out and Alex as tray-o had, rightly, not deemed powerchair replacement parts the best use of limited metal-factory resources. There was a limit to how many different things a pioneer society could manufacture. More important things than powerchairs had gone to the bottom of the list. Still, Jake missed his old chair.

Lau-Wah Mah's face gave nothing away. Did he know yet what had happened at the genetics lab? In his second year of his six-year term as governor, Mah was the third most important man in Mira, after his fellow triumvirates Mayor Shanti and Alex Cutler. Mah was a quiet, focused man with a smooth blank face like a peeled egg. So far he had let the other two, advised by Jake, make most of the decisions.

Jake couldn't remember when the triumvirate system had informally devolved to mean one Arab, one Anglo, and one Chinese, but he didn't like it. This wasn't the way he and Gail Cutler had designed the political system on Greentrees to work.

Well, nothing had happened as designed. How could it, when they'd discovered sentient Furs living on Greentrees, and then it had turned out that the Furs weren't native to Greentrees but imported, part of a vast biological experiment by another alien race at war with the real Furs. Mira City had been caught in the crossfire between these two technologically superior races. Jake and eight others had been kidnapped by the Furs to send them to the Vine planet to destroy the Vines' defenses, but of course the Fur plan had failed because Karim Mahjoub—

"Jake," Alex said gently, and he realized he'd been doing it again, letting his mind wander back to the vigorous past. Ah, it was no fun being old. He forced himself to pay attention to the here and now.

David Parker said, "We haven't had any radio communication from the ship. But I agree with Lau-Wah—I can't see why Karim would come in that slowly, when he can use the McAndrew Drive for rapid balanced deceleration much closer in. Why take the extra time?"

The mayor said tentatively, "Maybe to investigate what he's coming back to. After all, he's been gone thirty-nine years."

They all contemplated this. *Thirty-nine years*, Jake thought. And for Karim, how long? A year, maybe. Maybe less, depending on how much time they'd spent under McAndrew Drive. Karim and Lucy would still be around thirty years old. Lucy, whom he'd once held in his arms, kissed, loved . . . *Stay in the present.*

Alex said, "Caution could be the reason for Karim's radio silence, too. Waiting until we contact him."

"No, no," Jake said, suddenly glad to be paying attention. "It's not caution. There's no radio on the *Franz Mueller*. Remember, I told you all—it's a captured Fur ship! They use quee, and Greentrees no longer has that capacity. I told you!"

"I forgot," Alex said.

"You all have forgotten too much! I've tried for decades to keep up the war preparations for this city because I *told* you it would happen, but each year there's more and more slack, and if we get an actual Fur attack I don't know if anyone is prepared at all, and . . ."

Jake stopped. Wrong, wrong. He was ranting, sounding exactly like an old man no one would heed. And no one was, except Alex, who was listening out of compassion rather than belief. Even now, with a ship coming in . . .

Lau-Wah said, "What is the state of war preparations? Who is in charge of that?"

Mayor Shanti said uncertainly, "Isn't it Donald Halloran? Or, no, he died and so his assistant must have taken over. Alex?"

She shrugged, not looking at Jake. "I know we all received a com about it, but I can't remember the name. An Anglo, I think."

"Well, it would hardly be a New Quaker," Jake said curtly, and Alex laughed. A second later her face showed how much she regretted the laugh.

The mayor said, "I know it's serious, Jake. This ship . . . Alex, find out who the new defense admin is and call him here."

Alex nodded and opened a comlink. "Siddalee? Who's the defense admin since Donald Halloran died? . . . Well, find out and get him or her here, please." She closed her link.

And that was another thing, Jake thought—in his day, they could have called up the information by computer. But fewer and fewer computers still worked, and Greentrees simply did not have the resources to manufacture many replacements. What they did create or adapt was usually assigned to the genetics lab, but even there people had taken to keeping the bulk of their notes on paper. Mira City numbered—what?—maybe fifteen thousand people now (once he would have known the exact number), but that wasn't enough to sustain every aspect of a fully digital society. And a lot of those people were New Quakers, who weren't interested in machinery, and neither were Larry Smith's ridiculous Cheyenne . . . no, wait, Larry Smith was dead long ago, somebody else led the tribes, Larry had been the founder, when the Cheyenne were still learning how to live off the land and glorify it with the spirit dances Jake had attended once, at dawn in the—

He was wandering in time again.

"—evacuation if necessary," Mayor Shanti said.

"How would we do that?" Lau-Wah said. "Where could we evacuate that many people to?"

"Our people aren't exactly good at living off the land," Alex said. "Maybe the Cheyenne had the right idea all along. No, don't scowl at me, David, I was joking. There's Siddalee comming back."

She listened to her call, while Jake studied her. Such a strong face. Not pretty, exactly, although her slim body curved nicely. Her features were too big and angular for feminine beauty, especially her jaw, but she had thick glossy hair, brown only slightly touched with gray, and undeniably beautiful eyes. Deep gray, wide, fringed with black lashes. Expressive eyes. Too expressive, maybe; Alex was not good at hiding her feelings. She'd had a very bad time when her young husband was killed in a mining accident, but that was long ago and she seemed all right now.

"The new defense admin is named Jon McBain," Alex said. "Does anybody know him?"

No one did.

"Well, I do. Siddalee says he's out in the bush right now, doing a field survey. He's a xenobiologist who's supposed to be developing a microbial battery, but he—never mind. Siddalee's still trying to reach him directly."

Jake said, "The defense admin might be unreachable while Mira is *under attack?*"

"We're not under attack, Jake," Alex said soothingly.

"Not yet! Give it a few days!"

"Jake is right," the mayor said, looking from one to another as if afraid his opinion might be rejected. "We went slack and now we might have to pay for it . . . Allah willing, not too heavily. Alex, could you ask Siddalee to reach McBain any way she can and get him back here? Meanwhile, David, we need to go over what still works of our equipment in space and what we might be able to do with it. Alex, maybe you could do the same for the resources in the city. Lau-Wah, would you mind digging up the last approved set of evacuation plans so we know what's usable and what we need to devise new? David, you'll know the second that ship signals any-thing at all, by any method?"

"Yes."

"Good," Shanti said, smiling diffidently at Jake. "Jake, you're the only one who really knows the Furs. If they attack, what can we expect? Maybe you could start with background."

They were actually going to listen to him, thanks to Ashraf's timid courtesy. It almost made up for their criminal ignorance. But only "almost"—thirty-nine years of peace and hard pioneering work were no excuse for that ignorance.

Alex was staring at him hard. Silently she mouthed, *Don't rant.*

She was right, fuck it all. Jake had to be careful to sound focused, sound *right.* He chose his words carefully.

"Every single contact humans have had with the space-faring Furs was bellicose. They're apparently xenophobic to an almost unbelievable degree. They've been at war with the Vines for thousands of years, trying for genocide. When they discovered that the Vines, whose technology is bio-based rather than industrial or digital, had created clone colonies of Furs on Greentrees in order to develop some virus to neutralize them . . ." Jake fell silent, remembering those cloned Fur colonies. One practically too passive to feed themselves, one all female, one perpetually intoxicated by some parasite lodged in their brain . . .

"Jake," Alex prompted.

"I haven't lost track. The Furs killed every one of their own species in the Vine-created colonies. Just wiped them out, along with the Vines on Greentrees, because the created Furs were defective. They even tried to wipe out the control colony of Furs, who weren't defective, just because the Vines had made them. They got a lot of them but not all, because so many males were away hunting in the forest. The Greentrees-born Furs left are primitive but just as bloodthirsty as their space-faring cousins. The Cheyenne, as you know, are intermittently raided by the survivors. The only human who has ever been able to make contact with them is Nan Frayne.

"If the space Furs attack here, they'll be just as ruthless to us as they were to their own clones."

"Unless Karim has succeeded," Alex said quickly.

"Yes."

"That could be the—" David Parker's comlink shrilled.

Jake closed his eyes. This was about the ship; he knew it. How? No point in trying to figure it out; if there was one thing you knew when you were eighty-five, it was that not all knowledge operated rationally. He waited.

No one said anything for too long.

Jake opened his eyes. The other three sat gazing expectantly at Parker, who looked stunned. The physicist cleared his throat, tried to speak, failed. He tried again.

"That was the monitor on duty. The ship doesn't have a McAndrew Drive. It's not Fur, and it's not Karim Mahjoub, and it just radioed . . . not 'just,' of course, it took the signal some hours to come in from their distance out . . . I'm sorry, I'm not making sense." He stopped.

"David—" Alex said.

"The ship radioed. They're human. From Earth."

Stay calm, Alex told herself, and knew there wasn't a chance in the world that she would. *Well, then, fake it.*

"David, what was the exact message?"

He fumbled with his left ear. Alex remembered suddenly, irrelevantly, that David had done that even when they'd been children. "Shurong said—"

"Shurong?"

"My assistant. Shurong Ou. She said the message was short, just, 'This is the ship *Crucible,* from Earth, commanded by Julian Cabot Martin, Third Life Alliance. We—'"

"What did you just say?" Jake demanded in his quavery old voice. "Who?"

"Uh, 'Third Life Alliance.'"

"That was the organization in control of the Earth-Greentrees quee the last time we heard from Earth. Nearly fifty years ago. I remember the name. Gail and I had just—"

"Jake, it doesn't matter now," Alex said impatiently, and immediately regretted it. She should be more patient with the old man.

Lau-Wah said, "Go on, Dr. Parker."

David pulled at his ear. "Yes, ah, 'This is the ship *Crucible,* from Earth, commanded by Julian Cabot Martin, Third Life Alliance. We are a scientific and fact-finding mission, launched in response to your last quee informing Earth that sentient aliens have been discovered on Greentrees. Request permission to land.' Shurong said that the message was repeated in Chinese and then in what she presumed was Arabic."

"So they know the colony's history," Ashraf Shanti said, which struck Alex as silly. Why wouldn't they know it?

"David," she said, "I thought you told me once that if a ship had left Earth the same day that Mira City queed Earth about finding Furs, it would still be seventy years before anyone got here. It's only been forty-nine."

"*I* told you that," Jake said irritably, "and I said if a ship *like ours* left Earth the same day. We don't know what advances Earth has made in stellar drives. Anyway, they're here."

"Yes, they are," Ashraf said. "What do we want to tell them to do?"

Alex stopped herself from rolling her eyes. Ashraf was not, had never been, a strong leader. Well, you didn't want too strong a leader in Mira, you wanted someone who could shape consensus. Even so, Ashraf sometimes struck her as overly swayed by the last person who happened to speak forcefully. He was intelligent, certainly, but not . . . individual enough. She sometimes suspected that Lau-Wah, who was individual and who would probably be the next mayor, thought the same, although they had never discussed it.

Lau-Wah said quietly, "I see several choices. We can tell them to land near Mira City and prepare a welcome. We can ask them to land a few thousand miles away and meet them there, until we see for ourselves just who they are and what they want. We can send the shuttle up with a delegation to dock at their ship, either in orbit or farther out, and do an inspection before letting them land."

David, looking genuinely surprised, blurted, "But why would you distrust a scientific expedition?"

"I do not," Lau-Wah said. "But I wish to be sure they are a scientific expedition. Or at least, that they have no ideas of conquest. Conquest and war were the dominant themes on Earth, you know, when we received that last quee message, the one Jake mentioned about the Third Life Alliance having taken over the quee sender at Geneva."

Jake had fallen asleep, the sudden light sleep of the old. Alex nudged his foot with hers and he jerked awake. He would hate himself, and her, if he missed this.

She said, deliberately recapping, "Yes, I think you're right, Lau-Mah. We can tell them to land near Mira City, ask them to land a few thousand miles away and meet them there, or send the shuttle up with a delegation to dock at their ship in orbit or even farther out."

Jake said instantly, "Meet them as far out as you can."

Ashraf said hesitantly, "Won't that look belligerent?"

"Who cares?" Jake said with sudden and unexpected force. His old eyes darted across their faces. "Safety comes first!"

Lau-Mah said, "I'm not sure it matters where we meet them. If they're belligerent, a shuttle party won't stop them. And I don't think we want to risk the *Beta Vine*. We may need it later."

This made sense to Alex. Mira City had possessed only two starships, both fitted with the rapid-acceleration McAndrew Drive, both captured thirty-nine years ago from the enemy Furs. The *Beta Vine* orbited Greentrees with a skeleton crew of what passed for military, actually just some of the city's security force, plus a changing roster of scientists carrying out various experiments. The last time Alex had been upstairs on the *Beta Vine*, it had been overrun by a party of touring schoolchildren whose class had won some sort of all-city competition. The Fur ship was equipped with formidable weapons that humans had learned to use. Nothing in Mira could match the firepower on the *Beta Vine*—although of course any attacking Fur ship would presumably have at least as good weaponry. Those weapons, in fact, were one of the primary reasons Mira had become so slack on downstairs defense.

The other reason was that the second ship, the *Franz Mueller*, had left thirty-nine years ago to destroy the Fur empire from within. That had been the plan, anyway, launched the year after Alex was born. The Vines, those half-mythic aliens seen only by a handful of people still alive, had also been at war with the Furs. Out of their advanced biotech and a few thousand years of experimentation on their enemy, the Vines had created an infectious organism that was supposed to attack the Fur brain and render the entire species passive and harmless.

It had done just that, Jake insisted, on the small group of Furs Mira City encountered fifty years ago. Two of Jake's contemporaries, Karim Mahjoub and Lucy Lasky, had set out in the *Franz Mueller* with a load of infected Furs, to arrange for them to be picked up by space-faring Furs and so begin the systematic infection of the entire species. Aboard McAndrew Drive ships, which could reach nearly light speed at amazing accelerations, Karim and Lucy would age only a few years for the thirty-nine they'd been gone so far, just as Jake had aged only a few months for the eleven years he'd been gone on an alien ship the first time around.

That was the story, anyway.

Alex knew she wasn't the only one to doubt it. Not the actual events—she believed those (although other, younger Mirites who did not know Jake personally thought the entire history so much junk DNA). No, what Alex doubted was some of the interpretations of events. Were the "Vines" really so powerful, peaceful, and manipulative as all that? Had they really created a superinfectious microorganism, or whatever it had been, to declaw their enemy, rather than just wiping them out? What made Karim and Lucy think they could cajole a superadvanced enemy into picking up their own disgraced fellow soldiers, or that the enemy would be naive enough not to realize that the rescued Furs might be contagious? After all, the Furs supposedly knew that the Vines were master microbiologists. And if it did happen that way, why should Furs revenge themselves on humans rather than on Vines?

"You don't understand," Jake had said to her the one time she'd voiced these concerns to him. He'd clutched her arm with such desperate urgency, had become so wild-eyed in his broken power-chair. "I was there!"

"I know, I know," she'd soothed the old man, and hadn't brought up the subject again. But as tray-o, she had made her resource-allocation decisions with strong skepticism about the likelihood of invading aliens.

And it looked as if she'd been right. The *Crucible* held humans, not Furs.

She said, "We need to balance any danger from this new ship with creating a reasonable welcome. If we treat them too unfriendly, we run the risk of creating unpleasantness where there doesn't need to be any."

"Yes, that's true," Lau-Wah said. "Let me suggest this: We allow the *Crucible* to take a geosynchronous high orbit, and we send up the shuttle. Meanwhile, the *Beta Vine* orbits on the opposite side of the planet, safe from attack. We don't try to hide our ship, just keep it away. If the *Crucible* tries to get nearer either to Mira or to the *Beta Vine* after being warned not to, we've gained a valuable piece of information."

"And maybe gained it too late!" Jake said. His left hand began to tremble.

"That sounds right to me," Alex said. Gently she put her right hand over Jake's left. "Ashraf?"

The mayor looked uncertainly from Jake to Lau-Wah. Finally he said, "Yes . . . that sounds all right. David?"

The physicist, who didn't have a vote, looked startled to be asked. "Ah, yes, certainly . . . we have a second message coming in. It's . . . no, wait . . . it's a repeat of the first. 'This is the ship *Crucible*, from Earth, commanded by Julian Cabot Martin, Third Life Alliance. We are a scientific and fact-finding mission, launched in response to your last quee informing Earth that sentient aliens have been discovered on Greentrees. Request permission to land.' "

"Radio to Commander Martin," said Lau-Wah, "that Mira City welcomes his expedition, and that the *Crucible* has permission to advance to a high-orbit position for which we will give them the coordinates."

Jake shook his head, but so feebly that not even Alex could be sure it wasn't just another tremor. She squeezed his cold fingers, but even as she offered this wan comfort, a thrill ran through her. Mira was about to learn, finally, what had happened during the last fifty years on Earth. Alex, like everyone else she knew, was not particularly interested in Earth; there was enough on Greentrees to hold both mind and imagination. Still, Earth *was* humanity's home planet, and anyway the people from it would be excitingly different, with different ideas and technology . . .

"Oh!" she said suddenly, "I wonder what replacement parts they might have for some of our machinery. Or new machinery we can barter for!"

Lau-Wah smiled. "Spoken like a true tray-o, Alex."

But Jake only gazed at her bleakly, rheum in the corners of his sunken eyes.

3

DEEP SPACE

K arim and Lucy stared at the floor beneath the ship's bridge. The Fur vessel had no way to directly view outside space when the ship was in motion; the only transparent wall was the bridge floor and during full acceleration it sat directly against the mass-plate. Of course, during acceleration the plasma cloud generated by the drive would have made it impossible to see anything, anyway. But now they had stopped. The living quarters had slid along the pole to their maximum distance from the massplate, and between the heavy struts crisscrossing the floor was an actual, if partial, view of space.

It was a view of a Vine colony world.

The Vines had been at war with the Furs for thousands of years, each battle isolated by centuries from any retaliation by the temporal mechanics of moving at nearly c. The Furs had developed their technology using physics. The Vines had developed theirs using biology. In fact, according to the biologist George Fox, whom Lucy and Karim had left behind on Greentrees, the Vines were more plants than animals, although they were also partly highly organized biofilms. "Even on Terra," George had said, "bacteria swap genes all the time. Essentially, all of Earth is one single bacterial gene pool with amazing mutability, and a single organism can change up to fifteen percent of its DNA *daily*. Vines might just have taken that to the ultimate degree."

The Vines had created the virus infecting the imprisoned Furs.

Or, rather, the "virus analogue"; George had said it wasn't really a virus even as he had declined to say what it *was*. He didn't know. None of the humans did. They were flying blind, trusting the Vines because there was no alternative.

" 'The enemy of my enemy is my friend,' " Karim said suddenly.

"What?"

"Nothing. Just something Jake once told me. We need to move fast now."

"I know that," Lucy said curtly. She didn't like any mention of Jake. "Karim . . . I think that's the shield around the planet. The one George posited, made of genetically engineered spores."

"Yes," Karim said slowly, "I think you're right."

They both fell silent.

The planet was a featureless, mottled brown-green, partially under grayish cloud cover. There were no large patches of blue ocean. Surrounding the globe, far above it and far more arresting than anything on it, billowed a huge glittering cloud of . . . something . . . that caught the sunlight. Karim estimated the shield as extending more than a 150,000 kilometers. Its density he couldn't estimate at all; the tiny individual points of whatever-they-were seemed individually invisible until hit just so by sunlight. Individually, but not collectively. It was as if the planet had been loosely wrapped in floating golden dust.

Lucy said, "Look . . . here comes the elevator."

As the globe rotated beneath their feet, something gleamed at one emerging edge: an impossibly long, impossibly thin filament extending into space, a whisker on a planet-sized cat. The light caught the filament for a moment, then its rotation carried it to a different angle and it seemed to disappear.

"What George would give to get a handful of that spore cloud!" Lucy said.

"He can't have it. If we got close enough to capture spores, then the spores could capture us. Or whatever they did to snare all those Fur ships for the Vines."

"Do you think they really are spores? That eat metal?"

"I don't know," Karim said. "Enough speculation. Let's do it now. Our quee is sending every second."

"We hope," Lucy said quietly.

They gathered their weapons, the human guns and alien "wallers," which was what Lucy called the handheld curved batons that created small invisible walls of some energy fields they did not understand. The weapons, they thought, probably wouldn't be needed, and they were right. The fourteen prisoners docilely left their room; all it took was gentle tugs on their arms. Meekly the Furs allowed themselves to be led, two by two, to the shuttle, and shoved inside. From some dim memory of former lives, they even strapped themselves in. When Lucy saw that, she suddenly wanted to cry.

"They're so . . . so *gutted*. Mentally, emotionally. Karim . . ."

"They're so harmless, is what you mean. Don't become sentimental, Lucy."

"I'm not!"

"Good. These aliens wanted to destroy Greentrees. The rest of them still do."

He was overstating, but she didn't answer.

When all fourteen Furs sat quietly in the shuttle, which was parked as close as possible to the bay door, Karim closed the small craft. The quee, of course, was already loaded into the shuttle. He and Lucy returned to the bridge and he went through the procedure he'd practiced half a dozen times on Greentrees and five hundred times since in his mind: depressurize the shuttle bay, open the shuttle doors, back away with a sudden, brief burst of acceleration that tumbled the shuttle into space as neatly as a gravid fruit.

"I wish we knew for sure that the quee was sending," he said to Lucy.

It was her turn to be unemotional. They were keeping each other balanced. "Of course it's sending. The Furs set it up to send continuously when they tried to make us ambush the Vines, remember? They were tracking us. They still are, only they think we're a Fur ship. Now they'll follow that same quee to the shuttle."

"What if they're suspicious of the shuttle not being locked from the inside?"

"I don't know, Karim. How can anybody know? We're doing the best we can."

"Don't snap at me."

"I'm sorry," Lucy said, although it was clear to them both that she was not. Neither had expected it to be quite like this: shoving sick, helpless beings out into an empty sky, less as a Trojan horse than as a collection of alien Typhoid Marys. They'd taken enormous risks to do this. They'd expected to feel more heroic.

Karim took one last long look at the shuttle, floating in the void. Then he sat in the pilot's chair and engaged the McAndrew Drive. A "quee," Quantum Entangled Energy link, sent messages instantaneously across the galaxy. Already the Furs knew that one of their missing ships had stopped, and where. The *Franz Mueller* had had only one quee, and now it floated with the Furs in an area reasonably expected to be patrolled by a combatant watching an enemy output. The rescuers could be here very soon. Karim and Lucy needed to leave.

"Karim—here comes a ship!"

He jerked his head to see the display, such a sharp jerk that pain snapped through his neck. Ship's sensors had shown nothing coming into the star system with the huge accelerations of a McAndrew Drive. He'd been so careful!

The ship was accelerating toward them from the planet.

"It's a *Vine* ship," Lucy said. "But they don't know about us! They don't have any idea who we are!"

The entire Fur fleet used quee. The Vines, bio-based, did not, not even on captured Fur ships. They somehow disabled it, and then ignored its carcass. Karim had no idea why. No Vine except a small, star-faring, experimenting band even knew humanity existed, and all members of that band were dead.

"They can't locate us while they're accelerating," Karim said rapidly. "They're blind. We're leaving!"

Karim threw the ship into high acceleration. The massplate

beneath their feet slid so fast toward them that Karim felt a surge of adrenaline: *Danger! Duck!* screamed his hindbrain. But there wasn't even the slightest lurch. The floor rapidly reconfigured. Karim swerved sideways, and for a long, glorious second he thought he'd made it. The Vine ship couldn't see him. He was out.

But not fast enough. The Vines had fired toward the last place his ship stood, and he hadn't changed course fast enough. The glittering cloud, airy and insubstantial as cosmic handfuls of flung gold dust, flared around him. Then, with an acceleration of over a hundred gee, he was beyond it. Ten minutes passed. There was no pursuit.

The ship's alarms sounded.

"We're breached!" Lucy cried. "Suit up!"

The gongs clamored the distinctive blast: two short, two long. A Fur signal, meaning who-knew-what on a Fur world. But Karim and Lucy had heard it before, when the inevitable meteor had struck the *Franz Mueller* as she left Greentrees orbit. This time, the breach was multiple. Karim and Lucy barely had time to fasten suit and helmet before the air disappeared.

Then the ship stopped.

"Karim!"

"She isn't responding."

All at once, he felt strangely calm. He looked at Lucy through the clear bowl of his helmet. Not a human-made helmet but one that the dead Vines had created for humans. It was much superior to any human counterpart because it carried its own atmosphere-creating microorganisms sealed in the neck ring. Karim had tested the helmets weekly; they still worked. Surely these new Vines would recognize the handiwork of their own kind. Surely that would help.

Lucy said, dazed, "It was spores, wasn't it? Just like George said. They clung to the ship and ate through the metal until they found the drive."

"I don't know. Maybe. Probably. The displays have all gone dead."

"It happened so *fast*."

"They've had several thousand years to practice."

She took his hand. His calm had infected her, or maybe it was her own bravery. Lucy had always been brave. Without discussion, they walked from the bridge to the docking bay, where the Vine ship would join theirs and the aliens would come aboard.

He only hoped the Vines hadn't yet interfered with the shuttle full of infected Furs. And that he could find a way to explain to them the unthinkable consequences if they did.

4

MIRA CITY

Outside the Mausoleum, the anniversary celebration was still in full swing. Inside, the triumvirate worked on the message for David Parker's people to send to the *Crucible*. Then they composed a public announcement for MiraNet. Ashraf Shanti ended the emergency meeting, and Alex asked Siddalee Brown to take Jake home.

"Lau-Wah, wait. You, too, Ashraf," she said as they prepared to leave her small, cluttered office. They'd met there instead of the mayor's office because the latter faced the park, with all its anniversary noise: shouting, singing, laughter, dance music, firecrackers. Alex's office, on the opposite side of the ponderous building, had its one window open to a stretch of experimental plant beds. Even so, revelers had clearly been here before moving on to within earshot of the speech platform. In the crop beds were trampled flowers and overturned benches. There wasn't much actual debris; Mira City recycled everything possible and bottles, cans, and paper were too precious to waste. But various items of clothing littered the ground: was that a pile of wraps by the pond? Siddalee would grumble for days.

"Is something else wrong?" Ashraf said. He usually anticipated something wrong. Well, this time he was correct.

"Yes," Alex said. "While I was supposed to be giving a speech, I was at the genetics lab. Lau-Wah, four of those dissident kids from Hope of Heaven broke in and loosed a lion from its cage. It was menacing four of the Mira lab techs, also all Chinese. They—"

"Yat-Shing Wong?" Lau-Wah said, his face stony.

"Yes." So Lau-Wah already knew. Something, anyway.

"Who's that?" Ashraf said fearfully.

"A misguided idealist," Lau-Wah said. "Was anybody killed?"

"No, because . . . because . . ."

"Sit down, Alex. Do you want a glass of water?"

"I'm *fine*. It's just a lot for one day." A ship from Earth, the disproved surge of fear that the ship might have been Furs, the hatred at the lab: a hatred such as Alex hadn't suspected existed in Mira. Then the long, sleek, purple-blue body of the leaping lion, the girl with her ringed hands over her face, the spear arcing through the air and catching the lion in midflight. The alien Fur balanced on its jumping tail. Nan Frayne casually cruel in lacing the boy to her stick, with a supposed enemy of all humanity by her side.

"Tell it from the beginning," Lau-Wah said with a detachment that steadied her. She hated to appear weak.

When she'd finished, Ashraf said, "Where are the kids from Hope of Heaven now?"

"I turned all eight over to Guy until we decided what to say publicly about the ship. They were all there when Nan Frayne made her announcement. Ashraf, did you authorize her to bring a *Fur* to the city celebration?"

"She never asked. And I didn't anticipate it."

Alex managed a smile. "Well, no, one wouldn't."

Lau-Wah said, "Has the Fur left Mira?"

"I don't know," Ashraf said. "I didn't even know it was here."

Alex said, "My guess is that Nan Frayne vanished back into the wilderness with the Fur, before anyone from the Cheyenne delegation realized it had come."

"I'm glad," Ashraf said with sudden force, "that we only have this sort of event every fifty years."

Despite herself, Alex laughed. Lau-Wah didn't. He said, "I propose we comlink Security Chief Davenport to let the lab techs go. By now MiraNet has made the public announcement of the *Crucible*. I'd like permission from you two to talk to Yat-Shing Wong alone."

Alex said, "It's Wong Yat-Shing now. He says Hope of Heaven is reverting to 'true Chinese usage.'"

Lau-Wah nodded expressionlessly.

Ashraf said, "Certainly, Lau-Wah, talk to Mr. Wong alone if you think it will do any good. What do they want? No one in Mira is poor or oppressed!"

"No," Lau-Wah said. "I do not think that's the problem."

"Then what is?" Ashraf said, and Alex held her breath, waiting for the answer.

"I think they want to feel oppressed so they have a reason for feeling angry," Lau-Wah said quietly.

Ashraf looked honestly bewildered. "But why are they angry?"

Lau-Wah didn't answer. The silence spun itself out, and finally Alex said, "Because they feel at the bottom, don't they? Only I don't really see why. I'm sorry, Lau-Wah, but I don't see . . . there's so much here. Enough for everybody. We don't really have a 'bottom' in Mira."

"There's always a bottom. The definition of it just changes," Lau-Wah said. He didn't look at either of the others as he spoke. "You've never been much interested in Earth history, Alex. Fifty years ago what you still call 'the Chinese contingent' came here through the philanthropy of one man, Huang Ji-en. He rescued desperate immigrants and Chinese nationals who were being systematically persecuted, even tortured. On Greentrees that generation had a new chance and was grateful, but their grandchildren see only that we started with less education than the Arabs or the Quakers or the Cutler clan, and with much less capital investment in Mira, because Huang wished to pay for as many come to Greentrees as he could.

"All that has translated into less power now. Most Chinese are lab technicians but not lab owners. Farm workers but not farm owners, not because land isn't available but because machinery isn't. It is still a capitalist society, and Chinese control little working capital. Also, there is no open university here yet, and apprentice positions to the scientists, the physicians, the manufacturies' heads are limited. They seldom go to us. Nepotism is always strong in a pioneer society. That is perhaps natural, since family is necessary when there is so much to do, but it has not helped us Chinese. Yes, everyone has everything they need. But sometimes that doesn't satisfy."

Alex stared at Lau-Wah. This was the longest speech she'd ever heard him make. Ashraf opened his mouth to say something, then closed it again.

She said quietly, "Obviously you've thought about this a lot, Lau-Wah. I'm afraid I haven't. I wasn't paying attention, I guess. But what do you think should be done?"

"I will talk to Wong Yat-Shing."

"No, I mean about the larger situation. What do you suggest we—"

"I will talk to Wong Yat-Shing," Lau-Wah repeated, and this time the note of finality was unmistakable. Lau-Wah had said as much as he would; perhaps he thought he'd said too much. Alex had come up against this trait in him before: a sudden opening of a door to permit a clear glimpse of lucidly arranged thought, and then just as suddenly, the door closed again. Restricted: No Entry. It frustrated her enormously.

"Lau-Wah—"

"I will report to you both what I learn," Lau-Wah said, and left the room.

Alex and Ashraf stared at each other. "Do you think, Ashraf, that I should—"

"I think you and I should do nothing," Ashraf said. He shrugged slightly. "We have bigger problems, Alex. Fur ships, human ships. Lau-Wah can concern himself with his people's petty discontents."

There it was. The dismissal that Lau-Wah had spoken of, the relegation of the Chinese to an unimportant status—and from Ashraf Shanti, never the most perceptive of men but also not the most condescending. Ashraf didn't even see his own attitude. Was this "racism"? Maybe it was.

Should Alex discuss the whole situation with Jake? He'd seen these different ethnic groups on Earth, had recruited them for

Greentrees, had built Mira City with them, had observed them for fifty years. Whatever he had to say would be informed by background.

But . . . it might be *all* background. More and more, Jake's mind wandered into the past. He produced long, boring tales of incidents from a childhood Alex couldn't picture. Crowded cities, biowarfare, sparkle concerts, cars and trains, pollution masks, CO_2-level alerts, going to bed hungry . . . Alex had never known anyone involuntarily hungry, not her whole life. Jake's reminiscences were so irrelevant, and so depressing. It was hard to stay interested.

No, she didn't want to discuss Wong Yat-Shing with Jake.

She looked out again at the trampled experimental seed beds. By tomorrow the techs would have it looking good again. The gene-farm might even try out new flowers in the beds; Alex would enjoy gazing out at those. In their variations on native plants, the geneticists often came up with genuinely beautiful colors, shadings, and shapes.

By tomorrow everything would be restored to normal.

It took the *Crucible* eleven days to reach orbit around Greentrees. However the ship was powered, it wasn't by a McAndrew Drive. During that time, Commander Julian Cabot Martin proved willing to answer anything they asked him, although of course there was no way to know if his answers were truthful.

The ship, chartered and financed by the Third Life Alliance in Geneva, United Atlantic Federation, had left the solar system forty-seven years ago, five years in ship time. She carried no quee. The *Crucible* did not have power to spare for the enormous drain of a quee, since even though there had been advances in drive technology in fifty years, Earth was in such a bad state that launching the *Crucible* at all had been very difficult. In fact, Earth itself would never send quee messages again. The *Crucible* carried only fifty-six people, all of whom but three had been in cold sleep for the voyage. Thirty of those were scientists from various disciplines, eager to study the first sentient aliens humanity had ever found.

"Good luck," Siddalee Brown muttered. "That Nan Frayne is the only one who could help them do that, and I doubt she will."

Alex doubted it, too. "Only three people awake for five years! How did they stand it?"

Jake said, "You're used to people around you all the time. You like that. These people may be much different."

"I don't see that," Alex argued. "Earth is much more crowded than Mira. You've told me that over and over. It seems to me that this Julian Cabot Martin would be more accustomed to people, not less."

Jake didn't answer, merely got that sad, knowing look that appeared more and more on his wizened face. The three of them sat in Alex's house, which had somehow by degrees become Jake's house as well. Alex was not interested in home decorating, and her two-room apartment, rented from the city and convenient to the Mausoleum, had scarcely anything in it but the standard sturdy, utilitarian foamcast furniture it had come with. Alex never noticed. She only slept and dressed here, and sometimes not even that, staying overnight in her office. Jake had come to occupy the bedroom, and Siddalee had moved in a cot for Alex. It stood, rumpled and unmade, under the room's only adornment, a plaque awarded to Alex by the Mira City Council for exemplary service. Siddalee had rescued the plaque from under a pile of debris in Alex's office and had hung it on the apartment wall.

Today Siddalee had brought a cake from the new bakery on Friend Street. The bakery was Quaker, which meant it was owned by a single family who was more interested in providing a good product than in becoming rich. Flavored with the Greentrees spice tangmoss, sweetened with genemod honey from Terran bees, rich with sue-bird eggs, the cake was the best Alex had ever tasted. She'd eaten, greedily, three slices. The cake's sparse remains littered her foamcast table, where Katous was illegally licking them up.

"Alex, you shouldn't let that cat up on the table," Siddalee said disapprovingly.

"Oh, he's all right."

"He's way too fat."

"Probably," Alex said.

"Living is too easy on Greentrees," Jake said. "I remember when I was young and—"

"It's time for MiraNet," Alex said. She really couldn't take one more story about the Earth of seventy years ago.

"Turn it on," Siddalee said, and Alex opened the comlink.

MiraNet had started as a full-time computer site, largely self-operating. The program sorted through all news postings from anyone in the infant colony; prioritized them by sender, content, and urgency; and provided sophisticated graphics and pertinent deebee background. Alex could remember that version of MiraNet from her childhood. Over time, Mira's computers had slowly decayed, even more slowly become beyond replacement. MiraNet had added comlink broadcast, which provided audio but no visual. Now there were too many people, and too many colony survival priorities, to provide everyone with a computer. So MiraNet ran partly on computer, partly on audio-only comlinks, partly on short-wave radio. They were, Alex as tray-o knew all too well, going backwards.

It was only temporary, she told herself. The technology was not lost. Mira would again make computers. When they were caught up on the manufacturing 'bots necessary, when the train system was running, when they were ahead on medical supplies, when the farming equipment was adequate . . .

"The *Crucible* will reach Greentrees' orbit tomorrow and will be met by the Mira City shuttle," MiraNet announced. Alex wondered what views of the ship the Net was displaying. As tray-o she could have assigned herself a computer but had not; she was not corrupt enough to waste one in a private home when there were so few left. "This is the latest from Julian Cabot Martin:

" 'We are very eager to meet you,' " came the deep, formal voice now recognizable to everyone on Greentrees. " 'It has been a long, dull voyage. All of us are now awake and looking forward to stepping onto solid ground.' "

Jake said fretfully, "He never actually says anything, have you noticed that? All PR."

Alex didn't know what "PR" was, and didn't ask. "He just said they're all awake. That's new information, Jake."

"Now that cat's *lying* on your table, Alex," Siddalee said. "It's just not sanitary."

Alex shooed away Katous, who gave her a baleful look before stalking into a corner and lying on Alex's jacket, which she'd flung there the last time it rained.

"Mira Corp Consolidated Mining," continued MiraNet, "announced today another mining start north of the Avery Mountains, where naturally occurring tunnels and underground aquifers make it relatively easy to—"

Siddalee reached out and closed the link.

"Alex—" Jake began, but Alex immediately cut him off. "Put the link back on, Siddalee."

"Alex, you don't have to listen to any—"

"I said put it on!"

Siddalee reopened the comlink. Alex glowered; she hated the way people still, after all this time, assumed that any mention of anything connected with mining distressed her. How did they think she did her job as tray-o?

She wasn't distressed. What she chiefly felt now was guilt that she was not distressed. Kamal's death in that mining accident had been so long ago, and their marriage had been so troubled by—

"Alex!" Siddalee exclaimed, and she realized that the news item about the mining start had been interrupted.

"—just posted! Someone has burned a field camp twenty miles downriver, destroying the inflatables used by a Mira City research team as well as the riverside holding pens in which the team was breeding local fish and water animals. The team, which consists of three scientists and two apprentices, was away from camp at the time of the attack. No one was hurt. Juliana Levine, in charge of the effort, reports that in the rubble someone left a metal rod twisted into the shape of the ancient Chinese character for 'hope.' This artifact has been identified with the dissident village Hope of Heaven, which—"

"Oh, Lord help us," Siddalee said. "Them again!"

"Siddalee, comlink Lau-Wah and Ashraf and tell them I'll be at the Mausoleum in ten minutes."

"Alex, don't go running off like this! You don't even know where Lau-Wah and the mayor are!"

The comlink shrilled on override. "Alex," said Lau-Wah's calm voice, "I'm with Guy, on my way to the research camp. Ashraf has agreed to put me in charge of this problem. I'll be back by the time the shuttle returns to Greentrees tomorrow."

"Lau-Wah—"

"Thank you, Alex." The link went dead.

Alex stared at it. She had been effectively cut out of the action. Whatever it was.

Siddalee said, chewing her lip, "You have enough to do already, you know."

"So does Lau-Wah!"

"They're his people."

"That's just the wrong thinking, Siddalee! We're all our people! Everyone on Greentrees is people!" Alex said, aware that she sounded both overwrought and obscure. Damn it to hell! "Jake—"

But there was no help from Jake. He had fallen asleep, snoring gently in his chair, the gray cat on his lap.

The Mira City Welcoming Committee assembled at the shuttleport just after dawn. "Shuttleport," thought Alex, was a misnomer. Used only by scientists and the rotating skeleton crew of the orbiting *Beta Vine,* the shuttle usually rested under a huge inflatable, which had been moved every few years as the city expanded. When needed, it was rolled out of the inflatable, checked carefully, and flown upstairs. Space travel for its own sake held little glamour for her generation of Greenies; the planet itself was still too full of exciting unknowns.

This time, however, a small crowd had gathered to watch the

launch. Alex counted one robocam plus three people with hand-held recorders; MiraNet would have a lot of amateur postings. A few people carried flowers, which they presented shyly to Mayor Shanti.

"Here, the Earthmen might like these."

"Give them an advance taste of how beautiful Greentrees is."

"Thank you," Ashraf said, helplessly accepting the bouquets, one of which was not tied together and trailed stray blossoms as he climbed aboard the shuttle. "Here, Alex . . . take some of these!"

"Not me," Alex said. "They're your problem. I want to be able to shake hands." She grinned at him wickedly.

Guy Davenport stuck his head into the shuttle. "You all ready?"

"Yes," Alex said. "Let the recorders hum and the music soar."

He slammed the door, frowning. Stuffy prig.

An irrational exuberance had seized Alex. She was going up-stairs to greet aliens. Forget the Furs and the even more mythical Vines—these Terrans were alien enough for her. They came from a different planet, a different culture, a different time, even . . . the *Crucible* had left Earth nearly fifty years ago. There would be so much to learn, to marvel at. So many interesting unknowns! Yet, at the same time, the arriving aliens professed friendship, spoke English, and were too greatly outnumbered by her own people to be threatening. It seemed the ideal situation. As Alex strapped herself in, she hummed under her breath.

They were seven aboard the shuttle: Alex, Ashraf, the pilot, two security people, the president of the Mira City Council, and the head of the Scientists' League, who was actually a geologist but refused to give up this opportunity to any of the physicists desperate to examine the Terran ship. Alex gathered that this had caused a tempest in a test tube, but she didn't know the details.

"Ashraf," she said in a low voice just before takeoff, "did you hear from Lau-Wah? I didn't."

"No." Ashraf lay back in his seat with his eyes closed and antici-patory dread on his face. He had a weak stomach.

"Here we go!" Alex squealed.

"You sound like a ten-year-old."

"That's the first remotely sour thing I've ever heard you say. Welcome to the work crew."

Ashraf didn't answer, and the shuttle took off from Greentrees.

As they approached the *Crucible,* Alex craned her neck to get the best view. The council president, Michael Lomax, turned in his seat to smile at her. "Exciting, isn't it?"

Kate Arcola, the geologist, said, "It's impossible to get a sense of the ship's size until we're closer. No scale out here."

Alex nodded. A voice came over the link. "Welcome, Mira City delegation, to the *Crucible.* Docking instructions follow."

The shuttle slid into the ship's bay. Alex still had no sense of its size. As the bay pressurized, she peered through the shuttle window. No other craft present—surely the *Crucible* had its own shuttle? Maybe both craft wouldn't fit. They must have moved it somehow, perhaps taken it outside and attached it to the hull.

"Fully pressurized," said the link voice, and the senior security officer opened the shuttle door. By the time Alex disembarked, the Terran delegation had come through a far door and stood waiting.

She should have dressed better. They all should have dressed better. No one had really thought about it, as nobody in her generation really did; it was only the young who paid attention to dress. Alex, Ashraf, and Kate Arcola wore the usual bits of bright cloth tied over skinthins; Alex's was her customary modest and nonhampering short sarong, this one patterned green and yellow. Ashraf's knots were knobby, inexpert bumps. Michael Lomax, who was portly, wore a coverall, as did the security team and the pilot. *We look,* she thought, *like a bunch of weeds invading a manicured garden.*

The Terrans looked dazzling. And how beautiful they were! All five, three men and two women, were well over six feet tall, well muscled, with clear pale brown skins and large, strangely brilliant eyes. Genemod. Had to be, all of them. They wore matching "uniforms"—Alex had learned the word from her history software as a reluctant schoolgirl. The uniforms were tight black pants and long tunics sashed in gold and trimmed at the shoulders with some wide gold decorations that looked both useless and intimidating. All five had hair cropped into short perfect curls of various colors. The curls gleamed like glass.

One man stepped forward. Black hair, startlingly green eyes, glittering as a cat's. Unerringly he picked out Ashraf Shanti, who stood gaping with the rest of the Greenies, and made a strange, graceful, embarrassing motion that only after a moment did Alex register as a "bow."

"Welcome aboard," said that already famous deep voice. "We are very glad to become guests on your planet. I am General Julian Cabot Martin of Third Life Alliance, commander of the *Crucible*."

He straightened, his eyes sweeping over them, missing nothing. Ashraf nodded vigorously. "Welcome to Greentrees." He went on nodding, evidently uncertain what should come next.

Alex stepped forward and took the bouquet of flowers from Ashraf's slack grip. She held them out to Julian Cabot Martin.

"These are from Mira City," she said shyly. "A small token of what awaits you downstairs. We're glad you've come."

"As are we," Julian Martin said, and, for the first time, he smiled.

5

THE VINE SHIP

The Vines from the colony planet below needed no help in attaching their ship to the *Franz Mueller;* the designs were identical. Karim and Lucy waited on the far side of the short air lock/corridor that connected the two ships. Karim plucked pointlessly at his s-suit and ran his finger around the seal of his helmet.

"Maybe they'll bring a translator egg," Lucy said.

"They undoubtedly think we're Furs, so they might. If they don't just fumigate us first," Karim said. They were both counting on that not happening, however. The Vines were pacifists.

No—the Vines they'd already encountered had been pacifists. Thirty-nine years ago.

"As long as they don't fumigate the shuttle, too," Lucy said, and there was that bravery again. Lucy's best quality. Karim took her hand.

The air lock opened and three domed carts rolled into the *Franz Mueller* and stopped dead.

Karim was surprised at their boldness until he saw the curved baton mounted on the front of the lead cart. Identical to the one he and Lucy used with their captives, it erected a force-field wall (what force? He would love to know!) The Vines were protected from the Furs they had presumably expected to find on a Fur ship. Instead, they found two humans.

Very slowly, Karim turned his empty hands palm upward and

sat down on the deck. Lucy followed. The Vines, of course, displayed no reaction.

At first glance they looked like plants, although closer scrutiny showed they were not. Each had a "trunk" covered with soft, overlapping, reddish brown scales; "branches" that might have been arms or tentacles, adorned with flat "leaves"; and, in the bottom of the cart, a thick mass of intelligent biofilm. Maybe the biofilm was intelligent; maybe it was merely directed by some organ elsewhere. A Vine, biologist George Fox had said on Greentrees, was neither plant nor animal nor bacteria, but some non-DNA amalgamation of analogues of all three. They had carried species integration far beyond any Terran adaptation. It may have even, George had said, been their major evolutionary mechanism.

The Vines breathed a different atmosphere, which they renewed under the hard clear domes of their traveling carts. They did everything very slowly. Karim composed himself to wait. He was still holding Lucy's hand; the slim fingers trembled in his.

"We are human," Karim said, each word distinct. He pointed to himself, then Lucy. "We are human."

And there, thank Allah, it was: a translator egg attached to the third cart, which rolled toward him. It stopped several feet away, which was presumably the perimeter of the invisible wall. The egg would have stored on it only Fur, of course, not English. Karim's job now was to supply as much clear, simple English as the device, captured from the Furs, needed to learn the language. But that wasn't his first job.

Slowly he held up the drawing he had prepared. The Vines that humans had encountered before seemed not to talk but to communicate by chemical exchange. Yet they had apparently been able to observe and hear other creatures. "A possible evolutionary advantage," George had argued. "As they evolved, there must have been predators on their planet. They might have developed additional ways of detecting them besides what we would call smell. After all, they and not the predators emerged as the dominant life form."

So the Vines could see Karim's drawing. He held it up. It showed their two ships docked together, along with the shuttle a short distance away. He had filled the shuttle with tiny Furs. Then had come the difficult part: how to convey that the Furs were a diseased Trojan horse to infect their own kind? Karim hadn't had too much time to think about the problem. Finally he'd settled for a separate drawing of tiny Vines on the side of the screen, sending a stream of tiny dots into the Furs. Beside one dot he'd drawn a crude double helix. Furs, like humans but unlike Vines, were DNA-based, part of the same panspermic fertilization of this part of the galaxy when it had been young.

Would these alien beings read all that from a drawing by a creature they had never seen before?

They didn't react. Karim held up his screen until his arms ached, and then he laid it down in front of the immobile carts with their immobile inhabitants. Were they discussing it? George had speculated that they could communicate across alien atmospheres by shooting created, nonliving molecules to each other, but this had never been proved before the Furs killed all the Vines on Greentrees.

"We have to keep talking," Lucy said, "or they'll never get English. I am Lucy. He is Karim. We are humans. We come from a planet called Greentrees. Your people did come to Greentrees. We did see your people. This helmet is from your people. Our people are humans. I am Lucy . . ."

It went on for hours, until they were both hoarse. Over and over Karim pointed to the drawing of the tiny Furs in the tiny shuttle. "Do not go here. Your enemy is here. Your people did make these enemies dangerous to your enemies. Your people did want these enemies to go to your enemies. Your people"—over and over he pointed to his drawing of tiny Vines—"we did see your people."

"They have to realize from the drawing that we've seen Vines before!" Lucy said desperately, hoarsely.

"Your people here. Enemies of your people here. We are humans. I am Karim. She is Lucy. Hello, hello . . ."

He didn't know his throat could feel so sore.

Lucy sagged against him from weariness. "Karim, it's not working. And who knows how long before the Furs show up, with all of us still in weapon range!"

"Your people did want these enemies to go to your enemies . . . Hello . . . hello . . ."

"Hello," said the uninflected mechanical voice of the stolen Fur translator. "Hello, Lucy and Karim."

Action replaced the long hours of desperate monologue. "You come," the Vines said, and rolled out of the *Franz Mueller* back into their own ship. Lucy and Karim looked at each other.

"Why don't they leave us here? On our own ship, even if it's disabled?" Lucy said in a raspy whisper. Karim shook his head. If the Vines did that, everything he and Lucy had risked would count for nothing.

He was surprised by how much he minded that. He was prepared to die, if necessary, but not to die for nothing.

Lucy seemed to realize the answer to her own question almost as soon as she asked it. She stumbled to her feet and followed Karim across the joined air locks into the Vine ship.

They found themselves in a small, completely bare room. The door closed behind them and another one opened. All three Vines disappeared through it and Lucy and Karim were left alone.

"A holding pen," Karim guessed. "They thought they'd find Furs aboard our ship . . . At least there's a window. Or something. It might be a screen."

"Hell, it might be a VR parlor," Lucy groused. "Not that we have much choice of—oh my God! Karim, look!"

The Vine ship began to move away from the *Franz Mueller*.

He knew this from the bowing of the floor, but even more from the visuals on the window/screen. The distance between the two ships widened. Then a glittery beam shot toward the *Franz Mueller*, enveloping it in a thick golden cloud.

Lucy gasped, "It's . . . *dissolving*."

It took only five minutes. The cloud of microorganisms ate through the ship like acid on paper. Another five minutes and the cloud itself had vanished.

"Terminator genes," Karim said. "Or rapid sporization. Or . . ." He trailed off.

"They're taking us downstairs," Lucy said. "We're going into the cloud. This ship must be treated somehow to avoid being dissolved."

Karim hardly heard her. He couldn't seem to take in what had just happened. The technology, based on a terrifying mastery of biology, was too alien. More: the philosophy behind the actions was too alien. He couldn't even begin to guess what would happen next to him and Lucy, shipless.

But just as alien was his own reaction. Karim had been brought up by a father who prided himself on throwing off the bonds of old, superstitious, confining folkways. Ahmed Mahjoub had been an engineer, a citizen of the UAR willing to become a citizen of the stars, a scoffer at anything "primitive," including religion. He had brought up his sons to think the same way. Yet now, watching the Vine planet in its huge glittering shield of deadly microorganisms, it was not of his father that Karim thought but his grandfather, that fierce pious old man kneeling toward Mecca on the tattered, faded prayer rug he kept to warn himself against pride. Prayer had seemed to bring his grandfather courage and serenity in an increasingly dangerous world.

All at once, Karim envied him.

6

MIRA CITY

You've accomplished an amazing amount, sir," Julian Martin said to Jake. "For fifty years, it is impressive."

"Thank you," Jake said, and Alex thought, *Jake doesn't like him.*

The thought made her angry. There was no reason not to like Julian, nor the other Terrans, nor this party, which everyone else thought was wonderful.

The party was held in the Mausoleum, in the large empty space on the first floor used for whatever rare event couldn't be held outdoors. Siddalee had done wonders in a short time; her efficiency was, in Julian's favorite word, impressive. Of course, she'd had a lot of help. Everyone wanted to meet the Terrans, aid the Terrans, attend the party for the Terrans. Ashraf's assistant had been in charge of the invitation list, and by now the poor man had the grounddown, besieged look of a trapped frabbit.

Some giggling Arab girls had hung so many wildflowers on the Mausoleum's plain foamcast walls that it looked like a temporary garden. The park's heavy tables and benches had been moved inside and draped with wraps in a rainbow of bright colors, emptying many people's wardrobes. The tables were covered with little cakes and cookies in baskets woven of tangmoss vines; the baskets gave off their own spicy fragrance. Sturdy glasses of plant-based plastics held fruit ades, bennilin tea, and Terran coffee, which had needed only a little genetic modification to flourish on Greentrees. A music cube, still in working order after fifty years, played bright tunes. Everyone had dressed up, tying their wraps in interesting and, among the young, daring styles. All in all, Alex thought, nobody could offer a more elegant party, even on Terra.

Julian and Alex sat on a bench beside Jake's wheelchair. The old man was wrapped in a blanket; the night had turned unexpectedly chill. Julian said, "My people are overwhelmed with your kindness in housing all of us so promptly. You spared us months in inflatables."

"I remember living in those," Jake said, not smiling. "All your people are downstairs?"

"All but the few on the *Crucible* with your physicists. They requested a thorough grounding in the drive and weapons, you know, and of course we're happy to comply."

There, Alex smirked at Jake behind Julian's back. Jake had drawn up a private list of his "requirements" for the Terrans, and unfettered access to the ship had been one of them. Jake ignored her.

While still aboard the *Crucible,* Alex had questioned the Terrans about their ship. She'd tried to be brisk and professional to these intimidating aliens. "We're interested, of course, in an exchange of resources, Commander Mar . . . uh, Julian. What we have to offer you are all the biological adaptations we've made of Greentrees flora and fauna to human needs. We can save your geneticists decades of experimentation. And in exchange . . ." She'd waited expectantly.

"In exchange, my people will gladly see what can be adapted from the *Crucible* to Mira City's needs," Julian said, beckoning to a woman to step forward. "This is Lt. Aliya Mwakambe, my chief engineer. She'll be aiding you."

"Hello," Alex said. Lieutenant Mwakambe, almost a head taller than Alex, had rich brown skin and eyes even more beautiful than Julian Martin's, brilliant gold genemod eyes flecked with silver. Alex felt drab beside her but plunged ahead anyway. "Lieutenant, we can use—"

"This can wait, I think, Alex," said Ashraf, with his timid but unfailing courtesy. "Our guests haven't even arrived downstairs yet!" Everyone had laughed.

Now Alex spotted Lieutenant Mwakambe across the crowded

room, but a party didn't seem the right place to grill her, either. Alex turned again to Julian. "And is everyone who's downstairs here at the party?"

Julian glanced around. Knots of Terrans, immediately notice-able for height, beauty, and their sleek uniforms, stood talking to larger groups of admiring Greenies. Alex had met most of the sci-entists, but she couldn't yet keep them all straight.

Julian said, "My brother has not yet arrived. He's housed with Governor Mah, whom I also don't see."

There were two hundred people jammed into the Mausoleum. How could Julian know who was there and who was not? Yet Alex didn't doubt that he did.

She said, "I didn't realize your brother came with you! Is he a scientist?"

Julian smiled. "No. He's not a scientist."

Jake said, with sudden aggression, "This party must look pretty paltry to you, compared with diplomatic entertaining on Earth."

"On the contrary, it has a refreshing simplicity."

Simplicity? Alex looked again at the bright tables, lavish food—why, there were even "candles," newly reinvented and marketed by Chu Corporation. The pretty scented things weren't necessary for lighting, but they looked so festive! How was this party simple?

Jake said, "What are your plans, Commander Martin? Will you return to Earth with your research about the Furs, since Terra no longer has quee capacity? Or are you colonists here?"

Alex blinked. Colonists?

Julian said quietly, "We aren't yet sure of our plans, sir. Certainly some of the scientists, at least, will want to return, although of course they will be bringing data to a world a hundred years older than they left it. Some of us may remain on Greentrees. You are open to colonists, I assume?"

"Of course!" Alex said warmly.

"And now, if I may ask a few questions?" Julian was clearly ad-dressing Jake.

"Go ahead," he said ungraciously.

"I look around and I see much purple vegetation. Yet you named the planet 'Greentrees.' Why is that?"

Alex laughed. "The First Landing named it before they got here. They had probe reports that a rhodopsin analogue was the dominant photosynthesant, but they called it Greentrees anyway."

"I see," Julian said. "Pure planetary perversity."

"Something like that," Alex said. She was delighted with his alliterative phrase, but Julian was still addressing Jake, not her.

"I understand from Alex that you have been the most prominent voice in urging strong preparations to defend Greentrees against a possible Fur attack. I've been told the history of Greentrees, Vines, and Furs, and I think you are completely in the right. May I ask what you think we can do to help?"

Jake's face changed. Surprise, suspicion, triumph—emotions flitted across his wrinkled features with the defenselessness of the old. "You agree that a stronger defense is needed?"

"I think it should be Mira City's overriding priority. I recognize that I speak as a military man, but I can see it no other way."

Jake burst out, "I told you, Alex!"

She said to Julian, "You've made a friend."

"Friendship isn't my aim, and I doubt Mr. Holman's is to be bought that easily," Julian said gravely. "But I am intensely interested in his views on this."

"Ah, but dear Julian is interested in everything," said another voice, and Alex turned and stared.

The man who stood beside the bench was the most fantastic figure she had ever imagined. All over the room people had stopped talking to gape at him. Unlike the rest of the Terrans, he stood about five foot ten, and his eyes lacked their agate, catlike brilliance. They were gray, the color of Alex's own, and his hair was an unremarkable dark brown, worn long and tied back at the nape. But his clothes! He wore a jacket of some red material like animal fur, except it was not animal fur, padded at the shoulders and sewn with inserts of shiny white cloth. Tight white pants revealed everything about his genitals. Tall black boots, a short black cape, and some sort of hat with, of all things, a *feather* in it, like a Cheyenne only larger and more flamboyant. And gloves, although no one but Jake thought the Mausoleum was cold.

Julian said, "Alex, Mr. Holman, may I present my brother, Duncan Martin. Duncan, this is Jake Holman, organizer of the first expedition to Greentrees, and Alexandra Cutler, second consul of the triumvirate of Mira City."

"Consuls and triumvirates! Oh, Julian, I see that you have indeed come to the right place!"

Alex had been intending to say hello, but at Duncan Martin's voice she forgot. She had thought Julian's deep voice beautiful—it *was* beautiful—but Duncan's sounded scarcely human to her. It was musical not only in its inflections but in a sort of background chords, a harmony to the spoken tones . . . human vocal chords couldn't do that, could they? Was it genemod? The double tones somehow echoed in her ear, each syllable both distinct and resonating, a tenor vibrato of enormous power.

Duncan smiled at her and bowed. "My dear Madame Consul. And you, sir."

Jake said flatly, "Falstaff?"

"Oh, no, no! How could you think so? Mercutio, of course."

"Or a satire on Mercutio."

"Is there any other way to play it, really?"

Alex had no idea what they were talking about. She looked at Julian, who said expressionlessly, "My brother is an actor."

"Eternally," Duncan said. "All the world, and all that. You are a thespian, Mr. Holman?"

"No."

"A fan?"

"No."

"Pity. Well, we must take our audience where we find it. You, Madame Consul, must enjoy the theater."

"We don't use titles like 'consul,'" Alex blurted. "And we don't have a theater on Greentrees."

"Not as yet," Duncan said, and smiled at her so richly that she was once more robbed of speech. What was he? A joke? Or did he consider them to be a joke? But why should he want to laugh at Mira City, and why should Julian let him?

Julian was watching her. "My brother is always like this, Alex. In that he told the truth: to him the world always *is* a stage. If he were not so good an actor—when he isn't mocking himself, of course— someone would have murdered him long ago for his aggressive self-promotion."

"And who else should promote me?" Duncan asked. "Or the company I will found in Mira City? I assure you, Madame Cutler, that when you hear me give my King Lear, you will forgive me any small excesses."

"Unfortunately for public decorum," said Julian, "Duncan is right. You will forgive him anything."

Jake said nothing. Alex, at a complete loss how to reply, was saved by the arrival of Lau-Wah Mah. The Chinese man's calm was not even dented by the weird figure of Duncan Martin.

"I am Lau-Wah Mah, Commander Martin. Welcome to Greentrees."

"Thank you. We are delighted to be here. May I present my brother, Duncan Martin, who was just going to bring me a glass of tea. Would you care for one?"

"No, thank you. Hello, Mr. Martin."

"And farewell. I search in vain, I see, for the sweetest fruit of the royal grape."

All four people watched Duncan walk away, stop at another group, and introduce himself. Alex said, "What's a grape?"

"Terran fruit," Jake said, "often fermented to produce intoxicating beverages."

"Well, I can get Duncan a fizzie, I think. Or some Blue Lion. They're not officially offered at the party, of course, but I think that—"

"The last thing Duncan needs is more intoxication," Julian said. "Governor Mah, Alex has been showing me around. What your triumvirate has accomplished here is impressive."

Lau-Wah studied Julian. "We don't officially use the term 'triumvirate.' It just originated as a joke of Jake's. Ours is a pretty informal society."

"As ours is not. I'm sure you all perceived that. I suppose that manners, like everything else, go in cycles. When I left Earth, good society had gone formal again."

Good society? What was that? wondered Alex, aware that all her life she had essentially known only one society. But that wasn't right, was it, in light of what Lau-Wah had told her two weeks ago. Greentrees had more separate, and separated, societies than she had been aware of.

She said to Julian, "Why did your brother say that you came to the right place when he heard the words 'consul' and 'triumvirate'?"

"I have an interest in the history of ancient Rome."

"In the empire," Jake said flatly.

"No, more in the military movements of the republic."

Lau-Wah said, "I'm afraid you will find each successive generation on Greentrees less interested in Terran history than the one before. For our young people, Earth is so remote."

"Understandable," Julian said, "but regrettable. One thing Terran history teaches us is the necessity of being prepared for external attack. Mr. Holman was explaining to me the great importance of increasing fortification against the Furs."

Had Jake said that to Julian? Alex couldn't remember. But certainly Jake believed it.

Lau-Wah said, "I'm sure Jake has also explained to you the possibility that Furs may never attack here again, either because Karim's infected shipload of Furs has neutralized the threat, or because of the great distances and time dilations involved."

"Which are both much reduced by the McAndrew Drive," Julian said. "And, of course, the pronounced Fur territoriality and xenophobia argue in favor of attack."

How did he know so much about Furs, their ships, and the entire situation? The Terrans had only just arrived.

"You appear to know quite a lot about us," Jake said.

"I have accessed your library deebees, with Dr. Arcola's kind assistance."

Alex laughed. "I'm surprised the deebees still work."

Jake said, "When did you have time to do that, Commander?"

"Last night. Perhaps you are not aware, Mr. Holman, that I am genetically engineered to sleep only an hour or so each night?"

Stillness took everyone.

"Only an hour?" Alex finally blurted. "Night after night?"

Julian smiled. "Yes. A genemod developed after you left Terra, I believe."

"Don't you miss it?" The instant she said it, she knew how stupid the words sounded. Of course he didn't miss what he'd never known.

"I'm told a long sleep can be quite pleasant," Julian said. "But of course, life offers many different pleasures."

"It would seem there's a lot we don't know about you," Lau-Wah said, with such grave courtesy that Alex knew he, too, disliked Julian. Jake, Lau-Wah . . . what did they see that she was missing?

"I'm willing to answer any question you wish."

"May we have the same access to your library deebees that you have to ours?"

"Of course. In fact, your scientists aboard the *Crucible* already have that."

"Then perhaps," Lau-Wah said, "you can give us a brief version of life on Earth when you left it fifty years ago."

Ashraf Shanti had crept noiselessly into their little group. The three Greenies and Jake, who was both Terran and Greenie, waited for Julian's answer. His eyes, Alex saw, those glittering living emeralds, reflected all light. You couldn't see into them.

"You are very lucky to have been born on Greentrees," Julian said quietly, "or to have emigrated here. Very little of Earth is left livable. The CO_2 level is one point five percent at sea level, which is not breathable. Worldwide warming moved tropical diseases into northern areas, which had no defenses against them. Shifting populations led to food shortages, which in turn led to war, some of it by biological agents. When ninety percent of your ethnic group is predicted to perish anyway, you don't mind releasing pathogens that will kill a third of your people but also a third of the enemy. One way or another, billions died on Earth. The surviving population is about a half billion."

It sounded an immense number to Alex, but Jake gasped.

"There are tribes roaming in the wild lowlands, but civilization survives mostly in domed cities at higher altitudes. Those have preserved a perhaps high level of civilization, or at least of technology. Geneva is one such place. I was part of a coalition to unite these surviving city-states to do what we could to restore the planet, but we were bitterly opposed and our leader assassinated. It was thought expedient to offer me the command of this expedition, and I accepted. With gladness, I might add. It was the only way I saw to redeem my life from hopelessness."

Alex found herself moved. Such a position! To watch one's planet dying . . . She said warmly, "I think you were very brave to come here."

Julian did not respond to that. Lau-Wah said, "This can all be confirmed by the news files in the *Crucible*'s deebees, of course."

"Of course."

Ashraf spoke for the first time. "Commander, what are your plans now?"

Julian gazed at him. Alex couldn't help contrasting the two men: Julian so tall and grave in his black uniform, Ashraf slight and fidgety, dropping his gaze as if his question had been somehow impertinent. Not a fair contrast, she knew. Julian was genemod. To sleep only one hour each night . . . how much more he could accomplish while the rest of them snored time away!

Julian said, "With your permission, Mayor Shanti, my scientists will dispatch a contingent in our rover to meet with Nan Frayne and the Furs that live nomadically on Greentrees. They—"

"You already know about Nan Frayne!" Alex said.

"I've comlinked with her. She's willing to meet with me."

"She *is?*"

He smiled. "I think Dr. Farling, head of my xenobiology team, intrigued her with offers of information exchange."

Jake said pointedly, "Ashraf, did you authorize this?"

"Well, no, I . . . do you think that's necessary? I wasn't . . . I mean . . ."

"I'm very sorry if I've violated protocol," Julian said, concerned. "Dr. Farling hasn't left yet; shall I cancel the expedition?"

"No," Ashraf said, with sudden decisiveness. He stared at Jake. "I give my permission now."

There was a little silence. Alex shifted her glass of tea to her other hand. Julian continued.

"The rest of my scientists are eager to get started on their various field studies. The four physicists and their two assistants are already working with your people, and will remain in Mira City. And, of course, Chief Engineer Lieutenant Mwakambe meets soon with Alex. I myself, again with your permission, would like to see everything in the city. Alex, will you show me what you've accomplished here? It's so different from Geneva. So . . . beautiful."

She heard his voice break, a tiny break but real, and remorse washed over her. This must be so strange for him. They were not treating their guest very well, examining him like some field specimen! "Of course I will," she said.

"Thank you."

Hoping to lighten the mood, she said, "And your brother? What made Duncan come here? Merely to bring theater to a new planet?"

"With Duncan," Julian said, " 'theater' and 'merely' cannot be put in the same sentence. As I'm afraid you're about to discover."

"Attention, please, everyone!" shrilled a female voice. Oh, Lord, Alex thought, her third cousin Seena Bramlee. That was all they needed. Seena was one of the few members of the huge Cutler clan who had no profession. She spent her time arranging what social and cultural life Mira City had; Seena had, in fact, helped arrange this party. She lived off her accumulated credits, the result of her mother's canny loans of original equipment and subsequent granted land to the second and third generation of Mira's embryonic capitalists. Again Alex thought of Lau-Wah's uncharacteristic monologue about the subservient position of the Chinese settlers.

Seena clapped noisily for quiet. "We are extremely fortunate in having with us one of Terra's greatest, most acclaimed actors! And even more fortunate in that he has agreed to act for us a speech from a play by one William Shakespeare! Ladies and gentlemen, speeches chosen just for Greentrees from *The Temper*!"

"*Tempest,*" Jake muttered. "Jesus H. Christ."

Alex stared at him in surprise—was he upset because Duncan was going to act or because Seena had mispronounced the name? And why was a "tempest," a weather disturbance, a subject for an apparently famous play?

There was a long pause, and then Seena dimmed the Mausoleum lights to their energy-saving setting. In the gloom, Alex saw the few Quakers present, Dr. Jamison and Victoria Bly and Ezra Cunningham, sidle quietly toward the door. Did Quakers disapprove of theater? She knew they used no fizzies or caffeine or vids, but theater had never come up before on Greentrees. Alex found herself mildly curious.

A single light was switched on in a side hallway, and Duncan Martin walked a few paces into the room, within the circle of light. He had changed from his outlandish costume into a plain, dark robe of some rough material. And his face was different—how had he done that? His nose looked longer, his eyes darker somehow, or maybe it was just that now they swept levelly, judgingly over the watching crowd. He was taller, too—heeled boots? Or did he just look taller? Was that possible?

Then he began to speak.

"What is this place?" Duncan looked around, fearful and hopeful at once. Alex could not look away. That voice!

" 'Be not afeared; the isle is full of noises,
Sounds and sweet airs, that give delight and hurt
   not,' "

he said, and in the richness of his voice Alex *heard* them, the sweet
noises of Greentrees, the murmuring breeze in bamler trees and
the lowing of teelie herds and the deep cries of the sue-birds cir-
cling overhead at dusk.

> " 'Sometimes a thousand twanging instruments
> Will hum about mine ears, and sometimes voices
> That, if I then had waked after long sleep,
> Will make me sleep again: and then, in dreaming,
> The clouds we thought would open and show riches
> Ready to drop upon me, that, when I waked,
> I cried to dream again.
> But beseech you, sir, be merry; you have cause,
> So have we all, of joy; for our escape
> Is much beyond our loss.' "

Alex saw the Terra of Julian's words, the bleak planet destroyed by
humanity, from which the *Crucible* had, indeed, escaped.

> " 'Our hint of woe
> Is common; every day some sailor's wife,
> The masters of some merchant and the merchant
> Have just our theme of woe; but for the miracle,
> I mean our preservation, few in millions
> Can speak like us—' "

"One way or another, billions died on Earth."

> " '—then wisely, good sir, weigh
> Our sorrow with our comfort.
> Prithee, peace!' "

—and the word was a cry, a plea of anguished need that echoed in
the vast room: peace, peace, peace . . . Duncan's body shifted and
his tone changed again. He held out his hands.

" 'O, wonder!
How many goodly creatures are there here!
How beauteous mankind is! O brave new world,
That has such people in't!' "

Duncan's hands dropped. No one else moved. Even Seena Bramlee was silent.

"Thank you," Duncan said, and the spell vanished, leaving him once more just a man.

Alex whispered, "Is *that* what we've lost?"

A moment later she was ashamed. What a stupid remark! But her fingers were quietly circled, squeezed, released. Julian.

"If Duncan Martin forms a theater company," Lau-Wah said dryly, "no one else had better be in it. They will all look like idiots by comparison."

"No, he's too good to let that happen," Julian said, "which I should not of course say, since Duncan is my brother. But it's true."

"I can believe it," Jake said. "He must have been a sensation in holovids."

"He refused to make them. A debasement of art, you know. Thespian purity."

Jake laughed. Even Lau-Wah smiled.

Alex said nothing. She could still feel the warmth of Julian's hand around her own. The feeling was not at all welcome. That, she told herself, was one place she was not going. Never again, not since Kamal. No.

She drew away from Julian and walked forward to congratulate Duncan.

7

A VINE PLANET

The Vine ship went into orbit around their colony planet. Lucy and Karim had to guess this; they glimpsed neither ship nor planet. After a sensationless short time, their air lock opened onto a square, featureless metal box.

"You go in this," said the mechanical voice of a translator. "Then we go to our planet."

"It looks like a packing crate," Lucy said, somewhere between resentment and amusement. "Should we get in?"

"Is there another choice?" Karim said. He took her hand and moved forward. Both were still suited in Greentrees s-suits and Vine helmets. The packing crate slid closed behind them, and they felt it lift and move forward.

"I really don't like this, Karim."

"I suspect we're being put onto a shuttle. Lie down, Lucy, and brace yourself. Shuttles don't have McAndrew Drives."

He was right; a few minutes later acceleration flattened him. Five gees, maybe . . . no, more . . . how much could Vines stand? And did they know how much humans could? No, of course not; he and Lucy were the first humans these particular Vines had ever seen.

Sound screamed around them. "We're entering an atmosphere," he tried to say to Lucy, but couldn't. Then, abruptly, the pressure stopped at the same time as the sound.

"We're here," she quavered.

"You all right?"

"Yes. God, it's hot!"

"Adjust your suit," Karim said.

They waited. For three hours, nothing happened. Lucy and Karim didn't talk much. He hoped her thoughts were happier than his. They had no ship, no certainty of how they would be received here, and no idea whether the shipboard Vines had understood the urgency of leaving the infected Furs alone in their drifting shuttle. If he could be sure that last had been done, that the plan had a chance of working, then never seeing Greentrees again would be worth it.

When one side of the packing box finally slid open, Karim tensed. At least this featureless tiny room was familiar.

Lucy was already on her feet. She managed a smile inside her clear helmet. "Show time."

"Welcome at our planet," the translator said, and they blinked in the sudden light.

His first reaction was that the scale was wrong. Everything was huge. The Vines aboard ship had been shorter than humans, as had the ones that visited Greentrees. They must have been selected, or grown, for space flight, because the Vines surrounding the shuttle were twice Karim's height. He stood child-size among trunks of pulpy brown festooned with tentacles and broad, flat, pulpy projections. On a smaller scale those had looked like leaves, but enlarged they more resembled purplish deformed mushrooms. Tentacles and fungi—impossible not to think in Earth analogues!—were evenly dispersed down the trunks, rather than blossoming at the top like trees, and so did not block out the sun. It shone very bright and a bit too orange, larger than Sol.

The Vines were *everywhere*. They crowded beside each other, tentacles intertwined, especially near the ground. It was very quiet; no birds sang or called, no animals roared. Lucy stepped out of the box and Karim watched her sink to the ankles. Quickly she scrambled back.

"It's swampy!"

He bent to look. Yes, the ground was mud and water, not, as he had first thought, the thick layer of bacteria that had carpeted the

Vine ship. Those biofilms had seemed to be part of the interconnected Vine sentience. Did they exist on the planet, too? Or had
they been manufactured for space travel?

So many questions. "We need George Fox," Karim said, "or
some other biologist. I just don't *know* enough."

"Me neither."

Karim put one foot onto the swamp. After all, the translator had
said they were welcome here. He sank up to his ankle, but no farther. Around him the pulpy fungi/leaves/hands swayed in a sudden
breeze.

Lucy joined him and they stood there awkwardly, not certain what
to do next. The Vines provided no help. Finally he said, "Vines?"

"I am Vines," the translator answered.

He gathered himself for the major, necessary effort, searching
for the simplest words possible.

"We say to your people on ship that our shuttle carries your enemy. It carries some of your enemy—'Furs'—that your people make
sick. The sick is part of experiment your people make on our planet.
Many groups of Furs, many sicknesses. All sicknesses are different.
Your people try to make the enemy not dangerous and also not
killed. They did this. Our shuttle carries sick Furs from your people.
You must let the enemy find the sick enemy and get sick also. Then
they carry the sickness to all your enemy. Then the fighting stops."

No birdsong, no animal roar, no answer. The huge silent sen-
tients turned slightly. Karim realized they were phototropic.
"Dreaming in the sun," Beta Vine had said so long ago.

Lucy said desperately, "Vines? Do you understand?"

Nothing. What now? Karim looked helplessly at Lucy. She
shook her head.

When standing became tiring, they lowered themselves to sit on
the ground.

Twenty minutes later came the translator voice, "I understand."

They slept in the box, away from the rain that fell at dusk. Not
that they needed to escape the rain, which was light and warm,

but the box quickly became the only solid, nonvegetative, non-pulpy object around. In a squishy, silent word, the box was hard and metallic. Their boots rang on its floor. Karim was grateful it was there.

"Where's the shuttle?" Lucy asked once, but he didn't know. It had vanished.

The dark was the most complete either of them had ever seen. Clouds covered the sky, and there were no artificial lights, no lightning bugs, no marsh gas. It was as if he'd gone blind. He escaped as soon as possible into sleep, lying close to Lucy.

When he woke, it was morning. He was ravenous. Lucy still slept, in s-suit and helmet, spittle at the corners of her mouth. Karim's stomach growled, and he welcomed the sound because it *was* sound. But it wouldn't feed them.

He walked from the box a few feet into the swamp. Vines dwarfed him. Which one had the translator? It apparently didn't matter. George had said they communicated by exchanging molecules. Whatever one knew, they all knew. For how far? Yesterday the Vine had said "I," not "we." Was the whole planet one interconnected sentient animal-plant?

He looked up at the creature—creatures? Hating the way their size reduced him. "We are thirsty and hungry," he said carefully. "Humans must drink water and eat molecules. We cannot make our own food inside us." George had theorized that the Vines practiced an analogue of photosynthesis based not on chlorophyll but on a non-DNA equivalent of adapted bacteria.

"Humans must drink water and eat molecules. We cannot make our own food inside us. If we do not have food and water, we die."

Then he sat down to wait.

After fifteen minutes—he timed it with his s-suit—the translator said, "We must make you water. We must make you food. We must have piece of you."

Karim had expected this. They were master geneticists even working with life forms starting from radically different biological premises. But they could not work in a vacuum. He said, "I can remove my suit." He pantomimed this, awkwardly. "If I remove my suit, will I die? Is it safe for me?"

This time the wait was half an hour. Lucy joined him, sleepy and worried. "Food?"

"I ordered room service a while ago."

She smiled.

"You must remove your suit," the translator said.

"Is it safe?" Karim asked.

"We do not know."

Before he could stop her, Lucy had unfastened and stripped off one boot. "Lucy!"

"It makes more sense," she said coolly. "You're the physicist, and more able to get back to Greentrees alone than I would be. Let them experiment on me." She stuck out her leg.

Something formed in the swamp beside it.

Not the same sort of biofilm that had oozed out of Beta Vine's cart on Greentrees. Again, Karim realized that those Vines that went into space must have been genetically adapted for that mission—and why not? Genetic adaptation was what these aliens *did*. He watched as the semisolid slime, looking like nothing as much as vomit with purplish chunks in it, rose in a viscous wave to engulf Lucy's foot.

She held her foot steady. Minutes passed, and finally the wave receded, leaving her foot faintly coated with slickness. Then she did shudder.

"Karim . . . something to wipe it off . . ."

There was nothing. Finally he bent and ran his gloves over the slime, which didn't remove it all. Lucy put her boot back on.

He said, too roughly, "We'll have to wait now. They don't do anything quickly."

"I know."

They waited an hour, sitting on the edge of the box like, Karim thought bitterly, scared children outside a stern tutor's office. Then the closest Vine bent slightly toward them. One of its flat, pulpy, purplish "hands" began to curve into a bowl. The bowl filled with thick grayish liquid.

"No," Lucy half moaned. "Last time they made a clear hard cup like our helmets. Karim, I don't think I can drink from that."

He didn't answer. She knew as well as he that they had no choice.

He couldn't pick up the bowl fastened to the Vine's trunk; he had to bend his head to meet it. When they touched, his clear helmet reshaped itself to form a seal around the living bowl. Awkwardly, Karim lapped the gray fluid. It didn't taste bad, nor good. Almost instantly his belly felt full.

Lucy closed her eyes and did the same.

Afterwards, Karim felt obscurely ashamed. He tried to figure out why. Finally he realized that the shame was because they were so dependent. Because they were being treated like . . . what? Like pets, fed and occasionally talked to but otherwise ignored. Because he and Lucy were so clearly insignificant to this vast, intelligent, but seemingly incurious entity, which was more alien than anything Karim could have imagined. Because.

He said, "Vine? Can you hear me? Please tell me more about this planet!"

The translator didn't answer.

He walked in an ever-widening circle around the box, guided by the coordinator built into the wrist panel of his suit. Lucy declined to come with him. She sat in the box, staring at nothing. "I'm thinking," she snapped at him whenever he asked.

No matter how far he walked, the landscape didn't change. Was "landscape" even the right word? Towering Vines, in clumps of three or four or five, their intertwined tentacles sprawling between clumps and sinking halfway into the marsh. Each time Karim lifted a boot, the mud made a noise like someone strangling. His suit registered the temperature as 110 degrees Fahrenheit. Every dusk it rained. The sky remained overcast, varied only by the dead blackness of night. He never heard a single sound.

It was the silence that was the worst.

"May we go home?" he asked the Vine with the translator, who didn't answer.

Only once did it talk to them. At dusk of the second day, as he and Lucy lay down close to each other in the box, the inflexible voice of the translator said, "Our enemy in your shuttle is gone. The enemy took our enemy in your shuttle."

"They did!" Lucy exclaimed. "When? Do you think they'll infect the rest of your enemy?"

There was no answer.

Days passed.

Then weeks.

Karim's beard grew inside his helmet, first itchy and then long enough to tangle against his chin. He must, inside his suit, smell terrible. Lucy's face grew paler, then ashy, her eyes dull and unblinking. She ate only when necessary, and lost too much weight.

Karim walked twenty miles a day, slogging through the mud. How did Lucy stand it, never leaving the box? He was starting not to care.

The silence was his enemy. The silence, and the horrific fact that nothing ever changed. The same gray sky, the same gray rain, the same gray filling unsatisfying food, the same emptiness. And the same still, alien Vine, a single one planet-wide for all he knew, saying nothing.

This life must not appear to the Vine as it did to him. He knew that, kept reminding himself of that. Beta Vine, who was one of these creatures (or creature) had once told Dr. Shipley that Vines spent their time "dreaming in the sun." There must be thoughts going on in that vast intelligence. Information was exchanged through molecules, pheromones, whatever. Science, surely. Politics? Poetry? Religion? Jokes? Whatever there was, he and Lucy were shut out from it as completely as if they did not exist.

Scruffy ghosts on an alien world.

He lost track of time. More days passed. More weeks.

Eventually, standing ankle-deep in mud that was the same mud, the same creature, the same sky no matter where he went, he screamed at the closest clump of aliens. "I want to go home! Do you hear me? I want to go home!"

No response.

Tears poured down Karim's cheeks; he didn't know when they had started. He was deeply ashamed of the tears. His father would have hated for his son to cry; his grandfather would have scorned him for it. He threw up an arm to dash away the tears and struck his own helmet.

Anger felt better than tears.

He reached into the nearest clump of Vines and ripped off a tentacle.

"Does that make you want to take me home, *ebn sharmoota? Khaby labwa?* Does *that?*"

Another tentacles, a fistful of "leaves" that were like pulpy hands. They would retaliate now, they would kill him, or at least knock him down or out or into some molecularly induced pain. He waited, breathing heavily, ready to welcome the pain, to welcome anything that was different from this swampy, noiseless, gray hell, which wasn't even his hell but rather the paradise of aliens. *Hit me, Vines! Kill me!*

Nothing happened.

Slowly, panting eagerly, Karim realized that no matter what he did to how many Vines, nothing ever would happen.

Nothing.

Forever.

He stumbled back to the box. Lucy sat there, staring. It was a relief to scream at her; at least she wasn't nothing. "Can't you do anything but sit?"

She leaped up so suddenly that a part of his brain, still rational, realized that she welcomed fighting him, and probably for the same reason he'd attacked the Vines. "What the hell do you care what I do? You're never here!"

"I'm mapping this world. At least that's something."

"You're not mapping." She sneered. "You're just wandering around aimlessly like a lost little kid."

"I am not a child. Do not speak to me like one."

"Don't tell me how to speak! What are you doing now, reverting to your Arab roots here, powerful patriarchal male and submissive little woman? Well, I'm not wearing a veil, Karim, in case you didn't notice, and I'm not impressed by your lost Arabian manliness, and I'm not—"

He hit her.

He didn't know he was going to do it until his fist had connected with her belly, and he had never regretted anything so much in his entire life. She doubled over and then fell sideways, landing on the metal floor of the box with the loudest noise he'd heard in weeks. She gasped for air. He knelt beside her.

"Lucy, oh, Lucy, I'm so sorry, Lucy, please . . ."

She didn't, or couldn't, push him away. He took her in his arms and thought, *No more. This stops here.*

They talked about it in whispers, in a back corner of the box. Karim said, "Whatever the Vines were to us on Greentrees, however they united with us against the Furs, here they're our enemy."

"But they don't mean any—"

"Listen to me, Lucy. No, they don't mean to harm us. Maybe they don't even know that they are. But we can't live like them, or with them, or here. They're our enemy because we need to plan against them to get something we want and they don't."

"To take us home."

"Yes."

"But how?"

"I don't know yet. We don't have anything they want. But there must be some way. Something around here must change, sometime."

"Wait," Lucy said. "What about the mobiles? You remember, Karim, the little two-legged semisentients that . . . that pollinate them at mating time. We saw them on the Vine ship. The Vines loved them, Beta said. If we could capture a few and hold them for . . . well, for ransom . . ."

"Capture pollinators? Wouldn't that be like trying to hold bees for ransom?"

"I don't know," she said. "Maybe. What else can you think of?"

"Beta Vine liked my whistling." He felt foolish mentioning this. "Really liked it."

"Good. What else?"

"I don't think we have anything else. Unless something different turns up on the planet."

"Then you keep exploring. Tomorrow I'll go with you."

He sat in the impenetrable darkness, his back against the metal wall, and fought off despair. Whistling, aimless walking, pollinators who might appear, for all he knew, every two or three years. With these flimsy things, they were supposed to coerce aliens to launch a ship to the stars.

"We'll find a way, Karim," Lucy whispered.

"I know we will," he said, for her sake, and knew that what he'd thought before was not true. Was in fact heroic nonsense. It wasn't enough that the infected Furs had been picked up by their brethren. It wasn't enough that the plan to save Greentrees might succeed. Karim wanted to live, to go home, to walk once more with his own species on a planet with a place for him.

That, and that alone, would be enough.

8

MIRA CITY

The day after the welcoming party for the Terrans, Alex stood by the window in her messy apartment, moodily sipping bennilin tea. Jake lay asleep in the bedroom, its door still closed. Alex's nightshirt lay on her unmade cot, where Katous sniffed it delicately and rejected it, leaping gracefully to the floor and then onto the table. Alex stroked him absently, reflecting on the day ahead of her.

It was too full. Too much was happening at once. Here it was not even dawn yet, and already she wished the day were over.

Beyond the window the eastern sky shone pale at the horizon, dark above. The constellations were still faintly visible, all those sketchy forms she had loved to pick out as a child: the Starship and Allah's Wheel and the Double Helix with its blue zero-magnitude pole star, Gemma.

"Did you know, Katous," she asked the cat, "when I was twelve I could tell time to within fifteen minutes by the Double Helix? I had all the position changes memorized."

Katous ignored her and sniffed the table, looking for crumbs. Dark forms beyond the park took on the ghostly outlines of buildings.

Right after last night's party, Alex had sat down with the *Crucible*'s chief engineer, Lt. Aliya Mwakambe, to discuss what technology the Terrans could offer Mira City. As tray-o, Alex had hoped for much from this meeting. She'd been disappointed.

The computers aboard the Terran ship, seventy years more

advanced than those brought to Greentrees by Jake's original settlers, had little that was compatible with MiraNet. The *Crucible*'s
life-support system had been designed for self-sufficiency in space
and offered few usable innovations for planetary technology. Some
techniques and hardware could be adapted, but in the main, Mira's
concerns—mining, manufacturing, building—simply had no
counterparts on the warship.

That left medicine and defense. The formidable weapons aboard
the *Crucible* were certainly welcome additions to Greentrees orbital
defenses, but to be effective they needed to stay in orbit. Terran
medical advances, even more welcome, were not Alex's department.
She turned Lieutenant Mwakambe over to the genetics lab people
and tried to allay her disappointment.

Today's meetings also looked problematic. Alex had three of
them, scheduled in three widely separated places, one reachable
only by skimmer, and she hated flying. Oddly enough, the shuttle
didn't bother her, not even when it went screaming through the atmosphere. The view of Greentrees from ten thousand kilometers
up was fine; from a hundred meters it made her queasy and anxious. But there wasn't any choice. Jon McBain was in the Avery
Mountains, Lau-Wah was at Hope of Heaven, and Mira City's chief
energy engineer, Savannah Cutler, was sending frantic emergency
requisitions from the solar array twenty clicks south of the city.

Better get started.

Alex gulped the rest of her tea and opened the door. Julian Martin stood outside, gazing at the rising dawn.

"Good morning, Alex."

"Julian! What are you doing here?" Too late she remembered
that his society was—had been—more formal than hers and didn't
ask people why they were doing whatever they were doing. But he
didn't look offended. Hastily she shut the door behind her before
he could see her disorganized living quarters.

He gave his faint, close-lipped smile. "I was hoping I could accompany you on your rounds this morning."

"Rounds? How did you know I had to go anywhere?"

"You're the tray-o. I knew you must go somewhere, and I thought that if you were kind enough to let me accompany you, it would be a good way to see more of the city. You control resources, and resource allocation always indicates a culture's priorities."

She smiled to cover her irritation. He was absolutely right, of course, but . . . but what?

What if he thought she was doing a lousy job of resource allocation?

Ashamed of herself—what a time to be concentrating on her own petty reputation!—she nodded a bit too eagerly. "Yes, I see. Of course you can accompany me. It's a hectic day, I'm afraid. How did you know I'd start so early? Oh, of course, you didn't, you don't sleep much so you probably spent the night walking around looking at things anyway . . ." She was babbling. *Shut up, Alex.*

"Yes, I did walk around all night. It's still novel to me that Mira City is safe enough to do that. Where do we go first?"

"To pick up a rover."

He fell into step beside her. Today Julian wore a Threadmore coverall; it certainly hadn't taken him long to dip into Mira stores! There was no chance, however, that anyone would mistake him for a Greenie. His height and the startlingly green genemod eyes ensured that. Surreptitiously Alex ran her fingers through her hair, trying to remember if she'd combed it.

"The cars are powered by hydrogen fuel cells," Alex said, taking refuge in lecturing. "We have limited manufacturing capacity, of course, and fuel cells are class A, right up there with mining equipment. The only waste product is pure water. You could drink it. We have two goals here on Greentrees, Julian. To make the colony flourish, and not to disturb the ecology of Greentrees."

"You say 'we.' Are those your own goals, too, Alex?"

"Of course," she said, puzzled.

"Which goal is more important?"

"They're equally important."

"But if a situation came up in which you had to choose, which would you pick?"

She said stiffly, "No such situation has ever come up. If something would help Mira City flourish but would harm Greentrees, we find another way to accomplish the same goal."

"Is that your job as 'tray-o'?"

She didn't like the faint inflection his voice put on the word. "Yes. It is."

"I see." He stopped walking and looked directly at her. His deep voice changed: lightened somehow, and acquired a note of pleading. "I do see. Remember, Alex, this is all new to me. *You* are new to me, you Greenies, and how you think. It's all very different from Earth. Please be patient with my clumsy questions."

The humility in those brilliant eyes, gazing so straight into her own, was disconcerting. Alex felt herself redden. "Yes, uh, of course. Julian. Yes."

"Thank you." He resumed walking, and she trotted to keep up.

"Was Earth so very different?" she said, to say something.

"You have no idea. We had few resources to expend, and groups fought viciously and unceasingly for whatever there was. The only goal was survival."

She remembered what he'd said last night about Terra's wars: *"When ninety percent of your ethnic group is predicted to perish anyway, you don't mind releasing pathogens that will kill a third of your people but also a third of the enemy."*

"This is so beautiful," Julian said wistfully. "Look at those flower beds. Native or genemod?"

"Those are native. We call them roses."

"They aren't much like Terran roses."

She laughed. "Jake says that what happened was that the First Landers weren't linguists. They just sort of named things haphazardly, sometimes using Terran analogues, sometimes making up fanciful names, sometimes trying to be scientific. So by my generation, we've got this hodge-podge, and it's getting worse."

"You're first-generation Greentrees?"

"Thirty-second kid born here. Get in the car."

The four official Mira City vehicles sat under an inflatable so old that even its durable material had started to show wear. Each rover was a stripped-down base with tough all-terrain tractors, open sides, and a top that was itself an inflatable that could expand to the ground. More attention had been given to durability than to comfort. Julian folded himself into the too-small front seat. Even squeezed down, with his knees sticking up, he kept that air of slightly forbidding remoteness that exasperated and baffled Alex.

"It's a good design," he said, "light and roomy, if not exactly aesthetic. Duncan would not approve. I assume everything on the rover is recyclable?"

"Everything on Greentrees is recyclable. And we do. After all, nature is a one-hundred-percent efficient recycling machine; we're trying to do the same."

"With the tray-o as machine controls," he said, smiling. "What happens if *you* wear out?"

"I'm replaced."

"That would be impossible, I think. High-quality precision tools are always rare."

She felt herself redden again, this time with pleasure.

Julian chuckled. "Have I violated another cultural taboo? Are compliments discouraged?"

"Not if they're sincere," Alex said, not looking at him.

"I'm a good judge of people," Julian said austerely, "but I don't expect you to take that on faith. I'll prove it to you today. Just wait."

She said nothing, not sure what response would be appropriate. They drove out of Mira and Alex pointed out the small businesses, none yet open: bakeries, wrap shops, foamcast engineers. When they reached the river she named the manufactures, from soap to mining equipment, explaining which were privately owned and which operated through Mira Corp.

"And those buildings over there are the gene labs. We just had a major breakthrough in incorporating flu-vaccination genetics into our tubers."

"Flu? Really?"

"Well, we call it that. I don't know what you'd call it on Terra. Low-level respiratory infection, kids get it a lot."

"We call it flu," Julian said. "Although on Terra there are many—too many—strains that are not low level. Lethal, in fact."

"I think the First Landing encountered that here. Maybe. I'm not sure."

"You eat most of your vaccines in food?"

"Yes," she said, surprised. "Don't . . . didn't you?"

"No," he said, but explained no further. They drove across the open plain as the sun rose in a cloudless sky over the purple groundcover and tall, thin trees. Birds wheeled overhead, crying raucously. A herd of frabbits scampered in the distance. On Alex's cheeks the air felt cool and sweet.

She was so seldom out of Mira City that the plain seemed foreign to her, wild, something that should belong to the Cheyenne rather than to civilization. They passed a huge thicket of red creeper, the quick vine that could seize and paralyze a man while it leisurely devoured him. The geneticists had been experimenting with red creeper genes, but so far had found nothing useful to do with them.

"Look at the lions," Alex said, gesturing to a pair barely visible in the branches of a distant grove. Julian must have heard something in her voice, some trace of that harsh memory in the lab with Yat-Shing Wong, because he turned his head to look sharply at Alex. But all he said was, "Predatory?"

"Yes."

"Greentrees appears different outside of Mira City."

"Oh, yes," Alex said. She was glad when the solar array loomed into view on the horizon and she could resume lecture mode. "This is a stage-three energy project for Greentrees. The original settlers started with nuclear power from their Terran equipment—no, don't look at me like that, Julian, it was only a temporary plan. As soon as possible, energies based on nondamaging waste were put in place: wind, water, and geothermal. But the problem is, Greentrees has very little volcanic activity or steep temperature gradients. Wind is good—there's a big wind farm on the other side of the river, but—"

"Does the river have a name?" Julian asked. "I've never heard it called anything but 'the river.'"

"Neither have I," she said, startled. "I never thought about it before."

Julian smiled. "That says a great deal about Greentrees."

Alex wasn't sure what he meant and suddenly didn't want to know. She resumed lecturing.

"The solar tech is more expensive and harder to manufacture than wind, but we're doing it, although the results have proved disappointing thus far. We get about thirty-six percent efficiency."

"Better than we were getting on Earth," Julian said, surprising her. She hadn't expected green knowledge from him, given what he'd said about Terra. "Are you using a concentrator photovoltaic system?"

"Yes. It concentrates sunlight about five hundred times."

They had reached the solar array. Alex climbed out of the car, stretching her legs, watching Julian stare at the huge curved reflective dishes, each turning like an upraised flower to follow the sun. He said, "What's the subject of today's meeting?"

"Here it comes," Alex said resignedly.

Savannah Cutler strode across the purple groundcover from the admin building. Older than Alex by fifteen years, lean and fit and with short gray hair, Savannah had the brilliance of an inventor and the personality of a stone. Alex thought she remembered seeing Savannah smile once, but she couldn't be sure.

"Alex. We need more silicon allotment from both Mira Corps and SecSun. Right away."

"Hello, Savannah. This is Commander Julian Martin from Terra. Julian, my cousin Savannah Cutler, chief energy scientist for Mira City."

"Hello," Savannah said, barely glancing at Julian. A real live Terran didn't deter her. Nothing deterred Savannah. "Alex, we're simply not using this technology to its fullest because we can't get enough silicon for the dense-array cells. That idiot at SecSun doesn't have his new mining company organized enough to produce in the quantities we need, and you aren't allowing us a big enough share of what Mira Mining produces. If we could get a ration increase of only sixteen percent and a corresponding amount of boron for the P-cells . . ."

She launched into a long, precise, monotone recital of projected figures that Alex did not follow. Savannah never offered explanations of technicalities. She assumed that everyone understood them, and, if they didn't, they should. Alex waited her out.

"Savannah, put it in a three-page requisition argument addressed directly to me." She had learned over time that this was the only response, other than capitulation, that Savannah would accept.

"You'll have it in an hour," Savannah said, turned, and strode back to her foamcast bunker.

Julian gave Alex his faint, aloof smile. Alex said helplessly, "I know it only postpones the refusal. I can't allocate any more mining equipment. We need it elsewhere."

"You're basically a capitalist society?"

"A mixture. We're 'in transition,' Jake says. Still. Anyway, the shortfalls are why new companies like SecSun are starting up. They see a need and a chance to make money, and they're right. The problem is that every new mining company needs mining equipment, and the original stuff is worn out, and so that means a new company to make mining equipment. Which in turn needs things made by new companies, and the most basic resources, including manufacturing facilities and people, are limited."

"So you get the job of deciding who gets what. You know," Julian added thoughtfully, "that's not so different from wartime rationing. Greentrees may not be as alien to me as I expected."

"We're not at war," Alex said shortly.

"Why don't you have solar power satellites in orbit? Their collection efficiency on Earth was eighty-two percent, and you could beam the energy down here in either microwaves or laser."

"Let's get in the car," Alex said, "I'm already running late. Solar power satellites have to be run by computers. Our computer system is old and unreliable, and that's a really intricate manufacturing process that I'm postponing a bit longer. A strong and eco infrastructure comes first. With a Greentrees-based system, we don't absolutely have to have the computers."

Julian stared at her. "You track the dishes to follow the sun *by hand*?"

"No, but we can if we must. Any computer failure won't take down the energy system."

"I see. That's good."

She felt irrationally warmed by his praise. The warmth made it easier to explain the situation at Hope of Heaven, where she now headed the car. ". . . and so Lau-Wah's been dealing with the dissident crimes. He's there now with Yat-Shing Wong, or Wong Yat-Shing as he now calls himself. Ashraf is coming, too. I don't think you should be present at this meeting, Julian. It's not the sort of thing open to anyone."

"Of course not. Don't you have a justice system to deal with crimes? Courts and judges?"

"Of course we do. But Lau-Wah says this isn't a usual crime, or series of crimes, and we need to look at it more deeply."

"He's right."

Julian didn't say more, and Alex didn't ask what he meant. But after a moment she burst out, "The whole situation at Hope of Heaven doesn't make sense to me! We have so much still to do on Greentrees, and we need everyone to do it, and here these kids are destroying instead of building? And for what?"

"You really don't understand power, do you?"

That stopped her. She realized she never thought about power, not in the abstract. Energy, yes, but not power. You did what was needed to get a job done, and so did everybody else. Didn't they? Apparently, there was a lot more to it that she hadn't considered.

Why did Julian make her feel like such an innocent? She was not that.

Julian said quietly, "Alex, you need security at the solar array. I looked and there wasn't any. It would make a good target for your Chinese dissidents."

"Oh, shit."

"Precisely."

"I'll discuss it with Lau-Wah."

They drove in silence after that. Alex followed the river northwest. For the most part, the terrain heading toward the coast was gentle, and the rover didn't bump too much. She watched Julian note the herds of grazing teelies, heavy and slow and stupid, endlessly munching groundcover. Wildflowers, peasies and colburn and lacy moonrushes grew along the banks.

"A purple Eden," he said finally, and she was first pleased to recognize the Terran reference, and then irritated at her own pleasure. What did Terran references matter? This was Greentrees.

He added, "Why didn't you put Mira City downriver, on the coast? For sea fishing, for future shipping."

"Ground too marshy there. Hope of Heaven is situated at about the last stable ground before the river turns brackish and then spreads out into delta. There, that's Hope of Heaven straight ahead." Julian sat up straighter. "Beautiful, isn't it? That's what Mira City will look like one day."

"How so?"

"That's the third-generation design for Greentrees buildings. We started with inflatables: instant and imported from Terra. Then foamcast—durable, sprayed from Greentrees materials with Terran equipment. These structures here are all our own, in completely eco designs. Recyclability, comfort, and beauty."

She stopped the rover at the edge of the village, which consisted of maybe fifty houses, some community centers, and the small manufactories of new companies like Chu Corporation. The buildings were asymmetrical, to take advantage of prevailing winds and shifting light. Roof gardens of compost and mulch reduced storm runoff and cooled interiors. Power for the houses, although not yet the factories, was mostly solar. All plastics, including those for the many windows, were made of biodegradable plant kernels. Even the toilets were eco, using very little water and creating compost that, thanks to genemod microbes, actually smelled sweet. The entire town was light, airy, fragrant, an improbable cross between a latticed crystal and a garden soaring skyward in flashing windmill and graceful com tower.

Julian said quietly, "And I thought Mira City was beautiful," but for once Alex felt no pleasure at his compliment. Too much tension about what was happening here. Whatever it was.

"I'll just walk around and look at things," Julian said. Alex nodded.

The community center had been cleared of its usual activities. In the open central atrium, walled with lattices made of living tang-moss vines, Lau-Wah waited with Ashraf, Yat-Shing, and three other young Chinese. All wore the cheek tattoos recently adopted by Hope of Heaven, two stars and a crescent moon. Along the wall stood three of Mira City's security team, alert and grim. One of them, Alex noted, was Jade Liu, Guy Davenport's second-in-command.

Alex spoke to Ashraf and Lau-Wah. "Are these three under arrest for the burning of the research camp? Or for anything else?"

"No," Lau-Wah said. His peeled-egg face showed no emotion. "There isn't enough evidence linking them to the crime."

"Not enough evidence! MiraNet said there was a metal rod in the rubble, twisted into the Chinese character for 'hope'!"

"Anyone could have left that rod there," Lau-Wah said.

"But everyone knows—"

"We don't convict on rumor," Lau-Wah said, and now the knife in his voice, so at variance with his face, stopped her. Lau-Wah was right, of course. Alex struggled to master her outrage.

Ashraf, rubbing his ear, said, "Isn't Julian with you?"

"Commander Martin has no place here," Lau-Wah said.

"I agree," Alex said. She looked for the first time at the four young dissidents. Instead of the smirks she expected, they gazed back at her with a blank calm that struck her as far more deadly.

Lau-Wah said, "Even though there are no criminal charges, I have asked Mr. Wong to tell us anything at all that might be useful in solving this problem. He has declined."

Alex couldn't resist. "No political polemics, Wong?"

"We do not talk when no one listens," Wong said.

"I'm listening."

"You are incapable of actually hearing. All of you."

Ashraf said gently, "You could try."

"I do not lower myself to try."

"Lau-Wah," Alex said, "did Mr. Wong offer anything useful before you arrived?"

"No," Lau-Wah said.

"Not true," Wong said. "I told you what you yourself are. A traitor to your people, a tool wielded by the Anglos and Arabs, a man of secondhand visions and selfish actions, their selfishness exceeded only by their triteness."

Lau-Wah did not change expression. But Wong did; all at once his young face burst into such fiery hatred that Alex took an involuntary step backward. Wong spat something at Lau-Wah in Chinese, and then all three turned their backs on the triumvirate and bowed their heads toward the floor. It had been rehearsed, Alex realized. A perfect gesture of personal contempt.

She couldn't look at Lau-Wah. Ashraf said, "No," hesitantly and pointlessly. Only Lau-Wah kept his composure. How could he, in the face of such hatred?

"Major Liu, these men are not under arrest. They are free to go. Mr. Wong, even if you will not speak to me, remember that I have spoken to you. Remember my words." He strode toward the door.

Alex, trailed by Ashraf, trotted to catch up. Outside, she said, "What *were* your words? I don't like this unilateral dealing, Lau-Wah."

"It is not unilateral dealing. I merely told him that on behalf of the Chinese citizens of Greentrees, I will permit no more violence. Not because of Mira City but because violence of this sort always creates a backlash, and the hardworking Chinese here do not deserve that. No matter what injustices he thinks exist. I will not sacrifice the many to the misguided idealism of the few."

Misguided idealism.

"Lau-Wah—" she began heatedly, but he had outpaced her, heading for her car. By prearrangement, he would drive it back to Mira and she would fly in the skimmer to the Avery Mountains.

Alex looked after him, her stomach twisting. And not into the shape of hope.

In the foothills of the Avery Mountains, Jon McBain bubbled with enthusiasm. Alex had seldom seen him otherwise, but today he practically foamed. "You've never seen anything like this, Alex. We thought yesterday that it was a type-six biomass, but it's not. We don't know what it is. It . . . who's this?"

"Commander Julian Martin, Dr. Jon McBain, xenobiologist."

"Welcome to Greentrees," Jon said perfunctorily. "Alex, this will astonish you. Over there . . . come on!"

Alex was in no mood to be astonished. The skimmer ride had only worsened her stomach. It had been a silent ride; Julian had not been waiting for her outside the Hope of Heaven community center. He had showed up half an hour later with no explanation, no apology. And Jon McBain, now burbling on about microbes, was the replacement for the dead Donald Halloran. Jon had sent his regrets about the defense meeting because of these microbes. Alex wasn't even completely sure that Jon realized the unknown ship had turned out to be Terran and commanded by Julian, or that Jon would care if he did know. And this was Mira's defense admin!

Alex struggled to hold on to her temper. She followed Jon, who moved so fast he was almost running, across a broad flat field. Somewhere in the distance she could hear the river, but could not see it. It ran more swiftly here in the foothills, digging itself channels with many overhangs and shallow caves. Beyond, the Avery Mountains loomed against the sky.

Jon stopped by a low foamcast building. Beside it, a drilling rig squatted above a narrow hole from which protruded a shining metal rod.

"You won't believe this!" Jon burbled, oblivious to Alex's mood. "We sunk this shaft down a mile and a half, and there's apparently some sort of anaerobic microbes down there that don't use any form of photosynthesis. Well, that's not so odd, the literature records those even on Earth. They oxidize sulfide, methane, iron, or hydrogen, if there's any water, for energy. Some of them pump out really weird molecules. But these! Alex . . . listen!"

Jon pushed a button on a small piece of equipment that Alex couldn't name. Squinting, she saw that a very fine filament ran from the equipment to the top of the shining pole sunk in the shaft. The machinery began to emit regularly spaced, discordant tones. Jon waved his hand and the unpleasant noise grew louder, then very loud. Alex clapped her hands over her ears.

"Turn it off!"

He did. His eyes shone. "That's the sound of some sort of crystallization. The Elliner amp turns molecular action into sound. The microbes down there are acting on the pole. It took us three different alloys before we got one it didn't just eat through."

"Jon—"

"We have no idea what they're doing down there," he said happily. "But all our initial sims indicate some sort of basic catabolism we've never seen before!"

"That's wonderful," Alex said sarcastically, "but not wonderful enough to ignore a summons to the defense meeting in Mira."

"Oh, but it is! We might be dealing here with a whole new division of basic life. It isn't—"

"It isn't what this research station is supposed to be working on, Jon. What about the—"

"We have a Mira Corp grant for basic science, Alex."

"I know you do," she said, as evenly as possible. "But as a sideline. What about the battery?"

"Oh, that's coming along," Jon said. He didn't seem rebuked. "Come on, I'll show you."

He led the way to the foamcast building. Inside, two vast clear vats filled with grayish sludge churned quietly.

"This is a microbially powered battery, a prototype," Jon explained to Julian, the visitor. "A genetically altered form of *E. coli* converts sucrose into CO_2 and water. We snatch the freed electrons created by oxidation before they can be seized by intermediate compounds. We've altered the bacteria to allow constant contact between cell's interior and a microscopic mesh screen that—"

Alex stopped listening. Nothing new here; Jon had been this far along on her last visit. It was clear that all the team energies had gone into his new discovery, not the battery that was supposed to eventually provide a natural, safe, recyclable power for Mira City.

". . . goal of two million liters of liquid and perhaps twenty thousand tons of microbes, producing power at a rate of—"

As tray-o, Alex's job was to make Jon concentrate work on the battery, not on the unknown and irrelevant biomass. The problem was that Jon's concentration, a formidable force when focused, was not easy to direct. It went its own way, independent as a lion. And just as perverse.

". . . problem of microbial waste, which tends to turn the soup acidic, so we—"

Alex said abruptly, "Jon, I want you to report to Mira tomorrow afternoon for a defense meeting."

"But I—"

"No arguments, please." She turned and walked away. Rude . . . she was being very rude. Well, so what?

She hated being rude.

Another silent ride back to Mira. As the city came into view, Julian said, "Alex, stop the car."

Surprised by his urgent tone, she did.

He sat still so long that she grew alarmed. Finally he twisted in his cramped seat and turned on her the full brilliance of those green genemod eyes.

"I want you to listen to me carefully. Sometimes the observations of an outsider can be valuable in assessing a situation. Mira—"

"I know we're a bit disorganized," she snapped. "I'll take care of it!"

"I'm not talking about disorganization. I'm talking about total stupidity."

Alex gasped. "How dare you just—"

"Now you're angry. Do you see how easily I angered you? I want you to see it. I want you to see that you—all of you—are just reacting to each event as it comes along, without any remote idea of how it fits into the overall situation. Savannah Cutler, Jon McBain, Yat-Shing Wong, even you . . . everyone is interested in a single goal, constructive or destructive, but not working together for the good of Mira as a whole. I called that stupidity, and it *is* stupidity. Willful blindness is always stupid."

Rage boiled up in her, but then he took her hand and held it in a hard, impersonal grip that compelled her to listen.

"You're blind to at least three things, Alex. First, you don't see the necessity for clear authority. You let Savannah Cutler and Jon McBain and even Lau-Wah Mah decide issues that you should decide. Like all democratic meritocracies, you're afraid to exercise actual power. But you're at war with the Furs, or will soon be. War does not go well if leaders try to lead by letting every talented person have control over the ends, not just the means, of his own fiefdom."

"They're not—"

"They're running them as if they have fiefdoms. Second, you're blind to an inherent problem with meritocracies. They always breed aggression."

Alex blinked, too surprised to answer.

Julian gave her his half smile. His fingers still gripped hers. "You thought the opposite? That in a meritocracy, where everyone has a chance to rise from sheer talent, aggression is minimized? No. A meritocracy means competition, and the less you mitigate that competition with universally accepted norms of inherited privilege, the more aggressive and nasty the competition becomes."

"I don't believe that."

"Really? Who are causing more trouble here, the Arabs with their three-centuries-old tradition of stable inheritance of some change but not too much? Or the Chinese with their history of totally remaking politics and culture every forty years or so?"

Alex was silent. She didn't know much history of either the Arabs or the Chinese.

"You have a genuinely dangerous situation-in-the-making with the dissidents in Hope of Heaven. You're blind to how dangerous, because you're blind to Earth history. What Lau-Wah said to Wong was totally inadequate. The third thing you're blind to is how many weapons you have here on Greentrees that you should be readying for war, but instead don't even regard as weapons."

"Like what?" Alex said.

"Everything I saw today. The solar array concentrates sunlight five hundred times, and the dishes are manually directed. Turn them into the sky, or onto the ground, and you have an unexpected heat weapon. Those new microbes of McBain's destroyed the first two poles he inserted into the shaft—didn't you hear him say that? I asked him what the poles were made of. The microbes ate two of the toughest alloys I know, including the one the hull of my ship is made of. *Ate metal,* in minutes. That's a weapon."

She stared at him.

"In war, Alex, everything is a weapon. Food is a weapon, in how it's distributed or not distributed. I don't mean you should starve out Hope of Heaven, which anyway would be difficult to do on a planet as rich as this. I just mean that you should scrutinize all your resources, both for minimizing violence with the dissidents and waging warfare with the Furs. If you don't, you could lose it all to the enemy. You're not even *aware* of your resources, not all of them. And you should be.

"After all, you're the tray-o."

Alex sat quietly for a long moment. Ahead of her the white foamcast buildings of Mira City sparkled in the sunshine. The greenery of the farm and the gorgeous genemod colors of the flowers leaped out from the purple countryside. She could see people, small and purposeful, striding along the nearest streets. Wind turbines on a hill across the river flashed in the breeze.

You could lose it all.

"Julian," she said slowly, "I want you to attend all meetings of the triumvirate from now on. I'll fix it with Ashraf and Lau-Wah. From now on, you advise us."

It was only later, in the middle of another sleepless night, that Alex wondered about the meeting at Hope of Heaven. "Inadequate," Julian had called Lau-Wah's rebukes to the dissident vandals. But Julian hadn't been at the meeting; he'd been wandering around Hope of Heaven, returning late to the car.

So how had he known what Lau-Wah had said to Yat-Shing Wong?

A week later Julian laid out his plans for the defense of Mira City at a special meeting of the full city council. Alex scanned the faces of the council members: Quaker, Chinese, and Anglo men and women; Arab men. Most of the councillors, busy with their own jobs and families and lives, were used to meeting hastily a few times a year to agree to whatever the triumvirate put in front of them. This meeting was different, and the faces looked solemn, wary, scared. The Furs were such an old threat; many of the councillors had not even been born when the aliens had last appeared on Greentrees. And Julian, flanked by his chief aides and scientists but wearing Threadmores, probably looked to them almost as alien as the almost mythical Furs.

Alex's gaze found Jake and Lau-Wah, whose expressions of noncommittal reserve were so identical that, under other circumstances, she might have laughed. She went to sit beside Jake. From there she could view the audience without drawing attention to her scrutiny.

Ashraf began with a little clearing of his throat. "You all know why we're here. Commander Martin has some . . . some defense plans to show us. For Mira City." He considered. "And the rest of Greentrees. Ah, Commander Martin." Ashraf sat down on Alex's other side.

"Thank you, Mr. Mayor," Julian said easily, and Alex noted that although he had dressed like a Greenie, he spoke with the formality of a Terran. What would the council make of that combination?

"As most of you know, my team has spent the last week talking to you all, learning about the tremendous resources and talent here in Mira City. I want to thank you all for everything you've told us. If Terra had been this cooperative and this rich, she might not have got herself into the terminal state she has."

Julian was silent a moment. Pain flickered across his face. Beside Alex, Jake muttered, "Very nice. Flattery tempered by a stoic-but-visible bid for sympathy. He's good."

"Shut up," Alex whispered.

"I'd like to start by listing all of Mira's resources," Julian said. "Please bear with me if I recite things you all already know. I hope to be able to show how they will relate to two things: defending Mira when the Furs attack"—*when*, Alex noted, not *if*—"and contributing to all our safety through a city-wide evacuation that gives first priority to protecting your children."

A ripple ran over the audience. This was the first that most of them had heard about an evacuation. Julian discussed that first, mentioning the children over and over. The children's safety, feeding the children, keeping the enemy from seizing even one child, preparing for the return of the children after the attack had been repulsed.

As Julian talked, Alex felt herself drawn in. Julian's plans were detailed and direct. It would require an enormous, temporary diversion of resources from the day-to-day running of Mira, but the evacuation seemed possible.

Julian spoke more, and it seemed advantageous.

He spoke more, and it seemed necessary.

Around her, Alex could feel the council members drawn in. A few nodded, or spoke in low voices to each other. She turned her head to glance at Jake; his expression told her nothing.

Julian said, "That's the evacuation plan. But of course it does no good to get everyone out of the city if we then let the Furs take it. *But we will not permit that to happen.* While the evacuation occurs— in fact, from the first moment a Fur ship is sited—the defense strategy begins. I'd like to have my ship's captain start by explaining possible orbital defenses that—"

"One moment, please, Commander Martin," Lau-Wah said. "Before you go any further, I'd like to ask some questions."

"Certainly," Julian said warmly, but a little chill ran over Alex.

"I've listened to your plans for this 'evacuation.' They're very convincing. But they leave out a crucial point. All these 'rich resources' you're diverting from Mira City will make it very difficult to keep the city running day to day. Manufacturing will be disrupted, mining, transport, food production, even education of our young. Instead, everything will be concentrated on evacuation and, I presume, defense."

Alex saw a few heads nod around the room.

"Not everything," Julian said pleasantly. "If I've given that impression, please let me correct—"

"Concentrated on evacuation and defense," Lau-Wah interrupted, most uncharacteristically. "And also concentrated in *your* hands, not ours."

A mistake. Alex realized it as soon as Lau-Wah spoke, and sensed that he did, too. Julian had shown nothing but concern for Mira City, for all Greenies . . . there wasn't a "your" and "our" here! Why was Lau-Wah trying to make divisions where they didn't exist?

Just as Hope of Heaven was doing.

Immediately she pushed away the thought. Lau-Wah was in an entirely different category from the dissident troublemakers, Lau-Wah was as concerned about Mira as any of them, it wasn't jealousy of Julian that drove Lau-Wah, it *wasn't* . . .

Julian said nothing, standing dignified and silent.

Finally a young Chinese councilwoman, color high on her cheeks, said, "I think Commander Martin is concerned not with . . . with power but with all our safety."

Murmurs of assent ran around the room. Then someone in the back called, "Mr. Holman, what do you think?"

Alex swiveled to look at Jake.

The old man said, "I'd like to hear the rest of the defense plans."

People nodded. Jake's voice had been steady and neutral. But Alex knew. Jake had always been the one to want a strong defense of Mira. He liked what he'd heard so far, and if Julian could present counterattack plans with the same careful plausibility that he'd presented evacuation plans, and with the same humility, Jake would lend the weight of his approval to Julian's strategies.

"Thank you, Mr. Holman," Julian said quietly, with obvious deference. He began his defense presentation. Alex had heard most of it before, starting with what he'd told her on their first trip out to the solar array, to Jon McBain's camp, to Hope of Heaven.

As soon as the discussion of orbital and ground weapons began, the Quaker members of the council slipped from the room. They would, Alex knew, return when a vote was taken. She guessed they would vote for the evacuation, against the counterattack. There were not enough of them to carry the decision.

Julian had prevailed.

Jake was nodding openly now as Julian talked. So did several others. But when Alex searched for Lau-Wah, she couldn't find him. He must have slipped out quietly along with the Quakers.

Her stomach knotted, although she would have found it difficult to explain exactly why.

9

A VINE PLANET

Karim had taken to whistling.

Not from lightheartedness, or joy in music, or even the memory of Beta Vine's pleasure in Karim's whistling on Green-trees. That memory, in fact, kept him for several days from forming a single note. But finally he whistled just to have a sound, any sound, in the dead silence of the Vine colony world.

He whistled Grieg.

Around him the huge, pulpy, unmoving Vines stood soundless.

He whistled Strauss.

No echoes came from this world with no hard edges.

He whistled dance tunes from Earth, Moran and Parakinski and Jerzell, all dead centuries and light-years away.

The silence stretched on.

He ran through the Vines, under their protruding lengths that were not leaves nor tentacles nor arms but something alien to him, alien to the music. He ran until he couldn't whistle, and then until he couldn't move and had to drop to the squishy mud that was never puddle and never dry. He dropped panting and blind and furious, but he knew fury wouldn't help. Nothing helped. He was trapped here and he would die here and his and Lucy's DNA would decay and form the only anomaly on this living world that would not respond to their existence.

Above him the motionless leaves/tentacles/arms did nothing.

When he'd regained his breath, Karim again stood. So far his and Lucy's determination to escape this pulpy hell had come to nothing. But Karim still walked every day, covering enormous distances, afraid not to walk, afraid to sink into more nothingness than he already felt.

He walked.

He whistled, from despair, the cheerful rondo from Mozart's *Alla Turca*. Dah dah *dee* dah dah *dee* . . .

Something answered.

Karim gasped and stumbled. Grabbing the pulpy trunk of a Vine—or the Vine, if they were really all interconnected—he righted himself. Listening.

Nothing.

He had imagined it. He must have imagined it.

With lips that almost trembled too much to purse, he whistled the rondo again.

Something answered with a single long, high note.

All the displays on Karim's suit still worked. Shakily he checked the direction of the received sound and began walking that way. Every hundred yards he whistled again, licking dry lips and holding his breath afterward.

Each time, something answered.

He came to it: an irregular pit, maybe fifty meters across at its widest point, less than a meter down to the surface. Karim stepped closer.

Not water. Not the ubiquitous mud. The pit writhed with a biomass of some sort, a pinkish gray stew of . . . what? Bacteria, maybe; it looked vaguely like the biofilms that had coated the interior of the first Vine ship. Microorganisms of some alien, unknowable sort, either sentient in their own right or else the servant of the sentient Vines.

Karim knelt by the edge of the pit and peered in. The biomass stew was opaque; his scrutiny told him nothing. He squatted back on his heels and whistled the Mozart rondo.

The biomass answered with a single long note.

He stared at it. A tropism of some kind, automatic and mindless?

He whistled a dance tune, one of Cazzie Jerzell's upbeat, simple rhythms.

The biomass gave him back the tune.

Karim's eyes widened. He tried Chopin, a minor-key and difficult fragment. The pit answered with the single long note. Another Jerzell ditty, and it sang it back to him. Grieg, and the single note. Which, he realized, meant *no*. The pit wanted the Jerzell. He was whistling to an alien life form with lousy musical taste.

"What are you?" he whispered to it.

Nothing.

For the next half hour, until his lips would no longer pucker, Karim whistled. He tried to construct his experiment rationally, but too many emotions swamped him: relief, exhilaration, desperate hope. Something on this planet was responding to him.

He learned that if he whistled bright dance tunes, the mass rippled softly. If he sat silent with folded arms, it gave a low soft note until he began again. If he whistled anything complex or subtle, the pit sounded its high long *no*.

"You hear me, yes," Karim said hoarsely at the end of what had to be the strangest impromptu concert in the universe. "You at least hear me."

He brought Lucy, and the translator. Neither was any help. Lucy's apathy had grown until it was difficult to get her to move to the pit at all. When she saw it, she stared for a full silent minute, and then said, "It's just bacteria, like on the ship. So what?"

"I don't know yet." Annoyed, he took the translator from her, set it at the edge of the pit, and spoke into it for a good hour.

The pit answered only with its low insistent note demanding whistling.

Karim was frightened by the force of his rage. He saw it as a sign of how unbalanced this place had made him. He forced himself to go on speaking, setting the translator on the ground beside a towering Vine whose fronds dipped into the biomass below.

Neither pit nor Vine answered him.

"Damn them for infidels and whores!" Karim screamed. The rage broke. He grabbed the translator and hurled it into the pit, where it sank silently.

Karim and Lucy looked at each other, petrified.

But nothing happened. And *that,* he thought in despair, was the slogan of this planet. Slogan, motto, operating system, epitaph: *Nothing happened.*

"Look," Lucy whispered. "Oh, Karim . . . look!"

He turned to follow her pointing finger. A few meters along the perimeter of the pit, very close to its edge, something was growing. At first a blob, it slowly—how slowly, like everything else here!—took on form. It was a small Vine, about six feet high. Then it was a Vine with two long fronds and a bulbous growth on top. The trunk divided. It was, Karim thought dazedly, like watching a speeded-up holo of a plant growing and flowering. An hour later—at least he thought it took an hour, he forgot to time it—the Vine was shaped recognizably, built from living molecules, a representation crude but unmistakable, grown from the sludge in the pit.

Karim was staring at a sculpted plantlike creature that was himself.

As he stared, the creation began to whistle: Cazzie Jerzell's catchy dance tune "Under the April Moon."

Karim and Lucy circled the pit, stopping a few feet from the creature/sculpture/music box. Up close, it looked even cruder. Its "lips," an open circle of pulpy purple, didn't move as the whistling sounds emerged. But something, Karim thought dazedly, must be moving inside.

He said inanely, "Whistling sounds are easy to produce. Even wind does it."

Lucy gasped, "Is it alive?"

"I don't know. I mean, yes, it's alive, it's a plant as much as the Vines are plants, but . . . but I don't think it's sentient. Of itself."

"No," Lucy said. She looked from the whistling arboreal Karim to the pit, then to a nearby Vine, then back to the pit. "Karim . . ."

"What?" This was the most animation he'd seen from her in weeks.

"I think we have it wrong. Here, on the Vine ship, even on Greentrees."

"What do you mean?"

"I think . . . no, wait." She closed her eyes, as if in pain.

He waited.

"I think," she finally said, "that we were wrong when we assumed that Beta's biofilm arm was under his control on Greentrees. Or that the Vines on the ship controlled all that biofilm covering the floor. Or that these Vines here are master of this planet. I think we were wrong. The Vines are just machinery. Like our translators and computers and ships and skinsuits. Or maybe like the genemod working animals on Earth. Horses, maybe. The biofilm controls the Vines, not the other way around. The biofilm is the sentient master of this race.

"All this time we've been talking to the wrong end of the horse."

10

MIRA CITY

It came ripping through the sky, a huge black disk growing larger and larger and larger still, until it stretched horizon to horizon, shrieking metal and wailing wind. The bottom opened and red spilled out, a trickle at first, growing to a silent torrent. The red liquid flooded the streets of Mira City, higher and higher. People screamed and thrashed, faces contorted with terror as they went under, drowning in blood . . .

Alex woke and bolted upright on her cot. Sweat soaked her pajamas. Panting, she recoiled as a furry missile landed on the bed. Katous.

"Bad dream, cat."

Katous stared at her in the darkness, two impassive yellow eyes.

"Very bad dream."

She pushed away her blanket; no more sleep tonight. Evacuation drill day, starting in less than half an hour. Well, for her it wouldn't be a surprise night drill. Probably there were a lot more people awake who were supposed to be taken by "surprise."

One of them was Jake who, since his last stroke, was now apparently installed permanently in her apartment with a strong male nurse. At least it might be permanently; Alex wasn't home much. Siddalee had grudgingly supplemented the cot in Alex's office with a shower. Tonight, however, Jake's nurse had moved into Jake's bedroom, and Alex had slept at her "evacuation drill home point."

As her eyes adjusted to the dark, she saw that Jake sat at the table in his wheelchair. The snores of the deep-sleeping young came through the bedroom doorway.

"Have some tea, Alex."

She poured herself a cup, first using her sleeve to wipe the cup clean of yesterday's dregs. "Why are you awake already?"

"Why are you? Actually, it might give you time to comb your hair for once."

Even at his age, Jake appreciated female beauty. Alex, who seldom thought about her appearance, grinned at him. She sometimes wondered what women had decorated his younger life, but never asked. "Ready for the drill, Jake?"

"Yes." His eyes gleamed; Julian had planned well. "I just wish I weren't in the evac group with that idiot Duncan Martin."

"Is he an idiot?" Alex said. She hadn't been able to attend any of Duncan's theater pieces—too busy with the stepped-up defenses. But most people raved about Duncan as both performer and impressario, a term Alex had never heard of before he arrived.

"He's a wonderful actor," Jake said grudgingly. "His Prospero was first-rate. And he's found acting talent among young people and got them doing amazing things, not to mention working like beavers."

"What's a 'beaver'?"

"It's a . . . never mind, it's not important. I called him an idiot because he won't stop doing just what I did, and of course none of us can tolerate our own faults in anybody else. Duncan refers constantly to Earth. Only he berates us all for 'criminal neglect of our artistic past.' He doesn't seem to understand that we've been busy surviving."

"So make him understand." She sipped the hot tea gratefully.

"You cannot argue with dogmatism."

"Sure you can. Look at Julian, arguing with Lau-Wah."

Jake blinked at her from his old eyes. "You know, that's the first time I've heard you make a joke about that situation."

Alex scowled over the rim of her cup. She didn't know why she'd joked like that; it wasn't funny. Since the council meeting in which

Julian had laid out his defense plans, Lau-Wah and Julian had continued to be quietly, courteously, lethally at each other's throats. And Alex, as tray-o, was caught in the middle.

"To have the city act together to survive," Lau-Wah had said to her, "it must, by definition, act together. We are not doing that. It should be our first priority."

"All men act in self-interest," Julian had said to her, "and that's good. Self-interest, as opposed to fanatic idealism, leaves room for compromise. Governor Mah is trying to advance the prosperity of his Chinese constituency. But he will have to compromise that temporarily for the good of Greentrees as a whole."

Was Lau-Wah putting the good of his Chinese over the good of Mira? The question troubled Alex. But as the weeks wore on, and Lau-Wah and Julian argued over everything—mining priorities, weapons construction, emergency taxes for defense costs, degree of permissible disruption of Mira's infrastructure—she found herself siding more and more with Julian. Ashraf Shanti, pliable and nervous, had also been swayed by Julian's calm logic and ferocious intelligence. But Lau-Wah had grown increasingly remote, politely curt in a way that made Alex uncomfortable. Politics on Greentrees had been more open before now.

They had not prepared for war before now.

No, that wasn't true. Jake told her that thirty-nine years before, Mira had prepared lavishly for a war that hadn't happened. Alex didn't remember much about that; she'd been a small child. But those who did remember tended to side with Lau-Wah, except for Jake himself.

He was still grumbling about Duncan. "The trouble with actors is that they can't stop acting once they step off the stage. That man is nothing but layers of roles he's played, tattered into intermingled ribbons. One minute he's Falstaff, then Faust, then Don Quixote, then Jerome O'Dell . . ."

The names meant nothing to Alex.

". . . and if I have to hear one more time about the 'pleasant primitive naïveté of colonies' I'm going to . . . oh God, here he comes."

Alex leaned forward and wiped a thread of drool off Jake's face. Duncan passed the window and opened the unlocked door without knocking. "Are we ready?" he asked in that thrilling voice whose musical doubleness, harmonizing with itself, was indeed genemod. Julian had told Alex so. " 'Cry "Havoc!" and let slip the dogs of war.' "

"Not war quite yet," Jake said dryly. Next to Duncan's robust health, Jake looked even older and more tired. The last tiny stroke had partially paralyzed one side of Jake's face, increasing the drooling, although the stroke did not seem to have affected his thinking much or slowed down his speech. Tenderness swelled Alex's heart. The old man was very dear to her.

"Oh, but we must have war or Julian will be so disappointed," Duncan said blithely. "Now don't look shocked, Alex, you know it's true. He is a soldier, and why do men soldier except to war?"

"Julian doesn't want war," Jake snapped. "None of us do. Don't talk obscenities, Martin."

"As you say. Do I have time for a cup of tea before the festivities begin? What, no clean glasses? My dear, you are a deplorable housekeeper."

"She's not a housekeeper, she's a leader of a city-state!"

Alex stepped into the bickering. "Duncan, did you ever hold a position in Julian's command on Earth? Besides acting, I mean?"

"Of course not," Duncan said. "My brother is far too astute to let me control anything. Most artists barely control themselves. I see that there is no hope of hot tea, after all . . . ah, there's the siren!"

Alex hadn't expected it to be so loud. The sound tore through the air, and for a moment the horror of her nightmare rushed over her. She pushed it back, and shouted, "Jake, Duncan, you know what to do . . . see you later!"

" 'No one dast blame this man,' " Duncan said, which made no sense but Alex had no time to question him. She ran out the door toward the transport inflatable.

All four rovers were gone.

It actually took her a moment to remember. Julian had devised evacuation plans, contingency plans, backups for the contingencies. He'd worked day and night—literally, sleeping only for his own necessary hour in each twenty-four—to create the plans and broadcast them on MiraNet. Then he'd sent volunteers door-to-door to make sure everyone understood exactly what to do and where to go. He'd taken into account the elderly Arab women who would not leave the medina with men unrelated to them, the scientists and engineers who might be away from the city, the old and the infants and the sick and the recalcitrant. He tried to think of everything. The rovers were missing because in a worst-case scenario they might all be out in the bush.

"I forgot my tram number!" a young girl cried, running up to Alex. The girl shivered in a thin nightdress. Her eyes looked huge with fear, or possibly excitement. "Is it a real attack?"

"Act as if it is! Where are your parents?"

"I was sleeping at my friend Aleya's and when the siren came I ran home but my family already left and—"

"Children are supposed to stay with the family they're with when the alarm sounds! And where's your emergency pac?"

"I forgot it. Oh, Ms. Cutler, is it a real attack?" And this time there was no doubting her expression: the child was thrilled.

"Go back to your friend's family," Alex snapped, "and leave with them. Now!"

"What if they already left, too?"

"Oh, for . . . come with me!" This was not going as planned.

"I'll . . . look! There's Aimee's father!" She ran off.

Glad to be rid of her, Alex ran toward the tram tracks. Getting fifteen thousand people out of a city and as far away as possible, in groups as small as possible, had required construction and ingenuity. Tracks had been built leading thirty miles out in five different directions. Basic flatbed trams ferried groups of people to the end points, from which each group had a designated destination based on how far and how fast they could travel. Some ended up in the ubiquitous caves to the north of the city, across the river. Some traveled to remote valleys. Some robust groups had no end point at all; after a real attack, they would travel across the continent, if necessary. Barges on the river served the same purposes as the trams.

"They won't all escape," Julian had said somberly, "and some who do will be caught later. But this at least gives us a chance to keep humanity alive on Greentrees. And to fight back."

Alex caught the next tram, climbing up front with the driver. She was a priority red, able to take whatever transportation she needed. A potential fighter rather than a potential hider. At the moment, adrenaline pumping, she was glad.

This tram was full of people who had mostly remembered their evac pacs and who huddled quietly together in the predawn dark. Mostly Anglos, some Chinese. A few people recognized Alex and nodded. No one asked her if the attack was real, and no one looked either outraged or terrified. Maybe this would work, after all.

"You don't need a full-scale drill," Lau-Wah had argued. "You can test the plans without forcing the old and sick to stand up to evacuation. And without emptying the city of all essential services. And especially without the EMP. Getting everything running again—"

"The city gets emptied completely," Julian had answered.

Ashraf said, "What if, for instance, a woman is having a baby?"

"Then she'll have it in transit," Julian said. "I'm sure she would prefer that to having a newborn child captured by Furs."

Ashraf had said no more.

Alex jumped off the tram at the skimmer inflatable. Julian had not, thank heavens, also removed them as a contingency test. She'd comlinked for the skimmer to wait for her. The seats were all filled with scientists and engineers; Alex squatted on the floor for the short trip to the number three command bunker. Beside her squatted her tech, Natalie Bernstein, who was also supposed to have been in the rover.

"Here we go, Alex," Natalie said. Alex merely nodded back. Natalie was no more than twenty-two, and her head of short, wiry black curls looked as uncombed as Alex's. But her broad face shone with the same excitement as the void-brained teenage girl at the tram stop. However, Natalie was anything but void-brained. Smart and steady, she had been Alex's first choice for bunker tech, despite Natalie's youth.

Their bunker lay sixty miles northeast of Mira City. The site had been carefully chosen. Wild and heavily forested, close to a small tributary of the river, the terrain was nonetheless not too mountainous to reach by rover or to land a skimmer. Six such underground bunkers, deep enough and heavily enough shielded to withstand an alpha beam, were scattered within a three-hundred-mile radius. Ashraf, Lau-Wah, Alex, and Julian were all assigned to different bunkers to minimize leadership loss if the Furs attacked from orbit.

The four command bunkers, plus the two housing essential scientists, were linked by computer and by comlink. When Alex ran down the short flight of steps, Natalie's backup, Ben Stoller, was already there; someone stayed in each command post at all times. Ben, a muscular and quiet young man whose ears reddened when he was embarrassed, silently gave up his seat in front of the displays to Natalie and stood in the back of the tiny bunker.

Julian was already comming from his bunker. "Alex? How does it look in Mira?"

She peered over Natalie's shoulder. "Moving smoothly, from what I can see."

"That's what the reports say. Major Helf?"

"The ship is three hundred million clicks out," said the voice of Julian's physicist, Lucia Helf. Alex, staring at the back of Natalie's black curls, thought for a moment that Lucia Helf meant "ship" literally. But of course that was part of the drill. They were tracking a hypothetical Fur vessel bent on attack.

A Fur ship equipped with their version of a McAndrew Drive could come in decelerating at a hundred gees. It then needed time to cruise into orbit, perhaps reconnoiter, perhaps send down a shuttle . . . or perhaps not. No one knew exactly what the Furs would do. Whatever it was, however much time it took would equal the time available to evacuate Mira City. Maybe six hours from the time the orbital probes picked up the ship. Maybe six days. Maybe sixty days. The drill used the least possible time.

Paul Ramdi, an energy engineer, said over the open link, "All class red facilities shielded."

"Good," Julian said. "Mr. Ching?"

"I just heard from the mayor—bunker number two is sealed. Captain Quiles reports that Mira City is about half-empty."

Alex said, "Have the mines reported yet? And the water-treatment plant?"

"Not yet," Andy Ching said. She heard the excitement in his voice, so like the young girl in her nightgown. Andy, too, was very young. Julian had quietly insisted that the youthful generation of Chinese be represented in each command bunker.

Alex watched over Natalie's shoulder and her face darkened. "Julian—Lau-Wah isn't in his bunker."

Julian's voice said sharply, "Where is he?"

"They don't know. He didn't take a rover—well, they weren't there, you know that—Natalie says he's not answering his com-link."

"Two hundred fifty million clicks out," Lucia Helf said.

"Mines shielded now," Andy said.

Alex said to Natalie, "Tell them not to seal the bunker yet. Lau-Wah must have stopped to deal with some problem."

"Then why hasn't he reported in?" Julian said.

"I don't know."

They waited. The water-treatment plant reported in: shielding complete. Lau-Wah did not join his bunker.

When the hypothetical ship had reached orbit, Ashraf ordered Lau-Wah's bunker sealed. Alex heard his voice quaver and she thought of Jake. By now Jake should have reached his end point, a small hospital cave beside the tram track's termination, not very hard for the old and sick to get to. Not very safe, either. Duncan Martin had been assigned there by lottery as an able-bodied orderly, a military attack not having much need for the usual skills of actors. Alex wondered if, during an actual attack, Duncan would stay at the cave or would try to join a group running farther away.

"Shuttle descending," Lucia Helf said.

Julian had worked out strategies for attacking a Fur ship in orbit, using the *Beta Vine* or his own ship, the *Crucible*. Those strategies could not be tested. Nor could the plans for attacking a Fur shuttle. Depending on where a shuttle descended from orbit, Mira would deploy the solar array, lasers, mining explosives, all the meager resources (Julian said they were meager) of destruction that Greentrees would offer. If the shuttle headed directly for Mira City, Julian would execute the maneuver he was about to test now.

"The biggest problem is these 'force walls' you describe," Julian had said, and Alex had noted his phrasing. No one on Greentrees could produce an example of the force fields that could be created and dismantled with the flick of a curved stick, walling captives in and danger out as the Furs chose. So Julian believed in them only provisionally. That didn't stop him from defending against the fields, in the only way he could think of.

"Shuttle one hundred fifty meters above Mira," said Lucia Helf, with as much tension in her voice as if the thing had actually existed.

"Deploy EMP!" Julian said. "Now!"

Everything on Alex's display went dark.

The electro-magnetic pulse knocked out electricity, radio waves, microwaves, X-rays—everything from 10^{-4} nanometers to nearly a kilometer. It wiped computers clean. That was why days had been spent moving as much equipment as possible out of Mira City, beyond range, for this drill. Personal equipment, at least small items, was supposed to move out with the populace. The big equipment—mining, water treatment, all the infrastructure of civilization—had been shielded with lead and foamcast and stone and dirt. "We don't know what they have," Julian had said, "so we're going to remove as much as we can from Mira."

Gazing at the bunker displays, Alex saw that he had.

The command bunkers, now like most of the inhabitants, were beyond the EMP range. Immediately reports began flooding in from Ashraf and the others. "It worked, I think!"

"Nothing coming from Mira."

"Those bastards are now unarmed and vulnerable."

"Wait—here comes the comlink from the water-treatment plant, Suval Tremaine just walked outside to link . . . no problems! The shield held, all equipment functioning!"

"Mira Corp Mining Consortium report . . . all functioning fine."

Alex listened intently to the comlink chatter while watching Natalie's displays. She could hear Julian's half smile in his voice. "Security Chief Davenport reports the city down. We'll have to replace a lot of lighting and pumping chips, I'm afraid."

Alex, Natalie, and Ben grinned at one another. The chips had been removed, building by building, leaving only enough to indicate the range of the EMP. Also sacrificed had been some old, nearly obsolete but sophisticated machinery. The sacrifice was worth it.

And yet a shiver ran over Alex. Grins, congratulations, a fine celebratory glow . . . because they had succeeded, hypothetically at least, in rendering other beings helpless. Was that what war did?

She realized, dimly, that she didn't know anything about what war did. Not real, visceral knowledge. Well, how should she? How should any of them except Julian and his Terrans?

By now Guy Davenport's security force was moving back toward Mira City, carrying comlinks and reporting as they went. A skeleton force had been left in the city to prevent looting, if any Greentrees inhabitants had decided to risk remaining behind. Security's weapons wouldn't work, of course, but then neither would the looters'. Nobody had anticipated any real trouble.

Natalie gasped. Alex's attention snapped back to the audio comlink report.

"—shooting fire out of the nozzle! I've never seen anything—"

"Where the hell did they get flamethrowers?" Julian's voice demanded.

"Who?" Alex cried.

"—fire at the hospital! It's caught fire . . ."

The hospital was one of the third-generation buildings that Alex had been so proud to show Julian: graceful soaring wood, beauty to comfort the ill and dying. It had been built last year, to replace the utilitarian foamcast hospital. It stood at the very edge of Mira City, at the very edge of the EMP range.

"*Who?*" Alex demanded again.

"Hope of Heaven," Natalie said.

Abruptly a visual display came to life. Alex watched, frozen, as masked figures ran away from the hospital. Behind them, red and yellow flames danced gaily over the purplish wood of the graceful building. The airy rooms, Alex thought, where the sick could gaze out on the bright genemod flower beds. The meditation chapel, the operating rooms, the children's wing . . .

A blackened beam crashed to the ground, dragging with it part of a wall.

"—This is Jenson Cutler just arrived back in Mira City for MiraNet," said a shaky voice, "sending from the roof of a building to . . . to all of you. Masked people are burning the hospital . . . no, now they're shooting flames at another building down the street, I don't know what it is . . ." The robocam swiveled and Alex saw flames—so gorgeous, so cheerful looking!—hit another curved, soaring structure.

"SecSun Mining," she said aloud, to no one.

The building burned as joyously as the hospital.

"I'm going in," said another voice on another channel. "They can't just—"

"Do not advance!" came Guy Davenport's voice, more decisive than Alex had ever heard it. "You have no weapons. Stay where you are; that's an order."

"But they're . . . oh my God!"

"Sweet gravy Allah," came Jenson Cutler's voice, and Alex barely had time to note with some numb, inane part of her mind that her young third cousin had used a bastardized Arab oath before the robocam turned for yet another view.

Furs were running down the street.

When did the enemy land?

But of course they weren't space Furs. A moment later, the longest moment of her life, Alex realized her mistake. The Furs running toward the flamethrowers were Nan Frayne's wild Furs, inexplicably invading a temporarily prechip Mira City. The Hope of Heaven rebels—as the robocam zoomed in, Alex could see the Chinese character on their masks—turned the flamethrowers toward the Furs. The young humans weren't fast enough. The Furs darted behind foamcast buildings. They moved with incredible speed.

A spear arced through the air and caught a rebel in the chest.

Alex was back in the genetics lab, watching another spear fly into a midair lion, Nan Frayne's voice in her ear: *"There's a ship approaching Greentrees . . . you better go find out. I've got better things to do."*

Spears and lances were not affected by an EMP.

Another rebel went down, impaled through the chest, still screaming. The robocam swiveled wildly. Incoherent shouting, and then two more rebels dropped their flamethrowers and clapped their hands on top of their heads in surrender.

Then two more.

Alex stumbled toward the display for a closer look. Later, it seemed to her that it had all happened during that one clumsy step forward, although of course it couldn't have been that compressed. But that's the way she remembered it. Guy Davenport's security force rushing forward, taking the rebels prisoner. People spraying water on the fires; the pumping stations were not, thank heavens, computer controlled. And Nan Frayne's Furs melting away, disappearing as completely as if they had never been there at all, had been as hypothetical as the space Furs' ship, their shuttle, the nonexistent attack on a city not quite empty enough.

"Why didn't you tell us?" Ashraf demanded of Julian. The small man in his rumpled Threadmores looked surprisingly dignified. He neither fidgeted nor glanced around distractedly. His dark eyes stayed fixed on Julian's, and in them Alex saw less personal offense at being deposed than impersonal concern for the truth.

"Julian, If you brought in Nan Frayne and her Furs to protect Mira City, we should have known. Alex, Lau-Wah, and Guy, at a minimum."

At the mention of Lau-Wah, Alex bit her lip. Lau-Wah had never reported in to his bunker. He was still missing.

Julian said, "Ms. Frayne made it a condition of her cooperation that I tell no one. She said that was nonnegotiable. I believed her."

Alex believed it, too.

Julian continued, "I didn't know, of course, that Hope of Heaven would choose the Mira City drill to attack. I was protecting us against as many contingencies as I could. That's a strategy we had discussed and agreed on."

"*Us.*" Julian counted himself as one of them.

They were meeting in the Mausoleum, whose chips had been the first to be replaced. Ashraf's office, unlike Alex's, was painfully neat, and unexpectedly cheerful for the stark foamcast building. Bright woven rugs and hammered copper plates from Terra, precious antiques, hung on the white foamcast walls. Another rug, green with a geometric design, covered the floor. The basic foamcast furniture had been softened with cushions. Holo cubes of Ashraf's children played on his desk. The room had the warmth that Siddalee was always complaining Alex's office lacked, although Siddalee was no better at creating it than Alex herself.

She said to Julian, "How did you get Nan Frayne to post her Furs as guards? Those creatures have always resisted having anything to do with any human except her. They're as xenophobic as the space Furs."

Julian said, "They haven't ever understood before that the space Furs who destroyed their villages and much of their populace fifty years ago might return and finish the job."

Ashraf said, "And how did you make them understand that?"

"Nan Frayne did. My scientists tracked her down in their wilderness in the southern subcontinent. You gave permission for my biologists to do that, you know. The triumvirate did."

True. But Alex hadn't expected the Terran scientists to succeed.

She'd assumed that Nan would reject them, just as Nan had rejected all overtures from Mira's own scientists.

Alex said to Ashraf, "Without Julian's intervention, the Hope of Heaven rebels would have done much more damage."

"I know."

Julian said, "What are you going to do with them?"

Alex liked that. Julian had met her and Ashraf's interrogation forthrightly, saw when he'd been forgiven his secrecy, and now was not eager to lap up praise, even justified praise. Her respect for him grew.

Ashraf said, "The rebels will be charged with their crime. We don't have prisons, you know—we can't afford the resources or personnel. After a software trial, they'll be flown in the skimmer to a distant, sea-locked island with more than enough supplies for basic survival and left there."

"For how long?"

"That depends on the outcome of the trial."

It was what the Mira City law said, although such exile had never been actually done before. Alex tried not to flinch from the bleakness of the pictures in her mind: a few people, primitive huts, predatory animals, carefully hoarded medical supplies that must eventually run out.

Julian said, "And the rest of the dissidents in Hope of Heaven?"

Alex answered. "I don't know if you understand our legal system, Julian. It's probably different than what you knew on Earth before you left. We're built on the old English system of presumption of innocence. If the rebels who tried to burn Mira tell us that others were involved, or the others tell us they were, or the software finds evidence they were, then more people can be tried. If not, we can't blame or punish the others in Hope of Heaven, because how would we know who was part of the attack and who wasn't? We might punish innocent people. So only those seven we caught will be tried."

Julian looked from Ashraf to her, then out the window. Four stories below, children played in the park. Their shouts rose faintly on the sweet twilight air wafting through the window. In the dusk a few lights came on, then a few more. Mira City was coming back to electronic life.

"You're right," Julian said. "It's different from what I knew on Earth."

"Cai," Duncan said softly, "what are you doing?"

He said sharply, "Don't call me that."

"Julian, then. What, my dear brother, are you doing?"

"Just what you see. Go to bed, Duncan. Even you need an hour of sleep at night."

"As I thought you did, but I seldom see you actually do it."

Julian looked up from the screen propped on the foamcast table. The small apartment held nothing of Julian but his computer, on loan from Mira City, and four sets of clothes: two Terran uniforms and two Greentrees Threadmores, one of which he wore now. The rest of the closet, both narrow beds, three of four chairs, and much of the floor was heaped with Duncan's costumes, printed scripts, music cubes, notes, and props, a fantastic array of centuries, climes, and characters. A tricorne rested on a toga, red tights on armor, a gold-embroidered robe on a worn dark cloak. Duncan's new theater would be foamcast soon, and all this would move there, including Duncan.

He said in his musical voice, "I ask again, what are you doing with these people? No, don't repeat 'Just what you see.' I am not a moron, nor are you innocence, 'with naught to dread.'"

"I am helping these people," Julian said, without looking up from his screen.

"To do what?"

Julian switched off the screen, folded it, and put it in his pocket. "Good night, Duncan. I'm going for a walk."

"To the home of the lamentably plain and idealistic Alex? Now, *there* is an innocent." He peered closer at Julian. "Good God, you genuinely like her!"

"Yes. I do."

"I am amazed. I am astonished. I am several other adjectives beginning with 'a.' You genuinely like this planet, too, don't you, this primitive unsceptered isle?"

Julian didn't answer. But for a moment his green eyes blazed, like a sudden burst from a laser. He went out into the scented night.

11

A VINE PLANET

When darkness fell, Lucy and Karim did not return to their metal box. Instead they stayed beside the pit, lying with their arms around each other in a small clearing, gazing up at the clouded opaque sky. Lucy had left her powertorch on, and the fronds of nearby towering Vines looked like dark solid ghosts.

"Ghosts of sentience," she said, and shuddered.

"We can use this, Lucy," Karim said, more confidently than he felt.

"How?"

"The biomass responds to us, which is more than the Vines do."

"A Vine spoke when we first got here, through the translator," Lucy argued. "So if everything really is interconnected, then the biomass already knew about us. But it didn't help us then."

"I know. But it hadn't *seen* us. Or maybe it just . . . how would I know? But I think now I can bargain with it. Watching it make that thing, that plant that looked like me . . . I remembered something."

"What?"

He'd been saving this since he thought of it, almost reluctant to say it aloud, turning the thought over and over like a small boy with a smooth stone. Running his fingers over the polished surface that might hide anything inside.

"The biomass *grew* that plant image of me, the way it must grow the Vines. The way it grew those smaller, mobile versions of Vines that came to Greentrees, including Beta Vine. It can manufacture molecules, the way it manufactures our food or even the microbe we infected the Furs with. To do that, it must have genetic blueprints, or something like that, stored in its cells."

"Yeeesssss," Lucy said slowly, "or if not in its cells, then in the connections among them, like among brain cells . . . I don't know. George always said that even on Earth biofilms are full of substructures and capable of enormous plasticity."

"True. Back on Greentrees, Beta Vine gave Dr. Shipley something, and then—"

"The 'death flowers'!" Lucy breathed. "Jake had them put inside the quee when the Furs captured us! But what happened to them after that?"

"I don't know. We got too sick with the virus to care. And then afterward, when we recovered and the Furs got sick, it didn't seem important. You and I went out in space to deliver the infectious Furs. I imagine the 'death flowers' went back to Greentrees with Jake and Dr. Shipley."

"Dr. Shipley would have taken good care of them," Lucy said with sudden conviction. "He promised Beta Vine. Beta told him that the death flowers were the souls of himself and the other Vines that the Furs killed, and they needed to be returned—"

She stopped abruptly.

"To the 'genetic library,'" Karim finished. "I think the death flowers were genetic blueprints to re-create Beta and the others, their individual consciousness, or whatever the equivalent is for Vines. Beta emphasized how important they were to his race."

Lucy lay silent. Karim could feel her slight tremor in his arms. He tightened his hold.

She said, "Important enough to trade for our passage home?"

"I don't know."

She cried out in sudden anguish, "But you threw the translator into the pit!"

"I don't think it matters. Either it's still down there, or we'll work out a code. With whistles, maybe. Or knocks on the ground. We already know from Greentrees that they can understand pictures we draw."

"What if Dr. Shipley and Jake have both died? Decades have passed on Greentrees since we left, you know. Or at least will have passed by the time we get back. Our . . . the new generation could have thrown away the death flowers."

"I don't think scientists would do that. But even so, the chance of the flowers' being there might be enough to get us home."

"When do we tell the Vines? Should we—" Lucy screamed.

A huge frond came swooping down from thirty feet above them. Its shadow fell like some monstrous bird of prey across the circle of light cast by the powertorch. Before Karim could react, the tentacle had snaked around his wrist and yanked him to his feet. Lucy, too, was jerked upright.

"Come," said the monotonous, uninflected voice of the translator, a second before Karim saw it floating on the surface of the pit ten meters away. "Go."

"Where are we going?"

"You go home. We get death flowers. We go your planet."

The tentacles/fronds/biofilm living machines were pulling him along into the darkness. Lucy barely had time to stoop and snatch up the powertorch. The Vines handed him along, passed from Vine to Vine, like a pail in an old-fashioned bucket brigade. It was the fastest that Karim had ever known the aliens to do anything.

From hastily glimpsed particular configurations of Vines, confirmed by his suit compass, Karim knew that they were being moved back to the metal box. Human home base on this Vine world. The drop-off place from the ship's shuttle. And, presumably, its pickup site as well.

Thank you, Allah.

12

MIRA CITY

Alex sat at her desk, frowning at her screen, which displayed a report from Savannah Cutler at the solar array. The report, written in Savannah's usual scientific jargon, heavy with mathematics and light on explanations, seemed to be giving much increased power outages, along with elaborate projections for results from new operations. Alex hadn't authorized any resources for new operations. But Savannah's esoteric jottings somehow conveyed a sense of definite satisfaction, in itself alarming. Alex was halfway through when Siddalee Brown appeared in the doorway.

"Yes. What is it? I'm busy, Siddalee, this report from the solar array is gibberish. Why can't Savannah . . . it seems to say . . ."

Siddalee said nothing.

Silence from Siddalee was as unusual as satisfaction from Savannah, so Alex looked up. Siddalee slumped against the foamcast doorway. Her brown skin looked ashy, the color of half-burned tialin leaves. Alex jumped up.

"Siddalee! Are you all right? Do you need—"

"Lau-Wah Mah is dead."

Something pierced Alex's stomach. "No, he can't be," she said stupidly. "I'd know. Guy Davenport would have told—"

"Guy's outside, on his comlink. Emergency report, he's coming right in. Lau-Wah . . . they did things to him . . . he was tortured. I . . . he . . ." Siddalee began to cry.

Alex tried to help her to a chair, but Siddalee shook her off and went out of the room, sobbing and ashamed of sobbing. Mira's security chief appeared in her place, comlink still in hand.

No. It can't be. No.

"Alex," Guy said, and she knew it was so.

A strange calm took her then, a numb automatic response system. "What happened, Guy?"

"Some kids found the body on Moonthorn Bluff. About an hour ago."

Alex nodded. The bluff, a few miles upriver from Mira, was a popular place for hikes and picnics. The eco team had long ago cleared it of dangerous native plants like red creeper, installed underground supersonic transmitters that scared away large predators, and even planted a few hearty, genemod Terran fruit trees. A corpse could not stay there very long without being discovered.

Guy continued, "There was a heavy rain yesterday; he was dumped there sometime during the storm, probably in the middle of the night. Somebody wanted him found, and also wanted any tracks erased by rain. Alex, he was tortured pretty brutally."

"How? No, don't tell me yet. In a while. Soon." She wasn't making sense. "What else?"

"Beside him on the ground was one of those twisted iron bars in the shape of that Chinese character. Hope."

"Too easy," she said instantly. "If Hope of Heaven did it—"

"Who else could have?" Guy said, a sudden flash of anger on his placid middle-aged face.

"I don't know. Let me think." She couldn't think.

Guy came closer and put a hand on Alex's desk, to steady himself or to emphasize his point. "If you want to make a . . . I don't know what you'd call it . . . an action people have to take seriously—"

"A political statement," Alex said. She'd learned the phrase from Julian.

"Yes. Then you might do it this way. They're cocky now, those bastards in Hope of Heaven. We didn't go after them for the river-encampment attack, we didn't go after them for the evacuation-drill burnings, all we did was ship out a few low-level people. Now they think they can get away with anything!"

So Guy had already decided that Hope of Heaven was guilty.

They probably are, Alex thought through her numbness. Why didn't she want to admit it?

Because she didn't want to believe something like this could happen in Mira. Had happened.

All of a sudden, with every fiber of her body and mind, she wanted to talk to Jake.

"Guy, what is your team doing? What have you already done? Where's . . . where's Lau-Wah?"

"I had him taken to the crematorium. I called out my entire force on Mira patrol. I closed the road to all traffic to and from Hope of Heaven: road, river, air."

Alex wasn't sure that was legal. She said, "I'm calling an emergency meeting right now. Siddalee! Get Ashraf here, and the council and league heads, and Julian Martin. I'm going to get Jake Holman myself."

"Jake? Why do you want—"

"Because I do!" Alex snapped. "I'll be back in ten minutes!"

At a dead run, her apartment was only a few minutes from the Mausoleum; it was why she'd chosen it. Passersby stared to see their tray-o, red wrap hiked nearly to her hips, sprinting along the paths bordered by bright genemod flowers. But on a few faces, Alex glimpsed comprehension, plus something else. These were the people who had already heard about Lau-Wah; the kids who found him might easily have been been hysterical. The something else was fury.

She was gasping for breath when she burst through her own door. A neighbor stood, in tears, beside Jake's powerchair. She saw that the old man already knew.

"Alex," he said softly, indistinctly, the thin flesh on his face a sagging map of sorrow. "So it's started. We hoped, Gail and I and Shipley, that on Greentrees it never would.

"Wasn't that stupid of us?"

The meeting couldn't be held in Ashraf's serene office, under the bright copper plates and woven rugs. Eighty-eight people came or were summoned to the Mausoleum in the next half hour, far too many for the small office. Siddalee cleared and closed off the ground floor and had chairs carried in from anywhere chairs were to be found. People were there who probably had no right to be, but no one thought of that until later. There were no precedents. For fifty years there had not been a murder on Greentrees. The few—very few—serious assaults had all been personal, people with grudges against each other of love or family or property or something else horrifying but small.

This, everyone sensed, was not small.

Present was the full council, made up of the heads of the city sections. Since the various ethnic groups in Mira tended to live together, sections followed ethnic divisions. The Anglos and Chinese elected their councillors; the Arabs appointed theirs; Alex wasn't sure what the New Quakers did. The council was ordinarily a part-time, rubber-stamp bunch. Most civic concerns were taken care of by internal ethnic leaders, also now present, or by negotiation among the corporate and Mira City's corporate and municipal chiefs.

Those were all present, too. Mining Consortium, Scientists' League, Eco-adaptation, Farming, SunSec, Chu Corporation, Maubrey Limited, MiraNet, Cutler Enterprises. Alex, up front with Ashraf and Guy, looked out at a mixture of costumes she had not seen since the fiftieth First Landing celebration. Gray Quaker Threadmores. White Arab robes. A sea of brightly colored wraps tied a hundred different ways over black skinthins or, among the young, bare flesh. Jake sat in the back in his wheelchair, his knees covered with an ancient blue blanket that might, Alex suspected, have even come from Terra.

"What should I say?" Ashraf asked her. Sweat beaded his upper lip, although the day was cool and the thick-walled Mausoleum even cooler.

"Just say what happened!" Alex said, more harshly than she intended.

Once he'd risen, Ashraf seemed more definite. He gave the facts quickly and dryly, then let Guy Davenport take the floor.

The security chief looked odd, somehow. It took Alex a moment to realize why; he carried a heavy gun on his right hip.

Security had never carried guns in Mira City, not in Alex's memory. The armory was reasonably well stocked since Julian had increased defenses, but everyone knew there would be warning of a Fur attack from the orbital probes. Security would arm then. For its usual patrols, security carried tanglefoam and small microwave stunners. That was enough to subdue any small group of rowdy kids or light-fingered thieves.

Guy's gun was a Nimrod, with both laser and projectile capability.

"What the mayor said is exactly what happened," he told the silent crowd. "My force is questioning people now, in Mira City and at the bigger research stations and at Hope of Heaven."

The last three words startled Alex. Guy almost spat them. She looked at his usually genial middle-aged face, now contorted into—what?

Hatred.

Someone, Alex couldn't see whom, called from the back of the room, "Have you arrested anybody?"

"Not yet," Guy said.

Savannah Cutler stood. "What about security at the solar array?" Belatedly she added, "And other important facilities?"

Guy ran his hand through his thinning hair. "I don't have the people to cover everything, Savannah, and also find the bastards who did this. You have to remember, Greentrees hasn't ever—"

A babble of voices broke out, rising higher as no one listened to anyone else. Ashraf took an uncertain step forward. Then a voice in the crowd, loud and furious, said, "I don't propose to let everything I've worked for be burned down or chewed up by some murderous shitholes! We need someone here who understands this sort of thing. Where's Julian Martin?"

"Yes! Martin!"

"Julian Martin! He knew how to defend us last time!"

"Julian!"

And there he was, standing up in the back, taller than the Greenies. Alex was surprised to see that he wore his Terran uniform, black and gold. Was he emphasizing his difference from them?

Julian strode to the front of the room, which quieted. He waited a long moment before speaking.

"Guy Davenport's security force is doing a wonderful job on this criminal investigation."

The room erupted again, until Julian held up his hand. He looked gravely at Guy. "But as you yourself say, Captain Davenport, you don't have the personnel to pursue both the investigation and increased security. I stand ready to serve in whatever capacity you like, and under your command."

Guy looked a bit overwhelmed at the idea of commanding Julian. Tall, muscled, glittering Julian, who had controlled an alliance of whole nations on Terra, and potbellied, inexperienced Guy . . . Alex understood Guy's hesitation. But Guy pulled himself together, and said, almost gratefully, "If you could take over the security patrols, with a force you organize . . ."

"Yes," Julian said. And to the audience, "If you will each submit to me the names of men and women from your sections as candidates to be deputized, my crew and I will interview and assign them."

Ragged clapping broke out, growing louder and nearly unanimous. Julian's eyes swept the room. Alex knew suddenly that he was noting who did not clap.

Julian stepped back, his eyes signaling to Ashraf to again take the floor. The mayor said, "Lau-Wah's family has asked that there be no public funeral, and of course we respect their wishes. Now, if anyone else wants to say anything . . ."

Several people stood. They yielded courteously to each other, but not all of them were courteous in their speeches, which all had the same theme: they loved Greentrees and Mira City. Their families had prospered here. No rebel group was going to destroy that. There was no reason for anyone on Greentrees not to prosper if they worked hard. No one should be permitted to destroy the work of others. They loved Greentrees and Mira City . . .

Alex stopped listening, longing for it to be over.

Rain started somewhere after midnight. Alex couldn't sleep. She made herself a cup of bennilin tea, which calmed her not at all. In what had once been her bedroom, Jake snored. Alex couldn't remember why she had been so desperate to talk to Jake right after she'd heard about Lau-Wah. He had only added to her fear.

"I never thought we could change human nature," he'd said, his sadness clear through the slurred words and helpless drool. "Neither did your aunt Gail. But we hoped that in a new setting, with enough resources to go around, with no hunger or real poverty, we'd hoped . . ." The easy tears of the old filled his eyes, a sight so unlike Jake that Alex had been almost glad to go to the meeting, almost glad Jake was asleep now. He'd spent the evening in praise of Julian's plans for increased security, which Julian had discussed with him in apparently exhaustive detail.

Alex set down her half-drunk tea and stared at the rain streaking the window.

Julian.

Why had he chosen to wear his Terran uniform to the meeting? Had he known they would ask him to take over Mira City security?

Yes. Probably. But he had waited, courteously, to be asked, standing unnoticed in the back of the room.

Or had that been in order to make a more dramatic entrance when he was asked?

She was confusing Julian with Duncan, now deep into preparations for something called "Macbeth."

Julian, in his black-and-gold uniform . . .

Alex rested her forehead against the cool plastic window. All at once she thought of Karim Mahjoub and Lucy Lasky, whom she had never met, gone nearly forty years from Greentrees on a mission to render Furs harmless by poisoning them. A mission that might or might not have made all Julian's war preparation unnecessary.

Except that the war now seemed to be within Greentrees' own people.

Abruptly Alex flung on her hooded coat and went out into the rain. Water flew off the coat's soft plastic, so fast was she walking. A voice called, "Halt!"

"What? Who's that?"

A figure emerged from the wet gloom. "Security. State your name and business . . . oh, it's you, Alex. Okay."

Alex stepped closer and recognized another of her young cousins from the huge, tangled Cutler clan. Eileen Langholtz, whom Alex had never liked. Eileen was self-important; when she'd been a kid, Alex had often seen her bully other children.

"After this, Alex, you'll need to show me your ident."

"My what?"

"An identity card to be issued shortly," Eileen said with the smugness of superior knowledge. "Everyone will carry them and security will check to see that you do."

"Why?"

"Why?" Eileen seemed to be surprised by the question. She blinked rain off her eyelids. "Well, because . . . because Julian says so."

"Ah," Alex said. "Good night, Eileen."

"Wait—where are you going?"

Alex turned slowly. She looked Eileen over very carefully, from her hooded head to her booted feet. There was a slight bulge on her right hip. Alex walked off without answering. Whatever Eileen called after her was whipped away by wind and rain.

Alex pounded on Julian's door, which was locked. He opened it and stood aside wordlessly.

She had seen the apartment only once, and then it had been full of Duncan's things, vast messy heaps of fantastic garments bewildering in their colors, fabrics, and musty age. Now the tiny place was nearly sterile, the bedroom door closed, the table holding only a soft screen of a type Alex had never seen before.

"Why will Greentrees citizens carry identity cards and have their business questioned by security?"

He showed no surprise at her damp anger. "Because I need to know who has legitimate movements so I can determine who doesn't."

"We're not used to this sort of . . . of . . ."

"The term you're looking for is 'invasion of privacy.' And you're not used to terrorism, either. The former is necessary to control the latter."

"*Julian*—"

"Alex, let me ask you something before you yell at me again. Why is this terrorist situation happening at all on Greentrees? The root cause?"

He had touched her basic bewilderment. "Lau-Wah said—"

"No, not what Lau-Wah said. What *you* think."

"I don't know."

"I do. It's the same reason there should have been a large public funeral for Lau-Wah Mah."

"A funeral?" She was caught off guard. "What does a funeral—"

"And also the same reason your schools are deficient."

She said crossly, "I'm wet and tired and angry, Julian, and I'm not in the mood for riddles!"

"Of course you're not." Unexpectedly, he moved to her side and peeled off her coat, careful to not get rain on her wrap. He pulled out a chair for her, took the one opposite, and folded up his screen. His face looking up at her was so humble, so beseeching, that she was confused all over again. It felt silly to be standing. She sat.

"So what is the root cause of this . . . terrorism and no funeral and our bad schools?"

Silently Julian looked down at his own hands, spread palms down on the empty table. His fingers, she saw, were long and strong, the nails cut very short, and on his right hand he wore a simple gold ring set with a small chip of green stone.

When he looked up at her, his voice was gentler than she'd ever heard from him. "Forgive me, Alex. I have no right to come here and criticize the methods that have already built a colony more successful than anything has been on Earth for over two centuries. My only excuse is that in the short time I've been here, I've come to love Greentrees. It's everything Terra could have been and was not, to our own shame. I didn't expect to ever again feel that passionate attachment to a place that my people call homewardness. A completely inadequate word."

She saw, with a small shock, that he meant every word. Her anger drained away. She, too, loved Greentrees. And he'd said "ever again" about a passionate attachment to a place. That implied he'd loved some other place before, and lost it.

She said softly, "What did you mean, the same root cause for Lau-Wah's killing and no funeral for him and our schools?"

"You have forgotten your Terran past, all of you on this wonderful planet. You don't think it's important . . . but it *is*. It's everything, because only the past can provide enough pride and tenacity and strength for sacrifice to defeat a real enemy. A comfortable present is fine for getting people to cooperate, and building things together can fuel a shared future, but they aren't tough enough to power genuine war."

"I don't understand," Alex said.

"Then listen, and weigh each statement I make against your own experience." A gust of wind blew the rain against the window in a sudden sharp drumming. Julian didn't raise his voice, and Alex had to lean forward slightly to hear him.

"A man named Sallust wrote this, almost two and a half thousand years ago, when his city of Rome was at war: 'The division of the Roman state into warring factions originated some years before, as a result of peace and of that material prosperity which men regard as the greatest blessing.' Does that sound familiar?"

"Why, it's what Lau-Wah said. And Jake, too."

"Yes. Mira is such an easy planet, Alex. So rich and lush. Everyone from Earth, all those basically moral and fearful people who risked coming here, just wallowed in delight in the planet. But your generation was born here and doesn't know much about Earth, and the one after yours, Yat-Shing Wong's, knows even less. And doesn't care. You teach almost no history in your schools, no tradition, no patriotism."

She said, "There's so many practical subjects to take up the time—"

"I know. And the young aren't innately interested in old things. So you have almost no public rites. No elaborate parades, patriotic marches, public funerals for public figures. Those things aren't frivolous, Alex. They build cohesion among disparate groups of people, and that's necessary because your groups on Greentrees are naturally very disparate. Quakers, Arabs, Chinese—"

"Yes. But a dead past—"

"Can be put in the service of the living. You're fighting the strongest force known, Alex. Evolution."

"Evolution?" Once again she was confused.

"Human beings evolved to cooperate in groups *because* cooperation gives a group an edge over other groups. With that edge, you can get a bigger share of resources, better defend your dens, better survive. Animals cooperate in order to compete. Whenever there's competition, there are winners and losers. Some of those will be sore losers. It's built into the biology.

"So to get many different groups to cooperate, you can't just show them that their interests are similar, because sooner or later their interests will diverge when some one or two groups get more. To forge cohesion, you have to foster something shared that's larger than present interests. That something is a shared past, with all the history and pride and pomp that implies."

These were new ideas to Alex. She sat pondering them. It made sense, but . . .

"It sounds dangerous," she said.

"It is. Pride and history can be misused. But they're not as dangerous as ignorance." Julian's tone was grim. "Or war."

"We're supposed to be at war with Furs, not each other!"

"Yes. The highest good is to avoid war completely. A good leader does what he can to protect lives. If war can't be avoided, the next good is to minimize it, doing whatever is necessary to make it as small scale and quickly over as possible."

"I can see that," Alex said. All at once she felt shy. He knew so much, had experienced so much, and she was just what he'd implied about Greentrees: ignorant. She looked away, out the rainy window.

"During the First Punic War," Julian said quietly, "isolationists convinced the Roman Senate that only the nobility, not the common people, wanted war. As a result, Rome didn't act early enough. When she did finally act, the only recourse was total war. Much of Italy was destroyed. I don't want that to happen on Greentrees, not by Furs or rebels. Not here. Alex, do you know what Mayor Shanti was thinking at that meeting?"

"Ashraf? Not really."

"Captain Davenport? Amelie Lincoln? Selson Childers? Ismail Shanab? Yi Zhang?"

She knew all their names, their families, their resource-allocation requisitions. But what they were thinking? Alex shook her head.

"You should. You must. An effective leader knows what every single person at every single meeting is thinking, all the time."

"That's not possible!"

"You can come closer than you think. It just takes knowledge, attention, and practice."

"I don't know how."

"I'll teach you." He took her hand. She was startled by the warmth of his long fingers, and then by the warmth in herself.

She said, to cover her confusion, "I don't know if I can learn, Siddalee says I'm no good at observation. I don't notice things. As anybody who's ever seen my apartment can testify! Not like your place, it's spotless."

He accepted her clumsy attempt at lightheartedness. "My place wasn't spotless until Duncan moved out last week."

"I saw it before. He had an amazing collection of things." She laughed, an inane laugh. Why were they talking about Duncan? They'd been talking about the most important things in the world, survival and war and what mattered to people, and now they were talking about Duncan. Julian hadn't dropped her hand.

Silence fell.

More rain spattered against the window.

Alex said, to say something, "Jake says that Duncan is always acting a role."

"Jake has it backward."

"What do you mean?"

Julian smiled. "Duncan is always himself. For him, 'All the world's a stage' means that everyone else is an actor, a supporting player in his personal drama. He sees everyone as a fictional character, larger and more vital than we actually are. Some people find that very seductive, to be seen as more colorful, sharper edged. But not, I think, you. You'd rather be seen as you really are."

His tone was detached, almost impersonal, but his thumb had begun to rub her palm in small, slow circles.

"Alex? Am I right? Wouldn't you rather I saw you clear, as you are?"

She took her hand away, moved around the table, and moved into his arms, stiff as glass. Her voice came out hoarse.

"I didn't want to do this, Julian."

"Why not?"

"Because of what you just said. Because I want you to see me clear, and I think you do, and what I think you see is an unsophisticated provincial dazzled by a genemod Terran."

"No. Shall I tell you what I see?" He released her, and Alex didn't know if she was glad or sorry.

He said, "I'll tell you honestly. I see a person who is, yes, politically unsophisticated because her whole culture is, but enormously intelligent and capable of absorbing ideas. Most people are not. I see an administrator who is good with detail and also good at keeping in mind overall constructive goals and working tirelessly toward them. I see a person with only one moral failing, a too-easy sympathy with the powerless, to the point where it compromises justice. I see a woman whose weakling husband died and who's carrying around a secret load of guilt because she never really missed him and—"

"How did you know that!"

"—and I see a woman I'm falling in love with."

Alex stood very still. She and Julian stared at each other across a foot of space that was light-years, a seething pit, and nothing at all.

"Alex," he said in a tone she wouldn't have thought him capable of, beseeching and needful. Oh, that final assault of men—to need! But Julian's neediness, clear on his genemod and alien face, was not the whining and jealous need that Kamal's had been. Julian didn't want to clutch in a drowning grip; he wanted to connect. She crossed the light-years.

His arms tightened around her so hard that she was shaken. She'd forgotten this, made herself forget it, this wild rush of the blood. Warmth seeped through her entire body. Hungrily she raised her face and kissed him.

In bed he was tender and skillful. *Practiced,* she thought, but without cynicism. Then she didn't think at all.

When she woke again he was still beside her, though not asleep. She reached for him and that warm sweet rush started again. With it, incongruously, came the silly song young Greenies sang so often:

On Greentrees we are
For good, but is it good,
How would I know, all I know
For sure is yooouuu . . .

Alex laughed aloud: in delight, in sensual pleasure, in amused incongruity.

"What is it, Alex?"

She sang the ditty for him. Julian smiled, not his usual half smile but his rare, full grin, barely visible in the dawn light just creeping into the window set high in the ugly foamcast wall. He kissed her deeply.

Only later, much later, did Alex realize that she had not once thought of Kamal.

13

MIRA CITY

Twenty-nine of Julian's newly deputized security force were Chinese. The rest were Anglos and Arabs, except for three of the young men.

"There's some New Quakers to see you," Siddalee said to Alex.

She looked up from her cluttered desk. "Who?"

"Friend John Garnette and his wife." Siddalee pronounced "Friend" disapprovingly. She had often expressed her dislike of the title, especially when it was applied to her: "They aren't my friends. I barely know them." Most of Siddalee's attention, however, was on Alex, not on the Garnettes. "You're combing your hair every day now. And that's a new wrap."

"Show them in, Sidalee."

"A lot of changes around here."

"Show them in."

The Garnettes were middle-aged, with pale faces and sagging bodies. They both wore plain gray Threadmores, in keeping with the New Quaker call to simplicity, one of their four religious tenets. Simplicity, silence, truth, service.

"Thank you for seeing us, Friend Cutler. My name is John Garnette and this is my wife, Julie. We own the factory on P Street that supplies Mira City with pipes of all kinds."

"Oh, yes," Alex said. New Quakers frequently owned businesses; their emphasis on simplicity meant not that they refused education or possessions but that they refused to let their learning or possessions own them. Faith and family always came first. As businessmen they were unfailingly honest, hardworking, and efficient. "Mira would not run as well without your Quakers," Julian had said musingly. "Not even half as well."

At the thought of Julian, Alex felt a glow that she sternly suppressed. *Not now.*

"We have two children," John Garnette continued. "Alicia, eleven years old, and Simon, nineteen. It's about Simon that we've come."

Alex nodded. Now she knew what was coming.

"He's joined Friend Martin's personal police force," Garnette said, and Alex was startled by both the term and the force with which it was uttered. "Simon is learning to use weapons, to kill. We New Quakers believe in nonviolence, Friend Cutler, as you probably know. Every human being has the spark of the Divine Light within, and that means that violence against another is violence against God."

Their anguish was palpable, the ancient anguish of parents over wayward children they loved. Alex said gently, "Simon sees the situation differently, I'm afraid. He sees a threat to his city and feels a duty to defend it. He's acting out of his own personal conviction, and I know Quakers put enormous emphasis on action from conviction. On following your inner light."

"Yes," put in Julie Garnette, as if she could no longer restrain herself, "but truth comes most reliably to shared light. That's why we share our thoughts in meeting, until a consensus emerges! And that's why we . . . we . . ."

"Julie," her husband said softly. Silence fell.

Alex tried again. "Mira City—all of Greentrees—is under threat of destruction. Nonviolence, what you call a 'peace testimony,' is simply not going to work in this situation."

"Has it been tried?"

Alex held tightly to patience. "Yes. Both with the Furs fifty years ago and with Hope of Heaven months ago. Both responded with further violence. Our choices are to act now before our only recourse is total war, or to let ourselves be destroyed. I don't want that for Mira City and your son doesn't, either."

"He is training with Terran weapons, monstrous things, from Julian Martin's ship."

"I know. And with our own weapons. A defense force needs to have as many resources as it can."

"These young men and women are being turned into an army!"

"Yes," Alex said. "Mira City needs a defending army."

Garnette said quietly, "Do you know what William Penn wrote several hundred years ago, Friend Cutler? 'A good end cannot sanctify evil means, nor must we ever do evil that good may come of it.' Some truths do not change, no matter how much changes in Mira City."

Alex stood. "I'm sorry that I can't help you."

The Quakers left. "I wish you peace," Julie Garnette said over her shoulder, and Alex couldn't tell if it was a blessing or a riposte.

She felt oddly shaken. The Garnettes so clearly loved and despaired over their son. And yet Alex believed completely that what Simon Garnette was doing was not only right but necessary.

Julian's carefully selected defense force trained every day, in sections, while other sections guarded Mira and the nearby scientific and industrial facilities. There had been no further violence. Guy Davenport's investigation had turned up no information about who had killed Lau-Wah, or why. His family had scattered his ashes so privately that even Alex didn't know what location they had chosen.

Julian's soldiers heavily patrolled Hope of Heaven, day and night. The dissident settlement had been the first to receive the new identity cards. Rumors reached Alex that Hope of Heaven's citizens were stopped, harassed, and, on one occasion, beaten by Julian's men.

"Not true," Julian had told her. "They have strict orders against harassment of any kind. Those rumors are designed to turn public opinion against the new security measures, but it's not going to work. Although I will tell you that I've set up a computer tracking system for key suspects like Wong Yat-Shing. We know where he is and with whom at all times."

"A tracking system? With what computer power?"

"Mine. It's on the *Crucible*'s computer and goes through our Terran comsats."

How did such a tracking system work? Alex hadn't asked. Now she tried once more to concentrate on the resource-allocation reports on her screen. Ashraf appeared in the door.

"Alex, Julian has denied a permit for the Chinese New Year procession."

Denied? Permit? She rose again from her desk. "You're not making sense, Ashraf. We don't need permits in Mira for ethnic celebrations."

"He says permits are necessary now, and he can't issue one because a Chinese celebration right now would be a perfect cover for violence."

Something cold pricked Alex's belly. "Where is Julian?"

"I don't know. He comlinked." Ashraf tugged on his ear. "Carl Liu and Yi Kung are in my office right now, very angry. What should I tell them?"

Why was Ashraf so ineffectual? Lau-Wah would not have palmed this off on her. "Tell them there's been a mistake and you'll comlink them tonight."

"Yes," Ashraf said. And then, with sudden force, "New permits should be a council decision."

"I think the permits are the least of it," Alex said.

She found Julian at the genetics lab, installing increased security devices and guards. Alex had to show her own ident to get admitted. She didn't know whether to approve or rage.

"The Chinese New Year," she said to Julian. They were alone in the room, hastily vacated by technicians, unless you counted cages full of several hundred experimental frabbits. The small creatures, brown speckled with purple, hummed softly.

"What about the Chinese New Year?" Julian said.

"You denied Carl Liu a 'permit' to hold it."

"Yes. I did."

"In the first place," Alex said, "Mira doesn't issue permits for ethnic celebrations, they're a given. A right. In the second place, if we did start issuing permits, the council would have to approve it. And in the third place, if the council did approve permits, Ashraf would make those decisions, not you."

"All true," Julian said, "if we were not at war."

"We're not at war yet!"

"You're splitting hairs, Alex. We're preparing for war on two fronts, and I have the responsibility of preserving peace in Mira while we do it. A Chinese New Year is too much of a risk. Firecrackers, masks, crowds, intoxicants, general rowdiness. It could easily be perverted into an attack. But even so, I didn't make an end run around your council. They're not in session, but I called fully three-quarters of them personally and asked if at the next session they will grant me the power to replace civilian law with military law if I decide it's necessary to protect Mira City."

Alex said slowly, "And they said yes?"

"They said yes," Julian said. Behind him, frabbits rustled in the rows of cages on the walls.

"You asked three-quarters of the council."

"An informal poll, yes."

"You didn't ask Carl Liu and Yi Kung."

"No," Julian said. "I didn't."

"Why not?"

"I think you know why not."

"Carl and Yi are loyal to Mira, Julian. They always have been."

"I believe you. But I didn't want to put them in the position in the eyes of their own people of even looking like they accept hostilities toward Hope of Heaven. If it comes to that."

A frabbit poked its head through the bars of a cage. Alex stared at it, to keep from having to look at Julian. "Is it going to come to that? To hostilities toward Hope of Heaven?"

"Not if the council lets me carry out preventive measures," he said, with such concerned determination that once again she believed in him. He wanted to defend Greentrees, to save it. That involved hard choices. He had the courage to make them.

"Alex," he said softly, "I'm doing the best I can. But this isn't my colony. You know these people. If you think the Chinese New Year should be permitted, I'll be guided by your judgment."

"No, you're right," Alex said. "I'll tell Ashraf. No, I'll tell Carl and Yi myself. Ashraf is . . . I don't know why the Arabs chose him as mayor."

"Yes, you do—because they can control him as easily as you can," Julian said, "when it's an issue they care enough about to do so."

Alex's eyes widened. Was that true? But Julian had already returned to work, increasing security in the genetics lab.

At night, in bed, they never talked about Mira City or the war. They talked about themselves. Julian wanted to hear about growing up on Greentrees, in what he still called "this purple Eden."

"When I was born," Alex said, "the plains around Mira were dangerous. An uncle of mine, Arelo Huntingdon, was killed by a red creeper, and two children were mauled by a lion. We kids were kept pretty close after that. Mira was in a constant state of building, spraying foamcast and laying pipe and, of course, the farms with their new genemod trial crops all the time."

She smiled at the memory, lying in Julian's arms in the cramped narrow bed. His bedroom was as austere as the main room of his guest apartment. No pictures, no holo frames, not even a music cube. But the window was opened to an unexpectedly warm night, and she could see the stars.

He said, "How long after the First Landing were you born?"

"Five years. Eggs, sperm, and embryos had all been frozen for the trip out, of course, in case there was a problem with fertility due to the flight or even the new planet. But there wasn't, and my mother got pregnant as soon as the stay on conception was lifted."

"Why did they name you Alexandra?"

"I don't know."

"Did you know it's the feminine form of the name of a great general?"

"Really?" She traced an idle circle on his belly.

"You're named after Alexander the Great, who wept because he had no worlds left to conquer."

"There are always more worlds to conquer," Alex replied.

"Spoken like a true colonist. Your name means 'defender of men.'"

"I didn't know that," Alex said, as, it seemed to her, she was always saying to him. Her circles grew more insistent.

He said, "What happened to your parents?"

"They died when I was ten, of Weiler's disease. By that time Greentrees' microbes had begun to adapt to our bodies enough to use them as hosts. We call the colony's second decade the Plague Years. We developed vaccinations not quite as fast as Greentrees developed diseases."

In the darkness Julian stroked her hair. "What did your husband die of?"

"Stupidity."

"You don't want to talk about him."

"No. But I will." She rolled slightly away from Julian. How to compress her marriage into a few sentences? The initial thrill, both of passion and of daring to cross ethnic barriers. The dawning realization that Kamal was not what she thought him. The growth of desperation over the futile and arrogant years she tried to change him into what she wanted. The occasional good times, the little morning routines, the moments of forced sweetness when they both "tried," the bitter arguments. He loved gardening. He had a beautiful smile. He sniped at her, and later raged at her, because she saw that his scientific aspirations were not going to be reached. Because she was happy in her work and he was not. Because she couldn't reflect back to him his inflated picture of himself.

Finally she said tonelessly, "Kamal was a geneticist. We were married five years. He drowned inside a mine."

Julian said nothing, waiting.

"You really want to know, don't you? I think you already do."

"I know what I was told. I'd like to hear it from you."

She said, almost angrily, "We fought a lot. Kamal had a lot of work problems. Finally he created a hybrid wheat that he didn't test well enough. Actually, he hardly tested it at all. It got out of the farm, cross-fertilized with a native grass, and produced an off-spring that proved fatal to an insect analogue that fed on it. That could have affected an entire food chain. The eco-scientists caught it just in time. Kamal was taken off research, given small, safe tech jobs. He was outraged and we fought more. One day when he was testing water samples in an underground aquifer, he drowned."

"Did he kill himself?" Julian's tone held neither pity nor censure, and so Alex was able to answer.

"I don't know. Maybe."

"You blame yourself."

"Yes. No. Why do we always talk about me, Julian? Why don't you tell me about your childhood?" She realized how harsh she sounded and laid a hand on his bare thigh.

"Duncan and I grew up in a military family. Duncan is older—that surprises you?"

"Yes. He seems younger than you."

"He's three years older," Julian said, amused. "I'll put your mistake down to his childlike charm and not my haggard looks."

"You're genemod enough to not have haggard looks, aren't you?" She said this hesitantly; Greentrees had few or no cosmetic in-vitro genetic modifications. There was too much else to spend resources on.

"Yes. Duncan's voice is genemod, although our father expected it to be a commanding military instrument, not an actor's trick. We were both supposed to be soldiers. Duncan refused, and was disowned."

"And you ended up commanding the Third World Alliance. How did that happen?"

"Fortunes of war, backed by a lot of politics. As war always is. It would be hard to explain unless you knew more about Terran history."

There it was again—her ignorance of Terra. Alex was tired of hearing about it. She fingered the ring on his right hand, a gold band set with a small green gem. "Who gave you that ring?" She'd wanted to ask that for a long time.

"My mother. She—what's that noise?"

Outside the window sharp ringing cracks erupted. Julian moved faster than Alex thought possible. A gun appeared in his hand.

"Julian, where did you get—Julian!"

In one unbroken motion he had pulled her to the floor, thrust her with his leg under the bed, and stood out of sight of the window, naked, aiming his weapon at the door.

"They're firecrackers!" Alex sputtered. "For Chinese New Year!"

"The celebration was not permitted." She had never heard that tone from him before: low, level, absolutely without emotion.

"I know, but probably kids are marking the day anyway, beginning at midnight. For God's sake, Julian!" Alex crawled out from under the bed, rubbing her bruises. "It's just some harmless new thing Chu Corporation invented for celebrations. We had them at the fiftieth anniversary."

She could feel him staring at her, although she couldn't make out his eyes in the dark.

"Are you sure they're firecrackers?"

"Yes!"

"I'll check."

He must have believed her somewhat, because he stayed long enough to pull on his pants. He was back in a few minutes. Alex spent the time lying on her back in bed, gazing at the ceiling.

"You're right, just kids and firecrackers," he said, "I dispersed them."

Dispersed. What a word.

He added, "Firecrackers can easily be a cover for weapon fire. They won't do it again."

No, they wouldn't. Alex could imagine how Julian would have appeared to the Chinese kids.

Before she could say anything, he said, "I should have remembered about the firecrackers. Duncan requested their use in his play."

"Do you want to go to the play together?" Alex asked. They hadn't appeared anywhere in public together yet. They came together only late at night, after long days of endless work, for a few rushed hours. Waiting for his reply, Alex held her breath. *Stop it,* she told herself, *you're too old for these sort of silly tests,* but she didn't exhale.

"Yes," Julian said, "especially since you're the only reason I'd go at all. Which play is it, again?"

She tried to remember the strange name. "*Macbeth.* Why wouldn't you go?"

"There's so much work to do. And theater has never interested me. It's so unreal."

"Well, yes," said Alex, who had seen almost none of it. "But I thought plays and fiction were supposed to reveal great truths underlying life." So her school software had said, anyway.

"I think most of them are more concerned with how life should be rather than how it is." She heard the amusement in his voice.

"It's a big event for Mira."

"I know," he said, the amusement gone. "I've been setting up security for Duncan's theater. Too many people in one place."

She rose on one elbow. "Are you afraid that Hope of Heaven—"

"They won't get the opportunity," Julian said, with such finality that she was silenced. "But you're right; we have to go. Damn. Duncan's frivolities win again."

Alex hadn't known it was a contest.

The new Mira City Theater was an ugly foamcast box, the basic second-generation building design. Alex had grudgingly approved the materials Duncan said he needed to build the interior, although these had been surprisingly modest. Apparently "Shakespeare" was often performed on a bare platform, with minimal lighting. Just as well.

She noted the heavy security presence outside the theater. Julian's new troops wore strange clothing from off his ship: not black-and-gold uniforms like his but thin, flexible metallic garments with heavy boots, belts, and helmets. The big helmets made them look menacing. When she asked, Julian said briefly, "Battle gear. A lot of built-ins. The uniformed sections are well equipped."

"Are there sections without uniforms?"

"Oh, yes. And you shouldn't be able to tell who they are."

If the soldiers out of uniform were at the theater, Alex couldn't pick them out. She was dazzled by everyone's sartorial efforts. The evening was warm, and all but the oldest women had left off their thinskins. Wraps in yellow, crimson, cobalt blue had been tied to show off cleavage, legs, shoulders, bellies. The younger men wore wraps, too, although the older ones stuck to their Threadmores or to a loose pants-and-tunic combination that was comfortable in warm weather. Even this had been dressed up with antique family jewelry brought from Terra. Others had necklaces or barrettes of polished native stone. Many Arabs wore their flowing white robes; a few Chinese had carefully preserved jackets or cheongsams in gorgeous colors, ornamented with embroidery such as Alex had never imagined.

She wore a diamond necklace that had belonged to her mother. She'd washed and combed her hair and, at the last minute, pinned a flower in it. The approval in Julian's eyes warmed her.

Alex scanned the crowd. No Quakers, of course, or at least none of the older people she knew by sight. Siddalee had said some of the young Quakers were coming, in defiance of "simplicity." Fewer Chinese than she expected. In those that were there, Alex thought she caught a hint of defiance in their manner: *See, we're as good citizens of Mira as anybody else.*

Well, most of them were.

No one commented on or reacted to her attending with Julian. Probably they just assumed it was an official appearance, tray-o and defense chief. Alex didn't know if she was pleased or disappointed.

"Hello, Mayor Ashanti," Julian said. "Madame Ashanti."

"Hello," Ashraf said. He wore white robes. His wife walked behind him with some other Arab women, laughing behind their veils. Duncan had made arrangements for any Arab women who wished to be seated separately from the men. Alex wondered how many arguments had gone on in the medina between daughters who sat unveiled with their Anglo friends and mothers who objected, wives who wished to attend the play and husbands who objected, young women who upheld the old ways and their sisters who did not. Life in the medina was closed to Alex. But certainly she saw no signs of tension in Mrs. Shanti's group of women enjoying themselves.

Star Chu and a group of young Chinese walked by. They all had tattoos on their cheeks, in that absurd copying of Cheyenne absurdity. They smelled of Chu Corporation's new perfumes, delectable scents like the Greentree nights. None of them smiled.

Alex and Julian sat to one side of the stage, along with Ashraf and Jake. Had Lau-Wah not been murdered, Alex thought, would he have attended tonight?

She noticed the way Julian's eyes kept moving, studying each new group. A small multichannel comlink lodged in his left ear.

The inside of the theater was as stark as the outside: rows of foamcast benches before a plain platform sprayed to form three levels. A few leafy branches stood upright in buckets, suggesting a wood. Alex wasn't impressed.

"They're late," she said to Julian.

"Duncan's always late. He thinks it increases drama." His green eyes never stopped moving. What was he hearing on the comlink?

Alex turned away. She was determined to enjoy this *Macbeth*. She only hoped that it didn't require a lot of Terran history or culture to be understood.

The lights dimmed, a single circle of light shone on the stage, and a bleeding man staggered onto it. Alex's eyes widened; it looked so real! But beside her Julian murmured, "He's rearranged scenes again."

"Shhh!"

Four men entered, dressed in rough brown cloth, one of them wearing a small metal crown. Alex didn't recognize any of them.

Duncan, searching for anyone more interested in an archaic Terran art form than in war preparations, had recruited his part-time actors among techs, apprentices, nurses, farmers. Alex knew Duncan hadn't had a wide choice. "'What bloody man is that?'" said the man with the crown, and she wasn't transported to another time and place.

Still, the plot was comprehensible, even through the elaborate language. The king, also named Duncan, was in the middle of a war. One of his soldiers, Cawdor, had betrayed him and was going to be executed. Macbeth was another of Duncan's noble soldiers, and was going to be given Cawdor's title. Alex was proud of herself; she could follow the action.

The soldiers left, the lighting changed, and three fantastic figures entered, dressed in rags, with scales and wings like Chinese dragons. Alex stiffened.

But the three were apparently not supposed to be Chinese, or even to be real entities. They spoke of magic and weaved weirdly around the stage. A few people in the audience tittered. More shifted restlessly in their seats.

Then Duncan entered with another man, both dressed in armor. "'So fair and foul a day I have not seen,'" Duncan said in that double-toned voice, taut with hope and regret, layered with pain and satisfaction. Alex knew that doubt, that questioning: Was this a good day or a terrible one? Did I do the right thing? How will it turn out? If only things could have gone differently. *So fair and foul a day* . . .

Yes.

The audience quieted. In Duncan's presence, the witches grew not silly but menacing. They told him of things to come, and Alex shivered.

> "'If you can look into the seeds of time,
> And say which grain will grow and which will not,
> Speak then to me . . .'"

Grain. Kamal. And telling what will happen and what will not . . . if only they could do that about the Furs or Hope of

Heaven! Alex glanced at Julian. He stared straight ahead, expressionless.

Duncan said in that voice that vibrated along her spine:

"'And oftentimes, to win us to our harm,
The instruments of darkness tell us truths,
Win us with honest trifles, to betray's
In deepest consequence.'"

Alex was entranced. The crude theater melted away, and Scotland rose around her, dark and hooded. Women urged death, exulted in it, and men killed with weapons clutched in bare hands. Loyalty broke, spilling blood. Macbeth, haunted by his own soul, trusted no one:

"'Those I command move only in command,
Nothing in love; now do I feel my title
Hang loose about me, like a giant's robe,
Upon a dwarfish thief.'"

Macbeth stared straight at Alex. She turned to take Julian's arm, but he was no longer there. She'd been so absorbed in Duncan's magic that she hadn't noticed him leave.

When the play ended, Greentrees sat in silence a moment, then fell to thunderous, inadequate applause.

Alex elbowed through the crowd. The clapping went on and on. Duncan appeared with his company to bow deeply.

Julian stood outside, talking into his comlink. "Julian. What is it, what happened?"

"Yat-Shing Wong escaped. With two others."

"'Escaped'? What do you mean? Nobody was a prisoner!"

"I mean they left Hope of Heaven. Two of my young Greentrees soldiers are dead, killed by lances and spears. Furs."

"But why would wild Furs—"

"I don't know. I have to go down there, and I think you better come, too. And Mayor Shanti."

"Yes. Just let me tell—"

"My lieutenant will make an announcement, after Duncan has milked all his glory. Let me comlink Shanti."

Alex wished she'd worn a Threadmore. Numbly she pulled off the diamond necklace and sealed it in a fold of her wrap.

Two Greenies dead. Killed by wild Furs. Who were the young soldiers? Did she know their families?

Macbeth had left her mind. But not Julian's. As he climbed into the rover he said abruptly, as if it mattered, "Duncan rewrote much of the play."

"He did? That wasn't the story?"

"That *was* the story," Julian said. "But Duncan reassigned speeches. He gave himself all the best lines."

"In the beginning," she said, because it was a relief after all to talk about something else, anything else, "I had the impression he was performing directly to you and me. Your opinion is important to him."

Julian didn't answer. Ashraf hurried out, and they left for Hope of Heaven.

14

SPACE

The ship was indistinguishable from that other Vine ship that had brought Karim and Lucy away from the Greentrees system. Then the others had been with them, Gail and Dr. Shipley and George Fox and Jake, firmly in charge. Karim couldn't compute how many decades had passed since he and Lucy left Greentrees for the second time; he just didn't have the data on Vine-planet diurnal duration or on ship acceleration. When they reached Greentrees, would any of their old comrades even be alive?

It almost didn't matter. They were going home. They were escaping the silent, motionless, pulpy world of the Vines that, Karim knew, had nearly driven both him and Lucy mad. It was too alien for humanity. There had been no point of contact, none, except the one that eventually mattered: Some Vine "death flowers," genetic blueprints for their own dead, were on Greentrees and must be retrieved.

"I don't understand why," Lucy had whispered to Karim. "If they can code so much information in molecules right in their cells, why don't they already have the . . . the equivalent of a genescan for all their Vines killed on Greentrees?"

"I think it's more than a genescan. I think the death flowers somehow encode the Vines' experiences since they left their own planet," Karim whispered back. They didn't know if they were being overheard, or even if they could be overheard. The ship was completely familiar from the last voyage with Vines, and completely alien.

It was one large circular room perhaps a hundred yards across. The ship re-created what, this time out, Karim recognized as a compressed version of a Vine planet. Seething slime like that from the pit covered the entire floor and crept up the walls and onto the ceiling. Silent Vines, smaller than the ones on-planet, grew tumbled together in clumps, their branches or tentacles intertwined. Runners across the slime connected the various groups of Vines. The light was very bright, the room stiflingly hot and humid.

Near the air lock the slime had drawn back from a small patch of metal floor, pitted and corroded, and here the humans sat, beside the translator that Karim had thrown into the pit. Or maybe it was another translator. Unlike their planetary cousins, these Vines were interested in acquiring English. Genetically bred for space travel, Karim guessed. He and Lucy had gone through the wearying business of babbling for days in order to give the translator enough vocabulary and grammar to work with.

"When we come to Greentrees," the translator said, "our death flowers are on Greentrees." The translator gave out an uninflected monotone; nothing in its mechanical voice betrayed the anxiety that led the Vines to ask the same question over and over.

"Yes," Karim said, "your death flowers are on Greentrees," and hoped to Allah it was true. How much relativistic time had passed on Greentrees? Had Jake and Shipley preserved the death flowers?

They must have.

What would the Vines do if they hadn't?

Days passed, then weeks. At least, Karim guessed it was weeks. The ship never darkened for any artificial night. Karim knew from the bowing of the floor, necessary to compensate for tidal forces, that the ship was at maximum acceleration. Not long now, and he and Lucy would walk on a planet with color and sound and motion! Birds wheeling overhead, river rushing along, night insects humming . . . why hadn't he ever realized how alive Greentrees was, how vivid and precious!

The ship stopped.

He knew it only from the visual flattening of the floor. He shook Lucy, asleep on their metal patch free of slime. "Wake up! We're home!"

"We come not yet to Greentrees," said the translator.

"Not . . . at Greentrees? Where are we?"

"One, two planets before Greentrees. We see first."

That made sense. Accelerating, the ship drive created such a plasma cloud that no sensors worked. The ship flew blind. Of course the Vines would need to stop to reconnoiter before flying in.

The translator said, "An enemy ship orbits Greentrees."

Fear clenched Karim. Then he remembered. "No, that's our ship, the *Beta Vine*. I mean, it was a Fur ship but we captured it, just as we captured the other ship you destroyed when you picked us up. The same way you capture Fur ships!"

"Two ships orbits Greentrees. One is different."

Two ships?

"Different how?"

The translator didn't answer. Lucy said, "Karim . . ." and to the translator, "Is it a Fur ship, too? Your enemy?"

"We not know."

"What will you do?" Karim managed.

There was no answer, not for a very long time. The Vines, or the slime, or some unknowable combination of the two, were thinking.

Eventually, the ship accelerated. The Vines would not answer Karim's or Lucy's pleas for information. A short time later, the ship stopped again.

Karim couldn't keep his eyes open. He had woken from a good sleep only hours before; he wasn't tired. But all at once, he felt irresistibly drowsy. Before he slept, he had just time enough to realize he was being drugged, and to hear the expressionless voice of the translator say, "Good-bye, Karim and Lucy. Thank you."

They woke simultaneously. Karim looked down. He squeezed his eyes shut, opened them to look again. To his shame, tears came.

A planet spun beneath his feet.

He and Lucy floated in space, encased in a clear thick bubble of slime. They were naked. Nothing whatsoever was in the bubble with them. Thousands of miles below, Greentrees rotated, a spinning ball of blue and purple and white, real and gorgeous and unattainable as paradise.

15

HOPE OF HEAVEN

"Tell it from the beginning and omit nothing," Julian said to the scared young soldier.

"Yes, sir."

So young, Alex thought, and then realized he was not really a boy. He seemed so because he was pale and shaken. This did not happen on Greentrees. Whatever brief training Julian had given, it hadn't prepared this youth. Her people had not grown up with violence.

"*So fair and foul a day I have not seen.*"

"Should we wait for Guy Davenport?" Ashraf said.

"No," Julian said. "He can hear it later."

The four of them stood in a small concrete bunker that Julian must have had built for his troops. Alex hadn't known it existed. Outside, in the sweetly scented night, the graceful buildings of Hope of Heaven soared against a moonless sky. The bodies of the two dead soldiers, Shanab Mesbah and Mary Pesci, had already been loaded into the rover to be taken back to Mira City. Julian had examined them with a strange intensity.

"Shanab, Mary, and I were on duty until midnight," the soldier began. "I was crewing the monitors and they were doing foot patrol for Sector Six. That includes this edge of the settlement, the settlement farm, and a bit of the plain. Everything was quiet. Nothing on the displays. Then Shanab yelled, just once. I tried to comlink, but nobody answered. So I armed and ran to the location that their helmets registered."

Julian said sharply, "Did you report in and call for force augmentation?"

"Yes, sir. I followed all procedures, sir."

"What did you see as you ran? What did your helmet record?"

"I saw nothing, sir. The helmet recorded nothing. But Shanab and Mary lay on the ground, with the spears in their backs, like you saw. Then the force augmentation arrived, the closest personnel, Sergeant Harding and the other private. Their helmets didn't record anything, either. Sergeant Harding told me to call you, and he went back to his post, which was guarding the dissidents. But by the time he got there, Wong and the other two were gone."

"I'll talk to Sergeant Harding next," Julian said, so grimly that Alex glanced over at him. "He was derelict in his duty priorities. You, however, acted correctly. Resume your duties."

"Yes, sir." The man held out his arm, then clapped it to his chest. He turned to his displays.

Alex realized, belatedly, that she had just seen a "salute."

Julian said to her and Ashraf, "At bunker distance the helmets record and identify only metal. The Furs' spears are wood and stone. At closer proximity the helmets track infrared, but it would be too confusing to do that across a mile. Privates Mesbah and Pesci probably detected the approaching Furs but might have thought they were animals. Or maybe the Furs fired the spears from some equivalent of a bow. They might get enough distance that way so that neither infrared or night vision would make clear what was happening. Not to untested recruits, anyway. And then other Furs got Wong and the others away while Harding left his post."

"But why?" Alex said, at the same moment that Ashraf said, "Wasn't Sergeant Harding supposed to help? You said—"

"I said Harding should have sent augmentation, but his first duty was guarding dissidents and he knew that." Julian spoke more levelly than usual, his only sign of anger.

Alex repeated, "Why would the Furs kill two soldiers and steal Wong?"

"He wasn't 'stolen,'" Julian said, and she saw from his expression that she should have realized that. "The Furs are cooperating with the dissidents."

"But Furs *killed* the dissidents who tried to burn Mira during the evacuation drill! They were on our side!"

"I don't know how they were turned," Julian said.

Ashraf said, "We should look for Nan Frayne."

Something flickered behind Julian's eyes. "Yes," he said. "I'll take care of it."

"I don't understand," Alex said.

Ashraf said sadly, "None of us do. I can't just . . . Julian, what is it?"

Julian stood very still. Alex saw, for the first time ever, shock widen his green eyes. He raised his hand to his left ear.

"A ship. A ship detected just beyond the star system. A Fur ship."

Alex said sharply, "The *Franz Mueller*? Karim? Is it signaling?"

"The ship is not signaling. The probe says it's not the *Franz Mueller*. But it's a McAndrew Drive ship, the drive is off, it's just sitting there."

Looking at Julian's face, Alex thought, *He didn't think this would ever actually happen. Despite all his urgent preparations, he didn't really think it would happen.*

Then there was no time for the personal. Ashraf said, "What do we do?"

Alex said swiftly, "Order the evacuation of Mira City. For real this time. The Furs are finally here."

The original plan had been for Ashraf, Julian, and Alex to occupy different bunkers, in case one was destroyed. But only one rover stood outside Hope of Heaven. Most traffic went by river. Alex surveyed the displays in the Hope of Heaven security bunker and said, "Julian, can you direct defenses from here?"

"I already am."

"I can direct my part of the evacuation, too. Ashraf, you take the rover, your command bunker is the one closest to here. Julian, send an armed guard with him."

Ashraf said, "Is there even an evacuation plan for Hope of Heaven? They wouldn't be part of ours."

"I don't know," Alex said. "But they must monitor MiraNet. They'll learn about the ship and do whatever they do."

"But—" Ashraf began, but Alex was no longer listening. She was on the comlink and a display, directing the evacuation. She didn't notice when Ashraf left.

As she worked, Alex translated the data on her screen into pictures in her mind. Jake, being wheeled in his chair to the tram, arriving at the not-far-enough-away, inadequately hidden cave that was the best they could do for those who could not travel well.

Siddalee, grumbling and efficient, a sector captain who would check every building in her sector before she left Mira.

Guy Davenport, posting his security force, some of whose weapons wouldn't work if Julian used the EMP.

Kate Arcola, head of the Scientists' League, directing the shielding of Mira's infrastructure. Receiving and coordinating esoteric reports, passing on pertinent facts and conclusions to Julian, Ashraf, and Alex.

The Arab women in the medina, their veils white in the darkness as they boarded barges on the river.

Duncan and his actors, maybe still in costume and makeup, rushing from the new theater for their designated transport to their end points. Which of the maybe twenty thousand people on Greentrees, including Cheyenne, would survive the Fur attack? Which would not?

"*'If you can look into the seeds of time,*
And say which grain will grow and which will not,
Speak then to me...'"

Julian's uniformed tech said, "Enemy vessel moving, sir. Accelerating at five gee, ten, twenty... McAndrew Drive confirmed. Trajectory straight for Greentrees."

"Continue to monitor," Julian said.

On Alex's comlink, now stuck in her ear, Siddalee said, "Sector J is emptied out, Alex. How come this couldn't have happened by daylight? I'm getting on the tram now."

"Good luck, Siddalee."

"We're going to need it. I got a pregnant woman right next to me who's days away from giving birth. At least I hope it's days." She clicked off.

And, thought Alex, there was no better place for a pregnant woman to be than next to Siddalee Brown. Alex almost smiled.

Two hours later, Mira City was empty except for Davenport's security force, Julian's soldiers, and the few cranky civilians who had refused to leave. Julian had told her that every evacuation in history had these cranks; they weren't worth coercing. Alex, not liking his language, had nonetheless agreed. The holdouts were making their own choice.

"Enemy vessel decelerating," the tech said. Alex turned to watch the graphic display.

The Fur ship changed from a blur to a dot somewhere between Greentrees and Ven, the next planet out in the system. Then it began to move much more slowly.

"Vacuum drive off," the tech said. "It's moving under cruising power, sir."

"Position report," Julian said.

The tech rattled off a string of coordinates that Alex couldn't follow. But from the graphics she gathered that the *Beta Vine* and the *Crucible* were both keeping steady on the opposite side of Greentrees from the enemy ship. It was possible that the Furs didn't even know the other two ships, one a captured vessel of their own, even existed. Julian had surprise on his side.

He said, "Any signaling detected?"

"No signals on any wavelength. Wait . . . an orbital probe is doing a close fly-by . . . visual from the probe. Switching to magnified visual, sir."

Suddenly the screen showed the ship in blurry detail. The living quarters pod was nearly at the full length of the pole away from the superdense mass disk. A sudden burst of brightness came from the ship.

"What's that?" Alex said involuntarily.

The brightness resolved itself into tiny glittering flecks. The focused cloud of flecks grew bigger and bigger, and then the probe flew into them.

A few moments later the picture disappeared.

"Probe signal lost, sir."

"That was a weapon," Alex said, "but not a beam of any type. It was a glittery sort of *spray*."

Julian said, "*Beta Vine*. Enemy ship has destroyed an orbital probe. Stand by, prepare to attack."

"Enemy vessel stopping," the tech said.

A few minutes later, "Enemy vessel assuming high Greentrees orbit."

"*Crucible* and *Beta Vine*, match orbit speed with enemy one hundred eighty degrees offset," Julian said. "Stay behind planet until further orders. Alex, is there anything in the Furs' previous visit to Greentrees about a weapon like this? Or anything close to this?"

"Not that I ever heard of."

Julian spoke rapidly on another channel, ordering a deebees search. Alex knew the records from those early days of the colony were skimpy. People had just been too busy building and surviving to enter much information into the deebees. Although surely if the Furs had had anything as alien as this . . .

She said suddenly, "Jake might know. He's the only one still alive who went off-planet with the Furs, except of course Karim Mahjoub and Lucy Lasky." Who had been gone thirty-nine years and were probably dead.

"Comlink Jake," Julian said.

"I can't. His evac end point is in a cave; no signals will get through."

Julian was silent a moment. "Then go there, Alex. There's nothing more for you to do here, and I'll be in comlink at all times. You can talk to Jake best and you saw what happened to the probe. I'll get a rover here to take you."

Alex hesitated. This went contrary to all Julian's previous plans about preserving Mira leadership to direct unknown future actions. But she was far from her designated end point anyway, and Julian knew better than she how to handle this kind of situation. And—yes, admit it—she didn't want to look like a coward. "All right. Assign me a dedicated comlink channel."

The rover arrived in less than half an hour, driven not by any of Greentrees recruits usually used as drivers but by a Terran soldier. Alex had learned to read the shoulder insignia; this was a captain. She was surprised that Julian would spare such an important soldier to go with her.

"He can fight," Julian said briefly. "You drive."

Alex didn't argue. "That leaves just you and the tech here," Alex said, noticing for the first time that the tech was not that but one of the Terran scientists who had come with Julian on the *Crucible*. Well, the computer equipment in the bunker was Terran, also off Julian's ship.

"Comlink me as soon as you talk to Jake," Julian said. He didn't kiss her, but his eyes held so much feeling that Alex felt warmed.

It was daylight outside the bunker, a cool clear morning. Hope of Heaven, a mile across the plain where the river made a wide bend, looked no different for last night's murders, no different for Wong Yat-Shing's absence, no different for the presence of the Fur ship, silent in high orbit. The rebel settlement's graceful buildings rose from beds of bright flowers. Dew wetted the grass. Somewhere to Alex's left something small rustled in the purple groundcover. Sunlight sparkled on the river.

She got in the rover and drove as fast as possible toward the cave where Jake, feeble in his wheelchair, awaited war.

Jake's end point was pitifully visible. The tram tracks stopped only a hundred yards away. Security had done what it could to disguise the entrance with brush and to erase the signs of having wheeled or dragged patients from the tram end to the cave, but their efforts were pathetic. Jake was right; the sick and old were at the most disadvantage during fighting, and they endangered those who cared for them, as well. But what other choice was there? These were Greenies, and they could neither travel far nor be left behind. Alex climbed out of the rover, leaving the two soldiers behind, and started toward the cave.

"Halt! State your name and business!" a young voice called, and Alex was back in the horror of the night before, two young Greentrees soldiers bleeding on the ground with spears in their chests.

"Alex Cutler, tray-o," she said impatiently, "to see Jake Holman."

"Ms. Cutler?" the voice said, and a helmet poked around a clump of brush, followed by the guard.

Not a Terran highly technical helmet, Alex noted, and not armed very well. Don't waste valuable resources on the sick and the old. She should understand that, resource allocation was her business. And yet something in her cringed.

Then she saw that the girl was crying.

"What is it?" she said sharply. She'd comlinked with Ashraf and Julian just five minutes ago from the rover: no movement from the ship, nothing happening on the ground.

"I'm . . . I'm sorry," the girl sobbed. "I know I shouldn't . . . state your b-b-business."

Alex fished a handkerchief from a fold of her wrap. The girl, she saw, was young even by Julian's recruitment standards. But, no, this wasn't one of Julian's but an evacuation volunteer.

The girl blew her nose and wiped her eyes while Alex stood by helplessly. She was no good at this sort of thing. Finally the girl said, "Are the Furs attacking yet?"

"No. Why are you crying?"

"Mary Pesci was my sister."

Again the picture in the mind of the dead soldiers at Hope of Heaven. No escaping it, for any of Greentrees.

"Why did the wild Furs kill her?" the girl cried. "It doesn't make any sense!"

"Ms. Cutler," came the voice in her ear, "you are exposed in the open. Please move into the cave." Her new bodyguard.

Alex led the sobbing girl toward the cave. "What's your name?"

"T-T-Tira Pesci."

"Tira, how did you learn Mary was dead?"

"A friend c-comlinked me. It's . . . all over M-MiraNet."

Of course it was. This time, no EMP had knocked out communications. Yet.

"M-Mary was older th-than me. I couldn't qu-qu-qu—"

"I'm so sorry," Alex said helplessly.

"—qualify for Commander Martin's army."

"I'll find Jake Holman myself," Alex said.

"Y-yes. I'm back on d-duty." Tira left her at the mouth of the cave.

Poor child. The other dead kid, Mesbah Shanab, must also have a grieving family. Alex ducked through the brush, which scratched her face and arms. She wished savagely for Threadmores instead of this stupid wrap.

The cave was long and narrow. Powerlights illuminated the beds and wheelchairs lining both rough stone walls. Volunteers bent over some of the cots, feeding or tending patients. A few people nodded at Alex, but no one questioned her presence. She had, after all, been passed on through by their guard detail. Such as it was.

Her people, she realized all over again, were not of the right temperament or background to fight a war.

She found Jake asleep on a cot at the back of the cave. Duncan Martin sat reading in Jake's wheelchair.

"Ah, the fair Alexandra approaches. Are the dogs of war howling in our ears?"

"No. What are you doing here, Duncan? I hear there's a brisk trade in evac posts." She knew she was being rude; his jocularity angered her.

"This is my assigned post and I made no effort to trade it, you enchanting shrew. Although as the bard tells us, 'There's small choice in rotten apples.'"

She had no time to ponder the unknown in Duncan's character that led him to keep a duty both dangerous and tedious. "I want to talk to Jake, alone."

"Your wish is my command." He ambled off, readerscreen in hand.

Alex sat in the vacated wheelchair and shook Jake's shoulder. "Jake, wake up. It's Alex."

The old man woke instantly, staring wildly for a moment and then clearly remembering where he was. "Has it started?" His voice was thick and a little slurred, but there was no mistaking the intelligence in his eyes. He was still Jake.

"No. The Fur ship is just sitting in high orbit. Listen, I need you to think about something, dear, and it's important. The Fur ship happened to make orbit near one of our orbital probes. It gave us a clear picture. But when it got too close, the ship fired on it, not a laser or alpha beam or anything else we recognized. It seemed to be a sort of beam of . . . of glitter, a lot of little things that spread outward fast.

"And it didn't destroy on contact. The probe flew into the cloud and continued to send for another twelve seconds before the signal was lost. Actually, now that I think about it, maybe the probe wasn't destroyed but just the signal made to cease. We don't know. Anyway, you're the only one left alive from that first trip off-planet with the Furs. Do you know what that glittery beam is? Did you see anything like that, thirty-nine years ago?"

"No," Jake said. Alex wiped a thread of drool from his mouth. "But wait . . . George Fox said . . ."

"The biologist? That's right, he was with you. I remember meeting him when I was young."

"He died twenty years ago. Was the glittery cloud in full sunlight? Not occluded by Greentrees?"

"Not occluded."

"The Furs who captured us," Jake said slowly, "told us that we humans were supposed to destroy some sort of shield around a Vine planet. We never got that far, of course. But Beta Vine drew us a picture once and George thought it might be the shield. It showed a huge cloud of tiny dots completely surrounding the planet, with a space elevator that George thought might launch them. He theorized that the dots were spores or some microbe analogue—the Vines weren't DNA-based, remember, and they were master biochemists, to say the least. George thought the microbe-things might be the shield. That they might eat metal or something like that."

"But . . . that would make the ship up there a Vine ship, not a Fur one! Didn't you say that the Vines used captured Fur ships, not the other way around?"

"That's right. The Furs developed physics-based technology, the Vines developed biochemical tech." Jake laid a shaky hand on her arm. "But, Alex, remember that all this was decades ago by Greentrees time. With their McAndrew Drive ships, it's possible the whole situation up there has changed and Furs now recapture their own Vine-modified ships. Those *could* be Furs in orbit right now."

Alex nodded. She could see how the long speech had tired him. "All right. Thank you, Jake. I'll comlink Julian."

"Wait . . . a minute."

"What is it, dear? Do you need something?"

"It could not be Furs, too. It could be Vines. Don't let Julian . . . we already destroyed their innocent people once and they tried to help us anyway . . . Karim and Lucy . . . infection . . . don't let Julian . . ."

The easy tears of the old filled his eyes. Alex wiped them away, both moved and irritated. Too many tears today.

"If they're Vines, Julian won't hurt them. I've told him the whole Greentrees history."

"Good. Where are Lucy and Karim? Karim and my Lucy . . . if they succeeded in infecting the Furs . . . if . . . I don't know . . ."

"Just rest now, Jake."

"No rest. One more thing—"

She was impatient to go outside the cave and comlink Julian, but she said gently, "What, dear?"

"Get that idiot Duncan Martin away from me."

Alex sighed. Some things not even war changed.

16

SPACE

Karim dozed, and woke, and dozed again. Time had ceased to matter. There was only the endless slow descent in the membrane that encased them like eggs in an alien womb.

At first he and Lucy had been terrified, then excited. They'd tried to understand what was happening to them.

"The bubble's *alive*," Karim said. "A thick sheet of some living molecules, maybe with clear hard carapaces joined together on one side, the outside of the bubble. Keeping the air in." Neither he nor Lucy wore their Vine-made helmets. The helmets must have been stripped from them while they were unconscious. Without it, Karim's head felt new and deliciously light.

Lucy said, "But if the bubble is alive, what's it eating?"

"Sunlight. And my guess is that sunlight is also powering the descent. We're not falling, Lucy. We're descending to Greentrees at a slow, controlled rate. I think the molecules in the bubble are creating and emitting gases that propel us downward. As we move through thicker atmosphere, the side of the bubble toward Greentrees will give off tiny jets of gases to prevent free fall. We'll just float down."

"So we're really going home."

"Yes." He took her hand. Those small, fragile bones. Both of them were naked.

"But, Karim, why not just send us down in a shuttle?"

"I don't know."

"Why not go down with us in the shuttle, if the Vines really want those death flowers so much?"

"I don't know that, either."

They fell silent, encased in their living bubble, watching the planet turn below them. Impossibly beautiful, impossibly alive. Home.

That had been a while ago. Impossible to tell how long, because Karim didn't know if complete revolutions of the planet had occurred while he slept. He could only judge time by his stomach, which growled incessantly. He was ravenous.

"It isn't like the Vines to not provide us with food or water," Lucy said. "Usually they . . . well, you know. They took good physical care of us."

"Yes," Karim said. He, too, felt shame at his previous hatred of the Vines on their own planet. "But I'm not thirsty, are you?"

"No. Just hungry."

"They must be keeping us hydrated somehow, Lucy. And no food argues that the trip won't be longer than we can stand without eating."

"I suppose so," she said halfheartedly.

Karim slept again, and when he woke the bubble was drifting through cloud. He could see nothing. "We're in the atmosphere, Lucy." But she was still sleeping. The molecules of the bubble must be generating heat to keep them warm, as well as everything else it was doing. But why? Why not a shuttle?

Maybe he and Lucy were scouts. After all, it might have been decades since they'd left Greentrees. For all Karim or the Vines knew, Furs might have returned to Greentrees. They might have killed or enslaved all of Mira City. But if Karim and Lucy were scouts, how would the Vines upstairs find out what they reported? Was the bubble going to ascend again?

Maybe. And he, Lucy, and the bubble were all living things. No metal for probes to pick up, no speed to alert detection devices. They were coming in "under the radar," as people used to say when Karim had been at school in London, UAF, another lifetime ago.

Two lifetimes ago.

He watched the featureless filaments of cloud slide past. Where would he and Lucy come down? The Vines who'd sent them must realize that they couldn't survive long naked in the vast Greentrees wilderness. Humanity occupied only a tiny fraction of the planet. Surely the Vines would send their human scouts, if that's what they were, to somewhere inhabited. Mira City, most probably.

But what would he and Lucy find once they arrived there?

17

BUNKER THREE

The Fur ship—if it was a Fur ship—upstairs continued to do nothing. Alex comlinked with Julian and told him what Jake had said about the glittering "spore" weapon possibly being able to destroy metal. Then she climbed back into the rover. Her Terran bodyguard asked no questions. She had the vague impression that this was part of Julian's training. The soldier did not even offer his name.

"We're going on to Bunker Three," she told the man. That was her designated end point for as long as the Fur ship—if it *was* a Fur ship—stayed in orbit. She'd have complete displays there and, thank heavens, a Threadmore. The skimpy wrap annoyed her more and more. Duncan's *Macbeth* seemed to have been played in a distant past.

Two young soldiers dead on the ground, with bow-driven lances in their hearts. Mary Pesci's sister sobbing, weapon in hand.

She had almost reached the bunker when Ashraf comlinked.

"Alex. Hope of Heaven is burning."

"Hope of Heaven?" But it was Mira that had been fired, by dissidents. "What do you mean?"

"A . . . a mob came to Hope of Heaven. I believe they're led by relatives of those two dead kids. The Pescis and Shanabs are both large and successful families, you know. The mob is burning buildings and some of the wilder and angrier young men are beating people up."

Alex said sharply, "How do you know this? I have my MiraNet programming set to automatically flag and comlink me with any postings of violence on Greentrees!"

"MiraNet is down. I only know what's happening because one of my nephews is a soldier with Julian. He comlinked me."

"Why didn't Julian—"

"He's busy putting the mob down, ending the violence with his own soldiers. My nephew got wounded and so he could comlink me direct. He says Julian is—" Alex heard Ashraf reach for careful repetition "—'directing a successful operation, with a minimum of force and a maximum of persuasive strategies.' Nobody's been killed that my nephew knew about."

Alex said, "What did you mean 'MiraNet is down'?" The computer system is still working, I just got a report from Savannah at the solar array."

"I mean Julian took down the news part of the system. He says it was spreading untrue and inflammatory rumors. So his techs blocked it temporarily."

"Did you authorize that?"

"I didn't have to. Julian's using his military-law powers." Ashraf, Alex thought, didn't sound at all dismayed by this. In fact, she detected a small note of relief.

"Alex, do you think I should go to Hope of Heaven? I am the mayor."

"No. I think you should stay where you are and let Julian handle it. He knows how."

"All right." Now the relief was more than a trace. "Good-bye."

Everything major at Bunker Three was calm, proceeding as planned. Natalie Bernstein, backed by Ben Stoller, worked efficiently at the display console. Natalie had already set up a duty rotation and Ben had replenished the water supply and checked the external sensors. Alex's Terran bodyguard, saying only, "I stay outside," vanished into the forest.

Now all anybody on Greentrees had to do was wait.

———

Three days passed. Mira City remained empty except for Guy's security force and that segment of humanity that insisted on ignoring reality. These holdouts went quietly about the abandoned city, causing minimal problems. Security stopped two instances of petty looting. Someone forced the door on a grocery, took several items, and left money along with a list of his purchases. Someone was arrested for kindling a bonfire in the park. Someone with a retina authorization, who nonetheless was not supposed to be in the city, fed the animals at the genetic labs.

At the end points, too, only expected difficulties occurred. A pregnant Arab women gave birth, her doctor in attendance. A very old woman in Jake's cave finally died. Two teenage boys got into a fight and one's arm was broken. Someone broke into the food supply at End Point Thirty-two and ate more than his share of rations.

The groups that had elected to travel moved steadily away from Mira City, losing themselves in the wilderness but staying in comlink touch. Young and fit, these groups were moving faster than expected, living partly off the rich land. Mostly they moved north, into the mountains and away from the subcontinent legally belonging to the Cheyenne. Their reports sounded almost exhilarated.

Julian had managed to put down the mob at Hope of Heaven with, astonishingly, no loss of life. The rest of the dissidents in the settlement, however, were bitter about the attack. Most of them packed up and they, too, took off into the wilderness. Julian made no effort to stop them. They were for the most part young, strong, and since Wong Yat-Shing's escape with Nan Frayne's wild Furs, leaderless. Julian tracked them from orbit and told Alex and Ashraf that he didn't believe they represented any further threat to Mira.

In short, Alex thought wryly, humanity was carrying on in all its varied angers, loves, temperaments, and contradictions. The only difference was that 99 percent of Greenies were now doing these things outside of Mira, while an alien ship orbited silently overhead. A ship that might be Fur or might be Vine, and that seemed to have no interest in communicating with the planet it had presumably traveled many light-years to reach.

Two more days passed. Still nothing happened. Natalie organized three-handed card games. Alex played a few hands and then excused herself. Cards couldn't soothe her anxious restlessness. The Terran bodyguard—who, she finally learned, was named Captain Lewis—checked in at the bunker twice a day, impassive as rock.

People began to drift back into Mira, despite Julian's directives to stay out. They were tired of camping out, tired of washing in streams or not at all, and no war had materialized after all.

"It's a good Fur tactic," he told Alex grimly on comlink. "Lull us into a belief there's no real danger. People can't stay hyperalert forever."

"Maybe there is no danger," Alex said. "Those could be Vines up there, not Furs. Jake said—"

"I know what Jake said. But he also warned that Furs could have captured Vine weapons, or that glitter beam might not have even been a weapon, or Dr. Fox's theory could have been completely wrong."

"Yes," Alex admitted. "Julian—"

"What?"

"Nothing."

"You miss me," he said, his tone softening, "and I miss you. Very much, Alex."

It wasn't like him to be so open. A glow of pleasure warmed her. He didn't say anything more—she hadn't expected him to—but the glow lingered a long time afterward, and that night on her bunker pallet she dreamed of his hard, beautiful body on top of hers. The dream was so vivid that, to her embarrassment, she woke with her hand between her legs. Her orgasm was so powerful her entire body bucked. Ben, at the monotonous displays, either didn't notice or pretended not to. Natalie snored softly.

War, Julian had told her once, sharpened the appetites. Apparently it was true even when the only fighting was intrahuman, not with the enemy. The thought disquieted her, and she slept no more that night.

———————

The next day, Julian comlinked her and Ashraf on their secure channel. "They've launched a shuttle."

Alex had been outside her bunker, clearing rocks to stave off boredom. "When?"

"Ninety seconds ago. Present trajectory indicates possible landing site fifty miles southeast of Mira, in the Avery Mountains. Alex, alert Guy to clear Mira of as many returnees as he can, and get any dropped shields back up on infrastructure facilities. Ashraf, I'm giving you an open channel to all sector captains to explain the situation. Emphasize that this is not a drill." He clicked off.

Alex raced back inside, barking information at her techs. For the next half hour she worked frantically. Her displays, enslaved to Julian's, let her follow the shuttle's progress. A small black dot on the graphics, it moved steadily toward Greentrees.

Who was in it? Why was it landing there? The Avery Mountains held nothing except research stations.

Something teased her mind. Oh, yes, Jon McBain and his buried anaerobic microbes. She had heard nothing from McBain in months, not since Julian had replaced him, to his obvious relief, as defense minister. Either McBain's research on both anaerobes and the microbiotic battery had fizzled, or Alex's cold reception of the former had discouraged Jon from copying her in on his reports. He had never requested further resource allocation.

Why land there?

Why not? This group of aliens, Fur or Vine, would be new to Greentrees. They might want to confront a small group of humans before facing the planet's largest aggregation of them.

Alex's silent Terran bodyguard had slipped back into the bunker. Julian's tech was giving oral readings every thirty seconds. They were on audio in the bunker as a whole, while the secure channel remained in Alex's ear. "Trajectory unchanged, shuttle at X minus forty."

"Continue monitoring," Julian said.

"Trajectory unchanged, shuttle at X minus thirty."

In her ear Ashraf said, "Alex, who do you think they are?"

"I don't know." Even she knew this was no time for speculation.

"Trajectory unchanged, shuttle at X minus twenty."

The small black dot had moved well into the atmosphere.

And then Julian's calm voice, "Germanicus One, positions. Quintus One, begin run."

Positions? Run what?

And who were Germanicus and Quintus? Nothing else appeared on her graphic display.

"Julian, what's happening? Julian?"

He didn't answer.

Natalie suddenly swore, an unexpected burst of Terran profanity. "There's a block program in effect . . . wait, I just learned about this, my old teacher showed me how to . . . what the . . . there!"

Ben gasped.

Another graphic appeared on the display from behind Greentrees, moving with incredible speed toward the shuttle. The dot was a purple smear: a McAndrew Drive at full acceleration.

The Beta Vine.

Julian's voice, still completely calm, "Germanicus One, fire EMP."

Alex watched the shuttle dot shudder and suddenly plummet toward Greentrees.

The smeary dot moved faster and faster, the alien ship in orbit began to accelerate, and then—how fast!—the *Beta Vine* slammed into the orbiting ship.

Both dots disappeared from the screen.

The shuttle dot hit the ground.

"Enemy shuttle crashed at fourteen six by a hundred eight three, sir," said Julian's tech. "Enemy vessel destroyed by a direct hit. *Beta Vine* destroyed on suicide mission."

"Continue monitoring," Julian's voice said.

Alex stared in disbelief.

Ben said, "He . . . he . . . Julian . . . sacrificed the *Beta Vine*! And we don't even know who was on it or the shuttle! The bastard killed them all!"

Suddenly Ben stood up so fast that his chair toppled over. He swung around, fury on his face, and Alex turned with him. Captain Lewis stood with his feet braced slightly apart, a gun leveled at the tech's chest.

"Corporal Stoller," the bodyguard said, "you will refer to the commander of this army in respectful terms. And you will calm down."

The two men stared at each other. Alex stepped forward. "Stop it, both of you. Now."

Ben looked at her; the Terran did not. After a moment the young tech walked past them both, toward the door.

"Remain inside, Corporal. That's an order. Commander Martin will decide who to comlink about his military decisions, and when to take that action. You, too, ma'am."

Alex demanded, "Am I a prisoner?"

"No, ma'am. But you will remain inside until further word from Commander Martin."

Alex turned away and spoke on the secure channel. The soldier made no effort to stop her. Ben, after a moment of clench-fisted indecision, picked up his chair and resumed his place at his console.

"Julian," Alex said, "you just blew up the *Beta Vine*, the alien ship, and the shuttle. Why?"

"What happened?" came Ashraf's voice.

"Why?" Alex yelled.

Julian's voice was quieter than ever. "Alex is correct, Ashraf. I put out an EMP on the shuttle while it was still in range of the Mira equipment. And I sent the *Beta Vine* on a suicide mission into the enemy ship. At full acceleration, it outran the so-called 'glitter beam' as well as the more conventional weapons. I did it to keep Greentrees safe."

Alex cried, "But you don't even know if it was Furs or Vines aboard!"

"I couldn't take a chance. My job is to protect Greentrees."

"You may have killed a shipful of innocent beings! A species that's been our ally!"

"I take full responsibility for the decision."

Ashraf said, "Who was aboard the *Beta Vine*?"

"Only a pilot, who was a volunteer. Everyone else had already been removed. The pilot, a Terran named Lt. Suriah Poliakis, is now a military hero."

A Terran, not a Greenie.

Did it matter?

No.

Julian said, "The explosion may have been visible to anyone on Greentrees monitoring the alien vessel, including all our scientists. I'm going to make a general announcement now of what has happened. I will not be available on this channel. Alex, you can tell everyone to return to Mira City.

"The city is now safe."

He was a hero; he was a villain.

The city council met in the Mausoleum. It wasn't actually a meeting as much as a chaotic, two-day shouting match. Councillors barreled into the Mausoleum as soon as they returned from their evac end points. Citizens thronged the cool foamcast chamber, arguing so loudly that they had to be hushed in order for the actual councillors to be heard. There was no order, no protocol, no courtesy—except in Julian himself.

He stayed there ten hours a day for two days straight, occasionally taking low-voiced reports from his lieutenants but never leaving the room. He neither ate nor drank. He was calm, polite, and absolutely unshakable that he had done the right thing.

"You destroyed unknown beings, who might even have been our allies!" a woman shouted. Ungroomed and covered with dirt, she had obviously just arrived from some distant evac point. "Commander Martin, you're a murderer! We do not murder on Greentrees!"

"Madame," Julian replied in his soft, firm voice, "I regret your use of that term. I defended Mira City so that murder of many

Greentrees citizens—perhaps all Greentrees citizens—will *not* occur."

"You also destroyed the *Beta Vine*!" a man called. "Our only warship! What if the Furs return?"

The *Crucible* is a warship and it stands ready to defend you as well, or better, than could the *Beta Vine*."

"You suspended MiraNet without authorization!"

"My authorization was wartime necessity. I didn't know—none of us knew—how much the enemy could monitor our communication. The less they knew about our activities, the safer all of us were."

After a few hours of this, Alex noticed a shift in Julian. He stayed as calm and approachable as ever, but he stopped answering his critics. Instead, he let other people do it for him.

"He had to make a choice," Mohammed Akbar said, "between our ship or their attack, and he chose right. Which is more important, the *Beta Vine* or Mira City?"

"But he—"

"Which is more important," a woman said, "Mira City, with all our children's lives, or the aliens on that ship? I know which one I'd choose. I'd blow *you* up if you threatened my two kids!"

Children. Alex remembered Julian first introducing the evac and defense plans. Over and over he'd mentioned the children of Mira City: the children's safety, feeding the children, keeping the enemy from seizing even one child, preparing for the return of the children after the attack had been repulsed. Had he brought up children this time, either when he was answering criticism directly or in his now fewer, quiet comments? Alex couldn't remember.

A council member said, "It's Commander Martin we have to thank for putting down that mob from Hope of Heaven. They could have burned the whole city down! We'd have lost our homes, our businesses, everything."

Someone else, someone in the back, said slowly, "But the price is . . . is this: Commander Martin is in sole charge of Mira City."

"I am not," Julian said instantly. "And if the council votes for me to resign my position as your defense leader, I will do so immediately."

There was a long silence. Then Ashraf Shanti said, "I think we owe Julian Martin our lives."

More silence, but its quality had changed. Alex saw that the usually diffident mayor's words carried surprising weight, especially among the Arab businessmen who would now be able to resume normal commerce in the city. The tenor of the meeting had subtly changed.

It stayed changed. The criticisms and objections continued, but the forces behind Julian grew hourly. He had won again.

And Alex herself? *I trust him*, she thought, but at the same time she couldn't help thinking about the aliens—Furs or Vines?—that had died, as well as the young dissidents from Hope of Heaven. Was that what war did, mix up the good and the bad so that no matter how hard you thought about it, they couldn't be separated?

"So fair and foul a day I have not seen." Alex was surprised how the words of Duncan's play lingered in her mind. When she told Duncan this, he merely rolled his eyes, and said, "My dear lady, do not embarrass yourself by announcing your ignorance of the bard's timelessness. At least keep it decently to yourself."

Julian himself remained unperturbed even after the two-days' "meeting" officially ended. "Talk abates over time," he said. He permitted MiraNet to resume operations.

Everything else was resumed as well, mining and research and farming and the hundred other entities clamoring for a greater allocation of resources. Alex worked long days. Nights she spent with Julian. They were as sexually hungry with each other as ever, and sometimes as she wrapped her arms around his hard, muscled body just before she fell asleep, she thought: *This is happiness*. But at the same time, there was a faint remoteness about him that had not been there before. He always waited for her to sleep before he left her, needing almost no sleep himself. He went back to his office and worked, he told her. She woke alone.

A memorial service was held for Mary Pesci, Mesbah Shanab, Suriah Poliakis. All of Mira, it seemed, turned out for the ceremony. Ashraf spoke, calling the three "our first martyrs," and Alex watched Jake's old eyes widen with shock.

"They don't remember Erik Halberg. Or even Beta Vine!" he said to Alex.

"We don't seem to be too good at remembering," she said wryly, and only later realized that she and Jake had used different pronouns.

Alex drove out one day, without Julian, to look at Hope of Heaven. The dissident settlement remained mostly deserted. A few figures, spied in the distance, went indoors as soon as they saw her. Weeds grew in the bright flower beds. The burned buildings hadn't been touched, piles of charred timber fallen in on themselves. Debris, probably left by looters, blew in the street.

Where had they gone, those passionate and misguided young people who had caused so much pain? Pushing steadily north into the wilderness. No one had received any comlinks from them, or at least no one whom Alex knew. It was such a huge, untouched world. Had the rebels joined again with Wong Yat-Shing? Were they creating somewhere the justice they felt Mira City had denied them?

When Julian discovered she'd traveled alone and unguarded to Hope of Heaven, he was as angry as she'd ever seen him. "Even one rebel left could have killed you for the pure satisfaction of it. You were not even armed."

"I—"

"I'm restoring your bodyguard," he said coldly, and she hadn't argued. His anger was proof that he cared about her life. She didn't really believe she was in danger, but she treasured his caring. Alex reached out and put a warm hand on his shoulder. He was so much to her, and so much in himself: brilliant and experienced and hardworking on Mira City's behalf. And he had chosen her out of all the women he could have had, which was most of them outside of the medina.

Impulsively she moved into his arms and kissed his warm, responsive mouth.

Mira was lucky to have him. Alex was lucky to have him. And he was right, the negative talk was dying down.

Everything was going to be all right.

18

THE AVERY MOUNTAINS

After what Karim judged to have been a few days, his and Lucy's hunger abated. They watched with fascination as Greentrees rose leisurely to meet their bubble. The continents and seas became distinct. Then, near the end of the descent, one continent moved below them, covered with mountains and purplish vegetation. The vegetation became trees, the mountains individual low peaks and upland purple meadows. Bright masses appeared and became flowers. Thin silvery strands resolved themselves into rushing mountain streams. The mountains were above them instead of below, and then the trees were above them, and then they were down, touching the ground as lightly as a breeze.

Karim blinked back wetness in his eyes. The membrane collapsed around them, falling to the ground like a popped balloon. Karim stepped free of the slime and breathed deeply.

"I'd . . . I'd forgotten how sweet Greentrees always smells," he managed to get out. "Oh, Lucy . . ."

"I know," she whispered. And then, visibly pulling herself together, "Where are we?"

"I don't know. I think the best thing to do is walk downhill as much as possible and hope we come to the river. If the bubble did leave us anywhere near Mira, that's our best chance of locating it."

"What about the bubble?"

Karim looked at the tough slimy "fabric" lying quiet on the purple groundcover. "I don't know. I guess it will do whatever it's sup-posed to."

What it did was follow them. When they stopped to drink from a small stream, cupping their hands to hold the cool water, Lucy no-ticed the slime oozing through the rough plants. "Karim . . . I think it's trying to find out what the situation is on Greentrees. Whether there are humans still here, or Vines, or Furs, or what. It's gathering intelligence."

"Let it."

She actually smiled. "As if we could stop it."

A few minutes later she said suddenly, "Karim, stop."

"Do you need to—"

"No, of course not, I haven't eaten anything. And I'm *hungry.* Those are wild sunberries. They're edible for us, if you don't mind some diarrhea."

The second Lucy said "hungry," Karim was ravenous. They pulled off handfuls of the big purple berries and crammed them into their mouths. Then Lucy insisted on finding leaves large enough to wrap around their genitals.

"Lucy, it's late afternoon. We have to find either people or a shelter of some sort by nightfall." Greentrees had predators, some of them very dangerous. The decades Karim and Lucy had been gone wouldn't have changed that.

"I'm not going into a group of strange people stark naked."

He gave in. She was quick and efficient at fashioning rude cov-erings for them both. The leaves lent no warmth, but they wouldn't need it until nightfall. With almost no axial tilt, Greentrees was near tropical everywhere.

And so beautiful. He hadn't remembered just how beautiful. Not paradise itself could surpass this.

"Lucy, come on!"

"I'm coming . . . oh God, Karim, the berries."

He had it, too, in a sudden gut-churning attack. Hastily they re-tired behind separate bushes. When the diarrhea had passed, Karim felt considerably worse: weak and light-headed.

A beautiful planet, but he had grown up in civilization.

"Karim," Lucy said shakily, "l-look!"

She stood at the edge of a downward slope. Karim walked to her. Below lay the river, shining in the late afternoon sun, and beside it inflatables and scattered large equipment. Three tall metal poles stuck up from the ground, with lines running from their tops to a nearby inflatable.

"A research station!" Karim said. "Just in time, we—"

The warriors jumped out of the bushes.

For a shocked moment Karim couldn't take in what he was seeing. He had images in his brain of scientists: Threadmores, data displays, dried rations, comlinks. In front of him stood three men carrying bows and spears. They wore animal pelts trimmed with feathers and small stones. On their cheeks were tattooed moons, stars, and other small totems. Their long hair was braided: one dark and two reddish blond. Two of the spears pointed straight at Lucy and Karim.

Lucy said dryly, with the odd self-possession that could come over her in crisis, "So you Cheyenne are still on Greentrees. I'm Lucy Lasky and this is Karim Mahjoub. Have you ever heard of us?"

The dark-haired brave said, "No. Come with us."

Karim said, "What is your name?"

"You don't need to know it."

The other two motioned downhill with their spears, and Karim and Lucy started walking toward the research camp. Karim said, "We have just landed from space. There's a Vine ship in orbit around Greentrees."

No answer. Karim glanced over his shoulder, but the slime was invisible. It had sunk into the groundcover, or just had not followed.

He tried again. "I was with the original landers. I knew Larry Smith, your founder."

Nothing. Karim had a sudden queasy flashback of talking to Vines on their silent planet, with never an answer.

One more attempt. "I thought Mira Corp had a covenant with the Cheyenne. I thought Mira City was supposed to stay out of your affairs and in return you were supposed to stay on the sub-continent to the south."

Then the brave did laugh, a sound so ugly that Karim glanced at him, startled. But the man in animal skins said no more, and they all started down the hill to the research station by the river.

19

MIRA CITY

S iddalee Brown said, "There's a Cheyenne chief to see you."

Alex had been just about to leave the Mausoleum. It was very late, hours past sunset, but she'd had mountains of work to get through. She looked at Siddalee.

"A Cheyenne chief?"

"That's what I said," Siddalee said, not without satisfaction at Alex's startled expression, but with evident disapproval of a Cheyenne coming to the Mausoleum. "Crazy," Siddalee called them, and Alex was inclined to agree. Crazy romantics, bent on re-creating, on an alien planet, a nontechnological life that had vanished even from Terra centuries before any of them were born.

This one wasn't old enough to have come with the First Landing. About Alex's age, he wore hides trimmed with embroidery and small stones, painstakingly sewn into elaborate designs. The hours of work! His light brown braids hung over his shoulders, bound with cord. He carried a spear, and Alex could just imagine the reaction he had stirred walking the streets of Mira. Alone? Probably not. This was the envoy; his bodyguards waited outside.

Her own bodyguard moved from just outside her door, where he spent his days, to a position inside the room with his back to the wall and his eyes on the visitor. He was unobtrusive, but he was always there. Alex had argued with Julian about him, but she hadn't expected to win, and she hadn't.

"Welcome to Mira City. I am Alex Cutler, Technology Resource Allocation Officer."

"I know. I am Star Rising. I was here for the fiftieth anniversary of the First Landing."

And she hadn't recognized him. Alex reddened, even as a rogue part of her mind noted detachedly that this self-willed primitive had the same first name as Star Chu, ambitious young technophile.

"I am here," Star Rising said, "on behalf of the Cheyenne Council of Tribes. We protest the attacks by what you call 'wild Furs.' "

Alex couldn't remember the Cheyenne political structure—they had so little contact with Mira—but she had a vague idea that the Council of Tribes was some sort of overseer for many individual tribes and thus a very big deal. But Cheyenne and wild Furs had been skirmishing with each other, both sides armed with lances and bows, for decades now. Alex was bewildered. "Mayor Ashraf—"

"Is not in Mira City. So I come to you."

No putting this off on Ashraf. The chief had dignity, Alex would give him that: in his tone, his carriage. She said as respectfully as she could, "Mira City has no jurisdiction over your subcontinent, as of course you know. And we have no jurisdiction over the wild Furs. They were here on Greentrees before either your people or mine."

"Yes. But until now, they have not had Mira Corp weapons to use against us."

Alex stared at him.

"Yes. My people have been killed by Furs carrying these."

From a fold of his tunic he pulled a gun that Alex recognized at once. It was the sort now carried by Mira City's much expanded security, and it was not hard to put together from objects also made for other uses: small laser, various metal fittings. Only one place in Mira manufactured them and the numbers were strictly controlled.

She said, stupidly, "How did the Furs get them? Do you know?"

"No. Although of course someone in Mira must have given them. We assume it was Nan Frayne."

"She doesn't have access to them."

"Fifteen Cheyenne have been killed with these guns since the Great Wheel rose in the east. Many Furs have them, which means more Cheyenne will die. Ms. Cutler, my people are not violent. The essence of our lives is contemplative, appreciation of the gifts of the Great Spirit. But I promise you that we will not have on Greentrees a repeat of the Sand Creek massacre. No matter what it requires to defend ourselves."

Alex had never heard of Sand Creek, but she recognized a threat when she heard one. "Chief Star Rising, I promise to investigate this, starting with the manufacturer. Where can I reach you when I know something?"

"I travel back to the Council of Tribes. Find me on the journey." He left, walking more silently than she would have thought possible.

Alex sat behind her desk and thought. Yat-Shing Wong was still, presumably, alive. He and his dissidents had been spirited away from Julian's guard by Furs, the Furs who had left spears in two of Julian's soldiers. So perhaps Wong was supplying the Furs with arms.

The manager of the gun manufactury, which was owned by Mira Corps, was Chinese.

But the man, Michael Lin, had been solidly cooperative with Mira City in arming Julian's troops, in the evacuation, in everything she could think of. Alex trusted him. Lin had never said so outright—most Chinese did not—but she was sure he'd been opposed to what the dissidents had done.

But he was Chinese.

Why had the Furs helped Wong escape? What other motive could they have except exchange for arms? But how could that deal ever even have come about, given that when the dissidents had set fire to Mira during the evacuation drill, it had been Nan Frayne and her Furs that had stopped them?

None of it made any sense.

She needed to talk to Nan Frayne, which was probably impossible. Also to Michael Lin and Julian, and not by comlink. Lin first.

But the thought of seeing Julian, even with this to unload on him, made her blood run faster. Shameful, to think of such pleasure in the midst of such trouble. But she couldn't help it. She didn't want to help it.

But Michael Lin first.

On his narrow bed in Alex's apartment, Jake dreamed.

He lay awake in his childhood bedroom, his brother, Donnie, snoring softly beside him. The white curtains his mother had hung so carefully over the grimy windows blew in the night breeze, echoing Donnie's breathing: in, out, in, out. The room, never completely dark even though it faced the brick wall of a half-bombed building, bulged with gray lumps: his clothing thrown on the floor, Donnie's, a chair with one busted back slat. Nothing in the room shone as white as the curtains, backlit by the violent city. Jake watched them intently: in, out, in, out. It was Donnie's breathing, it was his own, it was his mother laboring in the next room with the baby that would kill her. In, out, the curtains blew. In, out, in, out . . .

Someone else moved around the room.

"Cal?" Jake quavered. Cal Johnson was his latest nurse, a hulking, sweet-tempered kid whom, Jake suddenly remembered, he'd told to go out for the night. Cal had started a romance with a sexy Chinese girl he'd met in the park.

"It's not Cal," said a female voice. "But don't worry, Mr. Holman, you are in no danger. No one will hurt you. However, you are coming quietly with us. Please don't make this difficult."

He couldn't see anything in Greentrees' damn darkness. This wasn't a violent, always lighted city, there were no gray lumpy chairs, white curtains backlit and blowing in, out, in . . .

Careful hands pressed tape over Jake's mouth and eyes. More movement in the darkness and he felt himself lifted in strong arms. Cal! he thought with a wash of hope, but knew it wasn't Cal. Jake tried to struggle but his own feeble attempts embarrassed him enough to stop. God, he hated being old!

He was carried outside; he could tell from the sudden scented breeze. Then placed into a rover. But rovers were open vehicles, surely someone would see . . . Hands gently forced him to lie flat on the floor. He began to count, trying to gauge how long the ride took, how fast the rover was going.

All of which proved unnecessary because when he was again carried inside and the tapes removed, he knew immediately where he was. Jake had been lowered onto an old armchair padded with blankets. Cots stood against narrow stone walls, beside neat supplies of food and medical equipment in plastic crates sealed tight against predators. His end point cave for a Mira City evacuation.

"I'm sorry if that trip was uncomfortable," the feminine voice said and he focused on her, a slight figure eerily lit by a single powertorch.

"I know you. You're Star Chu. Zongming Chu's granddaughter."

"Yes. I run Chu Corporation."

One of the few expanding businesses owned by Chinese, Alex had told Jake. All young people, smart and ambitious, making their way by offering third-generation luxuries like alcohol, fireworks, perfume, candles, soaps. Alex had spoken of Star Chu with admiration.

Jake peered at her more closely. In her twenties, slender, very pretty, with short black hair and red mouth. Dressed in a no-nonsense Threadmore, but there was a bracelet of shining green stones on her wrist and a tiny Cheyenne tattoo on her cheek.

"Why am I here, Star Chu?"

She wiped a thread of drool from his mouth.

"Don't do that." She wasn't Alex.

"All right. I'm sorry. You're here because there are some things you need to know, and Alex Cutler needs to know. We can't get to her because of her Terran bodyguard. So we're telling you and you can tell her. Believe me, Mr. Holman, I wouldn't have brought you here if the situation weren't so desperate."

Desperate. Fear pierced him. "Where's Cal?"

"We haven't hurt him. He's out with Rose Li, just as he told you, having a very good time. She'll keep him out for the whole night."

Poor Cal, thinking it was love.

Star continued, "There's someone here to see you. We're bringing him in."

To Jake's surprise, the young Chinese brought to him was bound hand and foot. Two Anglos walked on either side, one of them carrying a gun. Where had he gotten a gun? They were strictly controlled by Mira Corp.

The bound man had wild black hair and a surly expression. He glared at Jake. *Would kill me if he were loose,* Jake realized. He didn't recognize the captive.

"This is Yenmo Kang . . . I mean, Kang Yenmo. He's one of the three dissidents that Julian Martin abducted from Hope of Heaven."

That *Julian* abducted? Jake glanced scornfully at Star Chu, but she was staring at Kang. Her small red mouth pursed and her eyes sneered. She hated Kang . . . or else she was a better actor than even Duncan Martin.

Star continued, "The Hope of Heaven dissidents have not gone far away, Mr. Holman. Most are hiding just a few miles from Mira, scattered in small pockets. They contacted me because my cousin is with them. She's always been . . . that doesn't matter. Chu Corporation is not in agreement with violence. But I said I would listen to her, partly because she's family and partly because the situation in Chinese Mira has gotten so bad. After I listened to her, I listened to Kang, and now you will listen, too." She looked at Kang with marked dislike.

Kang said, "I talk to you only out of a desire for justice. You are all despicable. You, Star Chu, are a traitor to your people, a tool wielded by the Anglos and Arabs for their own riches. You, Jake Holman, are a worn-out exploiter who can never outlive the destruction you've caused. Hope of Heaven is trying to restore dignity and pride to the Chinese on Greentrees, and we will do whatever is necessary!"

Jake said, his voice stronger than he'd dared hope, "Forget the

rhetoric, Kang. I heard it a hundred years ago in a hundred different languages. What do you have to say that's new?"

"This," Kang said, black eyes blazing. "Wong Yat-Shing, Wu Po,
and I did not escape from Hope of Heaven with the help of wild
Furs, as all you Anglo-Arabs seem to believe. We were abducted by
Julian Martin's soldiers. And they would have killed us if we hadn't
killed them first."

Jake said scornfully, "Do you expect me to believe that three
Greenie kids killed armed Terran soldiers? You're not talking to another provincial, son. I'm *from* Terra."

Some of Kang's disdain fell away. Abruptly he sat on a bare cot,
facing Jake at eye level. His face glowed with sullen sincerity.

"It didn't happen that way. I'm going to start from the beginning, so you know it all. Julian Martin is trying to take over Mira
City, and he used Hope of Heaven to do it."

"So you believe," Jake said.

"It's true!" Kang said, and for just a moment Jake saw how
young he really was. "When we attacked Mira during the first evacuation, the drill, Nan Frayne and her fucking Furs stopped us. That
part's true. But they only did it because Julian Martin stationed
them there. His so-called scientists—and you should ask your own
scientists, Mr. Holman, how much 'research' those Terrans have actually shared since they got here—made contact with the wild
Furs. That's how the Frayne woman even knew there was an evacuation of Mira City. Fur spears work when nothing electronic will,
so Martin posted them in Mira hoping we'd attack. Right after that
you poor dupes all made him defense admin, didn't you? He
gained a lot of power from stopping us."

Jake said coldly, "There's no way Nan Frayne would cooperate
with Julian Martin. Let alone get wild Furs to help Mira. They
don't give a fucking fart about us."

"But Nan Frayne cares about those Furs. In return for her help
during the evacuation, Martin gave the Furs laser guns to use against
the Cheyenne."

Jake stared.

"That's right, Holman. I'm surprised you haven't heard about it already. Furs are killing Cheyenne with laser guns, made by his Terrans at a secret place about thirty miles from Mira. I've seen it . . . from a distance, anyway. Laser guns aren't hard to make and the parts are easily available on the black market."

Black market. Of course Mira City was large enough to have a black market. Jake should have realized it long ago, would have realized it if he weren't so feeble. He must tell Alex.

"Pay attention, Holman," Kang said. "Don't crash on me. After the evacuation drill, Hope of Heaven was watched night and day by Martin's new army. There were guards on Wong, Wu, and me night and day. Do you really think primitive Furs could get us away from Martin? His own men abducted us and they used Fur weapons to kill those two deluded Anglo-Arab 'soldiers' so it would look like Furs did it. And right after that you bastards in Mira voted to give Martin unlimited military rule."

"If Martin's Terrans had wanted to kill you, you'd be dead."

"We should be. That part was accident." Something behind his eyes shuddered slightly, an involuntary fear that Jake suddenly found convincing. "They got us out of Hope of Heaven walking and jammed us into a rover. All the Greenie soldiers were busy with their duties about the Fur ship coming in. The patrols were arranged so that nobody came near our house. I expected to die.

"But the rover malfunctioned when the EMP was set off, and we were still in Hope of Heaven. They must have mistimed something. The Terrans couldn't leave us in the dead rover, killed or not, without somebody eventually investigating when the Fur attack was over. So they pulled us out and made us march towards the river. Maybe they meant to let it carry our bodies away. Or maybe they were under orders to keep us alive in order to torture us for information."

Kang stopped and Jake saw him reliving it all: the weapons jammed against his head, the terrified forced march for the river.

"We were lucky, though. Some people had refused to evacuate. Someone in a house near the river saw what was happening, some true Chinese with honor and courage untouched by the corruption of Mira City. Three people ran out armed with anything: poles and garden hoes that were electronically inoperative and kitchen pans. *Pans.*"

Kang turned his head away briefly before resuming.

"The two Terrans weren't affected at all by the things thrown at them, of course. The Terrans turned and shot all three of them. A man, a woman, and a teenage girl. While the Terrans were briefly turned away, we jumped one of them. None of the Terrans expected *us* to attack—they have contempt for Greenies as fighters. So he wasn't prepared and we were lucky and killed him. Another one shot Wu. Wu's body turned into a shield for Wong and me, just long enough to get another Terran down. I wrestled with her for her gun, and I got it, and I killed her. The last Terran would have shot us both except that another Chinese had crept out of a house and he had a gun, too. The Terran swung around to shoot him and they killed each other. Then Wong and I ran."

Jake said nothing.

"I don't know what happened to any of the bodies. I guess Martin disposed of them all. Hope of Heaven was attacked by that mob from Mira because of the two Greenie kids Martin killed with spears, so it would have been easy to keep the Chinese deaths from Shanti and Cutler. Not that they'd have cared."

Star Chu said to Jake, "There's more, Mr. Holman. I have another source of information, another cousin. We Chinese are just as interrelated as the Cutlers, you know."

"I know," Jake said. He fought off dizziness.

"My cousin came to me weeks ago to tell me something. I didn't believe her then. She's old," Star said, and in the girl's voice Jake heard that the old were unbelievable, fanciful. "Also, sometimes not too . . . but I believe her now. She said . . ." The girl clenched her fists.

"Go on," Jake said.

"She said that during the first evacuation, the drill, she didn't leave Mira City. Most Chinese did leave, you know, the first time. We obeyed orders. But a lot stayed the second time. My old cousin hid in her *wei*. That's a kind of extra tiny room sprayed into foam-cast to hide in, often with hidden slits to see indoors and out by means of mirrors."

"A priest's hole," Jake said.

"A what?"

"Never mind."

"She was in there during the evac drill. She lived next door to Lau-Wah Mah. When the city was deserted, she saw a Terran carry out Mah's body, wrapped in a blanket or rug. He dropped it. Lau-Wah was a big man for a Chinese, and I guess Martin could only spare one person for this. The rug opened. An arm was torn off the body and the . . . the place between his legs all bloody."

Kang said, not without satisfaction, "The traitor had been tortured."

"He was a good man!" Star cried. She slapped Kang across the mouth. He lunged up but she shoved him back into the chair. Bound hand and foot, there was nothing he could do but sneer.

Star said to Jake, "I didn't believe my cousin then, like I told you. I thought that after Mah was found missing, she made up the story to get attention. She's like that. But after I heard from this piece of slime here . . . Mr. Holman, most Chinese in Mira City are not with the dissidents. We know we aren't treated as equals to Anglos or Arabs, but we have our own lives and our own businesses and we hope that in future generations we can change things. We do not believe in violence.

"But since Mah was taken and then his body deliberately left out so that people would think Hope of Heaven did it, and since the dissidents tried to burn Mira, and since Mary Pesci and Shanab Mesbah were killed . . . I don't think people like you know what it's like to be Chinese in Mira City. People shun us now. They whisper. Our kids get taunted in school and sometimes beat up. Arabs and

Anglos, except for Quakers, don't buy from our little businesses. Chu Corporation has had sales fall fifty percent. And we Chinese are afraid of what's to come. That mob marched only on Hope of Heaven, but Chinese Mira could be next.

"And Julian Martin is causing it! That's what you must see. This piece of shit here is at least right about that. Martin kills and manipulates in order to get power, and it's worked. He controls Greentrees. You must tell Alex Cutler and Mayor Shanti."

Clearly this girl didn't know that Alex was sleeping with Julian. "If you believe all this is true, Star, why don't you tell her yourself?"

"She's watched by that Terran bodyguard. If any Chinese got near her . . . I don't think I could get near her. But you live with her. And they're not watching you."

Of course not, Jake thought. He was too old and ineffective to worry about, unless Julian or anybody else happened to want a bit of historical information. Otherwise Jake mostly slept and drooled and stayed indoors, away from everything, which is why he hadn't even been aware of Mira's thriving black market . . . but why had he been so easily swayed by Julian Martin?

He was so tired.

Star said, "Do you believe me, Mr. Holman? Do you believe Kang?"

Jake said slowly, "I don't know. You have no real proof."

She cried, "But why else would wild Furs have helped Mira during the evacuation drill and then killed Mary Pesci and Shanab Mesbah during the real attack? Don't you see how Julian Martin has done everything to get control of Greentrees?"

"I need to think about all this, Star." And then, with deliberate pathos, "I'm an old man and very tired."

She said at once, "Of course you're tired. We'll take you back now. And when you've thought about it, you'll tell Alex Cutler. I know you're still the sharpest and most experienced mind in Mira."

Irrationally warmed by her praise—this girl was pretty good at manipulation herself—Jake let the tape again be put over his mouth and eyes. He would never be able to identify the big man who had lifted him. He felt himself being laid carefully on the floor of the rover, but he didn't feel the ride into Mira. By that time he was already asleep.

20

THE AVERY MOUNTAINS

Karim blinked at his first view of the inflatable.

From the outside it had appeared to be standard research-camp living quarters as he remembered them from fifty years ago: dull green, quick to erect, durable. Inside it was unrecognizable. The plastic walls and floor had all but disappeared under pelts and woven blankets. A small drum lay on its side, ornamented with feathers. Baskets held handmade tools and various dried foods. Somewhere outside someone was grilling meat; the smell made Karim's empty stomach growl.

Two braves sat in a corner, smoking. They rose quickly when the captives were brought in.

"We found them in the upland meadow," a captor said.

"An odd place for love," the oldest brave said. "And you didn't let them put on their clothes?"

"They weren't doing sex. They had no clothes."

The elder frowned. He had bright red hair and, under his suntan and wrinkles, the trace of freckles. Most of the Cheyenne in the First Landing, Karim remembered Jake telling him, had not actually come from that ethnic group at all. They were people rich enough to afford space passage who nonetheless wanted to live like primitives. Their blood had been American, Irish, German, English, Italian, all the defunct countries of the UAF. A few had even been Chinese.

None of this had made any sense to Karim. Without your place in the family, in the generations of the medina, how could you really know who you were?

"Who are you?" the elder asked.

"I am Karim Mahjoub and this is Lucy Lasky. Have you ever heard of us?"

"No."

"We're from the First Landing. We've been out in space," Karim said desperately.

Carefully the brave studied Karim, then Lucy. Finally he said, "They're crazy. Put them with the others."

Their captors motioned them out. Lucy stopped defiantly and plucked a pelt from a basket by the door. "I need this to cover myself, all right?"

The elder nodded and she took two pelts, handing one to Karim.

They were marched toward a smaller inflatable, probably originally supply storage. Inside on a bed of pelts sat two men and a woman, all bound. They stared at Lucy and Karim.

"You're not Cheyenne," one man said. He was small, blond, and intense. The other man was both younger and larger, obviously unshaven for at least a week. The woman was Chinese.

"No," Karim said as he and Lucy were pushed down to sit with the others. A brave bound their hands and feet and then the Cheyenne left. Five prisoners crowded the available space. Everyone jostled to find enough room.

"I'm Jon McBain, an energy researcher for Mira Corp," the blond man said. "This was my research station until we were taken over by those archaic lunatics out there."

Karim said, without hope, "I'm Karim Mahjoub and this is Lucy Lasky. Have you ever heard of—"

"Oh my God," McBain said. "Is it really you? Are you back?"

Karim lay bound in the darkness, unable to sleep. They had been fed, fish and game and some sort of fat mixed with dried fruit that had actually tasted pretty good. Karim and Lucy had gobbled ravenously, their hands untied long enough for that purpose, under watchful guard. Karim's belly stretched taut and full.

But not as full as his mind. Jon McBain and his two techs, Kent Landers and Kueilan Ma, had questioned him about his mission: had he really deposited the infected Furs in space? Had they been picked up by other Furs? Was it actually working, the Vine strategy to render their ancient enemy harmless?

Yes, and yes, and I don't know, Karim had said. And then McBain had told him there was a Fur ship in orbit, poised to attack Greentrees.

"No," Karim said, "it's a Vine ship! They sent us down first in . . . never mind. Does Jake Holman think it's a Fur ship? They might try to shoot it down with the *Beta Vine*! I have to get to him and tell him those are Vines upstairs!"

"We don't know what's happening in Mira City," McBain said. "The Cheyenne took over this camp a week ago and of course their moronic philosophy doesn't permit comlinks or MiraNet. We've had no news."

Dr. Shipley, Karim remembered, hadn't thought the Cheyenne moronic. *"They are interested in the sources of life,"* he'd told Karim once, *"and in living as close to it as they can. Of all the Plains Indians, the Cheyenne were the most high-minded."* It hadn't seemed high-minded to Karim, the scientist, back then, and it didn't now.

"I have to get to Mira City to tell Jake Holman!" he said to McBain.

"Mr. Holman? I don't think that's who you want, Mahjoub. He's an old man, and since his last stroke, I hear, not competent."

Jake Holman an old man. His last stroke.

Karim said with some difficulty, "Who runs Mira Corp?"

"You've been gone—what?—about forty years? A lot has happened."

The three scientists spent the next two hours taking turns relating the history of Greentrees. Long after everyone else slept, Karim lay awake trying to digest it all. Gail Cutler and George Fox and Dr. Shipley all dead. Nan Frayne living wild with Furs at war with the

Cheyenne. Julian Martin. Mira City evacuations. Defense plans and allocations. Hope of Heaven. Dissidents and rebellion. Arson and murder.

It was a long time before Karim could even doze, and his last thought before he did was, *I must get to Mira in time to tell them the ship in orbit is Vines, not Furs. I must get to Mira . . .*

21

MIRA CITY

Jake couldn't decide if he believed Star Chu and Yenmo Kang.

Star had brought him back to Alex's apartment; he woke in his own bed. His nurse, Cal Johnson, staggered in at dawn, looking happy and dazed. Jake had refused breakfast or a bath and Cal had fallen into the deep sleep of the sex-sated young. Alex, presumably, was in a similar state at Julian Martin's. Jake lay under a warm blanket, cold seeping down his spine.

If Star and Kang had told him the truth, Julian Martin was a monstrous tyrant who wanted to rule Greentrees as dictator and was well on the way to doing so. Jake had no trouble believing in the possibility. He was experienced enough with evil to recognize how far it could go, as Alex and Ashraf and the rest of these native-born Greenies were not. Julian Martin could destroy Mira in the name of ruling it. It had happened often enough on Earth.

In fact, it had almost happened on Greentrees. Forty years ago Rudy Scherer, Mira's security chief, had tried to exterminate the Vines despite Jake's orders to the contrary. Scherer had been driven by xenophobic paranoia, not by a desire for power, but Jake still should have remembered how easily military could go rogue. God, wouldn't he ever learn? Wouldn't any of them ever learn?

If it was true, then Martin had achieved enormous power in a short time. He had, if the Chinese youngsters were right, eliminated the one leader opposed to him, Lau-Wah Mah. Had eliminated Guy

Davenport's security force as anything but an auxiliary to his own Terran-led army. Had eliminated distrust of himself by the old tactic of setting minor local enemies against each other and then becoming a hero by restoring peace. Had eliminated MiraNet during crucial periods. Had eliminated the ship in orbit. Had eliminated the *Beta Vine,* leaving his own ship the *Crucible* the only warship around.

On the other hand, every one of those actions could be viewed as legitimate steps in a strong defense of Mira City.

Star and Kang might have fed Jake an artfully constructed story, one whose horrifying parts hung together for their own purposes. The Chinese felt abused and discriminated against, enough so to spawn Hope of Heaven. Wong Yat-Shing hated Mira. Even those Chinese who were not dissidents, Star said, felt apart from the Anglos and Arabs who mostly ran Greentrees. So ordinary Chinese citizens only needed to stand aside while dissidents created revolution from which their entire group would benefit. That, too, had happened often enough on Earth.

Should Jake tell all this to Alex and Ashraf?

He was under no illusions about either of them. Ashraf was a mild, amiable, diffident man who occupied the position he did because the Arabs of Mira City wanted him to. The Arabs and the vast Cutler family were Greentrees' richest people. They, along with the Quakers and Jake himself, had financed most of the First Landing and had owned most of the original colony. Jake was old, the Quakers did not mix in politics, and the Cutler family, scientific backbone of Greentrees, were much outnumbered by the Arabs. Ashraf Shanti was a figurehead whose individual integrity had never been tested because there had never been any divide between his own beliefs and the medina.

Alex was more complex.

She was capable, warm, generous, intelligent but not shrewd. An idealist, grown in the nurturing agar of Mira's long peace. And although as tray-o her job was to allocate resources, which she did very well, at heart she was not a person who counted costs. When something genuinely mattered to her, she committed utterly.

Jake remembered a conversation he'd had with her a few years ago. She had just become tray-o, put in the position in pretty much the same way Ashraf had, by her family's influence. She'd been telling Jake her plans for resource allocation. He, who had once long ago been a lawyer, listened, and said, "Your view of power is too maternal, Alex."

"Power? Maternal?"

"Tray-o is an inherently powerful position. By controlling resource allocation, you essentially control what gets done. You want to use power to nurture, to foster scientific and material growth wherever you think it should happen."

"Of course," she said, bewildered.

"A more accurate view of power was held by the Founding Fathers of old America. They—"

"Who?"

"It doesn't matter. These men put together a government that later became the basis for the whole United Atlantic Federation on Terra. Very important. That government was based on a view of power much different from your maternal nurturing. James Madison once said that the only way to keep order was to set ambition against ambition, interest against interest, as checks on each other."

Alex had said instantly, "I don't believe that."

"I know," Jake had said. "But you should. They were realists, Madison and Jefferson and Adams."

Since then, Alex had not changed. She still committed utterly, without reserve.

How much did Julian Martin matter to her?

How much compared to Mira City?

Were Star Chu and Yenmo Kang telling the truth?

Jake went around and around with it in his mind, and could see no clear answer. His head ached. He needed to get to the bathroom.

It was hard to do by himself, but possible. Laboriously he dragged himself from bed to wheelchair.

After the bathroom, he wheeled his old chair—the damn thing was sticking again—to the table, cut himself some bread, and spread it with caliberry jam. The knife trembled in his fingers. He tried to be careful; all he needed now was a bloody hand. Maybe the food would revive him enough to think more. On the cot against the wall, which had once been Alex's cot, Jake's nurse slept on, Katous on top of him. This new nurse, Cal Johnson, could sleep through a typhoon. Ah well, one had to take what one could get.

Jake was just finishing his meal, sticky jam on his chin and blanket, when Duncan Martin entered without knocking.

"Go away," Jake said. One of the few good things about being old was that you could abandon courtesy. "Go rehearse something."

"I must talk to you alone," Duncan said.

It got Jake's attention. No quips, no quotes, no specious "My dear man." Even that genemod actor's voice seemed muted, its thrilling tones not projected for self-aggrandizement. Duncan wore brown Threadmores, as if he'd tried to pass through the city unnoticed, and it wasn't even quite dawn.

Jake said, curious despite himself, "My nurse is asleep."

"Not good enough. And I don't want to be seen through the window. Come with me."

He grasped Jake's chair, wheeled him into the bedroom, and closed the door and window. Jake had dragged the bedclothes to the floor when he transferred himself, unaided, to his chair. Duncan let them lie and sat on the edge of the bed.

"Jake, I learned last night that Julian has armed the wild Furs against the Cheyenne."

Jake kept his face as blank as he could.

"How did you learn that?"

"One of my actors is a tech at that water-thing building by the river. He heard it from a scientific friend who comlinked from some remote place far south where a geologic survey of some kind is going on. This woman and her party came across a Cheyenne encampment full of corpses tied up in tanglefoam. They had apparently starved to death."

"Rumors," Jake said. "Thirdhand hearsay." His heart began to thud in his breast.

"Perhaps. But these naive people are so *truthful.*"

Jake said carefully, "Even if it's true, why do you think Julian was the one to arm the Furs and not, say, Hope of Heaven?"

Duncan's voice went flat. "Because I have seen it all before."

Jake forced himself to silence. If you waited long enough, most people would talk.

"Jake," Duncan finally said, leaning forward, "I have struggled with this. I know you don't believe me. Actor, sham, egoist, clown. I know what you think of me. However, those attributes have kept me alive and prosperous in a hellish Terra you cannot even begin to imagine."

Jake said quietly, "Don't be so sure."

Duncan got up and began to pace the tiny room. Three steps in one direction, five in the other. He didn't seem to realize he trampled Jake's bedclothes beneath his muddy boots.

"My choices were to leave Earth with Julian or be killed by his enemies if I stayed behind. They would have torn me and everybody else even faintly connected with him into screaming shreds. He was that hated. His Third Life Alliance did things to stay in power—"

A memory, fifty years old, stirred in Jake: *Third Life Alliance in charge in Geneva. War continues.* The last quee message Greentrees had ever received from Earth. "War against who?" Gail Cutler had asked, and no one had had an answer.

"—and I'll give you details if you like. Julian had control of bioweapons, secret police, a nuclear arsenal. He used them all."

"I don't need details," Jake said. A part of his mind was numb, he realized. A part was concerned with stupid fixations: Why were Duncan's boots muddy on a dry morning? His mind was protecting itself from full comprehension, and the implications of full comprehension.

"I hoped . . ." Abruptly Duncan stopped pacing. "Oh, what didn't I hope? That Julian had learned better. That he genuinely wanted a new start. I saw that his love for your pretty little planet was genuine, and maybe even his love for Alex. And so I hoped . . . When your Chinese consul's body turned up tortured, that looked like Julian. Still, I wasn't sure because, after all, there was Hope of Heaven. I was a fool—'Here's that which is too weak to be a sinner.' But now Julian's arming one group against another, as he's done so many times before. He has reinvented himself so many times that my poor acting is nothing next to it. Our name isn't even 'Martin,' let alone anything as aristocratic as 'Julian Cabot.' He was born Cai Fields in—did you hear that?"

"I don't hear anything," Jake managed to say.

"It was . . . oh gods! Old man, if you value your life pretend you're a vegetable, go slack and spastic, go—"

The bedroom door opened.

Duncan's body blocked Jake's view, but he knew what was happening even before he heard Julian's quiet voice. "Duncan."

"Julian! Oh God, I'm so glad you're here, I found Jake like this! Help me to—"

"An actor still. I commend you. But your skill is wasted. I know what you're doing here."

"Paying a call on Jake. But I found him like this! And his nurse is passed out, drunk maybe—"

Duncan moved aside. Jake lay flaccid in his chair, mouth open, eyes staring. Drool had accumulated on his chin and dampened his clothes. As quietly as he could, he let his bladder go.

Julian stepped around his brother. Jake glimpsed the armed men beyond him, in the main room, and knew Cal was already dead.

"Jake?" Julian said softly. "Are you acting for my benefit? Have you been taking lessons from my traitor brother?"

Jake willed himself to lie flaccid, staring, his right hand trembling only slightly.

Julian stepped closer. Jake sensed the moment that Julian smelled urine, and then feces. That handsome genemod nose twitched. He stared hard another long moment, then turned back to Duncan.

"So the stroke is genuine. But you didn't know about it before you chose to visit at this strange hour and by that devious river route. I never would have thought it of you. My own brother. My mistake," Julian said tonelessly.

"Cai, I swear—"

Duncan's body crumpled. Jake smelled burning human flesh.

"Dissolve the body and get the residue out of here with the nursemaid's," Julian said. "Hanson, code seventeen."

"Yes, sir. And that one?"

"No danger. Petrovski, make sure there are no signs we were here. Don't slip up."

"Yes, sir."

Julian left. Jake watched helplessly, twitching and drooling, sitting in his own wastes, as Petrovski wheeled him through the doorway. Behind him, Petrovski sprayed every inch of the room and bedclothes with a fine mist from a canister on his belt. Genemod selective enzymes, Jake guessed. They would eat every molecule that could possibly have come from a fingerprint, mud, hair, or whatever else they were engineered for. The only clue left behind would be the total absence of human passage, and Guy Davenport's colonial security force did not have the tech to detect that void. It had never been needed.

When Petrovski had finished, he closed the bedroom door silently. Now he would remove Jake and then spray the other room, where Duncan Martin and Cal Johnson had already been "dissolved" to "residue."

Jake struggled to breathe shallowly. His shit and piss smelled terrible. He was alive only because of Duncan's warning. Now he must stay alive, must continue to appear stroke-damaged enough so that Julian didn't hear otherwise, must tell Alex and Ashraf . . .

But he couldn't think clearly how to do that. All he could think of was Duncan's muddy boots. They were muddy because the actor had come stealthily along the river, trying to avoid public notice.

But Julian's men had been following him. Duncan had not realized his own brother would put him under surveillance. He had trusted Julian at least that far; Julian had not trusted him; Julian's cynicism had won.

Jake had to get to Alex.

22

THE AVERY MOUNTAINS

Karim's Cheyenne captors were apparently unacquainted with boredom. Scrupulous in feeding their captives, in taking them outside for piss breaks, even in allowing them an hour or so a day of supervised exercise, the Cheyenne nonetheless made no effort to relieve the boredom of sitting tied down day after day in a darkened inflatable with nothing to do. Nor would they answer any questions.

The Cheyenne themselves were always busy: hunting, smoking meat, scouting. At night they beat on drums and danced, or so it sounded to Karim, sleepless on the other side of the plastic wall.

"Until you came we were bored out of our minds," Jon McBain said to Lucy. Karim suspected that Lucy and possibly Kent still were. But Jon and the other tech, Kueilan, filled the time by encapsulating for Karim every advance in science since Karim had left decades ago. He listened eagerly, longing for a screen, or even pencil and paper.

But always Karim's thoughts returned to the ship in orbit. He had to tell Mira City that the ship was Vine, not Fur. He had to obtain for the Vines upstairs the death flowers they had come for. McBain, on the other hand, seemed never to think about the ship, the war, the Cheyenne, or imminent death. He talked excitedly and practically nonstop. Eventually he came to his own work.

"—when Alex Cutler renewed the allocation for the microbial battery. But then we discovered something so amazing I put the battery aside for the last months. Mira doesn't understand about pure research, the tray-o isn't a scientist after all, but for *this* . . . We found a unique biomass six, Karim. I know you're not a biologist, but it's an apparently huge cache of underground anaerobic bacteria producing completely novel molecules. The amazing part is a pole inserted inside the biomass began vibrating with enough repeated sequences that we hooked it to a computer. There are enough variations and a high enough signal-to-noise ratio that I think it's non-random process, a crystallization of some sort that we—"

"What did you say?" Karim demanded.

"I said a crystallization of a new—"

"Before that!"

Jon stared at Karim in the gloom. "Why?"

"Tell me again about the biomass."

Jon did. Lucy and Karim looked at each other. Finally Karim said, "I need to see that pit, Jon."

"It's not an open pit, it's a hidden biomass two clicks down that—why?"

"I'm not sure," Karim said slowly, "but it may be that the signal repetition isn't crystallization. It may be that it's communication."

"Communication? From *what*, for God's sake?"

Carefully, trying to control his own wild surmises, Karim told him.

23

MIRA CITY

When Alex woke in Julian's apartment, he was still not there. He hadn't returned at all during the night. That was unusual but not unprecedented; he was often away from Mira City on inspection of other defenses. Still, it was disappointing. Her body ached for him.

She padded to the bathroom, washed and dressed, and headed for a commissary. Julian never had anything to eat in his apartment. Food didn't interest him, except as a necessary fuel.

The morning was clear and fresh, a perfect purple Mira day. Dew still clung to the bright yellow petals on temlillies planted around the foamcast commissary. Inside, cheerful clatter and the scents of hot food met Alex. She showed her Mira Corp card, selected her breakfast, and sat alone at a table against the far wall, pondering why Hope of Heaven had armed the wild Furs against the Cheyenne.

"Hello, Alex," a Mira maintenance crew called, on their way out after breakfast. "Beautiful day." She waved at them.

Hope of Heaven would have nothing to gain from arming the wild Furs.

"Alex, maybe you could comb your hair one of these mornings," called an old school friend, also on her way out. She smiled and waved.

In fact, no one had anything to gain from arming wild Furs. Except, perhaps, Nan Frayne. Had that passionate and enigmatic old woman succeeded in an underhanded deal of some sort? But last evening Alex had talked to the gun manufacturer, Michael Lin, for a long time, and she believed him innocent. They'd gone to the warehouse and his inventory sheets tallied with both her inspection and the reports she had from his raw-material suppliers; no weapons were unaccounted for. Besides, what could Nan Frayne possibly offer in return?

A commotion arose beside the door. It spread from table to table. People gasped, rose, rushed out. Siddalee Brown pushed her way in and ran ponderously to Alex.

"Where've you been? There's another ship!"

"Another ship? A *third* ship?"

"Yes! Probes picked it up. Where's your comlink?"

Alex had forgotten it in Julian's bed, a measure of how disappointed she'd been by his absence. She stood unsteadily.

"Siddalee . . . where's Julian?"

Siddalee said accusingly, "He's giving the evacuation signal for Mira, since you weren't around to do it."

The siren started then, in blasting waves.

They won't go a third time, Alex thought with despairing clarity. People got tired of alarms, especially alarms that had so far resulted in no damage to Mira City except that caused by leaving it.

She pushed past Siddalee and dashed for the door. Outside, her fears were confirmed. Many people rushed for their designated transport to the end points, carrying ready-go bundles and children. But many people did not. These stood in small angry knots, gesticulating wildly. Over the sirens Alex couldn't hear what anyone said.

Her Terran bodyguard materialized beside her.

"I don't need—oh, fuck it!" Julian's apartment was nowhere near as close to the Mausoleum as her own. Alex was panting by the time she reached the huge ugly building. The Terran, damn him, wasn't even sweating. Alex thought of checking on Jake; her place was only a few steps away. But there was no time. And Jake had probably already left with Cal Johnson for his evac transport.

This time, the rover, her designated transport, was still housed in its inflatable. Her two techs, Natalie and Ben, waited impatiently inside. "Alex, where were you? We were just about to leave!"

"I'm here now. Ben, you drive. And give me your comlink . . . Julian?"

"Where were you?" his cool voice asked. "You didn't answer. And where are you now?"

"I'm on my way to my bunker. What do we know?"

"Is Captain Lewis with you?"

"Yes! *What do we know?*"

"Another McAndrew Drive ship, picked up by a probe beyond Cap. The probe stopped signaling seconds later, so I presume they destroyed it."

Now she heard something in his voice: too much coolness. He was shaken. He hadn't expected this.

None of them had expected this.

She said, "Why didn't this Fur ship arrive together with the first one? An armada?"

"I don't know. We have less than an hour."

Ashraf's voice said, "Alex, a lot of people in the medina aren't leaving. They just don't . . ." He couldn't find the right word.

Alex said grimly, "A lot of people outside the medina aren't leaving either, from what I saw. I'm going to use MiraNet to try to persuade them."

"Don't let it interfere with your primary duties of securing the infrastructure," Julian said.

Ashraf said, with the only malice Alex had ever heard from him, "This time we don't have an expendable warship to fight with."

"No," Julian said, so calmly that Alex thought perhaps Ashraf's comment hadn't been malicious after all. She had just heard it that way.

No one came near Jake during the chill hours before dawn.

He sat in his chair in the bedroom, afraid to move because he couldn't tell if Julian's men had all left. The darkness stretched on and on, and Jake drowned in his thoughts. It felt like that—as if every sentence of Duncan's that Jake remembered was a fresh flood, smothering him.

"Because I have seen it all before."

"He was that hated. His Third Life Alliance did things to stay in power—"

"When your Chinese consul's body turned up tortured . . ."

And then, mixed in with Duncan's words to Jake, Duncan's words on the stage in his resonant actor's voice:

> *"'And oftentimes, to win us to our harm,*
> *The instruments of darkness tell us truths,*
> *Win us with honest trifles, to betray's*
> *In deepest consequence.'"*

Jake, no less than Alex and Ashraf, had believed everything Julian told them. Jake, who had also seen it all before on Terra, and who should have known better. Jake had let that instrument of darkness tell Greentrees truths about her shoddy defenses, in order to win Greentrees to betrayal. And Greentrees had responded. *"'In deepest consequence.'"*

Jake, sitting in the theater, had thought at the time that Duncan was playing his Macbeth directly to Julian, wanting to impress his powerful brother. Now he realized that it had been Alex that Duncan played to. Warning her. Futile as warning a falling rock about gravity.

But he, Jake, should have seen. *"'In deepest consequence.'"*

When pale light finally fell into the window, he decided that Julian's men must have gone. Painfully Jake rolled his chair to the bedroom door, opened it, and peered out.

Nothing.

His bread and jam still sat on the table. The knife lay where he'd put it down when Duncan Martin had come in. Katous sat preening himself in the middle of the table. Alex's jacket was flung over a chair. The cot where Cal Johnson had snored stood empty, the bedclothes rumpled.

Jake leaned forward and peered past his own knees. No stains of any kind on the floor to show where two bodies had lain.

Had it all really happened?

He closed his eyes, made himself breathe steadily. Should he open the outer door? If Julian had left a guard, Jake's cover of stroke-induced imbecility would be gone. But why would Julian leave a guard? He believed Jake no threat, and Alex was with him.

At the thought of Alex in the bed of that bastard Jake felt red fury pulse through his brain. He fought it back. He needed to think as clearly as he could.

He would risk the door.

He got it open, struggling with his weak arms. Finally flinging the damn door wide, he inched his chair outside. Later than he thought; the sun had risen in a clear sky. People walked past on the way to the day's work.

"Help!" Jake cried as loud as he could. "Help—" A siren drowned him out.

The evacuation siren.

Now fury did take him. What was that fucking monster Julian doing now? Not for a minute did Jake believe that another ship had appeared in the Greentrees star system. It was a trick, a ruse like all Julian's others, to gain power and—

The siren went on and on, coming from the Mausoleum a few buildings away. Jake clapped his hands over his ears. Everything in him quivered with sensitivity, with age, with achiness. He had to get to Alex—

"Mr. Holman!" a large woman cried, halting in front of him. "Where's your nurse?" Siddalee Brown, Alex's assistant.

He couldn't make himself heard over the siren. Siddalee dashed inside, returned a minute later, and screamed, "Where's your nurse? You—"

The siren ceased. There would be thirty seconds of silence before it began again. Siddalee grabbed the arm of a teenage girl rushing past. "You! Get this man to the Sector Six tram and go with him to the end point!"

"But I—"

"I don't care where you're assigned! Now you're going with Mr. Holman!"

The girl's eyes widened. "Is that really Mr. Holman? All right!"

Siddalee rushed off. Jake grabbed the girl's arm. "Listen, I must find Alex Cutler. She—"

The siren started again.

The girl rushed into the apartment and appeared a moment later with Jake's ready bundle and Katous. She dumped both onto Jake's lap, along with her own ready bundle. "Can't leave your pet!" she yelled cheerfully and set off pushing his chair at nearly a run. Jake clung desperately to the arm's chair. Katous leaped off. A brief stop while the girl scooped him up and dumped him into her bundle sack, loosely knotting the ends. Katous yowled and clawed.

"Stop!" Jake cried. It did no good. The girl, her eyes bright with excitement, was determined to rescue him and the cat. They sped toward his designated transport and the hospital cave.

The siren screamed.

The first hour in her command bunker passed so swiftly that to Alex it seemed like a few minutes. She gave dozens of orders, starting on Ben's comlink during the top-speed trip in the rover. She received dozens of reports, formulated instant strategies, squeezed in two MiraNet pleas to evacuate. Once they arrived at the bunker, her techs worked frantically to monitor and verify. And all the while at the side of her mind Ashraf's words crouched like a patient predator: *This time we don't have an expendable warship.*

Julian's ship, the *Crucible,* had no McAndrew Drive. If it came out of hiding on the other side of the planet, it would be destroyed long before it could get close enough to fire. Would the defenses that Greentrees did have be enough?

Her tech said, "All research stations reported in except Jon McBain's, at the Avery Mountains. I can't comlink them at all."

"Keep trying," Alex said.

"Enemy vessel four hundred thousand clicks out, sir, and decelerating," said the expressionless voice of Julian's lieutenant, on audio in Alex's bunker.

"Continue monitoring."

"Two hundred thousand clicks out, decelerating."

"Continue monitoring."

"One hundred thousand clicks . . . fifty thousand clicks . . . thirty-five point three thousand clicks out, deceleration complete, vessel in stable Greentrees orbit."

Then a suspended time, not long enough.

"Enemy shuttle launched, sir."

"Standby to fire EMP."

"Standing by to fire EMP . . . sir, shuttle trajectory mapped. It will not land within EMP target zone."

Alex's gaze flew to the graphic display. The tiny dot representing the shuttle was not headed for Mira City but for the high Avery Mountains, far to the southwest.

Ashraf cried, "What are they doing?"

"Avoiding us," Julian said. "They don't know what weapons we've got now."

"Sir, second shuttle launched . . . trajectory for Mira City . . . wait, it's too fast to be a shuttle . . ."

"Focus solar array!" Julian said. "Focus all ground missiles . . . Code twenty-two! Repeat, code twenty-two! Fire as possible!"

Alex's graphic display, slaved to Julian's, erupted. Yellow lines ran from the solar display to a point that intersected with the projected "shuttle" trajectory. More dots launched themselves from the ground. When had Julian put ground missiles taken off the *Crucible*—they had to be off the *Crucible*, Mira had nothing like that!—onto Greentrees? And why hadn't Alex known about it?

The nonshuttle moved too fast. The solar array yellow lines never intersected with it. A bewildering pattern of lines appeared on the display, while data flashed past. All Alex could see was that some of the lines connected to the ground patch that was Mira.

A second later a missile line connected with the nonshuttle. Both disappeared.

"What happened?" Alex cried. "What was that?"

The lieutenant's voice said, "Unmanned enemy launch destroyed, sir. Enemy beams, unknown type, made hits on Mira City prior to destruction. All our ground missile sites nonoperable. Enemy shuttle landed high in the mountains, coordinates to follow. Enemy vessel maintaining orbit."

There was more, terse communications back and forth between Julian and others, but Alex didn't hear it. *Enemy beams, unknown type, made hits on Mira City prior to destruction.*

Mira City . . .

All those people who didn't leave . . .

All those people . . .

"Alex. Alex."

She was pulled out of her temporary paralysis by the insistence of Julian's voice.

"Alex, stay with me. Make sure all end points slated to move into the wilderness are doing it, and allow any others who want to go to also do so. When shielded facilities report in, advise each of the situation and tell them to keep shields in place. I may still need to EMP."

"Yes," Alex said. "All right."

All those people. Her people.

She set to work numbly, focusing on a few clear facts. The Furs were here. This time there was no doubt it was Furs. They'd destroyed much of Mira City. How much? Julian's security force in Mira would tell him. Her job was the people who had evacuated.

All those people.

24

THE AVERY MOUNTAINS

Karim and Jon McBain couldn't get near the biomass pole. The Cheyenne took them for their daily exercise to a different part of the upland meadow, standing guard as the captives, wrists still bound but ankles free, were permitted to walk or run in circles. Jon sped around at top speed, usually until he exhausted himself. Lucy, Karim, and Kent jogged, Karim feeling like a fool in the Cheyenne animal pelt that was still his only clothing. Kueilan didn't run. Instead she used her brief freedom to go through graceful yogalike contortions, her slim body bending so far backward that her long, filthy braid lay in loops on the ground. All of them smelled horrible, although it was only after the exercise period in the clean outside air that Karim really noticed their collective reek.

One day Jon took off toward the biomass pole at a dead run. He was easily, contemptuously caught, and all five captives were dumped back inside their inflatable.

"That was stupid," complained Kent. "I wanted to run more!"

"And what could you have accomplished anyway, Jon?" asked Kueilan reasonably. "The Cheyenne took away the computer. There's nothing but the pole sticking up from the ground."

"I don't know," Jon admitted sheepishly. "I just couldn't stand it anymore. Why are they even holding us here anyway? If we're hostages, for what and from who?"

"Well, I wish that brave hadn't been so rough," Kueilan said, rubbing her arm. "I'm going to have a bruise where they grabbed me."

Lucy said thoughtfully, "They're not usually rough. In fact, they usually don't touch us at all."

"They usually don't have some idiot like Jon making a break for it toward a pole," Kueilan replied crossly.

"No," Lucy said. "I think it's more than that. The Cheyenne seemed . . . not agitated, because they're never that, but somehow more uneasy. And last night there was a different quality to that drumming and dancing, more—I don't know—more urgent."

"I didn't notice it," Kent said.

"You were asleep," Kueilan said. "And snoring."

Karim respected Lucy's human antennae. "What do you think it meant, Lucy?"

"I don't know. Bad news of some sort for the Cheyenne."

Jon said, "Maybe the war with the wild Furs is going badly for them."

"It could be."

Kent said, "Let's just hope they don't take it out on us."

Karim said, for perhaps the hundredth time, "I've got to get to Mira City and warn them that the ship upstairs is Vine, not Fur."

No one said aloud that by this time, with Julian Martin in charge, the ship upstairs might no longer be anything.

"Wake up!" Lucy cried. "Everybody wake up!"

Karim bolted upright. He heard it then: yelling so heart-stopping that instinctively he strained against his bonds. The human yelling was followed by even louder noises that clearly were not human.

"My God," whispered Jon. "What's happening out there?"

Kueilan said, "It could be a wild Fur attack."

The five of them sat there in the darkness, unable to see one another until Jon fumbled the powertorch on.

"Kent, can you see out the door?"

"No, I—"

The inflatable door ripped open. A wild Fur darted inside, spear raised high. Karim saw the thing clearly, teeth bared and crest raised. *I'm going to die*. He groped for Lucy's hand, hoping numbly that being impaled was quick, please Allah let it not take too long . . .

"*Karim?*" a voice said incredulously. "*Karim Mahjoub?*"

A wiry old woman dressed in animal pelts, her skin as rough as the pelts under cropped gray hair, her strong arms holding a spear, stared at Karim. "*Lucy? Lucy Lasky?*"

"Who . . . who . . ." Karim stammered.

"My God," Lucy whispered. "It's Nan Frayne."

Nan Frayne? But Nan was a girl, barely out of her teens, she'd gone with them and Jake on their first trip off-planet, Karim had seen her only . . .

Only thirty-nine years ago.

"So you're back," Nan said, amused. She'd regained her composure; Karim had not. "What a stupid place to turn up. Get out of here, all of you." She said something to the wild Fur, who vanished. The yelling outside had stopped. Nan bent and deftly cut their bonds, one after the other.

"What is—"

"War is. My people are avenging themselves."

Nan vanished from the inflatable. Pulling Lucy to her feet, Karim followed Kent outside.

It was a moonless night. But by the Cheyenne's fire, burning bright, Karim could clearly see the bodies. The braves lay where they had fallen, one holding a bow but the others unarmed. Karim smelled burning flesh.

Burning, not pierced.

Karim stumbled closer. The brave lay face upward, his eyes open. In the middle of his chest was a laser burn, smoking away the clothing in a neat round hole and burning through to the heart. Two wild Furs hovered just beyond the firelight. They held guns in their hands.

Nan Frayne smiled at him. She made a strange, alien noise in her throat, and the Furs moved toward the bodies.

"You don't want to see this," Nan said with malicious defiance to Karim and Lucy. "My Furs aren't human, remember. And they're carnivores. I suggest you follow the river downstream until you reach Mira City. You'll be all right. I've told the Furs not to touch you as long as you stick to the river. Our war isn't with you."

"You're insane," Lucy gasped to Nan.

She smiled again. "Better get going, little Lucy. Give my regards to Jake if he hasn't croaked yet."

Karim grabbed Lucy's hand and pulled her away. The five humans stumbled in the dark toward the river. Karim could hear it, rushing downhill beyond a dark strand of trees.

They had just reached the woods, scratched and torn from underbrush, when the entire research station lit up like day. Karim could just see startled Furs raise their heads from the bodies on the ground. Above, the source of the light but itself a black shape against the stars, a craft slid silently down the sky.

"A shuttle," Lucy breathed. "The Vines!"

"Or the Furs," Jon said. "The real ones. It—" He fell silent.

Karim strained his eyes into the darkness. Small branches crossed his field of vision, dark lacy lines. For the rest of his life he remembered what he saw next as seen through those twigs, as if the scene were indivisible from that intricate living mesh. As if it could somehow screen him.

The shuttle landed, egg shaped with a long flexible tail, as were both Fur and Vine shuttles. Instantly the door opened. Armed Furs strode out, completely clad in clear space suits. Karim had not, whenever he'd encountered Furs, ever seen them wear anything except weapon sashes. These warriors were dressed as if they feared vacuum—or contamination.

The wild Furs stood still for a long moment, eerily frozen by this, their first look at their cousins from another world, another infinitely more technologically advanced time. The two with laser guns dangled them limply by their furred sides. The ones with spears held them poised aloft, unmoving until it was too late.

One of the space Furs must have done something. Every wild Fur crumpled to the ground, Nan Frayne with them. Without so much as breaking stride, the Furs picked up their primitive kin and carried them into the shuttle. Nan Frayne they left on the ground.

The shuttle door closed.

Karim said shakily, "The infection worked. The Furs are in negative-pressure space suits so nothing can contaminate them. The ones we left must have infected others with the virus, or how would these Furs suspect that either wild Furs or humans might still be able to harm them with microbes? We did it, Lucy, the infection has reached more of the space Furs—"

The entire research camp disappeared.

The shuttle's flexible tail moved slowly in an encompassing arc, and as it went, everything before it disappeared. Inflatables, pole leading down to the biomass, foamcast buildings, Cheyenne tents, fire and drying racks and the dead braves. And the body of Nan Frayne. Gone, as if it never existed.

No one spoke.

The shuttle lifted, and it was halfway up the sky before Jon McBain gasped, "I . . . I never saw anything like that before!"

Karim said grimly, "We did. Fifty years ago the Furs destroyed all the wild Fur villages in the same way. I mean, the wild Furs that had been created to test other versions of the Vine viruses to render them passive. The space Furs called them 'blasphemies' and wiped them out and their villages just like that."

Kueilan gave a small moan. She said, "If they use that thing on Mira City . . ."

Jon demanded, "But they didn't destroy the wild Furs! Why not, if what you say is true and last time they destroyed all the 'blasphemies'?"

Karim was thinking as fast as he could. "Maybe because these aren't blasphemies. They were the Vines' control group. They're whole and sound and the Furs want them—"

"*Why?*"

It was Lucy who answered. "Maybe for breeding stock. Maybe the Vine plan worked really well and the virus is spreading across their home world and even their colonies! Maybe they plan to use those males to reach more females because they need a larger gene pool. They know that they didn't get the control group last time because so many wild Furs were off hunting, not in the village when the space Furs wiped it out. Maybe our plan worked!"

"I hope so," Karim said. "But now the space Furs are *here* again. They want their uninfected cousins and I'm afraid they want . . ." He couldn't say it.

"Greentrees," Lucy said. He saw that she was following his line of thought and that she had to say it aloud, for her own sake. To get it out of her vulnerable mind, like a dangerous predator flushed into the open.

"The space Furs want . . . want G-Greentrees. Because they know that the virus isn't here among the wild Furs. They can see that— the wild Furs aren't passive and helpless. And Greentrees has air the Furs can breathe, has enough shared DNA to colonize. It . . . it's rich and lush and mostly empty. It's a prime colonization world for . . . for this uninfected group of Furs. Except . . . except . . ."

"Except for us," Karim said. "Except for humans."

25

A HOSPITAL CAVE

The teenage girl whom Siddalee Brown had put in charge of Jake didn't accompany him to his evacuation end point, as Siddalee had told her to. Instead the girl brought him as far as his designated transport, the stripped-down tram, and turned him over to the civilian sector captain. "This is Mr. Holman, he goes on here, I still have time to get to my own transport!" she screamed cheerfully over the siren. "Be careful with him, there's something wrong with him! He drools!" She ran off, waving back over her shoulder, a young careless figure excited by the unusual.

Something wrong with him. He drools.

Jake realized all at once that he had been a fool to try to talk to the girl, to let her see he was coherent. He was supposed to have had a massive debilitating stroke, and after the evacuation—or during it—Julian's men might well check to make sure that was true. If it wasn't, Jake was as dead as Duncan.

He made himself go floppy in his chair, arms dangling over the side, face blank. Eyes empty. Jake Holman, himself, gone.

The sector captain, a woman he didn't know but who of course knew him, looked shocked. From the corner of his deliberately empty eyes, Jake saw tears come to hers. Tenderly she folded his arms across his lap, which made Katous, still in the bag where the girl had tied him, begin clawing and yowling all over again.

The sirens stopped, leaving a too-spacious silence.

"What is—a cat!" the captain said. "Oh, Mr. Holman, we can't bring any animals . . ." She looked at him again with that sorrowful tenderness and said softly, "Well, maybe for you an exception. Leanne! You come here and take charge of Mr. Holman. Tie him better in that chair and hold on to it . . . this tram's going to start in a minute. From now on he's your only patient, you hear me?"

"Yes, ma'am," said Leanne, another teenage girl. The evac team used whomever it could get.

Jake closed his eyes. How long was he going to have to pretend to be reduced to imbecility? The rest of his life? That wasn't a life.

If he didn't pretend to be brain-dead, he also wouldn't have a life past the moment Julian discovered Jake was coherent.

If that was a Fur ship coming in, none of them were going to have any life anyway.

"Let's go!" the captain shouted. A last patient on a hospital bed was hoisted onto the tram, and it started forward.

In the end-point cave nothing had changed. Jake couldn't believe he'd sat there just hours ago with Star Chu and Yenmo Kang. The same cots lined the rough stone walls; the same boxes of medical supplies and evac rations were stacked everywhere. But now the cots were occupied, the boxes being opened. People bustled by his chair. Somewhere behind him some poor soul wailed incessantly, in pain or outrage or bewilderment.

His new teenage nurse, Leanne, had parked Jake's chair against the cave wall just inside the safety line. He faced the cave entrance, close enough to smell the brush pulled hastily over it as camouflage. It would fool nobody on the ground but probably looked natural from the air. The brush smelled spicy and clean. Purplish leaves quivered in a slight breeze from outside. Katous, the moment he had been let out of his sack, had bolted through the brush and disappeared.

Leanne said to someone Jake couldn't see, "How do I feed Mr. Holman? Does he need a tube inserted?"

Please, no.

"I don't know," a male voice answered. "Try a spoon and see if the swallow reflex is still working."

A few minutes later Leanne spooned soysynth into Jake's mouth. "He can swallow," she called joyfully over the purposeful low din of patients and caretakers.

"Good. Get him on a cot . . . no, wait, he'll have to stay there a little longer. We got two extras from Mira, somehow. Anybody know what's happening there? Did Mohammed report in?"

"No," Leanne said. Her young voice turned worried. "But if he'd heard anything from Mira, he would have. I wish I knew what was happening back there."

So do we all. Finally a Fur attack, after nearly forty years of mostly desultory preparation, and Jake must play a semi-vegetable. What he must do was warn Alex about Julian, he had to get to Alex! He had to—

He fell asleep.

When he woke, he lay on a cot in the same position in the cave and it was night. A powertorch farther in lent only a dim gloom up here. The leaves rustled quietly, smelling of Greentrees' sweet night air, and he dreamed of Lucy Lasky, young as she had been fifty years ago, laying her cool thin hand on his old heart.

"Jake?" the dream said.

He mumbled something at the sweet lithe figure and smiled in his sleep.

"*Jake?*"

It wasn't a dream.

Jake gasped and struggled to sit up, forgetting that he was supposed to be incapacitated. "*Lucy?* How—"

"Karim and I are back. We—"

"What are you doing here?" someone said sharply. "Who are you? You're not authorized for this end point!"

"I'm . . . never mind. Get me the person in charge."

Leanne said eagerly, "Are you from Mira? Is the evac over?"

"I'm not from Mira. Who's in charge here?"

"I am." The sector captain appeared from the depths of the cave. "Who are you?"

"I'm Lucy Lasky. Karim Mahjoub and I are back from—"

The woman drew a quick sharp breath. She peered closer. "You are her, aren't you! Oh my God . . . My father talked all the time about your plan! Did it work? Are the Furs infected?"

"Yes. But there are some here on Greentrees who are not. I need to talk to Jake Holman and then this Julian Martin. The situation is desperate."

The captain said gently, "Ms. Lasky, talking to Mr. Holman . . . I'm sorry, but he's had a debilitating stroke. He can no longer hear you or respond."

"But—" Lucy began, and Jake put a hand on her thigh. Just a small movement, shielded from the others by Lucy's thin body, and if she didn't understand it then she would go to Julian and all of Greentrees could end up destroyed. One little movement of his hand, and everything depended on it, and fuck it to hell, life shouldn't be that way. But it was.

"I see," Lucy said, and her hand briefly pressed his.

Jake thanked the gods he didn't believe in.

"I'll just sit with him a while, if that's all right," Lucy said. "We knew each other a long time ago."

"Of course," the sector captain said. "You can't reach Commander Martin anyway until the comlinks are open again." She and Leanne and everyone else left them alone.

"Jake," Lucy whispered sorrowfully, "You . . ." She stopped, embarrassed.

"I'm old," he whispered. "What did you expect?"

She merely shook her head, a slight shape standing beside his cot in the gloom. With the light behind her, Jake couldn't see her face, but she might be able to make out his. Furrows, white skimpy hair, rheumy sunken eyes. Old.

She said, "I always loved you, you know. Even though I left with Karim."

"Don't try to make amends for age, Lucy," he said, and was shocked to hear amusement in his voice. "It can't be done. What is happening out there? No, don't look like you're conversing; I'm supposed to be an imbecile and I'm dead if they find out I'm not."

He felt her go still. But in a moment she recovered—Lucy had always had that capacity, Jake remembered, a resilience hidden under her emotionalism. She said in a low voice, "We think the plan worked. We left the infected Furs by the Vine planet, the Vines confirmed that they were picked up, and we believe the infection spread. But now a Fur ship is in orbit. We saw the shuttle land and destroy a Cheyenne camp in the Avery Mountains. They used that same beam we saw before in the shuttle tail. Wild Furs had just attacked the Cheyenne. Nan Frayne is dead."

She saw that it was a lot for him to take in, and paused a moment, her head bent. A stronger breeze blew through the fragrant brush. Rain was coming. Jake thought of Nan Frayne, that difficult and enigmatic crusader among a species not her own, and closed his eyes.

Lucy's voice continued, "I think the Furs who landed in the shuttle are afraid humans could recontaminate them. They wore suits and helmets, which we never saw at all last time. Also, they took the wild Furs in the Cheyenne camp with them. Karim thinks this may be a shipful of Furs who feel cut off from their empire. They risk infection if they go home. He thinks they want the wild Furs for a bigger gene pool, and Greentrees for their own planet, and humans exterminated completely so there's no further risk of infection to them. Karim sent me to find Julian Ma—"

"No!"

Lucy said, "What?"

"Julian is the one trying to kill me. It's too long to explain now. But, Lucy, he wants to take over Greentrees, too. He'll kill me and Alex and probably you. I have to get to Alex to tell her everything!"

"I don't think you can go anywhere, Jake."

"Just watch me," he said grimly. "And you're going to help me. Where's Karim?"

"He and Jon McBain—that's a xenobiologist we were with after the Vines set us down, are—"

"The *Vines?*"

Lucy said, "I need to start at the beginning. I haven't told you all of it."

"Go ahead," Jake said. "But look like you're praying aloud or something, and make it as quick as you can."

She was not quite halfway through when the outside guard burst through the camouflage brush and turned on a powerlight. In the sudden glare Jake, blinking, saw that the boy was crying. The sector captain rushed up. "Mohammed! What do you think you're doing?"

"They got Mira City!" the boy said. "A runner just came, he saw it! The city is . . . is gone. No buildings, no people, no anything! It just isn't there, and neither is anybody who can tell what happened!"

"Oh my God," the sector captain said. Tears filled her eyes but she said to the boy in a severe tone designed to be bracing, "Go back outside on duty. Keep your comlink open to receive but *do not send.* Stay hidden yourself, so that you can't be seen from the air. Mohammed, did you hear me?"

"Yes, ma'am. My parents . . . they wouldn't leave Mira this time . . ."

"Go now, Mohammed. You're a soldier. Other lives depend on you."

"Yes, ma'am," the boy said and blundered out.

"Mira City gone," Lucy whispered. "Jake . . ."

"Most of the people are out," he said clearly, loud enough to be heard by the sector captain. She stared at him, astonished through her pain.

"Captain, I need to get out of here with Lucy Lasky. I can't explain now, but it's important. The most important thing in the world right now." Jake hated sounding sternly melodramatic, but this was the sort of woman who would respond to that—just as she, in turn, had known the boy would.

Lucy's hand tightened on his.

They left just after midnight. The sector captain went outside, commandeered Mohammed's comlink, and made an emergency call for a rover. She stumbled a few miles in the dark to do so, away from the cave, just as Mohammed had done earlier. Comlinks went through satellite. If the Furs were monitoring from orbital probes—and of course they were—they now knew where at least one human was, along with the three unavoidably exposed command bunkers; you couldn't command without communicating. The bunkers were underground and heavily shielded. The sector captain, as soon as she was done making her call, would not be at the site it had come from. It was the best they could do. Runners connected the sites closest to Mira, which included this hospital cave but not the bunkers.

It was to the second bunker that the captain sent her message, the command post that Lau-Wah Mah would have held. The Chinese community had not yet elected his replacement, although they should have. Too much dissension among them, too much fear. Ashraf Shanti had appointed a temporary person to do the administrative work, Lien Kao. He was a doctor.

The sector captain reached the bunker's outside guard, who relayed to Dr. Kao that Sector Six had a medical emergency. There was no caxitocin, a vital genemod heart drug, in the hospital cave. Without it two patients would die. Send a rover.

"A rover?" said the outraged guard, one of Julian's Terran soldiers. "Are you demented? The six rovers are all military commandeered, including the one here. The enemy has already attacked!"

"Take my request to Dr. Kao," the captain said. "Your rover is closest!" She crouched under a clump of bush, her hands shaking. It was cold and dark. She couldn't tell what strange lights might be in the sky behind the clouds, or what predators in the night.

"Madame—"

"It's Dr. Kao's decision! That's the chain of command!" Jake Holman had told her what to say.

"Wait," the voice said curtly.

"He may even prefer that Kao not have a rover," Mr. Holman had said to Lucy Lasky, which made no sense. Mr. Holman must have meant Commander Martin, but why wouldn't he want Dr. Kao to have a rover? And why had Mr. Holman pretended earlier to have had a massive stroke? He must have known that as soon as the

more urgent patients were dealt with, she'd have taken a medscan and found no traces in his brain. Why was she supposed to tell no one, no matter whom, that Mr. Holman was coherent?

The sector captain hadn't asked. She'd been a nurse for twenty-seven years, accustomed to taking orders from doctors. *A good nurse,* she told herself as she shivered under the cold bushes, and if she had to die doing this thing she didn't understand, she had had a good life. And she was doing it for Greentrees.

"Rover en route," her comlink finally said, such a long, long time later.

"Yes," she answered, knowing it wasn't military but not knowing what else to say. Immediately she turned off the telltale comlink and started groping her way, dim light-cells on the bottom of her shoes her only illumination, back through the night to her patients.

They left in the rover as soon as it arrived, in the middle of the night. The driver was one of Julian's Greentrees soldiers. She had been drugged the moment she touched the cave camouflage, disarmed, and tied onto Jake's cot before anyone but Jake, Lucy, and the sector captain realized she was there. A blanket was pulled over her body and head. To the other patients, it would look as if Jake were still there. Only the sector captain and the young guard Mohammed knew different.

"She wouldn't have listened to you if you were anyone else but Jake Holman," Lucy said. "You couldn't have pulled this off."

"If I were anyone else, I wouldn't be saddled with pulling it off," Jake said. He heard his words begin to slur from weariness. He was so tired. Lucy and the sector captain had hauled him into the rover, well covered with blankets. His wheelchair rode in the back. Lucy drove; this was one of the original rovers from the First Landing, designed to last as long as possible and carefully maintained for fifty years. Jake, however, would need to navigate. He knew where Alex's bunker was; few others did.

"Are you all right?" Lucy said. She was driving blind, lights and electronav both off, going by a compass lit by a shielded powerlight so dim that Jake still could not see her face. She'd changed from the animal pelts the Cheyenne had given her into a Threadmore from the hospital cave's supply. It was too big for her.

"I'm fine," Jake said curtly, although he wasn't. "It's starting to rain."

"Good. More cover."

They were silent a moment, while Jake gathered his questions. So many questions: about the Vine planet, the ship that had brought Lucy and Karim home, what they'd seen at the research station, what Karim and Jon McBain suspected. He'd just decided on what to ask Lucy first, or maybe what to tell her, when he fell asleep, the rain driving hard against the window of the rover lurching toward Alex.

26

THE AVERY MOUNTAINS

Karim and Jon waited several hours in the trees by the river, lying on their stomach under leaves and brush, until they were fairly sure the Furs were not coming back.

"Why should they?" Jon said heavily. "There's nothing to come back *to*. Nothing."

"No," Karim whispered.

"Mira City—"

"Wait." He had, Karim realized, become better at waiting. No waiting on Greentrees, under any circumstances, could equal the hellish weeks of waiting on the Vine planet. Months? Years?

He had sent Lucy to the end point where, Jon said, Jake Holman had been assigned. It was between the research station and Mira City, and Lucy could follow the river until she came to the tram tracks and then follow those. Kent and Kueilan would accompany Lucy as far as the tracks, then continue along the river to Mira City. Jon didn't know where either Alex Cutler's or Julian Martin's commander bunkers were located; that was apparently classified. So their best plan was for Kent and Kueilan to explain to a Mira City guard why they needed to see Commander Martin, and the guard could arrange it.

Karim heard the respect in Jon's voice when the biologist spoke of Julian Martin. Karim's hopes rose. Maybe a Terran-trained military commander *would* be able to fight the Furs. The Fur shuttle had landed somewhere higher in these mountains. Martin might be glad of Kent and Kueilan's information.

Meanwhile, he and Jon had something else to do.

They lay hidden the whole night and again the whole following day. No Furs returned. Surely, by now, at least Lucy would have reached her destination. Kent and Kueilan had ten miles farther to walk than did Lucy. Karim hoped all of them were warmer, less cramped, and better fed than he was. He hadn't eaten in thirty hours and his stomach ached with hunger.

The second night he and Jon crept out of their hiding place. Thick clouds and low rumblings promised rain. In the perfect darkness Karim followed Jon, feeling his way over the uneven ground, falling more than once.

"It was here," Jon finally whispered. "I know it was."

The pole above the biomass had been annihilated by the shuttle weapon, along with everything else. But Jon dropped to his knees and began a slow, shallow digging with a forked stick. First one place, then another a foot away, then a third. A fourth. Rain started and Karim heard Jon's teeth chatter.

"Here!" Jon finally cried. "The Fur beam took it off at ground level but the pole below ground is still here!"

"We don't have a computer to interpret signals," Karim began, but they'd been over all this before. The computer would come later, from Mira City, as soon as Kent and Kueilan reached there. Now Jon and Karim could only work with what they had.

When they'd cleared the pole down to a foot or so and rubbed off the dirt with their clothing, Karim began tapping. Three, pause. One, pause. Four, pause. One, pause. Five, pause. Nine, pause. Repeat.

Jon said, "Do you really think the biomass is sentient? That it will recognize pi?"

"If it's the same entity we found on the Vine planet, it will." Three, pause. One, pause. Four . . .

Nothing.

After several minutes of nothing, Karim said, "What's wrong with me! Of course pi won't mean anything to them . . . they use biology, not physics and mathematics, as their science! Jon, what can I send that will mean something . . . they aren't even DNA based!"

Jon thought. "They're anaerobic, but they're using something as electron acceptors for respiration. Maybe several somethings; some DNA microbial strains can switch metabolic pathways to use what's available. Maybe your alien critters—if that's really what's down there!—can do the same thing. So let's pick, say, iron. Send the ferric electron-shell numbers."

Karim did. He was on his sixth long pause between slow, careful repetitions when his hand, gently resting on the pole, felt it vibrate back.

"It's repeating the pattern. Jon, it's doing it."

"Try sulfur. The geologic survey showed there's some down there."

Karim did. The pole vibrated the same pattern back.

Jon said, "But how do we know it isn't just some form of . . . of echo? How do we establish sentience?"

"I don't know."

"I hate to say this, Karim, but no Terran or Greenie anaerobic microbes ever evolved to become so much as a multicellular organism, let alone sentient."

"These aren't Terran or Greenie. I'm going to send . . . owww!"

An electric current had run up the pole to his hand.

"Jon, they're ahead of us. They know you had electronic devices hooked up here before. They're trying to send to *us!*"

"Send what?"

"I don't know. Maybe pictures. We've got to have a computer."

"Wait a minute," Jon said. "In the river . . . I should have thought of this before!"

"Of what?"

"Nate Cutler. He's an ichthyologist. Strange old coot. He left devices in the river to monitor fish activity, some program of his own devising. He left them at two-mile intervals, including here. Hasn't been to check it in months. But there's at least some kind of computer inside."

"With a screen?"

"I doubt it."

"Pictures are how Beta Vine communicated with us before," Jon said. "But maybe this fish-counting tech will at least let us record what the mass sends."

They found Nate Cutler's device easily, even in the dark; a marker on the bank was unmistakable. Taking it apart, however, had to wait for daylight. At the first hint of light, Karim and Jon crawled back into their hiding place, wet and starving and exhausted. Karim wrapped himself protectively around the fish-counting device and fell into a heavy sleep troubled by faceless monsters.

The next day, still in hiding, they saw the Fur shuttle fly silently overhead, toward Mira City.

27

BUNKER THREE

The Fur ship in orbit launched no more unmanned missiles. Time passed for Alex in dazed horror, made worse by not being able to do anything. She couldn't send anyone to Mira City to assess the damage because there might be another attack. She couldn't receive reports from the critical facilities because, if they still stood, they were shielded against a possible EMP. End points were under comlink silence, to avoid enemy detection, until she contacted them. So, now, were Julian and Ashraf. It was as if all of Greentrees had ceased to exist except this bunker and its four people.

Natalie and Ben remained as quiet and sober as she. Her Terran bodyguard, Captain Lewis, spent most of his time outside. Probably assumed that Alex was safe inside the bunker, at least from anything he could protect her against.

By dawn of the third day she could no longer stand it. "I'm going outside."

Natalie looked up from her displays, which gave no new information. Her cap of black curls was limp and dirty, and black smudges sagged under her eyes. Not even the young people were sleeping well. Natalie said to Alex, "Ben is already outside."

"I know Ben is already outside," Alex snapped. Then, "I'm sorry, Natalie. We're all tense and bored. I know Ben is out getting water, but I'll stay close to the bunker, I'll stay under cover, and I'll leave the door open. If anything happens, shout and I'll hear you."

"All right," Natalie said, disapproval in her voice. She almost sounded like Siddalee.

Alex ascended the flight of foamcast steps to the surface and emerged through underbrush beneath a grove of tall purple trees. Her Terran bodyguard went with her, but she ignored him. Neither Ben nor Captain Lewis was anywhere in sight, and what kind of bodyguarding was *that*? She wished she could ask Julian; she wished she could just talk to Julian, just hear his voice.

But the fresh air seemed the most delightful sensation she'd ever experienced. It had rained overnight and dew sparkled on the groundcover. The world was pale luminescence; tiny lavender wildflowers had sprung up beneath the groundcover, just barely visible, and the sun, still below the horizon, brightened the sky to delicate silver-gray. Alex drew a deep breath.

So beautiful. Were humans going to lose it all to aliens too xenophobic to share an almost empty planet?

She lay full-length on the soft purple, under cover of the trees. Dew wet her Threadmores but didn't penetrate. Alex tried to empty her mind—just for five minutes, she told herself—but couldn't do it. Too many worries intruded. Was Julian safe? Was Jake? How many had died?

Her ear, pressed to the ground, heard the rumble of approaching machinery.

Alex jumped up and dashed for the bunker stairs. But before she descended, the rover came crashing through underbrush from the direction of the river and she saw that it was a human vehicle. She waited, knowing that Ben, fetching water, must have seen the rover and allowed it to pass. Where was Captain Lewis? She squinted. Two people inside . . .

Jake.

Forsaking caution, Alex ran toward the rover. Captain Lewis appeared from nowhere and reached the vehicle first, putting himself between it and Alex. She cried, "Don't shoot! That's Jake Holman! Jake, my God, what are you doing here? It's not safe, get this thing under those trees . . . what's happened!"

The woman driving looked about to faint. She was much younger than Alex, maybe thirty, slight and pretty and fragile. At the sight of her obvious illness, Lewis scowled but kept his weapon pointed at her. Why? She clearly wasn't a Fur, and she clearly wasn't dangerous.

The woman pushed open her door, her hand over her mouth as if about to vomit. She staggered and fell, and before Alex, running up, could catch her or even knew she was armed, the woman fired a gun into the Terran's chest.

Captain Lewis fell heavily to the ground.

Alex screamed. The woman, not staggering at all now, scrambled off the ground and said rapidly, "A lot has happened. Get Jake into your bunker, I'll put this . . . where is your own rover hidden?"

Ben came running up, carrying no water. He snapped, completely uncharacteristically, "Drive that rover into that grove . . . no, over there! Quick! It can be seen from the air, you know!"

"I know," the young woman said impatiently. "You, help get Jake into safety. Don't forget his chair, in the back of the rover. *And turn off all open comlinks in the bunker.*" She drove the rover off as soon as Jake was out.

Ben flung the old man over his shoulder. Alex, bewildered, followed them through the brush, down the steps, and inside. While Ben ran back for the chair, Alex knelt by Jake where he had been unceremoniously deposited on the floor, his back to the wall. "Jake! What are you doing here? Who's that woman? She *shot* Julian's lieutenant—"

"Have to . . . tell you . . . something . . . critical," Jake gasped. She gave him a minute to get his breath after being pushed and pulled. He looked terrible: weak, drooly, slack.

"Tell me! Good God, Jake, that woman killed my bodyguard! Who is she?"

Astonishingly, the old man grinned. "That's Lucy Lasky."

"*Lucy Lasky?*"

"Yep." His smile vanished. "Alex . . . there are things you need to know. About Julian Martin."

———

She curled into a corner of the bunker, pretending to be asleep. The others, a tight fit in the narrow space, talked in low tones. She could distinguish Jake's quavery rumble and Lucy's high, light tone, but no words. The links were all set to receive but not transmit. Natalie never took her eyes off the displays, but since nothing was changing, she also put in an occasional inaudible word. Alex didn't try to listen, didn't want to listen. They would call her if anything happened.

Just now she gave all her attention to her pain.

It was a real thing, like a parasite or a fetus, growing inside her. It was conceived the moment Jake had said, "Julian is a traitor," and it had grown ever since, taking over more and more of what she was. She didn't try to fight it, not yet. For now she merely endured it, examined it, tried to understand this alien thing tearing her insides.

Julian had abducted, tortured, killed Lau-Wah Mah.

Julian had betrayed Greentrees' trust, knowing that Hope of Heaven would attack Mira during the evacuation drill and permitting the attack so he could then put the rebellion down and be given military powers by a grateful Mira City.

Julian had armed the wild Furs against the Cheyenne.

Julian had destroyed the *Beta Vine* so that the only ship in orbit would be the *Crucible*, its sophisticated weapons aimed at Greentrees.

Julian had done all this, and more, on Terra.

Julian had killed Duncan, his own brother.

Julian had held Alex in his arms, caressed her body, made love to her, loved her . . .

Julian had abducted, tortured, killed Lau-Wah Mah.

Julian had betrayed . . .

Around and around, the pain growing stronger with each repetition, feeding on itself.

She tried to think of something else, someone else, tried to open her world again beyond her devouring self. She tried to think of Jake. He had been as devastated to learn of the Fur destruction of Mira City as she had been to learn about Julian. Tears had sprung into his old eyes and he had groped blindly with one hand, clawing the air as if he could shred the words Alex had just said. "Mira City?" he'd quavered. "Gone? Mira City?"

It had been Lucy who reached for the clawing hand and gripped it firmly, tenderly. Alex had been grateful to Lucy. She herself had nothing left to give.

Julian had abducted, tortured, killed Lau-Wah Mah.

Julian had betrayed . . .

Mira City. She must think of Mira City. Most of the people had left during the evacuation. If the Furs really wanted Greentrees, they would, afraid of further infection, hunt down all the rest of the humans and kill them. Mira City wasn't its buildings, it was its people, and Alex must find a way to defend them against the Furs, against Julian Martin . . .

Julian had abducted, tortured, killed Lau-Wah Mah.

Julian had betrayed . . .

Greentrees. She must subdue this pain, this adversary, and think of Greentrees. The pain was only personal; Greentrees was a whole world.

Julian had abducted, tortured . . .

"Alex!" the tech said. "Wake up! The Fur shuttle is moving!"

Alex rose. "I'm awake," she said. "Where is the shuttle headed?"

It flew south, away from Mira City, or what had once been Mira City. "It's going toward the Cheyenne subcontinent," Alex said. "The space Furs want to gather up more wild Furs before they all flee into the wilderness or hide or whatever they'll do. Or maybe they won't flee—they're highly xenophobic. Nan Frayne is—was—the only human they ever accepted. Maybe the wild Furs will welcome the space Furs with open arms. I have to tell Julian—"

She stopped.

Natalie said, "Alex—the Fur mother ship is dropping orbit!"

Jake spoke urgently. "Alex, break e-silence. *Now.* Do an all-comlink broadcast, including MiraNet. Tell everyone that Mira City has been annihilated by a Fur weapon, nothing left, and that the mother ship is descending to do the same thing from space to a much larger swath of Greentrees. Tell everyone to get underground, in caves or under overhangs or anything they can. Tell them to dig a pit if that's all they can do, and to cover the roof with dirt. Dirt, not branches!"

She stared at him.

"Do it!" Lucy Lasky said. "The beam somehow stops at the surface, it's everyone's only chance!"

Natalie said, "Enemy ship still dropping orbit."

Julian's voice said sharply over the link, "Alex, are you tracking? I'm not getting any transmissions from Bunker Three."

Alex froze.

Jake said to Natalie, "Open all comlinks, without exception. When they've been opened, no one should talk to or about me or Lucy. Julian doesn't know we're here. Alex, *go*."

They all looked at her. Weirdly, it wasn't Jake's weary and ruined face, or Lucy's stern and impossibly young one, that made it possible for Alex to move again. It was young Ben's, still in the Greenie version of a uniform, a corporal in Julian's army, his eyes fearful and naive and optimistic that Alex could do something. The eyes of Greentrees.

Julian had abducted, tortured, killed Lau-Wah Mah.

Julian had betrayed . . .

Alex's voice held steady, without a single break. "Open all comlinks, both ways, including MiraNet."

"They're all open," Natalie said.

"Attention, everyone who can hear this. This is Alex Cutler. The Fur ship has annihilated Mira City and is descending in orbit to annihilate a huge area of Greentrees' surface. We don't know how big. But you must take cover. Their weapon beam stops its destruction at the planetary surface. Get under stone or soil however you can, and do it *now*. We don't know how long we have. Find—"

"Alex!" Julian said on his private channel. "What the hell are you doing?"

"—a cave or an overhang on a stream bank. If there's nothing else, cover yourselves with rocks. Trees and brush won't protect you, and neither—"

"I didn't authorize this broadcast!"

"—neither will foamcast. The beam leaves stone, dirt, and water but nothing else. Find cover now, and stay under it until I broadcast again. Do not use your comlinks because that will give away your positions. Keep all comlinks—"

"Alex!"

"—on receive. We can survive this, my fellow Greenies, and we can and will reclaim our planet for ourselves. For now, *take cover*."

"Alex," said Julian's voice, and now his was deadly calm, "I cannot raise Captain Lewis. Why not?"

"I don't know," Alex said, and still her voice didn't quiver or break. "He went outside."

"Outside? I should still be able to link with him."

"I don't know why you can't."

Jake tugged at Natalie's Threadmore and made a quick slicing movement, surprisingly strong, with his hand. She cut off the comlink. Alex closed her eyes.

Jake said quietly, "He knows that you know."

"Yes," Alex answered. "He does."

The Fur ship descended to fifty clicks, a lower orbit than any human technology could have sustained. It made two more orbits of Greentrees. Then, silently and invisibly, it fired . . . something. On Alex's displays, the high-resolution digital images from orbit showed vegetation, and everything else, disappearing. The multicolored graphics represented different reflection properties, different material compositions, different temperatures. After the invisible beam passed over them, the images held only two shades: bare soil and bare stone.

"The beam's path is ten miles wide, north to south," Natalie said in a voice of forced calm. "It starts about a hundred miles east of Mira . . . east of where Mira *was*. It intersects that site and goes on to . . . wait, destruction has stopped."

Jake said, "They'll make another pass on the next orbit."

They did. This ten-mile-wide swath lay north of Mira, slightly overlapping the first path. Natalie said, "Destruction stopped, same three-hundred-mile length. They'll probably—"

All images vanished from all displays.

"What—"

Alex said calmly, "Julian has cut us off. He deslaved our monitors. Ashraf's, too, most likely. Now Julian is the only one receiving comsat information."

Jake nodded.

That was the moment the pain stopped.

Alex looked at Jake, at Lucy and Ben, at Natalie, who, Alex now saw, had been working through tears. Calculating rapidly, she realized that if the ship didn't change trajectory, and if its band of destruction kept moving north before the Furs began doing the same thing south of Mira, the beam would sweep over Bunker Three a few hours from now. It would destroy everything aboveground: the grove of trees where she had lain this morning, the tiny pale lavender wildflowers, the brush covering the bunker entrance, the body of Captain Lewis, whom Julian had assigned to watch her.

Alex eyed the bunker door. "We have to strip down one or both rovers to minimal essentials and bring them down, too. We're going to need them."

"For what?" Ben blurted.

"To fight the Furs."

The boy gaped. *"With what?"*

"I don't know yet," Alex said. "But we—"

Lucy broke in. "Maybe Karim and Jon—"

"—are going to fight the Furs with something," Alex finished steadily. "And fight Julian Martin, too, if we have to."

She stood a moment, thinking, and then amended her statement.

"When we have to."

28

THE AVERY MOUNTAINS

Nate Cutler's fish recorder proved disappointing. Karim hauled it out of the river and took it apart but couldn't find anything usable to translate the vibrating signals of the biomass into visuals. He and Jon had taken the device a quarter mile downriver, to a place where the river grew shallow, babbling and breaking on stretch of boulders. Here erosion had created an overhang, at least while water levels stayed low. They felt safe there, although while Karim tinkered, Jon peered out at the clear sky, watching for the Fur shuttle. It did not reappear.

"There's a comlink in this device, or at least the makings of one," Karim said. "But it's not transmitting."

"Julian Martin ordered all continuous transmission devices turned off," Jon replied. "It was part of the preparedness push. Gives away a research facility position."

"Microwave silence didn't save your camp."

"No. What else is in there? God, I'm hungry."

Karim said, "You ate more than half of those fruits."

"And will probably have diarrhea for my greed. What else is in that thing?"

"Not much, unless you want an accurate count of twenty-two different fish species. But I think I can set this comlink to receive continuously. That way if anything is broadcast from Mira, we'll get it."

"Good. Of course, we've already missed a few days' worth of broadcasts. Do you think we can—"

"No, Jon," Karim said patiently, for perhaps the eighth time. "We can't risk going to the biomass pole in broad daylight—if the pole is even still there. And anyway, we don't have any way to translate its signals into pictures, and pictures are the only way we're going to open real communication with the biomass."

Jon shifted on his hams. He was filthy, his blond hair matted, and he stank. Karim thought he himself probably smelled worse. It didn't matter.

"Tell me again," Jon said. "If the biomass is anaerobic, and if it spent its entire life two clicks underground on Greentrees, why do you think it's going to comprehend any pictures we send it? Let alone pictures of a space war?"

Karim put the jerry-rigged comlink on a flat rock in the river beyond the overhang, where it would be able to receive. He splashed back through the warm water and sat again under the safety of the overhang. Hypothetical safety. His stomach growled.

"I think—I hope—that this biomass is like the one I saw on the Vine planet. That one was open, because the atmosphere, whatever it was, wasn't oxygenated. Here the anaerobic biomass is deep belowground, for protection. But it's not native. It was brought here by the Vines before humans even colonized Greentrees. If that's so, either it's the sentient part of a Vine creature or else it's an extension of sentient Vines, maybe programmed like some sort of computer analogue. Either way, it may know things, have seen things or been told them, from before it was buried here."

"So you think it knows about the war with the Furs, the genetic experiments on Greentrees . . . but not, presumably, *us*. Think, Karim. If we came after the biomass was put down there by Vines, it has no idea we exist."

Karim said grimly, "It will know after we tell it."

"Here's another question for you, then." Jon sat up, looking like a wastrel gnome. "Why didn't the Vines ever tell Jake Holman, or anybody from that first contact with humans fifty years ago, about the biomass?"

"I think they didn't trust us enough." After a moment Karim added, remembering, "And they were right."

"And what do you suppose—"

Another voice started shouting.

Karim and Jon both jumped. Karim realized, a beat too late, that the voice came from the comlink, shouting only because he'd turned the volume up to be heard over the babbling river.

"—descending in orbit to annihilate a huge area of Greentrees' surface. We don't know how big. But you must take cover. Their weapon beam—"

"That's Alex Cutler!" Jon blurted.

"—stops its destruction at the planetary surface. Get under stone or soil however you can, and do it *now*. We don't know how long we have. Find a cave or an overhang on a stream bank. If there's nothing else, cover yourselves with rocks. Trees and brush won't protect you, and neither will foamcast. The beam leaves stone, dirt, and water but nothing else. Find cover now, and stay under it until I broadcast again. Do not use your comlinks because that will give away your positions. Keep all comlinks on receive. We can survive this, fellow Greenies, and we can and will reclaim our planet for ourselves. For now, *take cover*."

The message began to repeat. Jon and Karim, with one last glance at the sky, shrank even farther back under the overhang. After a long silence, Karim said, "I saw this beam once before. Here, on Greentrees, from a shuttle. I saw it vaporize an entire village of wild Furs instantaneously."

"Mira City is gone," Jon said numbly, and Karim realized that Jon might have family there. Not everyone had been away in space for thirty-nine years.

Jon said no more. He turned his face away, toward the dirt at their backs. Karim didn't intrude. Where his people came from, the ancient Terran city of Isfahan, men did not cry in front of outsiders.

The ship didn't reach them with its overlapping swaths of destruction until evening. Although it must have been in a very low orbit, Karim didn't see the ship. Nor did he feel anything pass above him. But the vegetation on the opposite riverbank began to disappear.

It was eerie and horrifying to watch. One moment bushes, trees, groundcover were there—and the next moment were not. It was almost a swiftly moving parody of a screen wipe, the kind children liked on their computers to erase schoolwork. A small animal of some type emerged from scrub, seemed to look directly across the river into Karim's eyes, and then silently ceased to exist.

Nothing existed for as far as he could see, except for rocks on bare brown soil. All the human building and planting and striving during that first joyous year on Greentrees . . . and during the fifty years since. All gone. Had Lucy reached Jake in time to learn about the Fur attack? To take cover in Jake's cave?

Had Kent and Kueilan, on their way to Mira City to bring back a computer, known to take cover? Had they been able to find any cover?

When Jon finally spoke, his voice was steadier than Karim had dared hope. "They do want Greentrees, Karim. You're right. They're wiping us out to have the planet for themselves."

"And to avoid being infected. They don't know that no one on Greentrees is a carrier."

"But they can't hope to get all the scattered Cheyenne, all the far research stations . . . God, we've even got a few research stations on another *continent*."

"They don't need to get everybody. Just most humans. They probably assume the rest will degenerate or die off, or at least pose no real threat. Certainly the Cheyenne, armed with spears, don't."

Jon spoke with a sudden, fierce energy. "Well, they're *wrong*. Thanks to Julian Martin. A lot of us were hidden at end points . . . maybe even most of us. Bunches went off into the wilderness. We have leadership in protected bunkers, and weapons hidden far from Mira, and a leader experienced in warfare!"

Karim nodded. But he didn't think bands of humans who had to stay physically hidden and electronically silent were going to pose much threat to Furs. Karim had seen Furs and their weapons; Jon had not. Nor could Karim have much faith in this Terran, Julian Martin. The man had anticipated well so far, but Martin had no idea what he was actually up against.

No, if humans were to stand any chance at all, it would be because of the biomass.

If Karim could find a way to communicate with it.

If the biomass was willing to help.

If the biomass knew of any way to help.

If—

The sky grew darker. Karim curled into a ball under the overhang, conserving heat against the coming night, courteously pretending he didn't know that Jon's tears had started again. His stomach rumbled; he was so hungry.

He tried not to think about Mira City.

Karim woke shivering after a fitful, cold night on the bare rock under the overhang. To think that he had hated the hothouse warmth of the Vine planet! Jon still lay curled in a filthy ball beside him. Slowly Karim rose, every muscle stiff, and ventured cautiously toward the river.

The sun, just breaking above the horizon, as yet offered no warmth. But at least the sun was the only thing in the sky. No alien ship annihilating everything beneath it. As far as Karim could see across the river, the landscape lay empty, inert, desolate.

Nothing to see, nothing to expect, nothing to eat.

Stiffly he clambered up the riverbank, to the top of the overhang. The view didn't change. A whole lot of nothing.

But at least here the damp was less. Karim sat down on a rock to await the sun. He doubted the Fur shuttle would return; there was nothing left here to destroy.

Warmth was just beginning to return to his flesh when he saw the rover top the horizon.

His first reaction was fear. But it was a rover, a human means of transport; surely the Furs couldn't have as yet commandeered rovers? Still, Karim ducked behind the rock he'd been sitting on until he was sure. Kent and Kueilan! He leaped up, waving wildly, and passed out from light-headedness. The next thing he knew Kueilan bent over him, forcing water through his lips. He shoved the flask away.

"Food!"

"Give him some of that soysynth," Kent said, and for a few minutes there was nothing in the world but Karim's primitive self, squatting on its hindquarters, chewing and grunting. *Good! Good!*

"Don't eat it too fast or it'll just come up again," Kueilan said severely. "You, too, Jon." But her hand rested compassionately on Karim's shoulder.

When he'd eaten enough, Karim gasped, "Tell me."

She knew what he wanted to hear. "The computer is in the rover. We took it and the rover from an end point by force, I'm afraid. They had no real defenses, it was a sort of pathetic hospital cave . . ." Her dark eyes shifted with some painful memory.

Kent said, "They didn't believe who we were or what we wanted. It was just after Alex Cutler's call to take cover, and we didn't know if you'd be wiped out by the Fur beam. It was just lucky you were under that overhang!"

"No, it wasn't luck," Karim said. But that part of the story could wait. "I don't think the Furs are coming back here—no reason. So we need to take the computer to the biomass right away, see if we can communicate, then get word to this Commander Julian Martin."

"Word of what?" Kent said, bewildered.

"I don't know yet! I won't know until we establish communication!"

Kueilan and Kent looked at him skeptically; obviously they had been talking over Karim's ideas and found an objection to it. Probably a lot of objections. Those would also have to wait.

The four of them piled into the rover. Karim saw Kent wrinkle his nose, and ignored it. River water, without soap, could only do so much, and Kent didn't smell all that much better himself. But at least they'd brought Karim a stolen Threadmore and he no longer had to wrap a Cheyenne pelt around his body.

At the biomass site, they dug more dirt loose from around the pole, this time aided by more than their hands. Kueilan set up the equipment. In less than twenty minutes she had a display vibrating with a complex but steady pattern of waves crosshatched with jagged lines.

Jon said, "That's baseline metabolic activity in the biomass, as translated into vibrations in the pole."

Karim said, "How far down did you say that thing is?"

"Point-three-five-seven miles for the main mass. Although it has extensions coming up higher. Remember, Karim, it could be an amazingly complex organism by now. Biofilms diversify, creating all sorts of internal structures and communication networks, all malleable as needed. The mass might even incorporate nonmicrobial elements like alga-analogues. It might help you to conceptualize it as a city rather than a single individual."

It would help most, Karim thought, for him to conceptualize it as Beta Vine, that long-dead helper of humanity. But the mass far under his feet wasn't Beta Vine, or any Vine. It was a vast unknown slime with which he was supposed to communicate.

"All right," he said to Kueilan, seated cross-legged on the bare ground before her controls, "last time we communicated, we sent electron-shell numbers for iron. Try those again."

Kueilan did. Almost immediately the display pattern altered to . . . something else. Karim squinted at it in the bright morning sunlight. Some fuzzy patches, some wavy lines, some irregular blobs . . .

"What's that?" Kueilan asked.

Jon said, "I don't know. It's *something*, I guess, in that it's different from what we had before, but I don't know what."

Karim said, "Try the shell pattern for sulfur. Last time the mass echoed that back to us."

Kueilan keyed it in. The incomprehensible display pattern changed to a different incomprehensible display pattern.

Karim smacked his hand into his fist in frustration. "There's no common starting point for interpretation!" He caught the skeptical look exchanged between Jon and Kent and remembered Jon's earlier words days ago, a lifetime ago: *"I hate to say this, Karim, but no Terran or Greenie anaerobic microbes ever evolved to become so much as a multicellular organism, let alone sentient."*

They were wrong. They hadn't seen the open biomass on the Vine planet, hadn't communicated with it, had never been off Greentrees. They just were wrong. This thing a third of a mile down was sentient, and Karim was going to find a way not only to prove that but also to wrestle the biomass into helping them defeat the Furs.

He said to Kueilan, "Send a picture, not numbers. What's stored in that system's deebees? Have you got a schematic of, say, a molecule of adenine?"

"Yes, there's a complete bio deebee," she said.

"Send that."

She did, and another incomprehensible visual came back.

Karim wasn't deterred. "Send a schematic for guanine."

Slowly he built up an informational picture of DNA, moving from the base proteins to the sugar-phosphate spines to the limits of his biological knowledge. DNA defined Furs as well as humans, of course. He was pondering how to proceed when Kueilan's display suddenly changed radically. The formless visuals were replaced by the clear drawing of a Fur, complete with bared murderous teeth.

"Oh my God!" Jon said.

Karim said rapidly, "That's the only DNA the biomass knows— so it *was* planted here before Vines knew there was such a thing as humans on Greentrees. It thinks we're Furs sending to it! Quick, send an image of a human before—"

The Fur on the display began to dance.

There was no other word for it. The savage, startlingly accurate drawing hopped and gyrated, moving more and more wildly until it was looping and bending in ways no actual Fur ever could. Then its head came off and danced separately, rejoined the body, gave way to separated dancing legs. The four humans stared, jaws gaping. Finally the Fur disappeared, replaced by tall thin trees dancing equally wildly. The trees disappeared. The screen filled with wavy lines undulating at manic speed. Then nothing at all.

Jon breathed, "What the hell was that!"

Kueilan said, "Now there isn't even basic metabolic patterns."

"You know," Kent said slowly, "if I didn't know better, I'd swear that last frenetic screen was the equivalent of *laughter*."

Karim said nothing. He felt stunned. Like Kent, he'd had the strong, irrational impression that the biomass simply was not taking their communication seriously. Not even when it thought the communicator was a Fur, its deadly and sworn enemy. What could that mean?

Jon said, with only a tiny touch of malice, "What now, Karim?"

But Karim had no idea what they should do now.

29

BUNKER THREE

Alex, Natalie, Ben, and Lucy worked feverishly to reassemble the rover. They'd been able to fit only one dismantled rover in the bunker. The other, the one Lucy and Jake had arrived in, had been vaporized when the Fur ship passed overhead. Since Julian had deslaved her monitors from his, Alex received no reports from the orbital probes or comsats. She could send on her comlink, but without a link to the comsats she had very limited range. She couldn't even receive reports. She was electronically blind.

It was the first time in her life that she had not been comlinked to much of the inhabited planet.

Julian knew where she was. He had weapons aboard the *Crucible* that, unlike the Fur beam from orbit, would destroy Bunker Three. Bombs, alpha beams. He also had the Greentrees skimmer, hidden far from Mira but under his control, along with his Terrans. He wouldn't fly the skimmer while the Fur ship was creating its paths of total destruction: too great a risk of losing it. But after that . . .

"He can't let you live, Alex," Jake said.

"I know. Nor you. Without us, he could deny my broadcast, say I'd been duped, he's so good at persuasion, he . . ." She'd had to turn away from Jake. But it had been only a momentary faltering, and she didn't allow herself another.

The rover seated four, and they were five. A young tech, an even younger and untried "soldier," a feeble old man, a woman who'd been off-planet for fifty years, and Alex herself, a middle-aged woman who'd lost the city she was supposed to protect. With this army, she was supposed to take on a technologically advanced species and a pitiless megalomaniac.

You worked with what you had. That was the essence of being a tray-o.

"Ben, bring that thing over there . . . no, not that one, the brown thing," Natalie said. She was the only one who was good with machinery. Ben supplied the muscle. Watching the girl work, her short dirty curls springing from her head in hectic spirals, Alex tried to plan, to maximize their resources, human and mechanical.

So much depended on so little.

They traveled by night, in electronic silence, through a landscape more empty than Alex could have imagined. She was almost glad she could see so little. In the dark, she could imagine there were still trees out there. Trees, bushes, the whole complex web of life, instead of nothingness.

Ben drove, pushing the rover as fast as it would go, Alex silent beside him. Natalie, Lucy, and Jake squeezed in the back. When Alex glanced back, she glimpsed Jake asleep with his head thrown back against the seat, drool at the corners of his mouth, Lucy's arms around him either in protection or to keep herself from toppling into Natalie.

Lucy and Jake had been lovers fifty years ago, when they were thirty-nine years closer to being the same age. Alex tried to wrap her mind around both the relativistic and emotional facts. What did Lucy feel now, cradling Jake's old and fragile body in her still strong, still young arms?

Alex pushed the question away. She couldn't afford the distraction. All her energy was needed to plan. Not even thoughts of Julian could be allowed to intrude, except as an enemy to defeat.

Oh, Julian . . .

No.

The first thing they needed was a safe hideout. Julian knew where Bunker Three was. As soon as he was sure the Fur shuttle had left the area, he would send the skimmer to destroy the bunker. He might even use the *Crucible* to fire an alpha beam from a low orbit, but Alex doubted it. The Fur mother ship was up there some-where, and Julian would try to keep the *Crucible* shielded from her by the planet. No, he would send the skimmer to destroy Bunker Three. But Alex would be gone.

To where?

The countryside around them, what she could see through one of the two night-vision helmets that had been aboard the rover, was completely denuded. No plants, no animals, nothing. Ben had been driving for nearly two hours at top speed, and they were still in the Furs' kill-clean zone.

Under Ben's thin helmet, clear except where the powerful vision strip crossed his eyes, tears dripped slowly.

Oh God. She couldn't cope with his falling apart. What did she really know about this boy? He was a good enough tech to serve as backup for Natalie. But he also was—had been—a corporal in Ju-lian's army and Julian had trusted him enough to post him in Bunker Three under the dead captain Lewis . . . Sudden cold trick-led along Alex's spine. Could she trust Ben?

Yes. The boy had had the sense to sort through what Lucy and Jake said—well, what Jake had said, anyway. "Mr. Holman" had enormous prestige among Ben's generation. Ben had believed Jake and had acted on his belief by helping Alex. Ben had recognized the truth about Julian much more quickly and objectively than had Alex. Maybe she should ask herself whether Ben could trust *her*.

He said, "Look over there, Alex, ninety degrees east."

It was a frabbit, hopping frantically across the blank landscape.

"We must be coming to the end of the kill-clean zone," Ben added, and a moment later she glimpsed, in zoom and infrared, the first tall treetops above the horizon.

When they entered the woods, Ben glanced over at her. From the backseat Lucy said, "We need a cave or something, Alex. To mask our thermal signature."

"We're a hundred miles from Mira"—*where Mira was, you*

mean, don't think of that now—"and the topography that close has been pretty well mapped. Julian has access to those deebees. He'll know where all the caves are. A cave won't work."

"Neither will being out in the open like this," Lucy said. A shrill undertone, born of tension and exhaustion, shot through her voice.

"I know that," Alex said, holding her own voice even. The effort steadied her.

Natalie said, "I know this area a little. My study group used to camp near here. If you turn north, you'll hit a large creek, a tributary of Mira's river. It's pretty wild here, with canyons and caves and overhangs. If we got down to the water, under a big enough overhang, our thermal signature won't be detected."

Lucy said, "What about the rover?"

Natalie said reluctantly, "We'd have to leave it topside. Cover it with a lot of branches. That's probably the best we can do."

"Turn north," Alex said.

They found the creek, and the rest was backbreaking, filthy work, barely finished before dawn. By weak powertorch they slid down steep banks, rattling loose rocks to the creekbed. Alex was grateful for her Threadmores; the durable fabric protected her from cuts although not from bruises. At the bottom they waded and stumbled along the edge of the rapids, afraid every minute of being carried away, until they found one of Natalie's overhangs. It wasn't ideal: not as deep as Alex would have liked, nor as dry. But time was running out. It would have to do.

Next came the aching drudgery of carrying down the equipment and supplies, hiding the rover, trying to cover as much as possible the signs of their slipping, bruising descents. Ben carried Jake, both of them white with fear and pain. When they finally finished, every part of Alex hurt. She was so tired she barely had strength to spread a blanket, in the driest place she could find, for Jake to lie on. The old man looked up at her with piteous, rheumy eyes.

"I'm so damn useless."

"No, you're not," she told him, her own eyes blurry from exhaustion. "You're our mastermind."

He snorted, and the next second he was asleep.

She spread her allotted blanket beside him, but Lucy appeared squatting beside her in the gloom.

"Alex, I need to comlink Karim."

"Comlink! Good God, Lucy, you know we can't do that! Julian will pick up every single electronic peep!"

"I know. But listen to me. Karim and Jon McBain are still by the biomass I told you and Jake about. Kueilan and Kent—those are two of Jon's people—were going to get a computer and bring it to the site so Karim could open communications with the mass. When he succeeds, I know what Karim will do. He'll go straight to Julian Martin to tell him about it. That can't happen—you can't give Julian Martin access to, or even any knowledge of, our only weapon! We must warn Karim!"

Alex peered at Lucy. All she saw was a dark blur. Alex could barely summon the energy to reply, and she had no energy for tact.

"Lucy, that's all crazy. Lunatic. You don't even know what Jon's biomass *is,* much less that it's any kind of weapon, much less . . . it's just crazy. You can't open a comlink to Karim. Jon's people wouldn't have crossed the kill zone with any computer—how? In what? Nobody would loan a research biologist's assistants a rover or computer at a time like this. *Think.* Karim can't reach Julian anyway . . . Julian's bunker is hundreds of miles from the Avery Mountains. Even if Karim and Jon are still alive, which I doubt—" She stopped herself, aware of the cruelty in her words.

"They're alive," Lucy said steadily. "I know."

"How?"

"I'd know if Karim were dead. I'd just know."

Alex heard the romantic fervor in Lucy's voice, the mystical lunacy, and the last of her patience snapped.

"Forget it, Lucy. I have no resources to spare for stupid reasoning or love-blinded daring. Go to sleep."

Instantly the small dark shape vanished. Falling asleep, Alex's last clear thought was, *I wonder if she was always that unstable. Jake would know.*

Hours later, when she awoke to bright harsh afternoon and the singing of the creek, Alex wished she had asked him. Natalie, Ben, and Jake still slept. Lucy Lasky was gone.

"The rover's still there," Ben said, clambering down the steep muddy bank. A shower of stones accompanied him. To Alex, Ben looked amazingly rested and energetic. Youth.

Natalie said, "So she walked? To where? What was she trying to do?"

Warn Karim, Alex thought but didn't say aloud. But not even a reckless Lucy Lasky could expect to walk several hundred miles through a denuded kill-clean zone without being detected, or could expect to reach Karim quickly enough to stop him from contacting Julian. If Karim were even alive. So where had Lucy gone? What was her plan?

Natalie said suddenly, "Oh . . ." She ducked into the deepest recesses of their pathetic hideout and rummaged among the equipment from off the rover. That woke Jake, who called querulously, "Alex? Alex?"

Alex went to him. "Just a minute, Jake, we've got a problem . . . Natalie?"

"She took the flare," Natalie said. "It's gone."

So that was it. The flare was microwave. It fired high into the sky and transmitted a distress message to the closest orbital comsat, which in turn routed it to its destination. If the user was incapable of recording either message or destination coordinates, the flare would automatically send an SOS to the Mausoleum on priority-one override. Except, of course, the Mausoleum no longer existed.

"Who took a flare?" Jake was demanding in his cracked, early-morning voice. "Who? Who?"

"Lucy," Alex said, to shut him up. "Natalie, how did Lucy even know what a flare was or how to work it? They didn't have them when she was on Greentrees! Chu Corporation only put them on the market two years ago!"

Chu Corporation. Which no longer existed, either.

Natalie said guiltily, "I showed her. I'm sorry, we were going over all the equipment."

"Lucy?" Jake croaked. "What did Lucy do? Alex? Alex?"

Alex explained to him. To her surprise, Jake didn't dismiss Lucy's ideas as deeply crazy.

"A biomass belonging to the Vines," he said thoughtfully. "If that's true . . . and if Lucy and Karim saw it on the Vine planet . . ."

He must have caught a glimpse of Alex's face.

"Alex, you weren't there. You never met Beta Vine, you never saw the inside of a Vine ship, you never experienced how different they are, how completely strange . . . and Karim is genuinely intelligent. If he can—"

"Can what?" she said acidly. "Can get a mess of bacteria buried miles in the ground to attack a starship? Jake, just because it's Lucy Lasky—"

"Listen!" Ben said abruptly. "Oh God, listen!"

Julian's voice, muted by the creek roar, filtered into the depression under the overhang.

It came from the comlink, set to receive continuously. Natalie had carefully propped it on a rock out in the open but safe from the creek. The link had been left on continuous receive. Julian was making an all-channel speech.

"—tragic loss that should only make those of us left determined to fight on all that harder. Alex Cutler embodied all that is best in Greentrees: courage, generosity, and, most of all, love for this beautiful planet. You know that I was not born here. But I share Alex's love for Greentrees; I share her commitment to its survival; I share her conviction, absolute to the bottom of her soul, that humanity *will survive* on this planet.

"No Furs are going to destroy any more of what you have all worked so hard to build. No Furs are going to take away from us what has been earned by effort, by passion, by human planning and thought, by love given tangible form in Greentrees' buildings and farms and research stations and communities.

"We will honor Alex Cutler's memory by rebuilding that which she loved. We will pass on to our children and our children's children that which has been paid for with Alex's life, with the lives of her techs Natalie Bernstein and Benjamin Stoller, and with our shared struggle against the alien enemy. We *will* prevail on Greentrees. I, though coming to you an outsider, cannot free myself of that conviction. This planet is ours, and we will keep it through faith, through cunning, through sacrifice, and through love of our home. We will not allow Greentrees to be forced from us. And the day will come when our children will live on our planet in peace and security. We will allow nothing else."

Bile rose in Alex's throat.

Julian had hit every note perfectly: love of Greentrees, concern for the children, fears of losing what everyone had worked for, inclusion of himself—but how diffidently!—as one of themselves.

Ben said, unnecessarily, "Julian wants everybody to think Alex is dead." Shock shimmered on his young face.

Alex said, "He's made a . . . a tactical error. I'm not dead yet."

"No," Jake said, "nor going to be. But it's only a tactical error if you respond wrongly."

"I'm going to make a broadcast of my own," Alex said, "and tell everyone not only that I'm alive but also exactly who and what Julian is!"

"That's what he wants you to do, Alex," Jake said. "That's the aim of his broadcast. Don't do it."

"And just let him have Greentrees?" Alex cried. "Let him do here the kinds of things he did on Earth? Torture and kill and suppress and—"

"No. Stop shouting, Alex, it hurts my head."

She looked at Jake, old and tired and streaked with dirt. Did he suddenly look so fragile because he was, or in order to manipulate her? She didn't know. Probably she had never known. He was smarter than she and more experienced—oh, so much more experienced!—at deception.

As was Julian. For a terrible moment she classed them together and hated them both, these Terrans who twisted her heart.

Jake said with sudden gentleness, "You need to plan, Alex. Now. We all need to create a plan. Sit here. Please." He waved his arm at the ground beside his chair.

Ben and Natalie, included in his feebly expansive gesture, readily sat on the muddy ground. Alex hesitated, then joined them.

"Here are our assets," Jake said, his voice suddenly stronger. "Julian doesn't know where you are. He can't even be sure you're still alive. He doesn't know what you'll do next."

None of those sounded much like assets to Alex, since she didn't know what she was going to do next, either.

Jake continued. "You have the means to broadcast when and if you choose. You have the space Furs."

"I have *what?*" Alex said.

"The Furs. Julian will have to fight them, and soon. If he doesn't, his grip on Greentrees power will start to slip. People turned to him because they perceived him as a strong military leader. Strong military leaders have to act militarily, or else people begin to doubt them. Julian is now enslaved to his own embryonic legend. You can use that."

Alex saw what Jake meant. At the same time, she wondered how anyone could think like that. What could Terra have been like?

"And now Julian has another priority," Jake said. Natalie and Ben hung on every word. "He had to flee. Since that broadcast started ten minutes ago, the space Furs know exactly where he is. Or rather, where he was—the broadcast was probably recorded and sent from his command bunker. Natalie—"

She was ahead of him, already wading out to retrieve the comlink. She accessed data and read the coordinates aloud.

"Yes," Alex said. "That's the position of Bunker One."

"So Julian is on the run. And the space Furs will be looking for him. Another asset you have, Alex: Julian's Terran force is only about fifty soldiers. He—"

Alex blurted, "He recruited an entire Greentrees army!"

"For now. But they're not well trained, and most of them will turn once they see what Julian is. As Ben here did."

Under his dirt, the boy flushed. Alex saw the pain on his young face, and the shame that he had, even for a while, served Julian. Jake moved on quickly.

"Those are your definite assets: Julian's uncertainty about you. The resulting element of surprise. Julian's split attention to escape the Furs. The potential to turn his Greentrees troops to you. Plus, you have an indefinite asset that might or might not be of use: the wild Furs."

Natalie said, "The wild Furs? But, Mr. Holman, with all due respect . . . they listen to no one. Except Nan Frayne, and Dr. Lasky said that she's dead."

"Yes," Jake said, and Alex saw that for a moment he wandered in some complex memory of a long-ago Nan Frayne. But this time he made it back from that distant country. In fact, Jake seemed to her sharper and more focused than she'd seen him in a long time.

"Yes, the wild Furs listened only to Nan Frayne. They're highly xenophobic, and the space Furs are their own species. But fifty years ago the space Furs also destroyed their villages and killed their kin. And right now, as Lucy's told us, the space Furs are carrying off wild Furs as captives, maybe for breeding stock to increase their limited gene pool of individuals uninfected by the virus *we* deliberately gave them. So the question is: Which will count more with the wild Furs? Their xenophobia against humans or their desire for revenge against their own kind?"

"Which?" breathed Ben. He looked enthralled as a child hearing a great story. God, he was young! Alex must remember that. Ben and Natalie both.

Her "army."

Jake said, "I don't know which will count as more important with the wild Furs. But I think we need to find out."

"How?" Ben said. "We don't even know where any wild Furs are! And how could we talk to them if we found some?"

"I don't know that yet," Jake said.

Alex said, "And this is a 'plan,' Jake? To fight both Furs and Julian?"

He snapped, "No, it's not a plan. I didn't say I had a plan—I said we needed to plan. This is how planning is done, Alex. What's your idea, to just give up? I thought you loved Greentrees!"

"I do." She remembered Julian saying, *"I share Alex's love for Greentrees . . ."*

After an uncomfortable silence Jake said, "I'm sorry."

Alex said, "I'm sorry, too. I'm just scared, Jake."

"I know. And Alex"—Jake shifted in his chair, looking suddenly taller—"that's an asset, too. You can admit truth. By now Julian is so enmeshed in his own grandiosity, need, self-promotion, and desperation that I doubt he can recognize reality, let alone admit it."

Alex didn't see how her own fear was an asset, but she didn't challenge Jake, instead she said humbly, "I am scared. And I don't know what to do next. I want to hear what you think, Jake, and you, Natalie and Ben. Also Lucy, if she comes back. Maybe out of all our scared ideas we can put together some sort of plan."

Jake smiled. "I'd like to suggest the first step. There's one other asset we have that I haven't yet mentioned. It might mean nothing—or everything."

30

THE AVERY MOUNTAINS

Karim sat well back in the shallow cave by the river, apart from the others, who respectfully left him alone. Jon, Kent, and Kueilan talked in low tones. Karim brooded.

He had spent hours trying to communicate with the biomass. He had sent pictures of humans; pictures of Furs and humans destroying each other; all the schematics Kueilan could devise of biological processes, counting patterns ranging from simple series of pulses (one, two, three, four) to complex iterative functions. The biomass had responded to all of it with nonsense. Sometimes they sent back distortions of the pictures. Sometimes schematics that Kueilan said were impossible, combining elements in physically impossible ways. Sometimes meaningless patterns. Sometimes the waves that, Karim became increasingly convinced, were laughter.

Jon said, in mingled frustration and consolation, "They're sentient, at least. They completed that last mathematical series correctly for two more numbers before going weird."

Kueilan twisted from her cross-legged seat in front of the small computer to look at Karim. "It's almost like . . . I know this will sound strange . . . but . . ."

"But what?" Karim snapped. They were all hungry, tired, angry.

"It's almost like they're little kids. Scribbling and fooling around."

Kent said, "Little kids who can extend iterative-function series?"

"Yes," she said stubbornly.

Karim considered. Kueilan was right. The biomass was playing, mocking them. Why? The mass on the Vine planet hadn't behaved like that. It had ignored him completely, until . . .

"Jon, how could we translate whistling into data to send down there?"

"Whistling?"

"Yes. When I was on the Vine planet, the biomass there responded when I whistled. More than responded—it was delighted. How can we send music down?"

Kueilan said skeptically, "Sound is all atmospheric waves. The pole we have conducting data can vibrate, of course, but on the other end that wouldn't—"

The pole began to dissolve.

Jon yelped. They had excavated two feet down to expose that much length of the buried pole. Now the pole tilted to one side, visibly growing softer, as if it were made of butter under the bright sun. The pole touched one side of the narrow hole. Then it grew softer still and dissolved, leaving only a slick residue that sank into the soil.

"What happened!" Jon yelled. He grabbed a sonic digger, loosened dirt at the bottom of the now empty hole, and flopped flat onto his stomach to reach down. Carefully he lifted dirt from around the spot where the deeper extension of the pole should have been. There was nothing. The pole was gone.

"Son of a bastard bitch!" he screamed.

"Be quieter!" Kueilan begged.

Karim stared at the hole. The biomass had grown tired of its games and dissolved the pole. Their one means of communication was gone.

There would be no Vine help in fighting the Furs.

"It wasn't your fault," Kueilan said to Karim. She knelt beside him in the deep shadow of the underhang, her hand on his. Kueilan's gentle, dirt-streaked face held only compassion, and her almond-shaped black eyes were gentle. "You shouldn't blame yourself, Karim."

"I'm not blaming myself," he said harshly, but of course he was, and she wasn't deterred. She said softly,

" 'To bear and not to own,
To act and not lay claim,
To do the work and let it go
Is what makes it stay.' "

"What's that?" He asked.

"The Tao Te Ching."

Karim smiled reluctantly. "There are parallel passages in the Koran. But what I need right now are instructions on disciplining unruly and unreachable alien microbes. Neither the Tao Te Ching nor the Koran contains that."

Kueilan laughed, a light musical sound, and Karim looked at her: almond eyes and slim curves. He was astonished and dismayed to feel the unmistakable signs of attraction. And Lucy missing or dead! How could he? How could—

Jon splashed toward them from the river shallows. "Karim! A flare!"

"A what?"

Kueilan said, "A microwaved distress message from a fired missile. Jon—targeted or general?"

"Targeted and encrypted. The comlink captured it. Is there an encryption program on that computer?"

Kueilan said, "Yes, but using it depends on how heavy the encryption is. It'll only handle up to class three."

Jon held out the comlink. Kueilan took it to the computer, stowed in the least damp place in the underhang, and transferred the data.

"It's a class three," she said. "Whoever sent it knew what equipment we have, or at least guessed pretty well . . . Here it comes."

Lucy's voice came urgently from the machine. "K, J, this is L. I got to my old lover all right. He told me—this is crucial—that you should not try to get to our boss. My lover says he can't be trusted, in the same way Rudy—remember him?—couldn't be trusted. Especially don't so much as hint at anything about our secret garden. My friends and I are going to come to—"

The message ended.

After a silence Kueilan said, "She didn't know how short flares are."

Jon said, "How did she know about them at all? Or to use a class-three encryption? And what does all that *mean?*"

Kent said logically, "Alex has techs with her. Someone helped Lucy. But what does she mean? Who's Rudy?"

Karim said slowly, "It's code. Not encryption, I mean she's talking in code because she knew the message would be intercepted. Lucy is warning us about Julian Martin. She's saying he's a murderer and a traitor, like Rudy Scherer was once, and not to tell Julian about the biomass."

Jon said, "*Julian?* He's done nothing but good for Greentrees!"

"And done it brilliantly," Kueilan agreed. "Lucy's wrong!"

"No," Karim said. "She says the information about Martin came from Jake Holman."

Silence while the others digested this. "*My old lover.*"

Finally Kueilan said, "I hate to say this, Karim, but Mr. Holman is so old now . . ."

Karim didn't answer. After the first visceral shock of hearing Lucy's voice, his mind raced. "*We're going to come to—*" she'd said. To where? Here? Lucy, unlike anyone else on Greentrees, had seen the biomass on the Vine planet: "*our secret garden.*" She'd believed it could help. And Jake had known Beta Vine. And Lucy hadn't said "We're going to go to—" No, she'd said, "We're going to *come* to—"

Karim said, "They're on their way here."

"What?" Jon said. "How do you know?"

"Because I know Lucy. And Jake."

Kueilan gazed at him with gentle doubt. Kent said, "Karim, I don't think they'd cross the kill-clean zone, even by night. Look how exposed they'd be. And if Julian Martin really is a traitor . . . why, he'd be trying to—" She stopped.

"To kill Alex," Jon finished. "I don't think I believe . . . but Kueilan's right about one thing. If Lucy and Alex tried to come here, they'd be completely vulnerable. No vegetation cover, and they'd give off a thermal signature from the rover."

All true. "Yes, but—"

Kueilan, their natural peacemaker, said, "If they're coming, we should wait for them. If they're not coming, we still don't have anywhere we can go. So I suggest we eat, and tomorrow we try again at the biomass to see if it has done something to reopen communications. I mean, if it feeds off metals, couldn't it also accrete them to create another pole? Or something else like a pole? Maybe it'll decide it wants to communicate again. Like a child wanting to play again. We don't really know what it will do, do we?"

She was right. Karim nodded gratefully. Nobody knew what the biomass might do. Or what Jake might do, either—in the old days, Jake had been the one to come up with plan after plan, saving their lives from murderous Furs.

Karim didn't let himself think about how old Jake must have grown since then, how feeble. He smiled at Kueilan.

31

ALONG A MOUNTAIN CREEK

Lucy returned so exhausted from walking that she practically fell down the muddy bank to the river. Ben climbed up the slope to cover as much damage as he could from Lucy's tracks. Jake was asleep in the back of the shallow depression. Alex and Natalie stared grimly at Lucy.

"I had to," Lucy mumbled. "Karim . . . Julian . . ." She was asleep.

When she woke, she told them more. Her previous note of apology had disappeared from her voice. She addressed Jake, now awake and sitting in his chair, as if Alex didn't exist.

"Jake, I had to warn Karim. This biomass could be the key. And Karim would have taken it straight to Julian Martin . . . you know him. Karim's not really a suspicious person, and Jon McBain's even worse. I did the only thing I could do, and I was careful to not let us be traced. I walked miles and miles before I fired the flare, and I set it for maximum flight before it released my message."

Natalie said angrily, "But the message itself was intercepted, including its coordinates. I told you that! Now Julian knows where Karim is, not to mention the biomass!"

"I coded the message."

"At class-three encryption! A child could break it!"

"No, I mean I coded it. No one but Karim will know what I was talking about."

Alex snorted.

"It's true," Lucy said, glaring at Alex. "And anyway, there's no time to argue about it. We have to start down there."

"Down where?" Alex demanded. She just realized that she didn't like Lucy.

"To Karim and the biomass!"

Natalie made a small noise. Alex opened her mouth but before she could blast Lucy for her arrogance, her assumption of command, and her stupidity, Jake spoke.

"Lucy, we already have a tentative plan, and it does involve going to the biomass. If you hadn't come back by now, we were going to do it without you. We—"

Alex stalked away from them, moving along the river.

She had argued with Jake for an hour last evening, until she couldn't stand it anymore. She'd been amazed at Jake's tenacity. He'd sat in his chair—weak, drooling, quavery voiced—and just kept *at* her. *"I'd like to suggest the first step. There's one other asset we have that I haven't yet mentioned. It might mean nothing—or everything."* Well, it meant nothing, in Alex's opinion. Jake's plan was just as wild-eyed and stupid as Lucy's flare. If it had been anyone but Jake, Alex wouldn't have listened for more than two minutes. But it was Jake, and so Alex had listened, and argued, and reasoned. To no end—Jake had remained firm about his insane idea.

Finally she had told him no.

And here he was telling the plan to Lucy as if Alex had agreed to it.

Alex plopped down on a rock jutting up from two inches of rushing river. Her boots and cuffs were wet, as was the rock. She was too upset to care. Lucy, Jake, Julian . . . no, don't think about Julian. Too much pain. Think only about defeating the Furs.

How did you avoid thinking about someone you loved who was probably trying to kill you?

"You can't think clearly just now," Jake had said last night, with compassion. Was he telling the truth or just trying to manipulate her again? Alex could no longer tell. Everything was too complicated, including her emotions.

Breathe deeply.

It was a glorious Greentrees morning. Fresh warm air blew above the sparkling river. The opposite bank was shaded by purple trees, the long thin leaves on their lower branches dangling into the water, which tugged at them in further elongation. Lacy moon-rushes turned their tiny bluish petals to the fading sun. Overhead a flock of sue-birds wheeled and cried. And dripping down the bank, an enormous red creeper, capable of tangling and digesting small animals, waited for its prey.

Something flew into sight on the distant horizon above the red creeper.

Alex shrank back against the riverbank. She ran back to the others, who had already seen it and were moving Jake's chair to the deepest part of the overhang. Natalie snatched up a breakfast bowl left to rinse in the river. With all their meager belongings they waited, hardly breathing, under the protection of dirt and rock.

The skimmer, flying very low, appeared over the top of the opposite bank, flew over the river, and disappeared.

Ben breathed, "if they saw the rover under those branches . . ."

"They didn't," Alex said. "Or they'd have landed." Hatred flooded her, caustic as lye. Julian had probably not been in the skimmer; he would be holed up somewhere in a new "command post" as primitive as Alex's own hideout. She was hiding from him, he was hiding from the Furs. But he'd risked at least two of his Terran soldiers in the skimmer to hunt her down.

Or maybe she was wrong. She had not responded with a broadcast of her own to Julian's announcement of her death. To that extent, anyway, she'd listened to Jake. So maybe Julian wasn't hunting her. Maybe he was hunting Furs. Or just scouting out his new planet, taken by treachery and murder and pointless destruction.

Ben said, "The skimmer is heading west."

"Good," Lucy said. "We need to drive mostly south."

Something else flashed above the river and was gone. "Oh my God!" Natalie cried. "That was a Fur shuttle!"

A second later they heard the explosion.

No one spoke. Then Alex said shakily, "Wait. If the shuttle had wanted to, it could have just annihilated the skimmer. But it exploded it instead. The Furs wanted it to register on human displays, so we would know . . . so we know . . ."

"Yes," Jake said. "And probably the Furs want the wreckage to
stay on the ground, too. It's a decoy to lure humans to check for
survivors. We're not going anywhere near it."

"But if there are survivors—" Ben began, and stopped.

Natalie said, "Commander Martin might come to look for his
survivors."

"No, Natalie," Jake said. "He won't do that."

Natalie looked puzzled. Alex said, "The Furs will have left surveillance equipment by the crash, Natalie. Julian will anticipate that."

Jake said to her, "Now you're starting to think like a soldier."
There was no pleasure in his voice.

Natalie said, "Then we can't stay here, either!"

Jake said, "Not unless you're willing to hide under a riverbank
twenty-four hours a day, every day." He spoke to Natalie but his
eyes were on Alex.

"All right, Jake," she said. "We'll leave now. But not all together."

They loaded Jake and his chair into the rover. Ben drove it south
along the creek, staying under tree cover as much as he could. Alex
watched them drive away and thought how brave both of them
were: the boy whose loyalties had been pulled and jerked like a
balky tree stump, and the old man who kept his frail body going by
the sheer will of his wily mind.

She might never see either of them again. They had the dangerous part of this insane mission, which included splitting up in order to increase survival odds for at least some of them. In the rover
Jake and Ben, heading for Karim's biomass, would be far more exposed than would the three others. Julian's skimmer was gone, but
the Furs still had one or more shuttles, plus who knew what sort of
land transport. The Fur mother ship orbited above Greentrees, as
did Julian's *Crucible*. Julian had the loyalty of all the humans on

Greentrees who didn't know what he had done, which was all the humans on Greentrees except five.

Maybe nine, if Lucy's "coded" message had indeed reached Karim and if Karim had indeed known what the hell Lucy meant. Alex doubted both these things.

The rover disappeared from sight. Alex slid back down the bank, where Natalie handed her a pack made up of as many essentials as each of them could carry. They'd buried everything else. Alex, Natalie, and Lucy were to stick to the creek, sheltering beside its wild banks and following it south to the rendezvous point with the rover. If, of course, the rover actually returned.

Natalie asked, "Do you really think Ben and Mr. Holman can get to Mira City?"

Alex glanced at the girl, then bit back her first sarcastic reply: *There is no Mira City to get to!* Natalie deserved more than that. She, too, had been incredibly brave and loyal.

"I hope so," Alex said gently. "Meanwhile, let's get going."

The three women started to walk along the creek.

32

MIRA CITY PLAIN

He drifted in and out of sleep, an old man who knew he confused past and present, thinking and dreaming. Beta Vine emerged from his shuttle for the first time in his little domed cart. Lucy Lasky scattered kisses on Jake's sleeping face. Alex's face became her aunt's, Gail's, dead for twenty years. Furs imprisoned humans, then more humans, then more and more until all of Terra howled inside cages with invisible force-field walls. And over all, Star Chu sang that ditty all the young people liked:

> "On Greentrees we are
> For good, but is it good,
> How would I know, all I know
> For sure is yooouuuuu . . .
> Yooouuuu . . .
> Yooouuuuu . . ."

"Mr. Holman," Ben said in his respectful young voice, "you said to wake you at the start of the kill-clean zone. We're here."

Jake forced open his eyes. Every bone ached from jostling along in the rover, even though Natalie had given him painkillers. The patch wasn't very effective because the effective ones also sedated, which Jake couldn't permit. Painfully he leaned forward to peer through the rover's mud-spattered windshield.

There was nothing whatsoever to see.

Ben had halted under a clump of purple trees. A few feet in front of them, all vegetation stopped. In all directions the plain was as blank as an empty display screen. No life, no remains of previous life. Sterile as a moon.

Incongruously, he thought of Alex's cat. Katous had gone with him to the hospital cave but had then run away. Undoubtedly the animal had been vaporized along with everything else. Alex had been fond of Katous.

A sue-bird flew through Jake's field of vision, squawking indignantly.

Stupidly cheered, Jake said, "How far to Mira City?"

Ben glanced at the rover's display. "Another hundred miles."

And nothing had annihilated them yet. "Go on."

Ben drove onto the blankness. And yet, Jake thought, it wasn't completely blank. Somewhere ahead were caves that had been end points for Mira City's evacuation. It was from one of those caves that Lucy had taken him. Were people still holed up there, rationing their supplies, waiting for instructions from Alex that were not going to come? End points closest to the city had been reserved for the old, the ill, the helpless. Jake doubted that Julian Martin would be mobilizing those Greenies anytime soon.

Jake suddenly wondered what had happened to Alex's efficient, perpetually disapproving assistant, Siddalee Brown. He'd always liked Siddalee.

Ben pushed the rover as fast as it would go. They were now exposed visually as well as thermally, perfect targets. Shooting fish in a barrel, Jake thought, on a planet that technically had never had either.

But nothing had annihilated them yet.

Sometime later, Ben again woke him. This time Jake heard tears in the boy's voice, which Jake tactfully ignored.

"This is where Mira City was, Mr. Holman. Right here."

Jake inched forward in his seat, and Ben suddenly stopped the rover and slid down the windshield.

Nothing. To Jake's left the river babbled and sang. The slight hill on the right horizon must be where the mausoleum had stood.

Nothing remained as a hint that a city had stood here—houses, manufactures, power plant, farm, genetics laboratories, parks, children. Not so much as a sapling.

But Ben's young eyes were stronger than Jake's. "Look, Mr. Holman—the groundcover's starting to come back." He pointed.

A faint patch of lavender, in a depression where the soil must be wetter. An embryonic swath of Greentrees' ubiquitous purple groundcover, tough as hide and adaptable as cockroaches. Give the plain two Terran months and it would again be in bloom, home to frebs and . . . and everything else native.

"Drive toward the iron mine, Ben. Do you know where it was?"

"My mother was a miner," Ben said, swinging the rover around.

The mine had been across river, away from the main section of the city that still rose in Jake's mind. Ben pushed the rover through relative shallows, once spanned by a bridge. A mile farther, the entrance hole still gaped in the low hillside, although the building that had fronted it had vanished. In that building Ben's mother would have directed the nanos that dug the tunnels, the robots that located the ore, and the trams that had carried it to the surface. It had been a big operation, Alex's pride, employing at full capacity as many as seventeen people.

"Mr. Holman, I can go in by myself. You told me where to find it."

"I want to go," Jake said. But that was sheer sentiment, nothing else. The less time he and Ben spent at the blank that had been Mira City, the better. Jake slowed everything down.

"No, you go ahead, Ben. Find it. Go quickly."

The boy leaped from the rover as if he'd been shot and ran toward the mine.

Ben might have played here as a child. He might have sometimes gone to work with his highly skilled mother and frolicked on the purple hillside above her head. The eco-team would have cleared the area of red creeper and other dangerous native flora and put one of their electronic fences in place against predatory fauna. Was she dead, Ben's miner mother? Had he played here with brothers and sisters now as dead as the city itself?

Jake tried to fight off sleep and failed. Again the disturbing dreams, Lucy and Duncan and Alex and Rudy Scherer all mixed together, yesterday indistinguishable from today. William Shipley, the Quaker doctor who had first put the box in a secret passage of the mine, lectured Jake. "We owe it to these people, Friend Jake. We promised them."

"They will never come back for them," Jake had argued. "Perpetual supercold storage is damn expensive!"

"Nonetheless, we will keep our promise," Shipley said tranquilly, and then the Quaker was shaking his shoulder. The doctor's hand on Jake's shoulder became Ben's hand, a plastic box about one cubic foot balanced awkwardly on his other hip.

"Mr. Holman, I found it. Just where you said." The boy had clearly willed himself to firmness. "Now please tell me what it is and what it will do."

Jake looked at him. Ben had earned that much. The only reason Jake hadn't explained before was that if they were captured, Jake hadn't wanted Ben to possess any knowledge for which he could be tortured.

"I'll tell you what it is, Ben. It's a supercold perpetual storage box, capable of preserving organic material for several millennia through fire, flood, quakes, everything but annihilating weaponry. Inside are Vine death flowers."

"Are what?"

Despite everything, Jake smiled. "We don't know what they are, either. But on their first trip to Greentrees, the Furs killed all the Vines that had landed here not long before. Before the Vines died, they tried to give us some genetic material they called their 'death flowers.' It didn't work; the Furs annihilated the death flowers, too. But later, when Karim and Lucy and I and others were aboard a Vine ship to—well, you know the story. The Furs annihilated those Vines, too. This time, however, when they gave humans their death flowers, we were able to keep them. When we returned to Greentrees, we hid them here in case any Vines ever came back for them, as the Vines had said would someday happen."

"But they never came," Ben said.

"No."

"So what are we going to do with these 'death flowers' now?" Ben said, somewhere between bewilderment and anger. "We just risked our lives to get this box—what good is it?"

"I don't know," Jake said. "That's what we're going to find out. Get back in the rover and drive."

They could have gone directly to the Avery Mountains, but instead they backtracked to pick up Alex, Lucy, and Natalie. Jake had argued against this; he wanted to reach Karim's biomass as soon as possible, and going back for the three women would add another day to the trip. But Alex had insisted and, to Jake's surprise, Lucy had for once agreed with Alex. Jake had given in. He had opposed Alex enough already. He knew, without wanting to think about it, how much pain she felt over Julian.

So Ben again drove at maximum speed across the kill-clean zone until he reached the relative safety of vegetation. Then he was forced to go much more slowly around or through thick stands of brush, red creeper, and purple trees. Once, rounding a copse to return to the river, the rover startled a herd of "elephants." The ponderous, placid, evil-smelling beasts, like no elephants Jake had ever seen on Terra, stared stupidly at the rover before returning to their grazing. Ben said hastily, "I'll move upwind."

"Can you make the rendezvous point before dark? I'd rather not use the lights."

"Mr. Holman, I'm not even sure where the rendezvous point *is*. We said ten miles down the creek from our camp, but that creek twists and doubles back and we weren't even sure Alex and the others could make ten miles today. Alex is pretty old, you know."

Alex was forty-five. Jake didn't point out that by Ben's calendar Jake himself must be fossilized. He felt fossilized.

The rover got tangled in a patch of red creeper. In the gathering gloom, Ben hadn't seen it in time. The predatory plant mistook the rover for some large animal and shot out its tendrils to capture it.

The tough vines wrapped themselves around any protuberances they could reach and started, much faster than anything on Earth, to climb toward the inhabitants.

Ben slid the side panels up. "There's a spray under the seat, Mr. Holman."

"Can't you just drive out? Surely the rover is stronger than a vine?"

"Yes, but when a friend of mine did that—" Ben suddenly faltered. The friend, Jake guessed, was probably dead. "—did that, he tore off the fuel cell water valve. Just hand me the spray."

Jake found it, a spray wand. Ben slid open the side shield an inch, stuck out the wand, and pushed.

Jake said, "How long does it take to kill the whole plant?"

"A few minutes. The eco-genemod team is—was—pretty good."

They waited in silence. Wild Furs materialized out of nowhere.

Ben gasped. Jake peered through the dirty windshield. Two ... three ... were there four? No, only three. They stood immobile, one in front of the rover and one by each side. All three carried laser guns.

"*Julian Martin gave the Furs laser guns to use against the Cheyenne—*" Yenmo Kang's despairing words.

Ben reached for his own gun.

"No," Jake said swiftly. "Don't fire. Don't move."

"You're not a soldier, Mr. Holman," said Ben, who'd been one for a few months. And then, in the first flash of bitterness Jake had seen from the boy, "You weren't ever a soldier."

"But I'm still Alex's senior adviser. And she's in command. *Don't move.*"

Please let Julian have made a fetish of the chain of command.

Apparently he had. Ben hesitated, dropped his hand.

Jake was acting on instinct, not thought, and he hated that. But there was no time to plan. "Slide down both side panels of the rover, Ben."

"But—"

"That's an order."

Ben obeyed. But Jake knew he wouldn't blindly obey too much longer; Ben had, after all, made up his own mind to believe Lucy and Jake about Julian. The boy was not completely broken to military obedience; he was a Greenie.

The three wild Furs didn't move. They were a fearsome sight in the deep dusk: powerfully muscled, heavily furred, their high-set third eyes scanning the sky and their thick balancing tails resting just beyond the patch of withered red creeper. Three laser guns pointed at the humans in the rover.

But the guns were only pointing, not firing.

Jake said, "Get out of the rover, Ben, very slowly. Let them see your every move. Lift out my chair and set it up in the clear, then put me in it."

"Why are you making us vulnerable to them?"

No more blind obedience. "If they wanted to attack, they'd have done so already. This is the most xenophobic species in the known galaxy. Our smell alone arouses rage in their hindbrains, or whatever the analogue is. If they're controlling that response, it's by an effort of will we can't even imagine. They want cooperation from us, and that's unprecedented."

"We don't need their cooperation."

Oh God, the bullheaded arrogance of even the meek young. Jake held his temper. "Yes, we do. Don't you see? They can lead us to space Furs."

Jake hoped that "lead·us to" didn't sound too exploitative. How much English had these aliens learned from Nan Frayne?

Ben moved slowly out of the rover, treading over the now-dead red creeper. Jake could read Ben's reluctance in every movement. The boy's very hair practically bristled. Not only Furs were xenophobic.

When Jake sat in his chair in the dark, he tugged Ben to sit on the ground beside him. Finally the Furs moved. One crouched and expertly built a small fire, starting it with a spark struck from a stone. The three lined up across the fire from the humans, tall menacing animals in the flickering light. Did the smoke mask the human smell? Jake hoped so.

The largest alien put away his laser and pulled his spear from its harness. Jake's nerves quivered. The Fur reached across the fire with the spear and slashed through the groundcover until he'd exposed bare ground. Then he made a single line in the dirt and uttered a single syllable: "Aaaaaannnnnttttttt."

"Nan. Nan Frayne," Jake guessed, and the Fur nodded clumsily, obviously not a native gesture. Jake felt Ben's surprised respect. Well, let the boy be impressed. Jake had already realized that these Furs must have been trained—socialized? recruited?—by Nan Frayne. Otherwise he and Ben would be carrion.

The Fur drew another line and uttered another syllable, this one too guttural to echo correctly. With his free hand he hit his own head.

"You," Jake hazarded; he could not reproduce the alien's name. The alien nodded, apparently willing to accept "you."

Many more lines in the dirt, and now the alien went back and added smaller rising lines to each. Jake was mystified until Ben said softly, "They're crests. He's drawing their males."

"Males. You males," Jake said. A nod. When Nan had taught them to understand a little English, had she also taught herself to differentiate the guttural Fur sounds? Then she had a better ear than Jake did.

The Fur drew more lines, this time without crests. "You women," Jake said. No nod. "You females." A nod. Nan had thought the sounds of "men" and "women" too close to use.

Now the Fur drew a circle, a line coming out of it, and a smaller circle. A McAndrew Drive ship, which the alien had certainly never seen. Nan again. He drew many crested lines coming from the ship and leading straight to the wild Fur females. Then savagely he erased the wild Fur males.

"Enemy," Jake hazarded. "You enemy. Kill you men. Take you females."

All three Furs nodded.

Exhilaration surged through Jake, which he carefully hid. He had the answer to his question. The wild Furs had chosen. Their xenophobia toward humans mattered less than their desire to regain the breeding females carried off to the space Furs' ship.

Or, rather, their xenophobia mattered less as long as the humans remained very careful to not provoke it. Submissive in posture, helpful to wild Fur goals. And downwind.

"Ben," he said softly, "we have a sort of ally."

They were late to the rendezvous point. It took a lot of picture drawing to communicate to the Furs that the humans would help the Furs against their enemy in the ship, that the rover was going to drive slowly to meet three more humans, that after that it was going to go to the place Nan Frayne had been killed. This last, which Jake had feared would be the most incomprehensible to the Furs, was actually accepted instantly. He had no idea why. Maybe he had stumbled on some death ritual, some expectation that he would commune with Nan's spirit. Maybe it seemed logical to them that he start his aid at a place where some females had been captured. Maybe it was the right conjunction of moons.

Ben had to use the rover's lights, after all. The three Furs disappeared; Jake assumed they were following. He let himself sleep, knowing he had to conserve his strength. The rover jostled him awake every few minutes. Nocturnal birds whistled, unseen creatures rustled the groundcover, and Greentrees' sweet, distinctive night smell drifted on the wind. Clouds covered and uncovered two small, high moons. And somewhere in the darkness, three aliens with revenge in their unknowable hearts trailed the human vehicle toward what Jake could only think of as an unholy alliance: dangerous. Temporary. And as unconscionable, in Jake's planning, as anything Julian Martin could ever have done, anywhere.

33

MOUNTAIN CREEKBED

Alex was so weary she could barely unfasten her pack. Natalie and Lucy didn't seem to feel the strain; they'd talked steadily as the three made their arduous way downriver. After a few miles Alex could barely breathe, let alone chat. They'd clambered over rocks, waded through shallows, climbed the riverbank when there was no footing below and then climbed back down when the water level permitted. Alex had fifteen years on Lucy, over twenty on Natalie. However, she'd made the rendezvous. She was here.

Another day, another muddy overhang.

When the rover appeared, Alex didn't hear it. She had sunk immediately into a sleep so profound that Natalie had to shake her whole torso to wake her.

"Alex . . . Alex! Wake up! They're back, Ben and Mr. Holman! They're alive!"

A moment to stagger back from that place of perfect rest. "Do . . . did they . . . the box?"

"They have it!" Now Alex could see that Natalie's dirty face glowed. The present triumph was enough for her.

Not so for Alex. She dragged herself up the riverbank yet one more time, filled with the desperate plan yet to come.

"Jake! Are you all right?"

"Of course I'm all right," he said. "Get in."

He looked terrible. Translucent flesh under the dirt and drool, jutting bones like chisels. His sunken eyes burned feverishly. He was living on sheer fierce will.

She leaned closer to him. He smelled awful, but then so did they all. "You can't go on like this, dear heart."

"The wild Furs have joined us."

At first Alex thought he was delusional; the words were spoken so quickly, with a frantic stare back over his shoulder. But Ben said, "It's true, Alex. Three wild Furs followed us here. Mr. Holman spoke to them."

"*How?*"

But Jake was repeating frantically, "Get in! Get in!" Natalie and Lucy hurried up with the packs, hastily assembled. The five of them jammed into the rover and Ben took off. Alex craned her neck behind. She saw no Furs.

Ben told the story over his shoulder as he drove, which he seemed now to do with ease, and without the fear of detection that haunted Alex. She kept glancing at the bare blue sky. Nothing.

The wild Furs were now their allies.

To do what, against two enemies with infinitely superior technology? No one said, and Alex decided not to ask the question. It would only be one more query without an answer.

Why do we think that bringing Vine "death flowers" to a Greentrees biomass buried far underground can help us?

Because Jake and Lucy want to do it.

Why do we think wild Furs armed with native spears and contraband laser guns can help us?

Because the Furs want to do it.

Why do we think that hurtling across the landscape at top speed, spewing visual and thermal trails, can help us?

Because Ben has gotten expert at driving the rover.

Alex rubbed her eyes with her filthy fists. All right, she had to stop this. It didn't help to tear down others' plans—no matter how stupid or far-fetched—unless one had something better to suggest instead. Alex had nothing to suggest. She was the tray-o, in charge of deploying resources, but how did you do that when essentially you had no real resources? Success went to the people with the best technology. Alex had learned that in decades of allocation administration. It was all she knew how to do.

Jake and Lucy were proceeding on some other assumption. What was it? Maybe something like: Success went to the people with the most daring. Could that be true? It didn't seem likely.

But nothing about this situation was likely. The best thing for her was to watch carefully how things developed until she had a clearer idea of what they all should, or could, do. Protest might as well wait until then. Conserve her strength.

She would need it if, eventually, she decided to oppose Jake and Lucy.

They stopped just short of the kill-clean zone to change the fuel cell. "Last one," Ben said when he climbed back into the rover.

Finally Alex saw the wild Furs. Out on the denuded plain, without cover, they were distant figures falling farther behind the speeding rover. How had they kept up before, with Ben driving as fast as the terrain allowed? But Ben had kept to the river; the Furs must have known shortcuts, routes accessible to feet but not vehicle. This was their natural turf.

No. It was not. Alex had to remind herself that the Furs were as alien to Greentrees as humans were. Or as native. This lot had been born here—but so had she.

"Slow down," she said to Ben. "You're losing our new allies."

"They can follow our tracks," Ben said. "We need to get under cover as soon as we can." He didn't slow.

He was right. Alex glanced behind. The wild Furs reappeared, moving at a steady lope. How long could they keep it up? It was remarkable how well they blended into even this blank landscape. Brown, shaggy—if they dropped flat she probably wouldn't notice them at fifty paces.

But such primitive camouflage wouldn't protect them from their cousins' annihilation beam fired from orbit.

Gradually the foothills of the Avery Mountains rose around them. Alex had once driven this way with Julian, to visit Jon McBain's research station. She'd been so eager to show Julian the battery Jon had supposedly been developing, and so irritated when she learned that Jon was devoting all his attention to these new bacteria. Buried anaerobes weren't impressive, and Alex had wanted to impress Julian. She had always been trying to impress Julian.

Lucy studied the rover's display coordinates. "Stop, Ben—*here*. This is the place."

Alex saw nothing except a narrow hole three feet deep.

Lucy hopped out of the rover and stared at the hole. "Where's the pole? They dug to expose the pole!"

The empty plain held nothing at all.

Jake croaked, "Find Karim. The river . . . they'd probably hide by the river. To wait for us."

Lucy got back into the rover. Ben drove toward the river. Over her shoulder Alex saw the three Furs lope toward the pathetic empty hole.

As the rover neared the river, Jon McBain clambered over the bank with an Arab who must be Karim Mahjoub. Lucy fell into Karim's arms. Two younger people followed, holding back slightly. The girl, Alex saw, was Chinese. She looked remarkably like Star Chu.

Had Star survived the annihilation of Mira City?

"You're alive," Jake said, and Alex saw that he spoke to Karim, standing beside the rover. The two stared at each other with looks that, under other circumstances, would have been comical. Surprise, compassion, distrust. They had not seen each other for thirty-nine years, from Jake's point of view. Less than one year, from Karim's. Even to Alex, Jake looked like a fanatical skeleton, animated by a last wild flare of dying life. What did he look like to Karim?

Lucy stood quietly watching both men.

Jake said softly, "Welcome home."

"Thank you."

"Where's the communication pole Lucy told us about?"

"The biomass dissolved it," Karim said.

Jake folded his hands across his concave belly and closed his eyes.

Alex said quickly, "We need to get under cover and then fill each other in on everything."

"What about the rover?" Ben said.

There was nowhere to conceal the rover. "Drive it farther along the river," Alex said, "and maybe you can find a place to get it down and hide it. If not, at least it will be farther from us."

"I'll walk back after I do," Ben said, and Alex saw his reluctance. He didn't want to leave his precious machine.

Eight were a tight squeeze under Jon McBain's overhang: Jake in his chair, Alex, Lucy, and Natalie, plus Jon, Karim, and the two techs, who were named Kent Landers and Kueilan Ma. Kueilan, Alex saw, avoided Lucy—what was that about? Kent, a quiet young man with a filthy red beard, gave them all bowls of soysynth and mentioned that their supplies were running low.

But it was Jon McBain, excitable Jon, who appeared completely unchanged by the shattering changes on Greentrees, who explained their failed attempts to communicate with the biomass. "It mocked us, Alex. I swear that's what it was doing! And then it just dissolved the pole!"

Kueilan added, "It seemed like a child, almost. Playing, not taking anything seriously."

Lucy said primly, "I think you're anthropomorphizing."

Kueilan, who seemed so gentle, snapped back, "But then you weren't here, were you?"

Jake, his head so sunk on his skinny breast that Alex had wondered if he were asleep, said suddenly, "I brought the death flowers from the Vine ship."

"What?" Karim said stupidly.

"The death flowers entrusted to William Shipley. We kept them in cryogenic storage, after you and Lucy left Greentrees. They're with us now."

Karim suddenly looked animated. Alex saw that despite whatever inexplicable tension existed between the two men about that

little space bitch Lucy, Karim still trusted and admired Jake. A plan
from Jake, no matter how desperate or dumb, raised Karim's hopes.

Her own rose slightly. Karim, after all, had seen and interacted
with Vines. The native Greenies, as Lucy had often pointed out so
acidly, had not.

Jon said excitedly, "I never would have believed the biomass
could communicate with us as much as it did—but I was wrong!
And if sentient Vines are somehow in symbiosis with giant biofilms
on their own planets . . . but how do we get the genetic material in
the death flowers in contact with the biomass? It's two miles down!"

But Jake had fallen asleep.

Alex said firmly, "We try that in the morning. We sleep now."

"But how do we—"

She tuned him out. Jon McBain was like a swarm of small biting
insects, persistent and vital and adaptable.

"Tomorrow," Kueilan said in her gentle voice, and Alex was
grateful.

Alex woke sometime during the night. She lay near Jake, bundled
up in most of their blankets in the driest part of the overhang. By
the light of three moons in a clear, starlight sky, Alex saw the out-
line of a small dark shape sitting beside him. Lucy. Evidently they'd
been talking.

"But has your life—until all this happened—been happy, Jake?"
Lucy asked softly.

A small silence. Then Jake's voice quavered, "As much as anyone's, I imagine."

"Did you ever think about me, all those decades?"

"Of course I did. Lucy, don't—"

"I won't. I just wanted to know."

Another silence. Alex breathed slowly out. Jake said finally, "It's
strange. The same things that draw people together end up tearing
them apart."

"Do you mean us?" Lucy said.

"No. I meant Alex and Julian."

Alex heard Lucy shift in the darkness. "Alex and Julian Martin? Jon McBain didn't tell us that!"

"Jon McBain wouldn't know. Or care. He spends his life in the field."

Lucy's voice grew harder. "So is that love affair going to interfere with Alex's fighting Julian for Greentrees?"

"No," Jake said, and Alex felt her vision clear again, her breath resume. "She's a Greenie through and through. She—"

"What did you mean," Lucy interrupted, "about the same thing that brought them together tearing them apart?"

This time Jake took longer to answer. Or maybe he was just tiring faster than Lucy. Eventually he said, "Alex is like most of her generation of Greenies. They aren't like us, Lucy. They grew up with Mira City's incredible generosity. Agricultural riches, mining riches, climactic riches . . . none of them have any idea how rich Greentrees is because they don't have any standard of comparison. They never saw Earth.

"So all of them, even the brightest, are a little naive. Used to enough of everything to go around, and then some. They've never seen naked, desperate want, or naked, desperate greed. Look at even the Hope of Heaven dissidents . . . they think they're the most dangerous and violent creatures ever to rise up in rebellion, and until Julian Martin showed up, they hadn't actually had a deliberate murder. Not one."

"I'm not following you," Lucy said. "What's that got to do with Alex and Julian?"

"I'll tell you, but then I need to sleep," Jake said, and Alex heard the weakness in his voice, the raspy exhaustion. "When you were a kid back on Terra, did you ever study a flock of chickens in school? Or model chicken behavior on a computer?"

"No."

"You were too young. There was an educational vogue for it when I was a kid." Jake fell silent, lost in some private, long-ago memory of a school Alex could not imagine.

"So?" Lucy said impatiently.

"So chickens really do establish a pecking order. Even if there's enough feed for all of them, even if they're awash in feed, they establish a power structure over who gets to eat when. So do mammals—dogs and all those extinct exotics, hyenas and lions and such. Hierarchy is hardwired into the brain, including ours. We don't seem able to get anything done until we establish it."

"I still don't—"

Jake's tone abruptly turned harsh. "You loved me once because I held power on Greentrees. Alex loved Julian for the same reason. You left me for Karim because you didn't like the way I used that power. Alex will oppose Julian for the same reason. Power is sexy, power of mind or body or political control. It's sexy because it says, 'I can control more than you can but, with you, I'm not going to. You're an exception.' Until, of course, suddenly you're not."

Lucy exploded, a hushed small violence in the dark. "That's ridiculous! You're leaving out genuine moral considerations, human decisions of right and wrong that—"

"Of course I am. I'm addressing the hardwiring underneath those things, and older than they are by millions of years. But still powerful."

"I didn't love you once, or Karim now, because of—"

"I don't want to argue, Lucy. I'm too old, and too tired. Believe what you want. But Alex could have just admired Julian, hero-worshipped him even, learned from him. She did those things, but she also loved him. Dazzled provincial woman and powerful seasoned warrior from beyond the mountains. Story as old as Sumeria."

"Don't you—"

"Good night, Lucy," Jake said, and at the weariness in his voice, even Lucy subsided, fuming.

Was Jake right? Had Alex loved Julian simply because she'd been dazzled by the head of an alluringly exotic and dangerous hierarchy? Had she really seen only what she'd wanted to see, not considering the implications of that dazzle?

Maybe, she thought painfully. But not exclusively. There was more, something else that Jake had missed. Alex was not, after all, alone in her enthrallment with Julian Martin. Most of Greentrees had worshipped him. Only a few, like Lau-Wah Mah, had seen Julian for the brutal schemer he was.

Mira City had been more than naive, more than hardwired for hierarchy. They had also been smug, so sure that the city they were creating needed no help from any Terran past. Mira had laughed at the Cheyenne, hanging on to dead ideas. In two generations, Terran history had been all but forgotten in Mira. Irrelevant, unnecessary. Let us do things our way. All those dead civilizations, their rises and wars and falls, had nothing to do with us. A waste of dee-bee space. And no one had believed that more casually, carelessly, and completely than Alex herself.

But Julian had been right, after all. Terran colony worlds needed to know Terran history. If they knew, they would be better able to recognize the subtlety of would-be conquerors, even without possessing the same brutality and ruthlessness. With surer knowledge of their shared past, maybe Mira City would not have welcomed Julian so trustingly into power.

Maybe Alex would not have welcomed him so trustingly into her bed.

Maybe Mira City would still be standing . . . no, that had been the Furs, not Julian! She needed to keep her conquerors straight.

Oh, Julian—

He still wanted control of Greentrees. He wasn't going to get it.

And so, teeth clenched, Alex fell asleep, and in her dreams Julian became a Fur and the Fur became Jake and Jake became her, until she woke in a clammy sweat, unsure who held power, who really wanted it, and who should have it over this gorgeous, generous, scarred planet that was her only home.

34

THE AVERY MOUNTAINS

Morning light revealed a whole camp of wild Furs across the river, upwind as far as possible while still able to watch the humans.

"They must have really good eyesight," Ben said after a cautious reconnoiter. "I think there are as many as two dozen, including maybe five or six females."

"Did you see technoweapons?" Alex asked.

"No, but we already know they have laser guns."

"They could have anything, including Terran weapons we don't know about," she said grimly. Julian.

Natalie said, "I thought the wild Furs lived in the southern subcontinent, with the Cheyenne."

"They used to," Kent said, "until all this started. I'd guess that they're here now to wage war."

Jon McBain, incredibly, seemed completely uninterested in the wild Furs. His total attention, and Karim's, was on the biomass. "I'm going over there now!"

Jake, spooning his breakfast unevenly into his mouth, said, "You'll wait. Minimize exposure."

"Wait for what?" Jon wasn't challenging, merely bewildered.

"Me."

Despite herself, Alex grinned.

Karim said, "We shouldn't all go to the biomass site, in case of an attack by . . . by anything. A backup group with a mix of skills should stay hidden here. Kent, Ben, Natalie, Lucy, maybe even Alex." He saw her face. "Well, not Alex. But to risk both you and Jake . . ."

"My decision," Alex said, and she saw that everyone, except possibly the oblivious Jon, heard the warning in her tone.

Karim flushed. "Sorry. I've been used to making decisions."

Alex said, "Jake, me, Jon, Karim, Ben, and Kueilan will drive to the biomass. Ben will then drive the rover back here and hide it again as best he can. Jon and Karim will try to communicate, Kueilan will do the computer, Jake will supply an historical context to any communication that actually results." And I will decide when to call a halt to this entire insane idea.

Lucy said, "I want to go, too."

Alex said, "No. If the worst happens and we're attacked, you're Karim's backup."

Lucy said coolly, "Who's yours?"

"Natalie," Alex said, and Natalie looked astonished. The truth, of course, was that if Alex, Jake, and Karim were wiped out, there was no backup. Julian would have his way with Greentrees.

What was Julian planning to do about the space Furs? Did he have a plan? And if so, did it have a chance of succeeding?

Natalie said, "What do you want me to do if the wild Furs come here and try to tell me something?"

"They won't," Jake said. "They're very hierarchical, Natalie. They will talk only to a male, and probably only to a male they perceive as leader from either age or strength. Kent, Ben, all of you, if one does approach you—this is important—do not look him in the eye, do not move suddenly or too close, stay downwind, do not do anything that could be interpreted as a challenge. Keep your eyes on the ground and point to me."

Jon said, "I see! You're acceptable because you're both respected and feeble! The whole genus *bolarius* engages in that behavior!"

Alex didn't know what was included in the genus bolarius and didn't ask.

Upwind, several Furs carrying long spears forded the river and climbed the bank.

By the time Ben had retrieved the rover from its hiding place and they'd driven to the biomass hole, the Furs stood waiting a hundred feet away, spears in one hand and laser guns in the other. Alex gasped when she saw that one effortlessly wore a huge shoulder-mounted weapon of some sort. "Jake, what is—"

"My guess is a missile-launcher of some sort. Terran. Heavy as hell. They're strong. Alex, *don't look at them.*"

She dropped her eyes. *Terran.* What had Julian intended the missile-launcher to be used for?

They had no indication that the wild Furs would employ it against Julian. Most likely they would not. These primitive allies were allies against the space Furs only. Not against Julian. It was important to remember that.

Jon, Karim, and Kueilan huddled around the hole, Jon talking furiously. Alex said to Ben, "Lift Jake into his chair before you go, and bring the chair to the hole. I'll take the supercooler."

They played out the pointless charade—*stop thinking of it like that!* But Alex couldn't help herself. In daylight the thing seemed more hopeless than ever before. Kueilan set up her computer, attached to nothing. Jake opened the cryogenic box that had been sealed for thirty-nine years.

Despite herself, Alex craned her neck to see. Inside lay a dozen or so packets of leaves, or leaflike things, of dull brown. They glistened, as if coated with something slimy. Karim lifted out four of them—how had he arrived at that number?—and dropped them in the hole.

"Now," Jon said, "everybody dance!"

They looked at him as if he were crazy.

Crazier.

"No, I mean it. Dancing or jumping will at least set up vibrations in the ground. It will let the biomass know we're here and maybe they'll get curious."

"Jon, they're point three five miles down," Kueilan said in her soft voice. From her, it didn't sound like a reproach.

"Yes, but maybe they have tendrils or veins or pseudopods or whatever you'd call them " Jon started jumping up and down. After a moment, Kueilan stood and started to dance gracefully. Karim looked uncertain until Kueilan took his hand and pulled him into her dance.

"Alex!" Jon called. "Jump!"

It couldn't get any nuttier than it already was.

Alex stamped one foot, over and over. She felt a perfect fool. After a moment Jake said, "Look at the Furs. No, don't look—just glance sideways."

The Furs were stamping their feet and banging their spear butts on the ground.

Alex stood still in sheer amazement. Jon said exuberantly, "It must have significance to them! We stumbled on a piece of their culture!" He kept on jumping.

But what significance? For all the humans knew, their manic jumping was issuing an invitation to war. Or a plea for rain. Alex closed her eyes and kept on stamping.

When they couldn't keep it up anymore, the four of them collapsed to the ground, panting, and stared at the hole. Nothing happened.

Of course nothing happened.

The wild Furs went on stamping spears and shaggy feet. Then they began to sing: a low, keening, dangerous sound that sent shivers along Alex's nerves. Jon said, "Oh—" but didn't finish his thought.

Jake, Alex saw, had fallen asleep in his chair.

Ben had been under instructions to return after two hours. When the rover pulled up, there had still been no change in the hole. "Leave the packets there," Karim said tiredly. "Alex, I want to stay."

"Me, too," Kueilan said, adding quickly, "with the computer." She blushed.

Oh, Alex thought. Kueilan's animosity toward Lucy was clear.

Alex said aloud, "No, there's no point in unnecessary exposure. You can check the hole later, Karim. Get in the rover."

The ride back was silent and dispirited. They left the Furs still stamping and keening. If the space Furs flew over in a shuttle, or if

Julian attacked with rovers on the ground, the wild Furs would have no cover. But surely they knew that.

The stamping and keening faded as the rover drove toward the river.

Hours later, as Alex sat trying to plan a plausible next move, Ben slid down the bank from guard duty. "Alex! Come quick! There's a wild Fur coming here from the biomass site!"

She stood so fast her ankle nearly twisted under her. "Just one? Armed?"

"Yes, but not the one with that launcher thing. What should I do?"

"Carry Jake up the bank. Carefully. Stay with him but keep your head lowered and don't—"

"I know. Mr. Holman! Mr. Holman!"

Poor Jake; Alex saw him wince with pain as Ben labored up the slope with the frail body in his strong young arms. Karim followed with Jake's chair. No women, Jake had said; it might be perceived as an insult to bring a woman to a war conference. He'd told her that the space Furs had female soldiers but the wild Furs, primitive, seemed to regard females as property. And a good thing, he'd added with an incongruous flash of mischief, or else they might not be incensed enough over the abduction of their women to join with humans.

Alex said, "Natalie, isn't there a zoomscope in your pack?"

"Yes!" Natalie said. "I'd forgotten!"

They had just put the 'scope together and poked it above the bank when their spying became unnecessary. Ben slid back down the bank and began splashing toward the rover, clumsily hidden downriver. "Mr. Holman says to get the rover for him, Karim, Kent, Dr. McBain, and Alex. Alex, look like a male!" He was gone.

Look like a male?

Natalie fumbled for a sunhat in her pack. Alex already wore Threadmores and boots; with Natalie's help she shoved her hair under her hat, smeared more mud on her face than was already there, and unzipped her Threadmores. Natalie shoved wadded-up blanket strips onto her shoulders and wrapped her waist thickly with cloth.

"Your hands," Kueilan said. "Do we have gloves?"

They didn't. Alex had small, dainty hands. Lucy said, "Bandage them. As if you were burned."

Natalie dived again into her pack.

Alex staggered up the bank just as the rover appeared. The wild Fur had already gone. Jake looked at her and cackled.

"It isn't funny," Alex said.

"Yes, it is."

"What did the Fur want?"

Jon burst out, "There's something growing at the site!"

"*Growing*? In the hole?"

"No!"

It was growing at the place where the wild Furs had spent hours stamping feet and spears.

The humans, warned and lectured by Jake, approached silently and slowly. Alex stayed behind the men as much as possible. They stopped several yards downwind from the wild Furs. Jake tried to propel his chair forward, but he wasn't strong enough. Alex, cursing her tray-o decision to keep scarce fuel cells for other uses, watched as Ben crept forward, head lowered and body stooped submissively, to push Jake forward.

An ooze lay on the soil.

That was all it was: a patch of slimy brownish ooze, glistening in the late-afternoon sun. When Jake's elongated shadow fell across it, Alex couldn't see the thing at all. Jon, excited beyond silence, began a whispered commentary.

"It looks simple, but biofilms can contain enormously complex structures. This one is anaerobic so that shine must be some sort of outer sealing layer. I must have been right about pseudopods extending up from the main mass. It probably metabolizes more than one or even two elements. The signaling structures—"

Karim said loudly, "Jake, I want to get the death flowers."

Jake nodded. The Furs did nothing.

Slowly Karim moved to the original hole. Alex muttered to Jon, "Won't the sun have spoiled them, or whatever? It's been hours."

"I don't know. But Karim's getting fresh ones off the rover. No—he's getting both."

It must have cost Karim much to move so slowly, bent over and nonthreatening. Even so, the Furs shuffled their feet and a low growl came from some, or all, of them. Karim stopped.

"Go ahead," Jake said levelly. He extended a stick that Alex hadn't noticed and began drawing on the ground.

Karim completed his tortuous circuit of rover, hole, humans. When he reached their small group, he actually sank to his knees and wobbled forward, carrying the supercooler, toward the slime. The growling grew louder. Alex held her breath.

Karim pushed the cooler within reach of Jake and crawled away. The top, loosened by Karim, slid off under Jake's feeble push. Alex realized that she had not been so close to one of the aliens since the day of the fifty-year-anniversary party, when Nan Frayne had brought one to the genetics lab. That alien had drawn its lips back from sharp, terrifying teeth. These did the same. The brown-red Fur covering their bodies was rough and matted except on the balancing tails, where muscles rippled impressively. Dark crests of silkier, stiffer hair rose from each shoulder.

Jake looked up at the largest Fur, down at his drawing, up at the Fur. The creature nodded clumsily. Slowly Jake bent over, grunting slightly, and pulled the Vine death flowers from their storage for the last thirty-nine years. Alex couldn't tell the ones that had been in the hole from the others. Jake tossed them all atop the slime.

For several minutes, Alex thought that nothing would happen. Another failure like yesterday's. But then the slime began to grow. Squinting, Alex could see it creeping up the sides of the packets and enveloping them, until the packets dissolved completely in the slime and something else began to take form on top of it.

Karim said suddenly, "Furs have been at war with Vines for millennia. If these wild ones recognize a Vine from descriptions by their ancestors—"

Recognize a Vine?

Karim was, Alex realized incredulously, right. From the death flowers—packets of genetic material, Jake had said—the slime was indeed growing a Vine. She had seen pictures in the deebees, taken by surveillors fifty years ago. This was the other alien species that had caught Greentrees in its crossfire. A Vine.

As it grew, a sort of upside-down bowl grew over it, also rising from the slime and covering the growing Vine like a clear dome. Jon blew out his breath. "Look at that! It's growing a biosphere to seal out oxygen and contain whatever atmosphere it's manufacturing in there! God, the adaptive mechanism—"

Alex tuned him out. The thing growing under its expanding dome was neither plant nor animal. Fleshy brown trunk, or torso, coated heavily with slime. Reddish brown branches, or arms, or tentacles. As Alex watched, these sprouted leaves, or hands, or thick broad plates with an unpleasantly pulpy look. No head grew. At about three feet, the forced rapid growth stopped—how much energy it must have taken! It had been like watching a speeded-up holo of some deformed botanical experiment.

The Furs didn't attack. They stood still as ever, their alien expressions unreadable.

Jake turned his chair slowly, painfully, toward the Vine and inched it forward. Not even Ben dared help him. Alex became aware of how heavily she was sweating beneath her hat and hand bandages. The day was not all that warm.

Jake began to draw on the bare ground in front of the Vine. Alex couldn't see the picture. Whatever it was, it had no effect on the Vine grown under its dome, which stood indifferent as purple Greentrees vegetation.

Jake said quietly, "Vines never do anything quickly."

Fifteen minutes later, Jake drew another picture. Alex couldn't see this one, either. But apparently Karim, taller and closer, could. She saw his back stiffen, and then a shudder ran over his whole body.

A shudder? A strong young man in his early thirties, who had already seen horrors Alex could not imagine? What was Jake drawing?

Fifteen minutes later, he drew something else.

Neither Vines nor Furs moved.

The sun sank closer to the horizon, tingeing a clear sky with the first streaks of color. Alex's stomach rumbled. Jake drew another picture.

Karim stiffened again.

Suddenly the Furs scattered and ran. Alex spun around and scanned the sky. From the direction of the Avery Mountains, a miniscule dark shape appeared against a streak of pink.

A Fur shuttle, coming this way.

Ben scrambled for Jake, to load him into the rover. But it was too late; too late for all of them. The rover could never outrun the shuttle. The space Furs would kill her, Jake, and all the others on the plain, including their wild cousins, all male. Greentrees would belong to Julian, or to the murderous aliens. It all ended here.

She started toward Jake, some stupid idea half-formed in her mind of protecting him with her body as long as possible. She never reached him. She stumbled and fell hard on her face, and then something powerful and fetid lifted her off her feet from behind and ran with her, but only a short distance. A pit yawned at her feet. She was thrown into it, landing on top of flesh that she didn't identify until more flesh was thrown on top of her. Alex yelled and tried to get up, but different arms seized her and Karim's voice said in her ear. "Lie still! The cover is fragile!"

A dark cover slid over the pit. Dirt rained down onto Alex's face, into her eyes and mouth. She spat it out, willing herself to not struggle. There was no room. The cover was fragile.

She had seen, just before it closed and darkened the pit completely, that the cover was made of crossed wooden beams, not substantial, covered with branches, which in turn were smothered with mud and rocks. Everything, she realized numbly, must have been hauled in last night from beyond the kill-clean zone. The dirt from the excavated pit must have been spread around the area to look natural. "Pits," plural—there were no wild Furs in this one.

The aliens had dug two, one to shelter their improvident human allies too stupid to think of this themselves.

The shuttle annihilation beam stopped at the ground's surface.

She said hoarsely, "Karim? Jon? Kent?"

"Yes," they answered. "And Ben. But they knocked him out."

"Jake?"

"No," Karim said, adding, "they kept him with them. In the other pit." Alex breathed again.

"I think," Jon said, "he's the only one they're interested in. Did you see the Vine, all of you? It shrank as soon as the shuttle was spotted! No, not shrank, it sort of dissolved and the residue sank into the ground . . . I'll bet it can just grow again after the danger is past!"

All of them in the ground, Vine and wild Furs and people, burrowing like animals to hide from the awesome technology of the invaders. And Jake, kept by the wild Furs with them, in case the unknowable humans suddenly erupted from their safe pit and stupidly killed themselves. The primitives had been protecting Jake from his own kind.

Which was horrifying because Alex, bile rising in her throat, suddenly knew what Jake had been drawing on the ground. Why Karim had shuddered. What Jake was planning to do to his protectors.

And she couldn't see any other course except to go along with him.

35

THE AVERY MOUNTAINS

irt in his mouth, in his eyes. His heart, alarmed by the lack of air, began to hammer and skip so much that Jake thought, *This is it. I'm going to die.*

A picture came to him, unbidden and incongruous: himself and his brother, Donnie, small children safe in his mother's arms. The picture was ridiculous; Jake had been half-grown when Donnie was born. But the picture had a force, an authority, that transcended fact. Soft light suffused it, and peace, and such sweetness that Jake almost felt a stab of disappointment when his heartbeat slowed and evened.

He wasn't going to die, after all. Not yet.

And he wasn't in his mother's arms—he was in a makeshift pit with a bunch of fetid, furry, murderous aliens, hiding from the lethal weapons of another bunch of fetid, furry, even more murderous aliens.

Light filtered into his dirt-blurred eyes and he realized that the aliens were opening the pit, were climbing out. Hairy arms with shockingly wet tentacles on the ends lifted him, not ungently, and set him on the ground. His chair was gone, annihilated. The computer was gone. The rover was gone.

"Jake!" Alex said, kneeling beside him. "Are you all right?"

Suddenly too weak to sit, he slumped over. Alex's strong young arms eased him to a lying position.

"I'm . . . fine."

"They're gone," she said, and he wasn't sure whether she meant the space Furs or the wild Furs until he glimpsed the latter standing impassive several yards upwind. Jake closed his eyes.

Someone said, "Ben's coming to," and Alex vanished.

She returned with water and food. Jake allowed her to help him sit up, sip and nibble. He needed every bit of strength he could muster.

Karim knelt beside Jake. He said excitedly, "It's growing again, Jake. The Vine."

He nodded. He'd expected this. The death flowers, as William Shipley had conjectured so long ago, were packets of information. Not just genomes, either. The Vines and their biofilms, in some symbiosis so alien that it couldn't really be defined in human terms, preserved information in atomic or molecular structure. All information. If Shipley and Jake were right, the vast underground biomass had used the death flowers to create a Vine that knew everything known to the Vines on that long-ago ship.

Those Vines had known a much younger Jake. Had known Karim and Lucy and the dead Dr. Shipley. Had known about Greentrees and the Vine-created biological experiments there, the wild Furs. Had known about the humans' capture by space Furs. Had participated in the Vine plot, centuries in the making and probably successful, to win the war against their ancient enemy.

The Vines on that ship had created and infected the humans, the inadvertent intermediate species, with a genetically tailored virus. The virus made the humans very sick; the elderly William Shipley had nearly died. Then the virus jumped species to the DNA-based Furs. There it didn't sicken in the same way. Instead, it lodged in the Furs' brain and rendered them so passive they operated on only a survival level. It also made them sexually irresistible to each other—which guaranteed maximum spread of the disease. Infected Furs would breed, and minimally care for their young. They would not invent, travel, or wage war. They would instead sit dreaming in the sun, as close to plants as their plantlike enemy could make them. Passive, impotent, tamed.

It was that death-in-life that the space Furs had fled to Green-trees to escape.

This newly growing Vine on Greentrees, product of information stored in the death flowers, already knew all that. It knew how to create the virus as the Vines on the ship had done, as a drinkable fluid that could use humans as intermediate host.

Beyond the lone Vine, Jake could see the wild Furs, standing with their spear butts on the ground and their contraband laser guns again in their other hands. Their river camp, merely a few miles away, included females, which the space Furs, if they had the chance, would abduct to their ship upstairs.

Karim rose. "I'm going over to the Vine, Jake. Although how we're going to communicate with it without the computer is—Alex will come to you in a minute. She's tending Ben, he has a nasty hit on the head. The Vine is about a foot tall now, can you see it? I'll turn you—"

"No," Jake said. "Don't."

Karim stopped, puzzled. Then, drawn by the drama of alien growth, he moved away. Jake could hear Jon McBain babbling in the background.

Then Alex knelt again beside him, holding out more water. After he'd drunk, she brought her face level with his. Her black-lashed gray eyes gazed steadily.

She'd guessed what was going to happen.

"You can't, Jake."

"I'm not . . . going to," he wheezed. "Vine is."

"You've told me the story over and over," Alex said. "Somebody, some human, has to drink it and get infected, then breathe on the wild Furs. You're the only one they'll let get close. And you're not strong enough this time around. Do you hear me? Last time you were in your forties, not your eighties! And anyway these Furs just saved all of our lives!"

"Do you have a better plan?"

She was silent.

He said feebly, "The wild Furs won't die."

"They might as well. And you *will* die."

"It's my time, Alex."

"Not yet!" she cried loudly, anguished enough that Kueilan, bent over Ben, looked up in fright. Alex dropped her voice. "It's not right, Jake."

He wasn't sure whether she meant his dying or his infecting the wild Furs, and he didn't want to waste precious energy asking. "The Vine will form a . . . bowl. Bring it to me."

"No," Alex said. And then, "Oh, Jake!"

"Have to." He closed his eyes.

Time passed, he wasn't sure how much. Surely he wouldn't fall asleep under these circumstances! And yet, he must have. When he opened his eyes again, it was because someone was lifting him, and somehow it was nearly dark.

"What . . . how . . ."

"Shhh, Jake, be quiet." Lucy . . . how could Lucy be here? They'd left her at the river camp! But in the gloom he could just make out her small, furrowed face as she stood beside him. Kent held him, walking toward the rover.

Jake pulled his head just high enough to glance above Kent's shoulder. The plain was empty—no Furs, no Vine, no computer. "Alex!"

"Back at camp already. You were asleep."

He said angrily, "I was drugged!" Alex holding out the cup of water, her gray eyes pained with her accurate guesses. Kueilan, with a medpack to bandage Alex's too-small hands, to tend to Ben's head. Medpacks included sedatives.

Lucy said, "She loves you like a daughter."

"She's the tray-o! She isn't supposed to love anyone enough to wreck war plans!"

Lucy said calmly, "Yes. You never did."

Kent lifted Jake into the backseat of the rover. Lucy and Kent climbed in front, driving. When the rover pulled away, all that was left on the bare plain were two shallow empty pits.

———

Alex sat a little apart from the others around the campfire, waiting. It wasn't much of a fire, a small faltering flame built on a large flat rock just beyond the overhang. Kent fed it steadily with small twigs. Whenever the wind shifted, smoke blew into their shallow protected cave, but there wasn't enough of it to cause anyone distress. Lucy had built the fire from some need of her own, and no one had objected.

A similar fire burned across and a quarter mile up the river, where the Furs did whatever it was Furs did in the evening.

Abruptly Alex said, "I'm going now." Kueilan stood and Alex added irritably, "Alone."

"Just partway," Kueilan said in her pretty, soothing voice.

"No." This was her mission.

Alex picked up the powertorch, switched it on low, and started to ford the river. It was low, partly due to the lack of rain. Still, as the water rose from her knees to thighs to waist, she felt a moment of panic. This was a mountain river—she could imagine a sudden rushing current knocking her off her feet. A strong hand gripped her elbow.

"Damn it, I said alone!"

"Too bad," Karim's voice said. "I'm here."

But once they'd reached the opposite bank, he let her go on alone. No males, she knew. Human males were definitely threatening to the wild Furs. The hope was that females were merely distasteful.

Alex shivered. From being clammy and soaked in the evening air? She hoped not. It had seemed to her around the fire that she'd felt the onset of symptoms and hence—she hoped—of contagion.

She walked along the opposite side of the river, picking her way among the wet stones. The eroded bank rose beside her, now steep and now falling into a low mass of rubble. The Greentrees nightsmell, sweet and poignant, competed with the dank stones and exposed soil. Once Alex stumbled and fell, and when she picked herself up again, her vision swam and sweat sprang out on her face and neck.

The Vines knew their molecular pathological business.

I approve, Alex thought, lurching again. The Vines were all a sort of tray-o, if you looked at it correctly. Using the resources they knew best, genetic manipulation. Just as she used technology and Julian used—

Don't think of Julian. One enemy at a time.

How close would the wild Furs let her get?

She couldn't see them anymore. Either they'd doused their fire at her approach or her vision was really going. Everything looked oddly green, not the normal purple it should be. But of course it was night, you couldn't see Greentrees' healthy purple at night, all you could see was dark until Julian arrived, he usually arrived deep into the night, slipping into bed beside her—

She fell into three inches of moving water and could not get up.

Julian—

But she wasn't close enough! She had to breathe on the Furs, she had to stumble into their camp and hope they didn't spear her before she could infect them, or maybe laser her with Julian's guns . . . Julian . . .

Alex tried to get up, failed. She closed her eyes. The river noise grew louder, became a roar, then a shrieking cacophony. It *hurt.* Alex cried out and flailed, trying to cover her ears. Somehow she couldn't manage it. But there was something else she was supposed to do, something important, something for Julian—

For Julian—

Karim's arms lifted her again. It hurt worse than lying on the wet stones and again she cried out. Damn Karim! But it wasn't Karim. The arms were furry and there was an odd smell, and there was something she was supposed to do for Julian—

Yes. Now she remembered.

Alex turned her face toward the face of the Fur carrying her, and breathed.

36

THE AVERY MOUNTAINS

Karim watched Alex stagger along the riverbed until he couldn't stand it any longer and had to turn away. It should have been him. He had argued that it should be him. But Alex, with Jake drugged, had simply ordered otherwise. She was the leader on Greentrees, in the absence of someone called Ashraf Shanti, whom Karim had never heard of. And Shanti was unavailable: out of com, missing, possibly dead. The scientist in him knew it had to be a woman; the man rebelled.

"I'm doing it," Alex said, and Lucy had nodded. Lucy! Why? Karim expected Lucy to side with him, and she had not, and before long he was going to find out why. No matter what personal quarrel it injected in the middle of a war.

Alex fell, lurched slowly upward. Karim clenched his fists.

Above the bank he heard the rover return with Jake, roaring along fast . . . too fast. Kent had stayed with Jake when the first group returned to the bank—too many for one trip, Alex had argued, especially with Ben injured. But Karim suspected that she simply wanted Jake away until the disease had begun to affect her and she had started along the river to the wild Furs. Lucy had driven back to pick up Jake and Kent. But why was the rover coming in so fast?

"Get in!" Lucy screamed over the edge of the riverbank. "They're coming! They know where we are!"

Who?

"Julian Martin! Get in, get in, damn it! They're not coming

from air, they've got rovers, they have these coordinates! Get in, everybody!"

Karim scrambled up the bank. His mind raced. If Lucy was right, rovers couldn't trace them if they kept comlink silence, but they could follow the physical tracks . . .

Kueilan said, "How do you know?"

"Open comlink from somebody called Siddalee Brown . . . get in! Get in!"

Who was Siddalee Brown? Whoever she was, she would be dead now if she'd sent an open comlink to Alex Cutler warning her that Julian Martin was on his way to her . . . How had this Brown person known that Alex wasn't already dead, as Martin had claimed? None of it made sense.

Kent sat in the backseat, holding Jake's frail body, leaving as much room as possible. But in a four-person vehicle they were eight, without Alex . . .

Without Alex.

"We can't leave Alex!" Kueilan cried, his own cry, but Karim already knew better. If they stayed, and Julian Martin was really on the way, they had no time to wait for Alex, who was probably better off than they were anyway. Julian might not look for her among wild Furs.

"They'll probably just return me to you," Alex had argued, before she'd stopped discussing and simply issued orders. "A female is a piece of lost property."

But no one really knew.

People scrambled into the rover. Natalie, to Karim's surprise, confronted Lucy. "I can drive along the river—Ben showed me the places to go. It'll cover the tracks."

Lucy said, "No, I'm—"

Natalie, twenty pounds heavier, simply shoved Lucy aside and took the wheel. Angry tears shone on Natalie's cheeks. A small detached part of Karim's mind registered this, as well as Natalie's tender glance over her shoulder at the injured Ben, his head wrapped in a bloody bandage, being cradled on Jon's lap much as Jake was on Kent's. Kueilan squeezed between them, half kneeling on the floor. Karim scrambled in beside Lucy in the front, the two of them squashed together on one seat, and Natalie took off down the riverbank into the shallows.

It was a ride so wild that later Karim would wonder how Jake and Ben survived it. But their two nurses cushioned them with Kent's and Jon's own bodies. Jon had the worst of it; Ben outweighed him by at least forty pounds.

Natalie drove expertly; she was a natural. The rover hurtled along in the gloom away from the wild Furs, toward the place Ben must have used to hide the rover. Wherever it was, Karim never saw it. When the last of daylight faded, Natalie switched on the rover's lights but kept them pointed downward, toward the river. They drove over rocks, through pools, through shallow rapids, keeping deep enough so that there would be no tracks. Water sloshed into the rover, then flooded its floor. Could the vehicle keep going this soaked? Evidently it could. Natalie had said there wasn't much left of the last fuel cell. What if it ran out?

"Jake?" Karim yelled once to Kent over the noise of the rover, the river, and Natalie's cursing.

"I don't know," Kent yelled back.

"I'm . . . fine," Jake said, and Karim thought again that whatever else Jake was, he was the bravest man Karim had ever known. Including himself.

I should not have let Alex . . .

"I'm going up," Natalie called, and Karim saw that the river had taken them out of the kill-clean zone. Tall tranquil purple trees bordered the banks, silhouetted faintly against the starlight. The rover wrenched itself and then drove, it seemed to Karim, straight upward. Surely it would tip . . . It didn't, and they were out. Natalie drove a while longer, then headed into a thick grove of trees and cut the engine.

Silence, shocking as gunfire.

Natalie twisted in her driver's seat, her hair dripping and wild. "Ben?"

"Passed out," Jon said from beneath Ben's bulk. "Probably a good thing."

Karim said, "Jake?"

Jake croaked, "I'm fine."

"Let's get out."

They climbed, bruised and soaking wet, from the rover. Kueilan, clutching her medkit, grabbed blankets and arranged them on the ground for Jake and Ben. Kent and Jon began gathering armloads of brush to further camouflage both rover and people.

Karim stumbled deeper into the trees, trying to see how much cover they actually had. The forest seemed pretty dense; they were probably safe for the moment. But they had little food, minimal weapons, no plan against Julian Martin. And Alex had been left behind.

Karim picked his way back to the others. Above, branches entwined in a thick canopy. A night bird cried, then fell silent. Greentrees' night smell surrounded him, sweetly spicy. God, how he'd missed that smell, that bird cry, in that other "forest," on the sterile Vine world! That hellish alien nightmare world . . .

Karim suddenly stood completely still among the trees. He knew now what he should have done at the biomass site.

Now that it was too late.

Or maybe not. He ran the rest of the short way to the rover, crashing into trees, tripping over roots. Beside the rover a powertorch shone downward, onto Ben's still figure. By its feeble light Karim grabbed Natalie's arm.

"Natalie, how much power is left in the rover? *How much?* We have to go back!"

37

THE AVERY MOUNTAINS

Something was wrong. Alex, weak and still feverish, couldn't at first find the words for what it was. She opened her eyes, was stabbed by blinding light, closed them again. Slowly she turned her head, which set off cascades of pain inside it. And when she opened her eyes again, she realized that turning her head had been futile. The light was everywhere. It was weak daylight.

She lay on a cot. That was what was wrong.

Cool dank cave walls rose a foot away on either side of the cot. Evidently her cot sat in an alcove inside a cave. A clean blanket covered Alex. She was naked. As she watched, helpless, weaker than she had ever been in her life, a hairy figure passed across her field of vision at the foot of the bed, outside the alcove. It was a Fur.

The odd, distinctive smell came to her a moment later. Furs, all right.

She tried to piece it together. Wild Furs didn't have cots and clean blankets. A space Fur? But the alien's pelt had been matted and dirty; she was sure she'd seen that much. And somehow the creature *moved* wild. But then shouldn't it be sick? She'd breathed on the Furs, the virus was supposed to be so contagious . . .

Alex strained to remember. *"They'll probably just return me to you,"* she had argued to Karim, before she'd stopped discussing and simply issued orders. *"A female is a piece of lost property."* Had that happened? Yes, she thought she remembered being picked up by the wild Fur, carried back along the river toward the human camp . . . then what? She couldn't remember.

Clenching her teeth, she tried to sit up, but fell back weakly on the cot. It rattled against the stone wall.

She had definitely seen a wild Fur, and now she realized that it had been accompanied by another figure, mostly hidden behind the alien. And the Fur had not looked sick. Either the incubation period was longer than Karim remembered, or else something had gone wrong. *"It's possible,"* said Jon, the biologist, *"that this group will be immune to the virus. They're several generations separated from the Fur group the Vines created the virus for, remember. Also on a different world. Viruses mutate and immune systems develop—the whole genetic thing at a microbial level changes amazingly fast. And your Vines on that ship had never actually seen the Furs created on Greentrees. They had only very old samples from the space Furs."*

She waited, unable to do anything else. Even if Jon was right, and the virus had failed to infect the wild Furs, where had they brought her? And why? And how did wild Furs have a human cot and blanket?

She examined the edge of the blanket. Alex was tray-o; she recognized goods produced anywhere in Mira City. This was from the Trimball manufacture, run by New Quakers. Strong, well made, durable, warm.

Now she remembered something else. The wild Fur that she'd briefly glimpsed, the dirty matted alien with the terrifying teeth and third eye on the top of its head—it had been crestless. A female. Now nothing at all made sense. Wild Fur females, the prey of the space Fur gene pool, were always kept away from danger. Not even Nan Frayne, Alex had understood, had been able to talk to a female. Unlike their technologically advanced cousins, wild Fur society was patriarchal and strictly gender divided. What was a female wild Fur doing observing Alex?

Julian Martin walked into the alcove. "Hello, Alex."

So much emotion swamped her that she thought she might faint. She did not.

"Don't stare at me with such hatred," Julian said. "You're too weak to spare the effort. No, you won't give your pneumonia, or whatever it is, to me, not even if it's caused by a Greentrees microbe. I've got immune-system genemods your biologists can't imagine."

Alex said nothing.

"I wasn't sure you were alive until I found Siddalee Brown. She'd had a tracer sewed into the Threadmore in your command bunker, did you know that? A new invention of Chu Corporation, infrasonic, nothing my equipment picked up. But she knew where you were, and she told me."

Bile rose in Alex's throat. Siddalee would never have told Julian voluntarily; she'd never trusted Julian. The image of Lau-Wah's tortured body rose in Alex's mind.

"Not that you've been much of a threat to me since the Fur attack," Julian said. "I expected you to make a broadcast, Alex. You didn't. That was Jake Holman's insight, wasn't it? Where is he?"

So it was Jake that Julian really wanted. Of course. Julian had to fight the space Furs for Greentrees. Jake was the only one who had successfully done that before. Julian wanted Jake's invaluable assistance. He didn't know about Karim and Lucy.

"I know that last incapacitating stroke of Holman's was faked," Julian said, "so don't try to pretend otherwise. I talked to that voidbrained teenaged girl who helped him to his transport during the evacuation. The one with your cat."

What faked incapacitating stroke? What teenage girl?

Julian said, "You don't have a poker face, Alex. You never did. You probably don't even know what poker is; they don't seem to play it on Greentrees. Never mind, darling. You just told me you don't know anything about Holman's playacting, and you were telling the truth. Do you know where Holman is?"

"Yes," Alex said. "Don't . . . Siddalee . . . Lau-Wah . . ."

He moved closer, bent toward her cot to stare at her. His crotch was level with her face. His brilliant green eyes under their thick black lashes glittered scornfully.

"So you're afraid of torture. You disappoint me, Alex. Although

I probably should have expected it of Greenie softness. All right, darling, no torture. I promise you a quick and merciful death if you tell me where Holman is."

Alex started to cry. Tears falling on the Quaker blanket, too weak to lift her head, she gave him the coordinates of the hospital-cave end point where Jake had been taken during the evacuation.

"No," he snapped. "We looked there!"

"After you looked. We saw . . . you," she blubbered. "We thought—Jake thought—you wouldn't have the manpower to check again . . ."

Julian stared at her a long time. Finally he nodded. "All right, Alex, I believe you. Provisionally. I'll check the cave."

She had bought Jake and Karim some time. To do what? Alex didn't know, couldn't think. She kept picturing Siddalee—faithful, picky, fatally maternal Siddalee . . .

And she, Alex Cutler, had loved Julian. She, Alexandra Hope Cutler, Mira City tray-o.

Now the tears of rage and shame were real.

They didn't stay in the cave, wherever it was. Alex, still wrapped only in her blanket, was dumped into a transport. The vehicle must be Terran, brought down from the *Crucible*; there was nothing like it on Greentrees. It was huge, a long rectangle evidently divided by internal partitions, since the section that held Alex was nowhere near the length of the whole.

She rode with five female wild Furs, all but one bound tightly with tanglefoam. They sat beside her and made a terrible keening noise as soon as the door closed, creating total darkness. The noise echoed off the transport's metal walls. Bodies shifted in the dark. They were all trying to move as far away from Alex as the cramped space would permit. Did she smell that bad to them?

Where were the males? What was Julian doing?

She tried to reason like him, although the effort brought yet more shame. The space Furs wanted wild Fur females. Therefore Julian was collecting them, as negotiating chips. He'd terrified the creatures into obeying him. What had he done with the males? Killed them, probably.

Or maybe not. Perhaps only the males had become infected by Alex, and had then died. Jon hadn't mentioned that anything like that could happen, and Alex didn't know enough biology to know if it was possible. But maybe it was, and Julian had collected the surviving females to return them to other wild Furs in order to consolidate his alliance with them. Julian didn't, after all, know that at least one group of wild Furs had become willing to throw in their lot with Jake.

Or maybe—

She gave it up. She didn't have enough information. She felt physically exhausted. Most important of all, she couldn't think like Julian. She wasn't Jake, able to anticipate and plan from somebody else's sickening viewpoint.

Alex was profoundly glad that she genuinely did not know where Jake was. Somehow they must have all escaped before Julian arrived at the river. When Julian found out that Jake was not at the end-point hospital cave, he was probably going to torture Alex for anything she did know. She shuddered.

Under torture, she knew, she would tell him about Karim and Lucy, about the biomass and the Vine it could grow, anything else to stop the pain. She wasn't that strong. But she couldn't tell Julian where Jake and Karim and the others had gone, because she honestly had no idea.

Clutching that thin comfort, she fell asleep in the jolting vehicle, surrounded by keening alien terror.

38

THE AVERY MOUNTAINS

The rover ran out of power somewhere short of the biomass site. With power went the lights. Karim looked up at the moonless sky, rapidly clouding over, and spat, *"Ebn sharmoota!"*

"I'm not going to ask what that means," Jon said wearily.

Natalie, who'd been driving more cautiously along the riverbed than her headlong hurl of a few hours ago, said, "We're only two miles from the site. I saw the display just before it went out."

"Then two miles it is," Jon said. "Let's go."

The three of them got out, carrying nothing except a powertorch set very low. The computer had been left behind when they fled Julian Martin; Karim doubted it was still there. Martin would have searched the area. They would have to manage without the computer.

How?

They trudged along the riverbed, slipping on the wet stones, until Natalie said, "This is silly. We can walk on the bank above just as well. If Commander Martin's men are still there, they're probably going to catch us either way."

Karim had been too tired to think of that himself. "Pick up a large rock first, each of you," he said. Gratefully he followed Natalie and Jon up the bank, carrying his rock. Walking was easier here, even though every so often one of them had to slide down the bank to check that they hadn't passed the site of their hidden camp.

By the time they reached the site, it had started to rain. Karim thought he couldn't get more soaked than he'd been from Natalie's wild drive in the riverbed, but he was wrong. Cold steady drizzle made his teeth chatter. He kept trudging on, flanked by Natalie and by Jon, uncharacteristically silent.

"I think this is where the camp was," Natalie said.

Jon descended the bank, climbing back up a moment later. "Everything's gone, including the computer. Natalie, Julian Martin's techs can access the deebees—"

"No," Natalie said. "I threw the computer into a pool before we left. They won't get anything out of that ruin."

"Good," Karim said. "Let's find the biomass hole."

They struck out away from the river. Jon said once, also uncharacteristically, "I'm so hungry I could eat the biomass."

"Don't think about it," Natalie said.

Karim wasn't thinking about food. He dropped to his knees, searching with the powertorch for some sign of the exact place the Vine had grown. He couldn't find anything. So he guessed. "Here. Start pounding."

They sat cross-legged by the site, the three of them hitting the ground repeatedly with their rocks. They weren't nearly as many as the wild Furs had been, stamping their feet and hitting their spear butts on the ground. But the vein of biomass—or pseudopod, or whatever it was—had come closer to the surface since that first summoning. Maybe it was still there.

Summoning. That was the right word. Sitting exhausted on the wet ground, hammering with a stone, Karim had a sudden vivid memory, so strong that for a blessed moment all else disappeared. He was with his *laleh* in his nursery in the medina, and she was reading him a wondrous tale of a genie summoned from a lamp. A boy was trapped alone in the dark and he found that if he rubbed an alien lamp . . .

"Here it comes!" Jon said, all the old excitement back in his voice. "Over there! Oh my dear gods . . ."

Karim shifted the powertorch. The Vine grew a few inches above the ground, along with its also-growing dome. Like nacre, Jon had said, or a coral reef. Nonliving protection.

"I've been giving its behavior a lot of thought," Jon burbled. "The playful refusal to communicate seriously before you gave it the death flowers, and its serious cooperation with us afterward. I think this thing might somehow divide its sentient functions in a way completely outside our conceptualization, with maybe memory residing in the biomass and what we might call interpretive and moral functions in the—"

"Not now, Jon," Natalie said. "*Please.*"

Karim waited as long as he could. The Vine was about a foot high now, much shorter than it had been during the previous communication. But Karim had no time.

He traced on the ground with the most pointed part of his rock, hoping the biomass could "read" the vibrations. It was a simple enough picture. One circle, one line, a lot of dots. Over and over he traced it, as the Vine continued to grow.

Please, Karim prayed silently to the Allah he didn't believe in, *please let it understand. And be willing to let us have them . . .*

Aladdin with his lamp. Three wishes . . .

Jon said, "Tell me again."

"Spores," Karim said. "These dots are supposed to represent the spores surrounding Vine planets." The circle was the planet. "The spores are apparently delivered upstairs by some sort of extruded-cable space elevator." The line, extending outward from the circle. "The spores float in a dormant state around the planet in dense clouds. When a ship enters the cloud, they apparently activate almost instantly and just dissolve any metal that hasn't been prepared against them. They metabolize metal for their biological processes. It's a shield, a world-spanning shield."

"But if this biomass here does give us these spores—"

"Be quiet, Jon," Natalie said, "for once!"

Jon subsided. Karim went on tracing on the barren ground. Surely the biomass and Vine knew it was barren, knew their ancient enemy had been through here with their annihilating devastation? Surely the alien thing knew that the Furs were enemies of humans, too? My enemy's enemy is my friend. But—

Karim pushed the "but" away. He couldn't afford it just now. He went on tracing. Circle, line, many dots . . .

"Let me take over a while," Natalie said kindly.

"No, I—"

"Look!" Jon said. "Look at the Vine!"

Three feet tall now, it was growing a deformed lump on the ground at its base. Jon shone the powertorch directly on the lump. It grew larger. Brown, slimy—as was everything associated with the Vines—it shimmered under the artificial light.

"Is it alive?" Natalie asked.

"I don't know," Jon said. "I . . . now look!"

The lump stopped growing. Simultaneously, Vine and dome began to dissolve. In a few minutes nothing remained except a slickness on the wet soil, which slowly sank underground, and the slimy brown lump.

Gingerly Karim touched it. What if it were another genetically engineered infection, this time one that would wipe out humans as well as Furs? It wasn't as if either species was any use to the biomass. But, no, the Vine/biomass didn't kill. Long ago, George Fox had speculated that the entire idea of killing was alien to a species that was essentially one large organism obtaining energy from something akin to photosynthesis. You didn't kill when everything on your entire world was you. It just wasn't in the genes.

Natalie said uncertainly, "I think it's a sac. A container of some sort. The spores might be inside."

"We have to test it," said Jon, the scientist.

"Not here. Under the overhang," Karim said. Now that they had the precious weapon—if it *was* a weapon—he cared again about possible detection by Julian Martin or by Furs. Now that they had a chance. Maybe.

A last chance. Because Karim doubted the Vines would emerge again from the underground biomass, no matter how hard anyone knocked. Partly because the biomass itself, two miles down, was safe no matter who won the warring above. Partly because the biomass had now given humans the only two weapons the Vines had, to Karim's knowledge, ever developed against the Furs.

But mostly, Karim realized, he thought the biomass would not emerge again because of Aladdin. Plodding through the rain, cold and shivering, he recognized his own demented logic. But the fairy tale of his *laleh* stayed brightly with him. Three wishes Aladdin had been granted. Send Karim and Lucy back to Greentrees. Infect Alex with a transmissible virus. Give Karim the spores. Three wishes.

The fairy tale was over. The genie had gone back into its alien bottle. Karim and the rest of the humans were now on their own.

Even Natalie, in weariness and cold, had miscalculated their trudge back toward the river. They stumbled across it not at their old camp-site but somewhere upriver. Or maybe downriver; there was no way to know. The overhang was less pronounced here, but everyone was too weary to go on. They settled in as well as they could.

"What's that in the river?" Jon said.

"I don't know," Karim said. "Go to sleep."

"Wait, there's another one . . . they're caught on that rock but they're going to float off in a minute. The river's rising with the rain."

"Rising?" Karim said. Of course it was. He'd been too bone-tired to think of that. He stumbled to his feet. "Get up, we can't stay here."

"I'm just going to have a look first."

"Jon!" Karim said, but he was too weary to really care. And Jon could hardly get any wetter. Karim and Natalie pulled themselves back up the bank. It was more exposed here, in the kill-clean zone, but that was better than being drowned. Maybe the rain would stop soon.

Jon appeared a few minutes later, dripping water. "Karim. They're all dead."

"Who?"

"The wild Furs. They're all dead, and the bodies are starting to float down the river from their camp. Or maybe they tried to cross to

this side first. I caught one and turned it over. Laser gun. Julian—"
He faltered for a moment. "Julian Martin killed them all."

"Alex?" Karim got out.

"I don't know. It's dark and the bodies are floating away! But—"
But probably.

Karim fumbled for the slimy brown sac nominally sheltered in
his Threadmore, needing to know that it was still there.

39

A TERRAN SHUTTLE

When the truck finally stopped, Alex expected Julian to haul her off for torture. But she didn't even see him. Evidently he hadn't yet heard from his soldiers checking the hospital cave near Mira City, where Alex had told him that Jake was hiding. It wouldn't be long until his soldiers reported in.

The side of the truck slid open. The female Furs immediately stopped keening, evidently frightened into silence. They shrank back against the metal wall.

A Terran soldier, tall and heavily armed, reached in and pulled Alex forward. As Alex's eyes adjusted, she saw that the soldier was a woman, genemod with glittering violet eyes. She must have been genemod for strength as well. She lifted Alex effortlessly and strode with her toward a shuttle.

Alex's heart stopped. They were going up to the *Crucible*.

But no, that made no sense. Julian wouldn't have dared a launch, not with the Furs upstairs in their own vastly superior, constantly monitoring ship. Undoubtedly the shuttle had been landed here, hidden, before the space Furs showed up to wreck whatever plans Julian had had for it. And now that she looked more closely, carried like a sack over the Terran soldier's shoulder, Alex saw that the shuttle wasn't like any reported by the initial Greentrees team inspecting the *Crucible*. So Julian had off-loaded it somewhere before approaching the planet—a moon, an asteroid—and brought it down sometime later.

The shuttle was big, larger than the truck. It had been parked very close to a hillside and then dug partway under it. Camouflage brush and sod covered the roof. Several odd-looking protuberances were probably weapons or surveillors; Alex recognized neither. Could the shuttle be easily brought forward for liftoff, or would that take a huge effort? She couldn't tell.

The Terran took her inside. She had a brief impression of displays, consoles, tables, intent people, before she was tossed into a closet and the door closed. Before Alex could react, it opened again, and the five female Furs, four tanglefoamed and one loose, were shoved in with her.

But at least this prison had light. And as Alex watched, the tanglefoam dissolved on the Furs, leaving them free. All of them began to keen.

Alex shrank into a corner. Five wild Furs loose, and her own smell not only disgusted them but brought out a deep, genetic xenophobia. Only apparently it didn't. The Furs ignored her, keening loudly.

Was the murderously xenophobic gene located on whatever was the equivalent of the Y chromosome?

No, that couldn't be true; the space Furs had female soldiers. She remembered Jake telling her so. So why weren't these Furs killing her from sheer biological imperative? She had no answer.

The door opened and two large bowls, one food and one water, were pushed in. Alex was suddenly ravenous. She crawled toward the bowl in the posture of extreme subservience Jake had recommended, half expecting to be cuffed or maimed. The females ignored both her and the food. Alex ate with her hands—basic Greentrees cereal, and how good it tasted!—and lapped water with her tongue. Feeling much better, she crawled meekly back to her position in the corner and studied the keening females.

One had dirty Fur much sparser and tattered than the others. Her tail wobbled as she leaned on it, and she rested her weight against the wall. One tentacle trembled. All right, Alex thought: Grandmother Fur.

Three of the others looked glossier, even under their dirt, with thicker fur and stronger tails. On one Alex spied a curious structure: a sort of bag distending from underneath the tail. In heat? Pregnant? Alex knew nothing of Fur reproductive procedures. But these looked to her as if they could be fertile females in their prime. Flora, Dora, Cora.

The smallest female, the one that had tended Alex before the Terrans had evidently decided the entire herd wasn't dangerous, had finer, silkier Fur and a strange bald spot on her chest. Accident, maybe, or prepubescent marker. Or maybe something else entirely, but Alex dubbed her Miranda. Youthful innocence.

" *'O brave new world, that has such people in it!'* " Duncan Martin's resonant genemod voice, and Julian beside her in the Mira City theater . . .

No. Not that now. She needed to learn as much as she could about the Furs. If she could persuade them to join her in some sort of attack . . .

This didn't look likely. The five keened more and then began a peculiar hopping motion, one bounce on their tail and then one on the left foot. Grandmother had trouble after a few of these, and she rested against the wall. The other four kept it up.

Alex hauled herself to her feet. The food felt queasy in her stomach, but not enough to throw it up. Her strength had at least started to return, as Karim had promised it would. He'd seen this Vine infection before, he'd reminded her. He'd had it. Humans did not die of it.

Alex tried a hop on her left foot. She had no tail, but she imitated the tail hop as best she could by bracing herself with one arm against the wall and using that for the alternate hop. She ululated, trying to hit the same pitch as the Furs' keening.

They all stopped and stared at her, baring their teeth.

What did that mean? At least she had their attention, for the first time. Tiring rapidly, Alex nonetheless hopped and keened a little longer. The female Furs watched her and then returned to their own mourning, if that's what it was. For all Alex knew, she was performing a rain dance. Or a mating display.

The six females hopped and wailed as long as Alex and Grandmother Fur could keep it up.

"Jake was not where you said he'd be," Julian said. "Where is he,
Alex?"

"I don't know."

He stood before her in yet another closet-sized room, hands
clasped easily, casually behind his back, long legs slightly apart.
The green eyes regarded her contemplatively. Julian wore the black
uniform in which he'd arrived from Terra, closely fitting his beautiful body. Alex, unbound in a chair in front of him, had been
stripped of her blanket. They were alone.

"I'll ask you again, Alex. I need Jake to defeat the Furs—who are,
incidentally, your enemy as well. I should think you'd remember
that. Where is Jake, Alex?"

"I don't know."

He unclasped his hands and raised one fist. The hand, Alex
noted numbly, with the green-stone gold ring. *"Who gave you that
ring?" "My mother . . ."* His ringed fist clutched something small
and metallic. He aimed it at her breasts and fired.

The pain was astonishing. Alex screamed and fell off the chair.
Writhing on the floor, she clawed at her chest, which was on fire,
burning through her skin to the nerves themselves . . .

"Don't claw like that, there's nothing there," Julian said calmly.
"That was a low setting, Alex, and a not-very-vulnerable area of
your body. I'll try your cunt next. Where is Jake?"

"I don't know!"

This time she passed out from the incredible pain, and when she
came to, it was still there. Julian raised his weapon.

"I don't know!" she babbled, tears and snot on her face. "I don't
know! Oh, Julian, don't . . . they left me to infect the Furs and I got
sick and when I came to I was here oh Julian please no . . ."

"Infect the Furs? What do you mean?"

She told him everything. Karim, Lucy, Vine, all of it. Once she
stopped and he fired again and she babbled on. She was still talking

when she realized that he was no longer there, he had heard enough and left the room. The pain did not leave. It took an hour for it to even lessen.

A soldier dumped her again in with the Furs. Alex cried out when she hit the floor. The door closed and she was dimly aware, through the red haze of agony, of the Furs clustered around her, making awful noises and odd smells.

They dribbled the cool drinking water on her breasts and crotch, and it helped a little. They tugged gently on her head hair; Alex never did figure out what that was supposed to do. They covered her with the one blanket and offered her lumps of cereal on the ends of filthy tentacles. Finally, when the pain eased enough for Alex to fall into despairing sleep, they resumed hopping and keening.

She woke in terror. The female Furs were all asleep, but Cora woke at her cry. The female removed the blanket and dribbled more water on Alex's wounds. Again she tugged gently on Alex's hair.

It didn't help. But in her shame and pain and helpless hatred, Alex found herself reaching out for Cora's tentacle. She got a foot instead, and held on, sobbing.

The alien let her, tugging softly on Alex's hair.

40

THE AVERY MOUNTAINS

Karim woke at dawn. The rain had stopped, and it was going to be a beautiful clear day. Too bad—rain might have provided at least minimal cover. He, Jon, and Natalie were exposed in the kill-clean zone and if Julian Martin had captured Alex, she might have told him anything.

Jon was already up. "We have two choices, Karim, as I see it. Follow the river up or down. It's our only cover. We can go back to the rover or towards Mira City."

Karim said acidly, "The rover's out of fuel and Mira City is gone."

"I know. We aren't looking for the rover or Mira City."

"What are we looking for?"

"Cheyenne."

Karim blinked and sat up slowly. The little biologist sank to his heels. His hair was so dirty it was no longer possible to even tell its color.

"Listen, Karim, it makes sense. We can't stay here. For those spores to do us any good, we have to use them on Julian Martin's weapons, or the space Furs, or both. We don't even know where either of them are. But Cheyenne can track anything—it's part of their lunatic lifestyle, hunting herds of wild animals to eat and wear. I'll bet the Cheyenne already know where both Martin's and the Furs' command places are. Or if they don't know, they can find them."

Karim stared at Jon. Filthy, diminutive, boiling with smug

excitement, Jon reminded Karim of a small boy playing soldier. Hadn't any of this death and destruction touched him?

No way to tell. And Karim didn't really care. He considered Jon's suggestion. "I thought the Cheyenne stuck to the southern subcontinent. That's what the original Greentrees charter gave them."

Jon, who had not been born when Karim had witnessed the original charter, waved this away. "Maybe once. But since they've gone to war with the wild Furs, they're around here, too, because the Furs are. That's due to Nan Frayne."

"And how the hell are we supposed to find them?"

"Well, I don't know that part," Jon said.

"Smoke signals," Natalie said.

Karim hadn't even known she was awake. She lay a few feet away, still curled in the fetal position against the night chill. Natalie uncurled and struggled stiffly to sit up.

Jon said, "What are smoke signals?"

"I found them in the library deebee. When I was on duty and bored one night. The Cheyenne make a fire and then put a blanket over it to control smoke puffs. They have a code in puffs."

"Do you know the code?"

"No," Natalie admitted.

"Then how—"

"No, wait," Jon said. "It might work. If we just release random puffs, or maybe a one-two-three-puff pattern, the Cheyenne might realize that someone is sending smoke signals. Someone inept. And I doubt that Julian Martin's men would recognize it as nonsense puffs. If they noticed it at all—and it wouldn't register on any surveillance equipment I know of—they'd probably assume it was Cheyenne. Or even wild Furs. Of no interest to them."

Karim considered. It didn't seem very hopeful, but on the other hand, he had nothing better to suggest. "Here?"

"We need wood for a fire, Karim," Jon said pointedly. "We need to leave the kill-clean zone."

"Then let's travel downriver, away from the others. For their safety."

Natalie said, "I'm going back upriver. To tell Mr. Holman about the spores. And to see to . . . everybody."

She meant Ben, Karim realized. He said, "Tell Kueilan we'll come for them as soon as we can."

Natalie gave him an odd look. Kueilan, Karim had said—not Lucy. It had slipped out, surprising even him. He flushed.

"All right," Natalie said neutrally. "But I'm not leaving until you test the spores." She laid something on the ground in front of Karim. A replacement part for something on the rover, he realized, made of some metallic alloy. Natalie, the tech, had thought to bring it with her last night.

Karim pulled out the slimed sac. How to do this without losing too many spores? And how many were too many? Carefully, controlling his distaste for the slime, he peeled back one corner of the lump. It proved to have layers, like the sweet dough his grandmother used to bake, on Terra. Karim peeled back more layers. Finally he exposed a few tiny, almost invisible brown specks.

"Shake them on the alleolater," Natalie suggested.

Karim did. The sparks suddenly glittered in the sunlight, exactly as he remembered the glitter around the *Franz Mueller*. The same delay of about ten minutes, and the alleolater suddenly melted.

"Hey!" Jon called happily. "Great!"

Natalie gave a sudden cry. Karim turned to see the fasteners on her Threadmore suddenly dissolve. The suit gaped open from neck to crotch, and Natalie clutched at it.

"Get upwind!" Jon cried, unnecessarily. He and Karim already squatted upwind of the glitters. Shakily Natalie held out her hand.

"Ben's mother's ring! From Terra! Gone!"

Karim gazed, fascinated, at her ringless hand. "How long . . . how far . . ."

No one knew.

Jon said, "Nobody move. Wait fifteen minutes and try something else metallic."

They did. They put metallic objects downwind, high and low, touching the ground where the alleolater had been. Everything dissolved, then some things dissolved, then nothing did. Natalie crossly tied tough vines, growing under the riverbank and so survivors of the kill-clean, around the waist of her Threadmore to keep it marginally closed. The material was too tough to puncture for laces.

Then Karim and Jon started downriver, toward Mira. Natalie went upriver, toward Jake and Ben and the useless rover.

Jon said, "You know, those spores are only dispersed on the wind, not dead. Whenever they touch metal, they'll dissolve it. Maybe forever. We've changed Greentrees ecology for all time. Anything metallic is at risk from now on, especially if we let out more of them and they can reproduce in this environment."

Karim hadn't realized that. Greentrees, left one day without anything metallic . . . How would they all live?

"Karim, did you hear me? Did you understand what I said?"

"I understand," Karim said. "The genie never goes all the way back into the bottle."

"What?"

"Never mind."

They saw no life during the long walk across the kill-clean zone, except that in the river. It was eerie to look at the desolate ground to the left, empty as the Terran moon, and then to turn one's head to the right and see fish darting in the bright river, red creeper climbing the bank, the occasional frabbit sunning itself on a rock or darting into a riverbank den. Left, death. Right, life.

Karim walked for a while with his eyes mostly closed.

"There!" Jon cried eventually. "Trees on the horizon!"

The edge of the kill-clean zone rose dramatically, a wall of purple sheared off as cleanly as a topiary hedge. Just before the tree line, Jon built a brushfire with green wood. "Good thing the powertorch didn't dissolve during our spore experiments," he said cheerfully. "Natalie thought of burying it, I didn't."

"She's the tech," Karim said dully. His energy was nearly gone. How did Jon McBain do it? Nothing to eat but some wild fruit they'd just picked, which was already turning Karim's bowels sour.

No sleep. Grinding anxiety. And Jon was bouncing around as if he were at his own intact field station.

How was Jake holding up? And Kueilan, Lucy, and the others?

"It's putting out lots of smoke," Jon said, studying the fire critically. "Give me the blanket."

Karim, who'd been sitting on the filthy thing, handed it to Jon. "Don't set it on fire. Wait, Jon, before you start—I'm going to hide the sac. Just in case we . . . just in case."

When the sac was hidden under a rock, Jon began covering and uncovering the fire. One puff of smoke, wait. Two puffs, wait. Three puffs, wait. "Wouldn't it be funny if I'm actually saying something? Maybe 'You smell bad'?"

"Hilarious," Karim said sourly.

He fell asleep. Exhaustion was just too great. The sleep, dreamless, was so deep that it took Jon's shaking him vigorously to waken. "Karim!"

"Sleeeeppp . . ."

"No! Look!"

Resentfully Karim opened his eyes. The sun was high in the sky and Karim was ringed by six Cheyenne braves, dressed in some sort of animal hides sewn with tiny glittering stones and bedraggled feathers. Two of the braves had dirty blond braids, one had bright red hair, and one looked at least part Chinese. They carried spears, bows, and wickedly sharp knives. Their left cheeks were tattooed with tiny moons, stars, and what looked like lipstick cases but probably weren't. None of them spoke.

"Hello," Karim said, feeling like an absolute fool. He lay on the ground, gut churning with diarrhea from wild fruit, looking up at six characters left over from four hundred years ago on another planet.

One of the braves said, "What the hell do you think you're doing?"

41

TERRAN SHUTTLE BUNKER

By the next day, pain had left Alex unless she touched the tortured areas. She sat huddled in her blanket, holding it a little away from her breasts, and tried to think why she was still alive. Julian had promised her a "quick merciful death" if she told him everything she knew, and she had. He knew now about Karim, Lucy, and the biomass. Her information hadn't included Jake's location, but only because she didn't know it.

That's why she was still alive. Julian wanted Jake's expertise in dealing with the Furs, and maybe Karim's in dealing with the biomass. Julian would pick up Karim and Lucy at the biomass site, force them to tell him where Jake was, and capture Jake. Then he would use her to make Jake cooperate with him. He couldn't torture Jake; the old man was too frail. But if he threatened to torture Alex, Jake would help him.

Or would he?

Alex hoped not. Once Jake had put Greentrees first, when he was much younger. But now, weak and close to dying, loving Alex like the daughter he'd never had . . . now? Would Jake help Julian conquer not only Furs but his own people, in exchange for Alex's life?

No, she decided. Jake would realize that Alex's reprieve would be only temporary. Julian would kill her anyway. Jake would know there was no way he could really save Alex from death.

But from torture . . .

She buried her face in her hands. Dora looked up and held out the bowl of now dirty water.

None of the female Furs seemed to react to Alex's presence. They didn't recoil from her smell; they carried on drinking, shitting in one corner, and picking unseen grubs or nits from each other's fur. They ate the findings. They "talked" to each other in low growls and muted roars. Alex had no idea how intelligent they actually were; dogs, cats, and frabbits could respond to each other's distress without true sentience. But Alex felt that, within their unknown limits, they were being kind to her.

Maybe in wild females the Fur xenophobic response was tempered by their socialization. Or maybe the socialization of males exaggerated the response. Or maybe—

She had no real idea.

Gently Alex pushed away the bowl of water. A piece of decayed organic matter floated in it. Alex didn't like to think how it might have got there.

She forced herself to eat more of the mushy cereal. Cora and Flora had dipped their "hands" into it but hadn't actually eaten any. Alex needed the energy, even if it made her sick . . .

Made her sick. Suddenly she remembered Julian in the cave: *"No, you won't give your pneumonia, or whatever it is, to me, not even if it's caused by a Greentrees microbe. I've got immune-system genemods your biologists can't imagine."* But she didn't have a Greentrees microbe. She had a genetically tailored microbe designed to infect human and Fur DNA both. Maybe she had infected Julian!

She tried to remember what Karim had told her about the contagious period. Had she still been contagious when he took her from the Furs? Were Julian and his soldiers even now vomiting their guts out in the rest of the bunker beyond this fetid cell? Was that why no one had brought fresh food or water?

Hope surged in Alex. If everyone else was incapacitated, and if she could get the female Furs to help her break down the door—

She staggered to her feet, letting the blanket fall to the ground. The Furs looked up but didn't stop eating grubs from each other's pelts. The tail, Alex noted, seemed an especially fertile feeding ground. She held her stomach in check.

Leaning against the cell door, she pantomimed pushing hard. The Furs ignored her.

Alex walked to Cora, who had comforted her last night, and took her hand. She tugged gently. Cora stood, her alien expression unreadable.

Alex led Cora to the door and again pushed. Cora sat back down and resumed grubbing on Miranda's tail.

Again Alex tugged Cora up, then Miranda. They both came with her, but neither would push. They sat down again.

Frustration took Alex. These stupid creatures, they wouldn't even *try . . .*

The door opened from the outside, knocking Alex over. A soldier in the black Terran uniform entered, sweeping his gaze contemptuously over the prisoners. Despite himself, his nostrils flared with their strange smell. He set down two bowls, water and food, and gathered up the old ones.

Alex scarcely noticed his hasty departure. She was too busy staring at the Furs. The females lacked visible noses, let alone flaring nostrils, but their reaction was unmistakable. They clapped their tentacled arms over their necks and turned away from the door, huddling against the far wall. After the soldier left, they removed their arms from what Alex guessed to be holes hidden by the ragged fur. Then all five waved at the air.

Alex had just learned two things. She had not infected Julian and his Terran troops. And it was only male humans who smelled terrible to Furs.

That fit, in a peculiar sort of way. Obviously sex differences were greater among wild Furs than among space Furs, or even among humans. Some of those differences seemed to be biological, not cultural. Wild female Furs were less aggressive than males (or else

Alex would be dead). They were less xenophobic. This was an alien species, equipped with alien biology, and to that biology, female humans smelled vastly different from human males.

Then she learned a third thing. Grandma Fur got laboriously to her two feet and one balancing tail. She lumbered to the door and imitated Alex's pantomime pushing. Then she looked directly at Alex from her two frontal eyes and clumsily, a clearly learned gesture, shook her head from side to side.

No. It won't help.

The Furs and she could communicate.

She couldn't use language. The vocal chords, or whatever Furs had, were too different. For all she knew, the hearing perceptions were equally different. Nonetheless, Alex couldn't stop herself from speaking aloud as she tried to make herself understood with gestures.

"Alex," she said, pointing to herself. Then, "Furs."

Cora and Miranda gazed at her, unreadable. Dora and Flora went on grooming each other. Grandmother was asleep.

"Them," Alex said, pointing to the door. "Bad! Kill!" She pantomimed stabbing herself and then cautiously stabbing in Miranda's general direction. Maybe protection of the cub would stir Cora. It didn't. They watched her, impassive except for an occasional baring of teeth that made Alex nervous. Threat? Yawn? Critical review of her acting?

How had Nan Frayne built such trust and understanding with these aliens?

Through months, years, decades. Alex probably had hours.

She tried again, pantomiming all of them crashing the door and running free. Cora reached for the water bowl; Miranda crawled onto Grandmother Fur, waking her.

Not a success.

When Cora had drunk her fill, Alex dipped her hand in the water and then into cereal. Jake, Ben had said, had used drawings to communicate with the male Furs. Karim had used drawings to communicate with the Vine.

"Furs," she said, dripping cereal from one finger in the shape of a tailed biped with three eyes. Laboriously she drew five of these, one smaller than the others.

Miranda drew close to watch.

Encouraged, Alex drew a human stick figure with cereal blobs for breasts, then pointed to herself. "Alex."

Now Cora and Grandmother gazed at the cereal-smeared floor.

Alex was running out of room. She scrunched herself against the door to free floor space, and sketched three human males. She gave them what she hoped looked like guns, although they were mostly cereal blobs. Then she shouted, "*Zzzzzzzzzz!*" hastily drew lines from the humans to herself and the Furs, and smeared all six figures out of existence. For emphasis she flopped over, looking dead.

Miranda and Cora tentatively tasted the cereal rubbed across the floor and spat it out.

Alex groaned. It wasn't working. Either female Furs were less intelligent than males, or they were so much more passive they didn't care if they died, or their perceptions were so different from humans that the pictures had been meaningless to them.

"Stupid creatures! As long as the door stays shut, you don't even think about how much danger you're in!"

Grandmother Fur dipped one tentacle in the water and then in the cereal.

Alex watched, gaping, as the old Fur drew five Furs, less expertly than even Alex's sorry attempts, but nonetheless recognizable. Then she drew four crested male Furs beside them, carrying "guns." She looked at Alex.

"Your males aren't going to rescue you! They're either infected or dead!"

No. That wasn't what Grandmother had meant.

Alex looked again at the crude cereal smears. The male Furs each had a slash across their "torsos." No wild Fur wore a sash. These were space Furs, set to carry off the Fur females. That's why there were four of them; Grandmother knew she was too old to breed.

Alex gazed at the alien, unreadable expression. As if on cue, the other four Furs leaped up and began their hopping and keening routine. Grandmother went on gazing at Alex, who warned herself against anthropomorphization but nonetheless thought that the old female's eyes held a warning: *You will only make it worse.*

Alex wasn't sure it could get worse.

42

ALONG THE RIVER

L ying flat on his back and looking up at the Cheyenne hunting party, Karim had a sudden memory of Dr. Shipley describing a Cheyenne chief, White Buffalo or Antelope or something like that (Karim had never seen either animal), who was shot down during a massacre by old-style Americans. The chief had stood in front of his dwelling, arms crossed, and sung a death song: "Nothing lives as long as the earth and the mountains." Shipley had recited this admiringly, adding that the original Cheyenne had been among the most spiritual and high-minded of all Indians, devoted to what Shipley had called "the splendor of the mysterious fullness from which all creation must come."

These braves didn't look very spiritual to Karim. They scowled down at him in their ludicrously pretentious, technologically irrelevant clothing. The Cheyenne tribe on Greentrees had been a voluntary association; most of the settlers buying their way in had come from Caucasian, Negroid, or even Asian stock. Their leader, the romantically demented Larry Smith, had changed his name to Blue Waters. Their culture was deliberately re-created, not inherited.

Could they actually track?

Jon McBain jumped right in. "We're so glad to see you! The smoke signals were just to attract your attention; the method was described in a deebee. I'm Dr. Jon McBain, a xenobiologist. This is Karim Mahjoub, he was . . . well, never mind that. We'd like to propose an alliance."

The six braves turned as one to leave.

Jon grabbed the closest sleeve, and Karim tensed. But the brave merely stared stonily at Jon, who hastily released the animal-hide sleeve. Karim staggered to his feet.

"We have proof that Julian Martin and his Terran soldiers armed the wild Furs against the Cheyenne. Now we're trying to destroy Martin."

The braves turned around.

It was hard to tell from their demeanor which one was the leader. But the same blond who had originally said, "What the hell do you think you're doing?" now said simply, "Why?" Karim concentrated on him.

"We want to destroy Julian Martin because he has killed Greentrees citizens, and tried to set groups of citizens against each other, and illegally armed Furs against your people, and tortured and killed one of our leaders, and kidnapped another. We sent the smoke signals because we need your help finding the abducted woman, Alex Cutler."

No response. But the brave went on listening.

"We were told that you can track anything," Karim continued desperately. "Alex Cutler was taken by Julian Martin's soldiers from a place upriver two nights ago. They had rovers, probably two of them. They—"

"And when she was taken, your Alex Cutler was with the band of wild Furs on the river," the brave said impassively.

So they had been watching. The Cheyenne had had spies, scouts . . . how? The human and Fur camps, a quarter mile apart, had both been in the kill-clean zone. There was no cover, no trees or brush . . . the Cheyenne had either scouted along the riverbed itself or crept by night so silently over the blank landscape that not even the wild Furs had detected them.

Karim's spirits rose.

"Yes," he said to the blond brave. "Alex was sick. She deliberately sickened herself with a disease we hoped to give to the wild Furs."

"Why?"

"So their females would carry it back upstairs—I mean, so the space Furs would take the wild females—they've been doing that, you know—to their spaceship and the space Furs would in turn become infected. We're at war with them, no less than you must be. They've killed Cheyenne and Mira City alike."

Again no response. Karim realized how far-fetched and convoluted his story sounded. And he hadn't even mentioned the biomass or the Vine . . . Jake should be doing this. Jake had always been the negotiator, the mastermind, the manipulator.

Jon blurted, "If you help us track Alex Cutler, it would help us both! Don't you want to punish Julian Martin for arming the wild Furs against you?"

Karim saw, as Jon did not, the sudden flash of contempt in the blond brave's eyes. Karim said quickly, "Not punishment. Cutting off the flow of arms to the wild Furs, before it grows to include Terran weapons not even Mira City can—could have—matched."

Something passed among the six men: not glances but some subtle shift of body weight, almost imperceptible alteration of stance. The blond brave said, "My name is River Cloud."

Relief made Karim's knees wobble.

The Cheyenne were as direct and efficient as even Jake could have wished, and as silent as Karim wished Jon could be. River Cloud listened to the expanded version of Karim's story and issued orders to his war party. Two of them took off in one direction, two more in another, and the remaining brave down the riverbank.

"Where are they going?" Jon said.

"To find Alex Cutler, to find Jake Holman, and to catch fish. You are hungry."

Karim was more than that. Now that someone else was safely in charge, he felt himself slipping into weakness greater than he'd ever imagined. It was an effort to stand. Impassively, River Cloud led him to a deadfall Karim had not noticed and motioned to him to crawl within. Instantly Karim and Jon fell asleep. When Karim woke it was night and a mess of cooked fish lay beside him, wrapped neatly in leaves. He and Jon devoured them, then crawled out of their den to find River Cloud seated on the riverbank with three of the braves.

What was the protocol here? Karim sat down, hoping any offense would be attributed to his unspiritual and misguided ignorance and not to malice. He needed River Cloud.

The blond brave said, "Jake Holman and the five people with him, three women and two men, are safe. They will stay where they are. Running Bush will hunt game for them, since they cannot feed themselves."

River Cloud's contempt was clear. Karim confined himself to "Yes," and put a restraining hand on Jon's arm.

River Cloud continued, "Julian Martin is being tracked. What do you plan to do when we find him?"

Should he tell the Cheyenne about the spores? Karim was aware of his rising anger at the brave's disdain. But anger wasn't a good reason to impress. And the Cheyenne might take the spore sac for their own use. No, better to look the fool, however painful that was.

He mumbled, "We don't have a plan yet."

Jon said, "Where are the space Furs? Did you find them?"

"We have known where they are since they landed," River Cloud said. "They don't leave their shuttle in the Avery Mountains, except to fly it in search of wild Fur females. And then they wear space suits. They are afraid of contracting your microbial disease. But you don't know if you can still infect them, do you?"

"How do you know that?" Karim said quickly.

"Because Julian Martin shot the male wild Furs before the disease could develop. And he took the females away. Your proof has all vanished."

So the Cheyenne had witnessed the massacre. They had seen Alex carried off by Julian, and apparently seen the wild females taken, too. They'd already understood more of the situation than Karim had thought possible.

Jon burst out, "How much do you know about microbial diseases? I thought you were trying to live like savages!"

River Cloud said coldly, "We learn what we must about the white man's world in order to protect ourselves against it. My grandfather was First Landing, a geneticist."

"But if—"

"Enough, Jon," Karim said, and Jon subsided.

River Cloud said no more. Karim found himself revising his opinion of the Cheyenne. However ludicrous and romantic their culture in a star-faring age, they had survived in greater numbers than had Mira City. The Cheyenne, unlike Jake and Karim and presumably Alex, were fed and housed and informed about their enemies.

And Karim sensed in them, bone-tipped spears and all, a stony relentlessness, an implacability, that might in the long run be far more dangerous to Julian Martin than Karim's own rage, than Jake's shifting expediencies, even than the space Furs' desperate bid to take over Greentrees.

One of the other two braves returned in the morning, conferred with River Cloud, and disappeared again.

"Julian Martin is hiding in the Isfahan Mountains, along the Black River," River Cloud said to Karim. "Those are our names. I don't know what you call them."

Karim wondered what River Cloud would say if he knew that "Isfahan" had been the name of an ancient Arabic city. What Arab-turned-Cheyenne two generations ago had named it?

"Martin has constructed a lodge out of a large military shuttle," River Cloud continued. "It is heavily defended."

"Take us there," Karim said.

River Cloud studied him. "No."

"No? Why not?"

"Because you have some plan that you have not told us. We do not ally without trust."

Karim locked gazes with the blond brave. River Cloud was taller than he by two or three inches. They were probably the same age, although Karim had been born fifty years earlier. He felt every one of those five decades now.

What would Jake do?

Oddly enough, it was not Jake's but Lucy's face that rose in front of him. Lucy, idealistic always, who had once left Jake for Karim because Jake had lied and cheated. Which was what Jake would also do now, if he were making this decision.

But Karim was not Jake.

"Yes," Karim said steadily, "we have a plan. And I will trust you with it. Did your grandfather ever teach you what a spore is?"

43

TERRAN SHUTTLE BUNKER

Two more days passed. Alex and the female Furs were fed and watered, although only Alex ate. Once each day a Terran soldier threw a pail of some sort of slop over the human and alien shit deposited in one corner, and it all dissolved, eaten by genemod bacteria with built-in terminator genes. The smell did not noticeably improve.

Alex would have gone on trying to communicate with Cora and Miranda, if only for something to do, but the Furs seemed to have lost interest. They made no response to anything Alex drew, pantomimed, or said. Perhaps Grandmother Fur had told them to ignore Alex. Or maybe the females were just getting too weak to bother. How long could they go without eating at all? Already they all looked scrawnier under their thick, dirty pelts.

Alex tore and twisted her blanket into a crude wrap. When that was finished, she had nothing to do. She slept as much as possible, lying beside the door with her nose turned away from the Furs.

On the third day, the door opened and a Terran soldier in full battle gear tanglefoamed the Furs.

Alex tried to force her way between him and the door. With a glance of amusement behind his clear helmet, he backhanded her and she crashed to the floor. Efficiently he dragged the five bound female Furs from the room and slammed the door.

Four female Furs.

When her vision cleared from her hard fall, Alex saw that

Grandmother had been tanglefoamed but not taken away. The old alien roared and wriggled against her bonds. When she found she couldn't budge them, the roaring changed to the high keening, one bound foot trying vainly to hop against the floor.

Alex hovered nearby. She couldn't touch the tanglefoam or she would be caught in it, too. Before she could think of anything to ease the alien's distress, the Terran soldier returned, seized Alex's arm, and dragged her from the room.

"Where are you taking the Furs? What are you going to do with the old one? Let me go, you—"

The Terran soldier ignored her, opening the door of the second cell and thrusting her through it. Julian Martin waited inside.

Fear stilled Alex. This tiny room was where Julian had tortured her before. But this time there was no chair, and Julian held no weapon. His nostrils flared.

"You stink of them, Alex."

"Where . . . where are you taking them?"

"To be 'wed in another key,' " he said, and she recognized the mockery of Duncan's voice. Then he said in his own, "I wanted to say good-bye."

Good-bye? Again the fear. To quell it, she concentrated on one object, using it to push all emotion out of her mind. Julian's ring, green gem on a gold band. *"Who gave you that ring?" "My mother . . ."*

He said, "I'll be gone for a few days, until I bring Jake back here. I wanted to say good-bye to you."

A sense of unreality swept over Alex, so strong that for just a moment the room blurred. Julian meant it. He had tortured her, tried to kill her, imprisoned her, and probably meant to do all these things again. Now he wanted to say good-bye to her before a few days' trip, like any lover leaving to check a research station. And yet he was not insane, not in any sense that Alex understood the word. His brilliant green eyes, constantly alert because he'd lived with treachery so long that he could never be careless, regarded her keenly. He saw everything, and interpreted it accurately.

"You think it's strange that I want to say good-bye. But, Alex, this is a dangerous universe. I thought I'd taught you that much, at least. Anything could happen, and I might not return. Is it so odd that I'd want to say good-bye to someone I loved, the first person to introduce me to this gorgeous planet?"

She said nothing.

"Because it *is* gorgeous, you know. You never saw Terra, or you'd realize how breathtaking Greentrees is. 'Sounds and sweet airs, that give delight and hurt not . . .'"

"Don't!"

He smiled. "All right. My sensitive plant. Do you remember when I told you that the highest morality is to protect lives, to avoid having to fight at all? I'm doing that now. Only a few humans will die—as only relatively few have died so far—so that the rest can live in the peace and prosperity I can bring to Greentrees. And I will, Alex. I didn't think I could love a place the way I love this planet, not ever again."

His green eyes had softened. Alex stared dumbly. He meant it.

Julian moved toward her. She flinched, but he seemed to ignore that. His lips brushed her cheek, then he turned and left.

A moment later the same Terran soldier tossed her back with Grandmother Fur.

Hours later, the shuttle shuddered. Alex looked up from the water bowl she held to Grandmother's mouth, carefully avoiding contact with the tanglefoam. Was the shuttle lifting off? Impossible, half buried in the hillside! What was happening?

The walls started to dissolve.

They thinned, wobbled, grew holes. Now Alex could hear shrieking, an eardrum-stabbing whoop like nothing on Greentrees. Through a hole in the dissolving wall—how could the shuttle be *dissolving?*—she saw the Terran soldier who had shoved her around. He held a weapon of some sort that had just sagged forward like a limp penis. More whooping, and a stone-tipped spear pierced the soldier, not dressed in battle gear, through the heart.

Alex ran forward, stopped. She had no idea what was happening or what she should do. More wall dissolved, and her cell was open. So was nearly the entire shuttle. Six Terran soldiers, caught inside and without armor, lay dead on the now-dirt floor, arrows or spears in their bodies.

Grandmother Fur began keening.

A Cheyenne brave emerged from a clump of trees and ran to her, faster and more graceful than she would have thought possible. "Where are the other Terrans?" he said, not even winded.

Alex could only shake her head.

"Julian Martin?"

"I . . . don't know."

The brave spied Grandmother Fur and drew another arrow from his quiver.

"No, please, she's just an old female! Julian took the other Furs but left her because she's too old to breed! And she's tied in tangle-foam!"

The brave sheathed his arrow. "Where did he take the female enemy?"

"I don't know. He only said he'd be gone a few days. No wait, I think he—who are you? What did you do here?"

The brave sped off.

Alex's knees gave way and she sunk to the ground. Nothing made any sense. A moment later she saw, beside the body of a dead Terran, a pile of pinkish goo, rapidly sinking into the soil. Hastily Alex smeared her hands with it before it all disappeared. The goo had been in a metal spray wand, now dissolved, on the soldier's belt, now also dissolved. It was the only antidote for tanglefoam. She wiped her hands on Grandmother and freed her.

The two of them waited, bewildered, for whatever came next.

Two figures, much less graceful than the Cheyenne brave, jogged into view.

"Karim!" Alex ran forward and embraced him, then Jon McBain. "How did you . . . who . . . Jake . . ."

"We'll tell you everything," Jon said breathlessly. "Are you all right? What did—"

Karim demanded, "Where's Julian Martin?"

"I don't know for sure, but I think he's gone after Jake. I didn't tell him where Jake is because I don't know, but I couldn't help . . . he also took four Fur females of breeding age and left *her*—" Alex looked around, but Grandmother was gone.

Karim grabbed her hand. "We've got to get to Martin before he finds Jake. I can stop Martin now, Alex. I've got the sporcs that—"

"The what? Where's Jake?"

"Not now. Run!"

He pulled her along. Parked at least a quarter mile away was a rover. Four Cheyenne braves waited quietly alongside.

"We had to leave it here, way upwind," Jon panted, out of breath. This explained nothing. "Get in!" He scrambled into the driver's seat.

Karim said to one of the braves, "You ride, too. It will be faster."

The brave, who wore blond braids, said coldly, "Cheyenne do not need white men's devices."

"You'll slow us down!"

He didn't even answer. Three Cheyenne melted into the trees. The blond brave said contemptuously, "Martin's tracks are clear. He's driving some very large machine. Follow me." He loped off.

"Supercilious bastard," Jon said cheerfully. "That was River Cloud. Come on, Alex, we have a long way to go and a lot to tell."

She got in. Suddenly Grandmother Fur limped behind the rover. "Stop, Jon! Wait a minute!"

Jon stopped, goggling at the creature. Grandmother gazed fearfully at Alex—to Alex, anyway, it looked like fear. And why not? If the Cheyenne scorned rovers, they at least knew what they were disdaining. To a wild Fur, the rover must be a terrifying mystery. But Grandmother wanted to follow her daughters. Her sheer bravery was dazzling. Alex opened the rover door.

"God, no, Alex, the Cheyenne will have a fit!" Jon said.

"Let them," Alex answered, and Grandmother stumbled in.

Julian was easy to follow; they wouldn't even have needed the blond brave to lead. Alex suspected that Julian was driving the same truck that had brought her and the Furs to the shuttle bunker. It left a wide trail of broken brush and broken tree branches. Even after the forest gave way to plain, the truck's treads were visible on the purple groundcover, which hadn't had time to spring back. On the plain, Alex felt exposed, but the brave ahead never faltered in his steady, tireless lope. Jon drove steadily a few hundred yards behind, while Karim, in the other front seat, shouted over his shoulder to Alex.

He told her about the spores.

She heard the triumph in his young voice—she, after all, had ridiculed his biomass hopes—but was too dazed to respond. There was too much to take in.

Julian had killed the male wild Furs, before they had even a chance of becoming infected.

Siddalee Brown had sewn an infrasonic tracer into Alex's Threadmore, and Julian had made Siddalee confess. Made her . . . oh God, the tiny metal thing in Julian's hand and the horrifying pain . . . Siddalee . . .

Natalie, warned by Siddalee just before her capture, had gotten Jake and the others away before Julian arrived at the river campsite.

Karim had contacted the Vine a second time.

The Vine had actually produced a . . . a spore that could . . . the same as the shield around Vine planets . . . it apparently never decayed . . . never . . .

She whispered, "*All* metal on Greentrees?"

Somehow Karim heard her. "Eventually. Not right away."

"But Karim—"

"Shhhh! River Cloud's doubling back!"

The brave loped to the rover, saw Grandmother Fur, and stopped. His mouth curved in anger, the first emotion Alex had seen from any Cheyenne. Grandmother bared her teeth and her three eyes glittered.

River Cloud said, "The desecration lies just ahead." It took Alex a moment to realize he meant the kill-clean zone. "Stay hidden here until we return."

Karim said, "We haven't got the time! If Martin gets to Jake Holman before we do—"

"He's not heading toward Jake Holman. We veered away from the river long ago. Martin's truck is driving toward the Fur shuttle in the mountains."

Jon cried, "He's going straight to the space Furs! But how can he expect to take *them* on?"

Alex thought rapidly. In a startling, vivid moment she saw suddenly what Julian was going to do: all of it, the whole plan, laid out before her as clear and detailed as a bright holo image. She could enter the holo as if it were three-dimensional, could walk around in it, could inspect every glowing aspect. At last, after all Julian's exhortations, she had begun to think like him.

It sickened her.

She said slowly, "He's going to use the *Crucible*."

"What?" Karim said.

"He's going to put out the four wild Fur females as bait. He doesn't know where the Fur shuttle is, hasn't dared expose himself enough to look for it. When the space Furs move the shuttle to get the females, he's going to send an order up to the *Crucible*. She's probably somewhere on this side of the planet in a low orbit while the Fur ship is on the other side. Julian waited for that configuration. The *Crucible* will blast the entire mountain with an alpha beam or some equivalent."

Jon said, "But if he does that, the mother ship will destroy the *Crucible*. They have more advanced weapons and are magnitudes faster! The Fur ship has McAndrew Drive!"

"Julian knows that," Alex said. She remembered Julian at that first party for him in the Mausoleum, explaining how Terra had destroyed most of her population: *"When ninety percent of your ethnic group is predicted to perish anyway, you don't mind releasing pathogens that will kill a third of your people but also a third of the enemy."*

Jon went on arguing. "But the soldiers on the *Crucible* know that they'd die. They wouldn't follow the order!"

Karim, born Terran and not Greenie, said grimly, "Yes, they would."

Jon said, "Then I don't see how we—"

Karim interrupted him. "We can release the spores as soon as possible onto Julian's truck. That'll take it all out—comlink to the *Crucible,* weapons, truck, everything. The Cheyenne can get close enough upwind to scatter the spores—"

"Maybe," Jon said doubtfully, "but I doubt it. Martin has probably got sophisticated thermal-signature detectors. I don't think anything human can get closer to him than maybe five miles, and that's nowhere near close enough to count reliably on wind dispersal. Anyway, if the *Crucible* does take out the whole mountain, we'd go with it."

Anything human.

Alex had thought she'd felt sick before, when she understood Julian's plan. It was nothing to what she felt now. She looked at Grandmother Fur.

No. She couldn't do it.

She couldn't see any other choice.

And she couldn't give Grandmother Fur a choice. If she did, even if Alex could somehow communicate enough in the short time left—the old alien might refuse. And then they all would die, killed by Julian Martin seeking power, or killed by the space Furs seeking uncontaminated real estate.

Grandmother Fur, unreadable, looked at Alex. Alex got out of the rover and gestured. The alien followed her, looking around. For her daughters, most likely, and her granddaughter.

Flora. Dora. Cora. Miranda.

O brave new world that has such people in it.

Hating herself, fighting down the bile rising in her throat, Alex said to Karim, "Give me the spore sac."

44

THE AVERY MOUNTAINS

River Cloud reluctantly agreed to guide the old female wild Fur. The space Fur shuttle, he told Karim, was in a mountain meadow several miles above Jon McBain's research station along the river. The Cheyenne had known its location two days after it landed. That was why they'd captured the station; it made a convenient base to keep watch on the shuttle-fortress. The inexplicable arrival of Lucy and Karim had startled the Cheyenne but not upset them: just two more crazy whites.

Karim watched Alex with the female Fur. The two sat on the ground in a small clearing. Late afternoon light slanted through the branches of the tall purple trees. Greentrees' night scent, which Karim had so longed for on the hellish Vine world, came to him on the breeze, still faint. Tiny white night flowers began to open.

Alex bent her head over the metal object, the second, she was using for her demonstration to the old Fur.

Karim wished savagely for a computer. If he could figure likely orbits for the *Crucible* and for the Fur McAndrew Drive ship, likely weapon trajectories . . . as it was, he was reduced to guessing that Martin would wait until dark to attack. Hardly a technologically sophisticated guess.

Better get accustomed to it.

Alex rose and walked toward him. At the sight of her face, Karim looked away. He had seen Jake in moral anguish. Dr. Shipley, Lucy. He had never seen anyone look as terrible as Alex at this moment.

"She's ready."

"I'll get River Cloud. Alex, are you sure this alien can—"

But Alex had already walked away, her back to him.

River Cloud gestured at the old female Fur, and she limped after him. Karim watched until they both disappeared in the trees. River Cloud's braves melted after him.

They had found no cave to shelter in, even in this area rich in caves. But the Cheyenne braves had arranged one of their deadfall shelters for the hapless Greenies. Jon and Alex crawled into it. Night came, moonless but clear.

Karim remained outside the deadfall. No fire, no powertorch to draw attention. But either they were far enough away from the Fur shuttle-fortress to escape Martin's detection and attack or they weren't. Karim fumbled in the darkness to find a thick, strong tree trunk. When he did, he climbed it, scraping himself bloody, until he was above most of the forest canopy and could see the starlit sky.

How far had River Cloud and the alien gotten by now? Was River Cloud on his way back?

Karim could see it clearly in his mind. River Cloud and the female Fur making their way through the forest, sworn enemies traveling together. Somewhere behind, the three other braves followed. Or maybe there were more than three by now; Karim didn't know how Cheyenne summoned their own. Probably not by smoke signals, judging from the braves' reaction to Jon's earlier brainstorm.

River Cloud would follow the track of Julian Martin's truck, and then, when Martin had stopped the truck somewhere safe and sent a Terran guard on foot with the female Furs up the mountain, River Cloud would not follow. The Cheyenne would stay at least five miles away from wherever Martin stopped, out of detection range. But the old Fur would not.

There, the Cheyenne would point. *They're that way. Your kin.* And the alien, hopeful, would go toward Martin. His thermal-signature detectors would pick her up, and ignore her. Another wild Fur. Nothing to pay attention to. The Terran soldiers were in full battle gear, with major weaponry on the truck. Martin had armed the wild Furs mostly with laser guns, and this one was not even carrying that. No threat.

Meanwhile, the Terran guard, probably one soldier, had forced the other four females up the mountain, toward the space-Fur shuttle. It, of course, might have more sophisticated equipment. But it would detect no electronic signals; Martin would have thought of that. The space Furs would detect four Furs trailed by a human, and then the human would leave. Prowling primitive humans warring with wild Furs, the invaders would think. They must have detected a lot of such Cheyenne-Fur interactions. They would eliminate the male primitives after they had finished with the more dangerous humans. Then the planet would be theirs.

Karim shifted on his thick, high branch. A small moon rose above the horizon.

Had River Cloud left the old Fur yet? Probably. The Cheyenne had started back toward Karim, traveling fast and low. Karim could see the grandmother Fur pushing on, hastening through the brush as fast as she could to where she thought her daughters were. Poor old horror. She limped faster.

Now the four fertile females were alone. Were they tanglefoamed? It would keep them from wandering off. But tanglefoam would be too strong an indication of human intervention. No, they were free. So they started to flee back down the mountain. But they've been detected by the shuttle. Do the space Furs know their primitive cousins are female? Do they know that wild females don't get left exposed and alone by their males? It would depend on how closely the space Furs had observed the habits of their potential sexual slaves.

Karim's own great-great-grandfather had kept an *andarun* of four wives and six concubines.

A second moon rose against the stars. The first traveled quickly westward in its low orbit.

He pictured the four bewildered aliens, starting back down the mountain. They don't get far—or maybe they do. Maybe the wild Furs refuse the bait, or don't detect it, in which case Martin would have to recapture the females and try again.

Miles away, he visualized, the old alien does not see her daughters. They're captive in that metal house, as she and they had been captive in the other metal house before the magic powder melted it. The magic powder that the human female gave her. These humans had hurt that human female, too. She had wanted their metal house to melt. And the old alien wants her daughters free.

She unclenches her tentacles and tears open the spore sac, as Alex had shown her. She dumps it over herself.

Tiny dark spores cling, invisible, without reflected light, to her pelt. More are blown toward Martin's truck. River Cloud has carefully left the alien upwind of the Terran camp.

And now the Fur shuttle lifts from its hidden location. Once before Karim had seen it pass over the river, a silent black shape against the stars. A hole in the sky. It follows the fleeing females easily, and sets down beside them. Furs emerge, completely suited, cousins of the terrified females from light-years and millennia of advancement away. The soldiers do . . . what? Stun the females from a distance? Throw up one of their invisible electronic walls to stop them? Are they making the Fur equivalent of superior laughter?

Whatever they do, the old Fur has not done her part first. Please Allah, she has not yet opened the spore sac. Because first Julian Martin must give the order to the *Crucible,* and that ship must swoop down as fast as it can toward the Fur shuttle, now that Martin knows where it is. Martin must have his metal equipment intact long enough to give that order, but no longer. Karim and Alex had to trust River Cloud to estimate the timing of everybody and release the old female Fur at the right time. Release her, deceive her, direct her to Martin instead of her lost children.

Please Allah, let Alex have guessed right about Martin's plans . . . Karim found he was praying.

A light streaked across the sky. One quick flash, like a meteor, and then the entire sky exploded into light. Karim's tree shook and he hung on for life itself. A noise that deafened him, and then an echo of the noise, and an echo of the echo.

Cries below him. Someone switched a powertorch on heedless

full beam, and Karim glimpsed Jon far below, tiny as an insect. Not Alex. He waited.

Nothing.

Then they had figured wrong! The Furs hadn't—

A second flash of light, higher, soundless.

Karim closed his eyes. It had happened. Alex had guessed right. The *Crucible*, on Martin's orders, had hit the Fur shuttle with an alpha beam, taking out half the mountain. Then the Fur mother ship, able to accelerate almost instantly to more than a hundred gees, had come roaring down and destroyed the sacrificial decoy in orbit.

All Julian Martin had left were his troops on the ground.

All the space Furs had left were the aliens in orbit.

The old Fur hunting for her children, still walking but already dead, was going to take care of both menaces, and never know it.

Karim began to climb painfully down the tree. Eventually River Cloud would return with his braves. Alex had still not appeared. She was still lying in the deadfall shelter, or had stumbled off somewhere into the forest to be alone. Karim would have to deal with her soon.

But not yet. That was more pain than he could face just yet.

45

THE AVERY MOUNTAINS

Alex couldn't sleep. She had waited in a small clearing in the forest, sitting on the ground, arms clasped around her knees. The huge flash lit up the sky and shook the ground, followed by the lesser flash. When she knew the Fur shuttle and the *Crucible* were both gone, a strange calm descended over her, an unexpected and eerie caesura.

It felt almost as if she were separated from her body. Her body made its way back to Jon and Karim, spoke to them, arranged a watch rotation with herself taking the first shift. Her body switched off Jon's powertorch and instead built a small fire, to keep off night chill and scare away predators. Her body noticed Karim's relief that she was functioning properly, as well as Jon's clumsy attempts to restrain his triumph from some misguided motive of sparing her.

And yet all the while, Alex was someone other than her body, some detached entity observing herself from the outside. It wasn't a painful schism, just a peculiar one. And she couldn't sleep. It felt as if she might never sleep again.

Jon, rubbing his eyes, relieved her watch after a few hours. Alex lay down by the fire and the snoring Karim, and stared up at the stars. She was awake when one of River Cloud's braves, the redhead, returned.

"What happened?" she said calmly. "Where's River Cloud?"

The brave sat in the firelight, looking no different from when he'd left. No blood on him, scarcely any dirt. For the first time, however, she saw one of the Cheyenne look tired.

He said succinctly, "The animal released the spores. Everything metal dissolved. We killed the enemy whites easily. Julian Martin was not there, and River Cloud has gone to find him." The brave stretched out and fell instantly asleep beside Karim.

Not there. Julian Martin was not there. Gone to find him.

Jon said, "It worked! Martin couldn't have known we were coming or anything about the spores . . . it's just bad luck that he himself was gone before the Cheyenne got there. Do you think he went to find Jake Holman?"

Alex watched herself say evenly, "He wouldn't know where to look. I couldn't tell him where Jake and the others went because I didn't know until you told me. It's a big continent. I doubt Julian went to search blindly for Jake, and Jake's too smart to have put out an electronic signal."

"Then we don't know where Martin went."

"My best guess is back to his shuttle-bunker. He doesn't know it was destroyed." Or that Alex was no longer in it. Had he gone back to do something more to her?

"Yes," Jon said. "Well, the Cheyenne will find him. I'm convinced they can find anything."

Alex gazed at the sleeping brave. She couldn't remember his name, if she'd ever known it. She reached out to shake him awake.

He sat up before her hand even touched him, knife in hand. Alex stayed very still, awed by his reflexes and unwilling to test them further. The brave said, "What?"

"What's your name?"

He stared at her coldly, but he answered. "Gray Bird."

Some instinct told her not to issue a direct order. "Gray Bird, I think Julian Martin may have gone back to the shuttle-bunker where he held me captive."

"That is where River Cloud seeks him."

"And I want to ask you something. What happened to the old female wild Fur with the spores?"

Something shifted behind his eyes, which, she now noticed, were a pale watery blue in the flickering firelight. "That animal is dead."

"Did you kill her? Any of you Cheyenne?"

"No. One of the Terrans shot her before their weapons dissolved."

"So she didn't even know her daughters weren't there."

He studied her. "She knew."

Alex didn't ask why he thought that. She said, because she couldn't help herself, "We betrayed her. I betrayed her. She thought I was helping her but I didn't keep the bargain. I used her. Used all five of them and they're dead."

"Yes," Gray Bird said, "we know. That is what white men do."

Anger flooded Alex. *You're as white as I am!* She wanted to yell to this blue-eyed redheaded fake. *My history is your history, you cannot shed it just because you call yourself Cheyenne and embrace some antiquated tribal life, that will not restore your innocence or spare you history—*

It was Julian who had insisted you cannot evade history. Or remain innocent and still survive.

She made no answer to the brave. Instead she let Jon carry out his watch duty and lay down on the opposite side of the fire.

She did not sleep.

Morning dawned spectacularly red, and the haze continued even after sunrise. "Dust from the alpha-beam attack," Jon said. "We'll probably see atmospheric effects for a long time."

Gray Bird moved their camp to the edge of the kill-clean zone. Alex didn't question him. She trudged behind the brave for hours until they were clear of the forest, and then she stood and blinked.

To her left was a mountain-sized pile of rubble, hazy with dust. The air tasted gritty here, out of the filter of trees. Alex's eyes watered. The *Crucible*'s alpha beam had shattered acres and acres, starting avalanches of rock and reducing wooded slopes to slag and flinders.

By comparison, the Furs' annihilation beam was clean and orderly. Where the terrible rubble stopped, the sterile plain began, empty and denuded. But not, Alex saw, completely so. The purple groundcover was starting to grow again in stubbly patches. She even saw the first shoots of what would be a deadly red creeper.

Something moved on the horizon.

Alex glanced at Gray Bird, but he didn't seem alarmed. He set about building a fire. As the thing on the horizon came closer, Alex saw that it was a herd of some sort. In the kill-clean zone? What were the animals eating? Squinting, she realized that it wasn't a herd at all; it was a parade.

Then she was running to meet them.

Three of the big herd animals the Cheyenne called "elephants," although Jake had told her they bore no relation to the Terran mammals of that name. Greenie elephants were placid, stupid herbivores domesticated by the first generation of Cheyenne. They smelled awful; that was their defense against predators. The Cheyenne prided themselves on tolerating the odor.

Two of the lumbering beasts had their armored backs loaded with gear. The third, led by two Cheyenne women, dragged a travois made of branches lashed together on which lay Jake Holman, cushioned with blankets.

"Jake!" Alex cried. "Natalie! Ben!"

They were all there, looking thin, weary, and filthy. Kent, Kueilan, Lucy. Two braves walked silently beside the caravan, which seemed to be made up mostly of women and children. Gray Bird greeted the braves and the three conferred apart from the others.

Alex fell on her knees beside Jake. "Are you all right?"

"Yes," he quavered. "You?"

"I—" She couldn't go on.

"The Cheyenne told us. Everything. It's over, Alex."

"Not quite."

"No," he agreed, and went into a coughing fit.

The grit in the air. Alex gave orders to have his travois drawn under the trees, where the leaves would filter some of the dust. It turned out the elephants wouldn't go under trees, so the travois was unhooked and Kent and Jon pulled it. Ben still had a bloody bandage on his head and seemed edgy and nervous. Natalie hung beside him, loving and tactful. Kueilan asked about fires.

"Build cooking fires in the kill-clean zone, apart from the trees; we'll make a smaller one in here at night for Jake. What do you have to cook?"

"Some things the Cheyenne women gave us, plus a glenning a brave just shot on the way here," Kueilan said. "They've been good about sharing their food. Alex . . . do you want a . . . a less skimpy blanket to wear?"

For the first time in days Alex became aware of how she must look. She still wore the "wrap" she had made from the blanket in her prison cell, plus a pair of boots taken from a dead Terran soldier. She had not bathed in . . . how long? She couldn't remember. Kueilan must have washed in the river; the girl looked clean, her long black hair in a neat plait, and her Threadmores were as whole and durable as ever.

"I'm fine," Alex said, idiotically.

"You look like you should sleep."

"Don't fuss over me, Kueilan. Fuss over Karim."

"Lucy's doing that," Kueilan said neutrally.

Alex busied herself with food, fires, security, knowing all the while that none of it was necessary. Kueilan was better at creating comfort than she was, and the Cheyenne better at security. Alex went to sit by Jake, but he was asleep. The old man looked frail and papery, as if he could blow away on the freshening wind.

The wind *was* freshening.

The first metal dissolved in midafternoon, just before the rain started. It was Ben's laser gun. Ben sat, with Natalie close by, on a fallen log at the edge of the tree line, chewing on a hard piece of something the Cheyenne called pemmican, a revolting mixture of dried meat, fat, and wild berries. His laser gun lay beside him. Alex happened to be watching when the metal started to ooze, then dissolved to nothing.

"Hey!" Ben cried, even though he had been told what might be coming.

"It's starting, Karim," Lucy said.

"Yes. Greentrees will be . . . different."

Which was an understatement if Alex ever heard one.

The spores were self-replicating, Jon had decided, flourishing whenever they had food, going dormant when they did not. "Food" included most metals, including natural metallic ores. The Vines had not known what metals their enemies the Furs could create, and so the Vines had shielded their planet with a spore cloud of voracious, catholic tastes.

The "cloud" on Greentrees would grow slowly but inexorably. Blown by the wind, feeding where it could, it waited to attack any technology based on metal. Laser guns, cooking pots, starships, spoons, computers, solar arrays, hair clips, batteries, comlinks, rovers, rings, manufactury looms, nails, mining equipment—everything Alex had allocated and hoarded and funded and counted and tracked as tray-o was shortly going to pass out of existence.

Greentrees could not loft the spores into space. She lacked a space elevator, a shuttle, even missiles. But the Fur ship still in orbit could not send anything down. The minute a shuttle approached the planet, it would begin to dissolve. Nor, after the spores had had time for sufficient replication (how much time?), could the Fur ship itself risk assuming a low enough orbit to fire its kill-clean beam.

It probably wouldn't take the Furs upstairs long to learn that. Their ship, with whatever uninfected Furs were still aboard, would leave orbit. They would have to find another planet to colonize, if they could. Their home planet and who knew how many colony worlds had been infected by the Vines' diabolical viral weapon, and now Greentrees was infected in a different way. The war here was over. The Furs had lost.

But Alex wasn't sure exactly who had won.

"Jake wants to see you," Lucy said.

It was nightfall again. A brisk wind blew, dissolving things. The Cheyenne women, amazingly efficient, had erected an entire tented village on the empty plain just before the kill-clean zone ended and the forest began. Fires burned, children played, food cooked, braves stood watch. The spores would make very little difference to the Cheyenne. They already functioned in the Stone Age.

That was not what Alex had wanted for Mira City.

She walked toward the trees. She still had not slept. Exhaustion hung over her like a smell—like the elephants, like the wild Furs. But rest would not come. Bloodshot in the eyes and wobbly in the knees, she stumbled through the forest to the second camp set up for Jake, sheltered a little from the dust.

Julian Martin stood by the fire.

His hands were bound behind his back and a strip of animal hide around his ankles let him walk but not run or kick. Gray Bird stood on one side of him, River Cloud on the other. A long jagged wound ran from one shoulder down Julian's arm, bloodying his black uniform. But he stood easily, arrogantly, and smiled when he saw her.

"Hello, Alex."

Jake sat wrapped in hides and propped against a tree by the fire, Karim and Jon standing beside him. For once, Jon stayed quiet. Karim looked at Alex's face and then away.

"Alex," Jake said, "there is something we have to decide. With you. Julian is the last of the Terrans left alive. The Cheyenne . . . Julian is the last. Ashraf is dead. He—"

"How do you know Ashraf is dead?" Alex got the words out somehow.

Julian said, "I told them so."

Jake continued, "You're in charge on Greentrees now. In charge of what's left of Mira City's population, anyway, which I suspect is actually quite a lot, scattered around. You can decide to keep Julian in custody until we build a judicial system again, but I don't think that's wise. He will always be dangerous." Jake paused, swallowed with difficulty—Alex, her vision preternaturally and painfully clear, saw his Adam's apple move in his withered throat—and said, "The Cheyenne want him."

It took a moment for the words to register.

River Cloud said, "He is ours. He armed the wild Furs against us, he and the woman Nan Frayne. The Cheyenne nation agrees to help you learn to survive in harmony with the Great Spirit and from His bounty, but only if you give us this man. He is ours."

Alex looked at Julian. He smiled easily at her.

He *smiled*.

"What . . . what will you do to him?"

Jake said quickly, "They won't tell you that."

Because Jake had instructed them not to. What else was part of this unholy bargain? Survival skills in exchange for—

Torture. That's what it would come to. The old Terran Cheyenne had tortured their prisoners to death.

She saw Lau-Wah Mah's body. Siddalee Brown's. Felt again the small silver weapon in Julian's hand in the tiny cell in his shuttle.

She said to River Cloud, "You can have him only if you execute him right now, here, in front of me. Now."

River Cloud hesitated.

"That's the only way," Alex said. "I'm sorry, River Cloud, but I can't. I can't."

"He is ours," River Cloud repeated.

No, he's not, she wanted to say. No more yours than Mira City's, than Yat-Shing Wong's, than Siddalee Brown's, than Grandmother Fur's. Than all the people he killed or caused to be killed. And Julian was hers, too, because she had believed in him and helped him, as had Jake and Ashraf and so many more. They hadn't known. They hadn't seen far enough ahead. None of them had.

> " 'If you can look into the seeds of time,
> And say which grain will grow and which will not,
> Speak then to me . . .' "

But she could not agree to torture. She simply could not, and live herself.

"No," she told River Cloud.

He picked up his spear and walked off. Gray Bird followed.

"Wait," Alex said. "Wait—"

A silent movement from Jake, a smell of burning flesh, and Julian's tall body crumpled to the ground.

Jake held a laser gun in his trembling, wrinkled hand. A plastic box, in which it had been preserved, lay open on his lap. As Alex stared, the gun began to dissolve.

"He wanted to die," Jake said to Alex. "He wanted it. River Cloud, stay a minute, listen to me—"

Alex didn't listen. She knelt beside Julian. He had fallen backward and lay face up on the forest floor. The brilliant green eyes were open. A half smile still remained on his face; Jake had been right. Julian had wanted to die. *"You're named after Alexander the Great,"* she heard his teasing voice say, *"who wept because he had no worlds left to conquer." "There are always worlds to conquer,"* Alex had replied, but not for Julian. Not without his army, his ship, his weapons, his power.

If Alex had had a gun, she realized, she would have shot him herself. From compassion, from revenge, from justice, from expedience—she could no longer tell her reasons apart.

Alex reached to close Julian's eyes, stopped. She couldn't touch him. Her gaze, suddenly blurred, snagged on the green stone on the ground beside his hand. The metal band must have dissolved. *"Who gave you that ring?" "My mother . . ."*

She stood and walked away from the body. Behind her, Jake began to negotiate with the Cheyenne. She heard the telltale note in his voice, as she had so many times before: bargaining, manipulating, persuading, compromising. Necessary work, and now more than ever before in Greentrees' brief history. Without the Cheyenne skills, mass survival on even this fertile and lush planet would not be easy.

Although Alex had no doubt now that the remnant of Mira City would survive, with or without the Cheyenne. Mira had survived wild Furs and space Furs and Vines and being caught in the crossfire of an alien war. They had even survived Julian Martin, which had been harder than the various aliens. There was nothing in the universe, Alex had learned, as dangerous to humans as they were to each other. Jake was deftly negotiating that danger right now. But Alex didn't listen.

She walked to the bustling nomadic village, lay down beside the nearest fire, and slept.

46

THE AVERY MOUNTAINS

The Cheyenne left as abruptly as they had come, loading up the malodorous "elephants" and trekking into a light blowing rain that, Karim was sure, was spreading spores even faster than anticipated. River Cloud spoke only once to Karim.

"Tell Alex Cutler, when she wakes, that she was wrong. We do not torture our prisoners. Not everything from Terran Cheyenne was worth keeping."

"River Cloud, won't you stay with us a little longer? We need to learn so much . . ."

"Gray Bird and his wife will stay behind to teach you." River Cloud pointed. "Look."

Kueilan was helping a Cheyenne girl take down a tent. They were trying to keep the inside dry, difficult in the drizzly wind. Kueilan wore her own Greenie boots with a fringed dress of soft tanned leather embroidered with tiny stones. The girl, barely past puberty, wore moccasins and a Threadmore with its fasteners dissolved, cinched around her waist with a strip of rawhide. Around her neck on a leather string hung a glossy plastic Chinese character that, Karim knew, meant "hope."

River Cloud said dryly, "Gray Bird and his wife have no children." He strode away.

When Kueilan had finished with the tent, Karim said, "I'd like to talk to you."

She flushed slightly. "Here?"

"No." He led her into the trees, stopping under one that provided shelter and privacy. Kueilan's hair, unbound, fell glossy and fresh-smelling to her shoulders. Her black eyes tilted upward at the corners, their expression, Karim thought, as gentle as a kitten's.

"Well?" she said.

He wasn't sure how to begin. "Lucy . . . Lucy and I . . ."

"Where is Lucy?"

"With Jake." The words came then. "She's always been with Jake. In her mind, I mean. She only came into space with me because they'd had some sort of quarrel, I don't know what. But it's Jake she—"

Kueilan said, shocked, "Mr. Holman's an old old man!"

"I know." Karim ran his hand through his hair. Unlike Kueilan's, it was filthy. "But to Lucy and me . . . We knew him so well before, Kueilan. When he was still young. He's an extraordinary person. Lucy—" as he spoke the words, Karim suddenly realized how true they were "—Lucy needs the extraordinary. Needs it. Nothing else matters to her, really."

"Not even you?"

"No."

Kueilan's eyes searched his. She said, "Yat-Shing Wong's my cousin."

He was disoriented. "What?"

"Yat-Shing Wong, a Hope of Heaven dissident. He was my cousin. Karim, what kind of Mira City are you and Alex and Mr. Holman going to rebuild?"

"I don't know what you mean. What does this have to do with—"

"It has everything to do with it," she said, and all at once Karim saw that his gentle kitten had become a tiger. Not that Kueilan, Greentrees born, would recognize a tiger.

"We Chinese could hope to become techs, like me, in the old Mira City. But usually no more than that, because opportunity was so tied to shareholding in Mira Corp, which in turn was tied to First Landing wealth. Are you going to construct that sort of colony again?"

Karim stared at her. "Kueilan, I'm a physicist, not a—"

"You're a First Lander's nephew, an Arab of the house of ibn

Saud. You never thought about this because you were already at the top of the social order."

"I never thought about this because I haven't been on-planet! For more than twice your entire lifetime I've been in space!"

She smiled, her small red mouth forming a close-lipped O, and Karim saw how she differed from Lucy. Kueilan had humor, and she didn't need to push every idealistic principle until it broke. Or every person.

Jake, even at his age, knew how to push back.

Kueilan said, "Yes, you were out in space. But Greentrees will need to be different now, Karim. Are you going to help Alex make it different?"

"Yes, I suppose so."

She laughed. "Which means you don't really care. That's all right. That's enough. As long as you won't be fighting for the old order." She reached up and kissed him.

Jake sat on a pile of animal-hide rugs in the one tent the Cheyenne had left behind, bleakly regarding its sapling supports. The tent was surprisingly snug, and roomier than he'd thought possible from the outside. But it was a tent, a primitive design made with primitive technology, and the pemmican Lucy had softened in stream water for him was primitive, too.

Jake had once commanded a starship.

Alex stirred in her sleep. She smelled vile, too, although that was only temporary. Her exhausted sleep, which had already lasted fourteen hours, was profound and, Jake hoped, dreamless. Karim, Jon McBain, and Natalie had buried Julian Martin while Alex slept; she had at least been spared that. Jake had told them to keep the grave unmarked and its location to themselves.

"You have to eat, Jake," Lucy said.

"It smells bad."

"It's nourishment. You have to bolster your strength. Mira City needs you."

She spoke, Jake saw, with complete conviction. Lucy genuinely believed that Mira City—which no longer even existed—needed a drooling old man who fell asleep at unpredictable intervals.

"Nobody but you could have negotiated River Cloud into promising us as much help as he did. Nobody. You're amazing."

Jake snorted. But the flattery was very pleasant.

Pleasant enough to put up with the inevitable friction between Alex and Lucy? Alex, his de-facto daughter, always bullied Jake about his health. And now Lucy, for whom no relationship label could sum up their convoluted joint history, was going to do the same thing.

"If we take good enough care of you," Lucy said, "you can direct the rebuilding of Mira City."

"Can I come in?" said Jon McBain, drawing aside the tent flap and coming in. "I want to show you and Alex something!"

"Alex is still asleep," Lucy said reprovingly. "Keep your voice lower."

"Show to you, then, Jake," McBain said excitedly. He irritated Jake. Always excited, always talking, the microbiologist seemed to lack all sense of social awareness. Whatever he was interested in, he assumed everyone else was interested in, too. Or should be.

"This is just a rough sketch, of course," McBain said, and held out a piece of tree.

Bark. It was a flattened roll of peeled tree bark, with a drawing on it in charcoal. Jon McBain had once designed energy systems on holo-computers.

"See, it uses ceramics, not metal. Structural ceramics, which I'm confident we can produce from borides and silicides, will be strong enough for a hydraulic system. Once we have this basic engine—and this is just the simplest prototype, of course—there's no reason we can't use it to manufacture plant-based plastics, and then use the plastics to—"

He talked on while Jake nibbled on the pemmican. Despite himself, he was impressed. He was no scientist, but the engine looked feasible. And Mira City had physicists like Karim, had other scientists . . . Jake had sent Natalie and Ben, now well enough to travel, west to the closest evacuation end point outside the kill-clean zone. The prevailing winds blew east. If Natalie and Ben could find a functioning comlink before the spores became widely dispersed, they would make an all-frequency broadcast. Its dual message would be simple: Come home because the war is over. And bury everything metal in sealed plastic containers.

"—resistant to oxidation and decomposition, and we can approach the brittleness problem by—"

Yes, this ceramic technology might work. *"You can direct the rebuilding of Mira City,"* Lucy had said, conveniently leaving out Alex. But perhaps Mira could be rebuilt. Differently, yes: new technology, new priorities, and, inevitably, new social structures. Not that any of that would eliminate future strife, future folly, future failures. Jake was too old and too experienced to believe that.

Still, the ceramic engine looked promising.

The same spores that made the ceramic technology necessary now protected Greentrees from any more invaders, Fur or human.

The Cheyenne tent kept out the rain very well.

"—high-strain-rate superplastic ceramic, not right away, of course, but after the—"

Jake bit into the pemmican. It wasn't bad.

EPILOGUE: MIRA CITY

Alex stood on the platform erected at one end of the park and surveyed the crowd gathered to hear the fifty-third anniversary speeches.

It was a satisfyingly large crowd, more people than she'd expected. Farmers had come in from the countryside, considerately leaving their elephants in a stockyard pen downwind. Several ceramics workers still wore their tough Threadmores, blackened with foundry soot and fastened with the new ceramic buttons from Chu Corporation. The New Quakers, as always, clustered together on one side. Several Arab women sat among them. Now that the medina was gone, the Quaker-sponsored course at the Exchange Center in sewing with bone needles had proved surprisingly popular with the older Arab women.

Behind her on the platform Jake called, "Remember to yell, Alex. No mike."

"Don't yell like that," Lucy said severely. "You already sound hoarse!"

Alex ignored them both. She scanned the crowd to get a rough count. Maybe as many as three thousand. Of course, the herders couldn't leave their glennings nor the breeders their frabbits, on which so much depended. Clothing, meat, sundries like the bone needles. And runners, the young people who in the absence of trams or horses carried goods among the nodes of this looser, more far-flung Mira City, were mostly in the field. But other industries had declared the day a holiday and closed entirely. The Scientists' League was there, and the Carpenters' Guild, and the flourishing Zhou Lighting Company, which had scored such an early success with oil lamps that it had cornered the market.

A breeze blew cooking smells to the platform. The communal kitchen had been working for days to prepare this feast. Every ceramic pot on every ceramic stove simmered with spicy delicacies. Alex's mouth watered.

The band struck up Greentrees' newly adopted anthem, "We're Still Here." Alex knew all the words, which were ungainly and moving, but she couldn't distinguish them over the instruments. Wood flutes, a ceramic horn of some type, a few guitars, and a drum. Several people stood; more didn't.

A ripple ran over the crowd and people spun around and laughed. Two messages were coming in simultaneously. Against the clear eastern sky, green smoke puffs—the coloring was another Zhou Company success—rose. Alex, like everyone else over the age of four, read the green symbols easily. They came from the upriver Hamoud Fish Farms.

(fish) (unable) (ship) (greetings) (as a result of the foregoing) (Hamoud staff) (ship) (greetings) (Mira City)

What made it funny was the other message, flashing from tower to tower via Jon McBain's polished glass-and-ceramic mirrors all the way from the coastal ichthyologist research station:

(fish) (Mira Ichthyologist Research Station) (ship) (greetings) (Mira City)

Alex smiled. The joke was pretty lame, but laughter hadn't been too plentiful in the last two and a half years. Too many people had died. But more had survived than she'd dared hope, those who had evacuated Mira when they were supposed to and then stayed hidden during the brief, terrible war with the space Furs. About half of

Greentrees' population had slowly staggered back from the places they'd fled to. More had chosen to move even farther away and build new frontier towns.

At first there had been no housing for the returnees, no hospital for the sick, little food, and no metal to try to re-create the familiar. Everything had had to be rethought. They could not have done it at all in a harsher environment. But this was Greentrees: lush, generous, beautiful wherever humanity had not scarred her.

So now Alex looked out at wooden structures with dovetailed joints; stone structures with that old Roman staple, the key arch; tents and lodges decorated with Chinese characters. This Mira City had none of the soaring grace and ecologically correct harmony she had once envisioned. This Mira City was eclectic, crude, makeshift, evolving, vital.

And here.

The band had long since finished its anthem. "Begin!" Jake called. "What are you waiting for?"

Alex held up her hand. The crowd quieted. She picked out individual faces: Star Chu. Kent Landers. Savannah Cutler. Salah Hadijeh. Ben Stoller and Natalie Bernstein. And off to one side, River Cloud with three young braves, all being much admired by a mixed gaggle of teenage girls.

But it wasn't the faces that were here that Alex proposed to talk about.

"As mayor of Mira City, I'd like to welcome you all to the ceremony commemorating the fifty-third anniversary of the First Landing. But before I talk about the wonderful things in our past and in our future, I want to begin as every public meeting in Mira City begins.

"So that we remember them always, and remember what we owe them, these are the martyrs who gave their lives so that we might live in peace on Greentrees:

"Lau-Wah Mah."

The crowd echoed solemnly, "We remember Lau-Wah Mah."

"Nan Frayne."

"We remember Nan Frayne."

"Ashraf Shanti."

· "We remember Ashraf Shanti."

"Duncan Martin." Even now her throat tightened at the surname.

"We remember Duncan Martin."

"Siddalee Brown."

"We remember Siddalee Brown."

"Mary Pesci and Mesbah Shanab."

"We remember Mary Pesci and Mesbah Shanab."

"Burning Tree of the Cheyenne."

"We remember Burning Tree of the Cheyenne."

"Grandmother of the wild Furs."

"We remember Grandmother of the wild Furs."

"Miranda of the wild Furs . . ."

Miranda. Alex could never escape memory. *"History defines us,"* Julian always said. Duncan Martin on a vanished stage, in his thrilling voice: " 'O brave new world that has such people in it . . .' " Alex looked out across the solemn, chanting crowd.

"We remember Miranda of the wild Furs."

Such people in it . . .

Yes.